REBEL ROUSERS

A Novel by
CARROLL C. JONES

Carroll C. Jones (signature)

Jan-Carol
Publishing, Inc
"every story needs a book."

Rebel Rousers
Carroll C. Jones

Published November 2015
Little Creek Books
Imprint of Jan-Carol Publishing, Inc
Copyright © Carroll C. Jones
Front Cover Illustration: Edie Hutchins Burnette
Design: Tara Sizemore

This is a work of fiction. All names, characters, and events are the product of the author's imagination.

This book may not be reproduced in whole or part, in any manner whatsoever without written permission, with the exception of brief quotations within book reviews or articles.

ISBN: 978-1-939289-79-7
Library of Congress Control Number: 2015956458

You may contact the publisher at:
Jan-Carol Publishing, Inc
PO Box 701
Johnson City, TN 37605
publisher@jancarolpublishing.com
jancarolpublishing.com

This book is dedicated to all of the Hargroves—past and present—who have made a difference in the Forks of Pigeon settlement.

Letter to the Reader

The ending of my first novel, *Master of the East Fork*, left the principal characters blissfully returning their wedding vows before a church full of family and friends. It was more than a decade prior to the opening cannon barrages of the American Civil War, and the newlyweds, Basil and Julia Edmunston, had the world at their feet and only sweet dreams filling their heads. These dreams entailed a loving life together on an immense farm in the heart of North Carolina's rugged western mountains. Little did the couple realize a ruinous war lie ahead—one that would disrupt their happiness and present unfathomable hardships, changing their lives forever.

In this book, *Rebel Rousers*, the saga of Basil Edmunston's family continues as the Civil War erupts in all of its horrible fury. Accordingly, original characters who have matured in years and new ones, such as Hack Hartgrove and the Bee Woman, become immediately immersed in the wartime drama. In order to soften the many scenes of military conflict, I have endeavored to weave wefts of romance throughout the historical fabric of the story. Yet no matter my efforts along these lines, realistic battle scenes and intertwining streaks of meanness or acts of cruelty introduced by the antagonist, Amos Bugg, will likely create anxious moments for readers.

I sincerely hope you will read *Rebel Rousers* to see how Basil and Julia Edmunston and their family and neighbors fared during the time when civil warfare intruded into Haywood County's East Fork River region. You surely will not be disappointed.

Best regards,
Carroll C. Jones

Author's Note

The scenic lands along the upper Pigeon River and its tributaries have a rich and intriguing history. Although these had been Native Indian hunting grounds for millennia, by the end of the eighteenth century the Cherokee had been pushed out and white settlers were beginning to penetrate the wilderness setting. Reliable historical resources have allowed me to create fictional characters and to imagine fanciful stories based on some of the actual pioneering families who tamed the wilds surrounding Forks of Pigeon (present-day Bethel, North Carolina). The specific names of individual characters portrayed in the book, although common to the area, have been made up for the most part. And no representations made or tales told within these pages should be construed as anything other than historical fiction....
Carroll C. Jones

Acknowledgements

The historical setting and fabric of *Rebel Rousers* is based on extensive study and research supporting the publications of my previous works of historical non-fiction: *The 25th North Carolina Troops in the Civil War*, *Rooted Deep in the Pigeon Valley*, and *Captain Lenoir's Diary*. All of the source materials cited in those publications are applicable in this one as well.

I remain very grateful to the descendants of Captain Thomas Isaac Lenoir—especially to Mary Michal, her brother Joe, and the late Emily Terrell and her husband Hugh K.—who were so supportive of my initial work on the Lenoir family, including the loan and use of the Captain's treasured Civil War diary. It was, after all, Thomas Isaac Lenoir whose personage and circumstances offered the inspiration for Basil Edmunston, a principal character in *Master of the East Fork* and the patriarch in this sequel, *Rebel Rousers*.

And finally there is another person who I would like to recognize for her unfailing devotion and support. She has listened to me read aloud the chapters in this book so often that I can now detect a touch of Scotch-Irish inflection mixed in with her beautiful Brazilian accent. My wife, Maria, is special in so many ways!

Foreword

By Kathy Nanney Ross

The inspiration for Carroll Jones's writing comes from a love of history, based on his childhood experiences in the upper Pigeon Valley of Haywood County. There his Hargrove, Cathey, Moore and Shook ancestors settled, building community out of wilderness, braving hardship and deprivation, and instilling in their descendents a love of the land and its stories. After publishing three historical nonfiction books, two of which focus on the experiences of Haywood County men during the Civil War, Carroll blended his extensive knowledge of the past and the actual pioneers to create his first novel, *Master of the East Fork*. It is a story about young Basil Edmunston, who is summoned from university to the mountains of North Carolina to manage his family's vast lands and the tenants and slaves who work them. Trials, troubles and romance immediately beset the youthful master and don't cease until the book's final pages are turned.

Rebel Rousers is the sequel to the original fictional tale, and in this novel Carroll revisits the East Fork of the Pigeon River setting some fourteen years later. Basil Edmunston has matured and he and his wife Julia are the proud parents of two daughters in addition to their adopted son, Rufus. They possess a thriving and vast mountain farming operation worked by their slave and tenant families and have earned the respect of their community. Just when Basil is about to enjoy the fruits of his accomplishments, simmering national political tensions erupt into Civil War. Though nearing middle age, Basil cannot avoid his obligations to the Confederacy. Nor can his son Rufus escape overwhelming responsibilities at home and what will become a brutal thrust into manhood.

With his father away at the war, Rufus must cope with the heavy duties of the farm, from establishing leadership over the slaves and tenants to ensuring crops are harvested and sold. He must also juggle the growing threat of a community bully whose brutality is fueled by the troubles of war. And, if not quite sufficiently burdened, Rufus must wrestle his burgeoning emotions, both passionate and affectionate, for the miller's beautiful daughter.

However, war's upheaval and its dreadful consequences work in such a tangled way that the roles of Basil and his son are reversed. Rufus will come to realize that death is capricious and arbitrary, at home as well as on the battlefield. He will also find that the worst evils of humanity raise their vile natures at home as readily as in warfare—and that sometimes, moments of kindness emerge in the most horrific circumstances.

Based on his study of the 25th North Carolina Troops, Carroll creates a fictional narrative based on the actual record of a company of highlanders organized from Haywood County. The unit saw action from the swamplands of eastern North and South Carolina to the hellish crater of Petersburg and the bloody banks of Antietam Run. His extensive research into local history allows him to take readers back to the nineteenth century and immerse them in the daily lives and struggles of Haywood pioneers. Throughout the story alternating sensual exposures, both sharp and real, provide the mood and backdrop for the characters' actions. Among these are the musty scents of a water mill, the warm surroundings of a busy general store serving as the heart of the community, and vivid scenes of conflict and gore that gradually reveal the folly of battle.

Readers will meet memorable characters in addition to the heroic Rufus and his best friend Hack Hartgrove. There is the Bee Woman, an eccentric healer whose life is unorthodox and free; also, a slave who will offer the ultimate sacrifice for the enslaver; and a preacher whose sermons are fueled more by emotion than the Word. Surprising character dramas include the nobility of an unnamed Yankee soldier, kindness of northern sympathizers, and the depravity of local renegades let loose on a society whose men are gone to war. All of this, and much more, is deftly woven into the sturdy fabric of a story that, while fictional, reflects the horror and heroism of the time of secession.

Carroll Jones blends unique story-telling and crafty writing with historical facts and regional lifestyles to create a superb, thought-provoking novel, *Rebel Rousers*. His book reminds us how the lines between joy and sorrow, good and evil, and justice and vengeance can blur. As a good historical novel should, *Rebel Rousers* transports us back in time and teaches us about our past without sacrificing a compelling story. Enjoy.

Kathy Nanney Ross has spent the last 28 years in Haywood County and is fascinated by the history of the region, as well as that of her own home territory, the Broad River and Bald Mountain territory of Henderson County. She is a former reporter and news editor for *The Mountaineer*, Haywood County's community newspaper, and continues to write the occasional column or story. For five years she wrote a weekly historical feature for that publication. She also contributed chapters on religion, education, agriculture, and natural history for the book *Haywood County: Portrait of a Mountain Community*. She is married to farmer Steve Ross and the mother of three sons.

Contents

Chapter 1	Foolery in South Carolina	1
Chapter 2	Dream Girl	10
Chapter 3	The Bee Woman	18
Chapter 4	Ruckus at the Mill	30
Chapter 5	Shucking for Love	40
Chapter 6	On Thin Ice	51
Chapter 7	The Music of War	59
Chapter 8	The Heart of a Lion	71
Chapter 9	Stuck in Everlasting Fire	81
Chapter 10	Undoing the Intent	91
Chapter 11	Oceans of Bluecoats	99
Chapter 12	A Regrettable Task	107
Chapter 13	Under the Good Dunkers' Care	114
Chapter 14	Glimmer in the Basement	123
Chapter 15	Glimpse into a Yank's Soul	131
Chapter 16	A Mite Partial to Her	142
Chapter 17	Sneak Attack at Gum Swamp	149
Chapter 18	An Irritating Itch	161
Chapter 19	Ten Muskets–Five Balls	170
Chapter 20	A Hollow Victory	177
Chapter 21	Reb's Angel	185
Chapter 22	Big Ol' Yankee Moles	196
Chapter 23	The Bloody Cauldron	205
Chapter 24	Yankee Eggnog	214
Chapter 25	Drama on Hare's Hill	224
Chapter 26	In a Pig's Sty	236
Chapter 27	A Helluva Git	246
Chapter 28	Shining Rock	254
Chapter 29	Bugg Hunting	262
Chapter 30	We Who?	270
Chapter 31	An Eloquent Proposal	277

Chapter 1

FOOLERY IN SOUTH CAROLINA

The gangly blond lad prowled the aisles eyeing the twists of tobacco, assorted delicious candies, and profusion of other goods that jammed the storekeeper's shelves. Along with several other fidgety customers, he was there at Deaver's General Store awaiting the arrival of the post carrier to the rural outpost of Forks of Pigeon, tucked away in North Carolina's secluded western mountains. By happenstance, it was the young man's fifteenth birthday. But on this particular cold and rainy spring afternoon of April 13th, 1861, his father had dispatched him to learn of any breaking war news out of South Carolina.

Lingering close at his side was a Negro slave boy, who was thoroughly enjoying the excursion. The stout African youth glanced with saucer-sized eyes over to his much taller companion and queried, "What you's wants, Rufus?"

However, before the curious African could be satisfied with an answer, the heavy wooden door of the establishment suddenly burst open, and the postman rushed in. And like worker bees drawn to their queen, the loitering patrons instinctively swarmed around the letter carrier.

"Okay, folks, holt on jest a minute now! Let me git my way over to the fire, so's to dry out a bit." With the heavy dripping mail bag still draped over his shoulder, he edged his way through the throng and over to the nearest of the store's two huge fireplaces. The noisy crowd anxiously followed him and watched as he squeezed up close to the flaming logs and shucked off as much wetness as he could. All eyes remained fixed on the man's every move. Stomping heavily in place on the puncheon floor, he at once put down the mail pouch, shed his wide-brimmed hat and sopping great coat, and proceeded to briskly rub his hands together over the warm flames.

Finally, the postman turned around and looked upon the gawking audience with wild eyes. After taking a deep breath and teasing with dramatic pause for long seconds, he at last exclaimed at the top of his lungs, "They done did it! Yestidy morning, General Beauregard's artillery guns fired on Fort Sumter, and by God they's ain't let up nary bit yet! They's sure 'nuff ain't!"

News of the bombardment by Confederate troops on the Federal fortification at South Carolina's Charleston harbor spread like wildfire throughout the Southern states—both those officially in rebellion and those contemplating the drastic measure, such as North Carolina. At nearby Asheville, the commercial center and gateway to the remote North Carolina mountains, telegraph messages of the attack on Fort Sumter streamed in throughout the day from the capital cities of the Carolinas—Raleigh and Columbia.

Of course the news brought by the harried letter carrier was dated when he finally arrived at Forks of Pigeon, after the long day's ride from Asheville. Those gathered at Deaver's Store on this nasty spring day had no way of knowing the United States' forces had already raised a white flag of surrender. Nor did they fully comprehend the significance of the rash actions undertaken in South Carolina to preserve a precarious way of life and an economy founded on the backs of African slaves. Included in the eager audience listening intently to the shocking news were the two naïve teenagers, Rufus Edmunston and his slave companion, Jesse.

Rufus was savvy enough to realize that the information he was carrying back to his father was highly important, primarily because of the gravity of the discussions he had overheard after the surprising announcement of the Fort Sumter business. His grandfather, Colonel Deaver, and his Uncle

Burton Deaver—joint proprietors of the store—had pulled him aside and insisted that he rush back home, at once, to break the news to his father. So after jumping on their mounts—Rufus on his black-maned gray mare and Jesse on an old plow mule—the two youths rode in the cold rain, hurrying up the East Fork River road toward home, just a few miles away.

"Jess, I don't know exactly what all this here war news means fer us," Rufus began explaining, as he hunched in the saddle and pulled the brim of his floppy hat over his brow. Soaking wet, with his flaxen locks hanging in strings to his shoulders, he carried on with the enlightening chatter, "So far, North Carolina has steered clear of declaring itself fer the Confederacy, I reckon. And I'm not right sure if this latest craziness at Charleston will change things up or not. Colonel Deaver—and Father too—are still set right firm against seceding from the Union, leastwise, far as I can tell."

"What you's means, 'succeeding,' Rufus?" a perplexed Jesse asked.

"That's 'seceding,' Jess. It means—uh—well, say if our state, North Carolina, no longer hankers to be included in our country—you know, the United States of America—why, then they can just decide to get out. A few Southern states have already dropped out—or seceded—and have formed themselves up into a confederacy of sorts, called the Confederate States. You getting all this?"

"Yes, I's believes so. Will this se—seceding be's much diff'rent to us East Fork folk, somehows?"

They kept on riding as Rufus pondered Jesse's question. Fact of the matter was, he had not given the political considerations of the day too much attention or thought. Since the election of President Abraham Lincoln, the Republican from Illinois, his father and the Deavers and all the neighbors were constantly debating the ramifications of the election and the intentions of the newly elected President. This was especially so after a few of the Deep South states formally declared their separation from the United States. Uninterested and uninvited, Rufus had remained comfortably detached from the contentious arguments. Until now, he had not seriously studied these strange goings-on so far removed from his geographical sphere of knowledge and interest. Lost in deep contemplation, Jesse had to jar him back to the discussion at hand.

"Rufus, did you hear my question I axed you's?"

"What? Oh yeah—sorry, Jess. I was just ciphering on what you said. Can't rightly say fer sure if secession will affect us much atall here in Haywood County. But I'm sure Father will have a strong idee on that, though. I'll be sure to let you know what he allows." With that said, the two unlikely friends fell into a thoughtful silence as they plodded in the rain along the river road back to the Den.

The 'Den' was the unpretentious ancient log structure where Rufus lived. Overlooking the brawling East Fork of the Pigeon River, the cabin was centered amidst some five thousand acres of rugged land his parents owned. Eleven more tenant farms were carved out of the immense Edmunston plantation, which was secluded deep in the Blue Ridge Mountains just west of Asheville—the region's largest town. His father, Basil Edmunston, had moved to Haywood County in 1846 as a twenty-year-old, unmarried man, whereupon he had dubbed the old cabin the 'Bachelor's Den.' Then, upon his subsequent marriage to Colonel Joseph Deaver's beautiful young daughter, Julia, a year and a half later, he had promptly re-branded his quarters. Dropping the 'Bachelor's' for obvious reasons, the place simply became known to all as the Den.

Rufus had actually been adopted as a toddler by Basil and Julia, after his natural mother was tragically killed by her estranged husband and Rufus's natural father, Sam Beck. It had been an awful thing all around—Altha Beck's murder—and had led to Basil's revengeful pursuit of the no-good Beck and their ensuing life-or-death battle. The crazed killer was justly consigned to the hellish environs of the devil, and Basil himself barely survived the fight. During his lengthy convalescence, a dormant flame of affection he had always held for Julia was rekindled as she steadfastly nursed him back to life. Eventually, they were married and, in addition to their beloved adopted son, Rufus, their marital partnership had also engendered two lovely and lively daughters—Mary and Emily.

As Rufus and Jesse approached the Den, they spotted Basil in the barnyard on the far side of the creek. Gathered around him, they could see, were a few slaves clapping and laughing to high heaven. Keen to learn what all the commotion was about and to pass along the exciting war news, the boys gave a quick kick to their mounts and rode straight away over to the barn.

"Oh, Father, you don't know how funny you look," the boys heard little Emily cry out in hilarity, as they approached the scene. Both of Rufus's younger sisters, Mary and Emily—ages twelve and ten respectively—were there amongst several of the African slaves, hooting and hollering at their father who was obviously the center of attention. Strapped to the bottom of Basil's boots were large wooden paddles that he was using to wade around on the sea of slimy manure and mud surrounding the barn. Tall, stout, and still ruggedly handsome with a full mane of graying dark hair, Basil was hopping and sliding to and fro, while singing a merry tune to the amusement of the gathered onlookers.

Plop...plop...plop. "See how easy it is, boys," Basil called out to Rufus and Jesse who had just ridden up. "These here are my manure pumps. That's what I'm going to call them anyhow. Made them myself this morning. See here—it's just like walking on two little rafts floating on top of all this stinking, muddy manure. They work kind of like snowshoes—the same idea. Why, before you know it, folks around here are going to start thinking that the Savior Himself has returned in the guise of a poor East Fork farmer. Now, it's not everyone who can walk on shit, is it?" he joked, feigning seriousness until a foolish smile cracked over his face. "Come on down off that horse, Rufus, and give these here pumps a try, why don't you?"

Well, Rufus could hardly believe his eyes and ears and did not even attempt to respond. Nor did he make a move to try out his father's new-fangled manure pumps. He just shook his head and smiled with embarrassment at Basil. Likewise, Jesse was grinning bigger than a possum at the silly proceedings. It was not often Rufus saw his father act a fool like this. As a matter of fact, very seldom had he witnessed such jovial, high-spirited buffoonery as that exhibited by his father on this wet dreary day. So he just let Basil carry on, entertaining the girls and the slaves in the rain. He judged that the exciting news he was carrying back from the store would have a sudden sobering effect on his father. And the last thing he wanted to do was spoil the fun for the girls—and his father too.

A short while later, Rufus and Basil—who was still sopping wet and smelling worse than his livestock—found themselves lodged in front of the fireplace. The father was beat and worn-out from his clownish exertions on the manure pumps, but he still listened intently as his son repeated the scarce details that had been offered by the postman. Rufus, being satisfied that an accurate account had been delivered, then proceeded to relay another important message from his Grandfather Deaver.

"Grandfather said to tell you that he and Uncle Burton want to discuss this serious turn-of-events tomorrow. He said you should go to church tomorrow with Mother—it will be good for you, he said." Rufus then paused for a brief second to catch his father's reaction.

Basil, not known to be a church-going man, did not even flinch at the veiled rebuke. So his son continued, "Said he'll catch-up with you after the preaching lets out. He 'spects the fence-straddling days may be over—that's exactly what he said." Rufus hushed up and awaited his father's response, fully expecting a whole bunch of probing questions.

Elsewhere, a distracting racket was arising from the kitchen. The space was a lean-to addition to the cabin and featured a great iron stove where the slave cook, Jenny, prepared all their meals. One whole side of the spacious room was taken up by a ponderous loom, a high spinning wheel, and several textile projects in various stages of completion. Julia and the girls were gathered in the cozy area, and their loud giggling and sounds of merry conversation—mostly at Basil's expense—intruded into the serious air of the father and son's weighty discussions.

Basil tried to ignore the kitchen riot, while deliberating on what Rufus had just told him. But before pronouncing to his son what he allowed about the defiant acts of rebellion, he rose up out of his chair and leaned over to poke up the fire. As he did so, Rufus noticed the mud and cakes of manure still clinging to his father's britches.

"Shooo, Father! Ye better not let Mother catch you wearing those filthy clothes in here," an animated Rufus chided with a chuckle.

Basil took one quick look down at himself and agreed wholeheartedly with his son. "Hah! For goodness sake! Must have carried the whole barnyard in here with me—reckon? Let's take these off right now," he muttered, and then grunted as he undertook to disrobe. Turning his head toward the kitchen, Basil gave loud warning of his intentions to the fairer sex, "Keep your eyes closed, girls! I'm undressing!"

Almost instantaneously, a boisterous cackling noise erupted beyond the log barrier and playful derisive chants gave answer. "Father's dressing—Father's dressing," Emily responded.

And Mary added, "Let's all go see Father with his clothes off. Here we come, ready or not."

"Very funny, girls—that's very funny!" Basil countered. "Best you stay in there with your mother. Just give me a minute now."

Julia—aging gracefully and still as beautiful and blonde as the first day Basil fixed his eyes on her at Deaver's Store—chimed in so everyone could hear, "We're all coming out, dear. Won't you show us those lovely white legs of yours?" And with that, the kitchen cacophony rose to a higher level, almost a roar. Mercifully, however, the girls did not make good on their threats, and they let their poor father be.

After slipping into some fresh clothes, Basil sat down again with his son in front of the popping fire and shared some of his innermost thoughts. "That's just plain foolery by South Carolina, Rufus. Those hotheads down there—the likes of Rhett and Calhoun—have already driven their state to secede and join the so-called Confederation of States. By instigating that cannonade against Fort Sumter and the Federal troops stationed there, they're forcing their state's rights and slavery positions down President Lincoln's throat. What a fool thing to do—and Lincoln's surely not going to stand for it! No sir, he's not going to tolerate it, atall."

Remembering Jesse's earlier question to him, Rufus jumped in and queried his father, "Seems to me like that cannon fire is a long ways off from here though. What difference is it going to make for us farmers here on the East Fork? I mean—reckon it's going to change things hereabouts any?"

Basil replied without hesitation, "Can't say for sure, son. But if our representatives in Washington City finally come to their senses and pass Crittenden's compromise bills, then the slavery question would be settled satisfactorily for most reasonable thinkers here in the South. It would establish boundary lines for future slave states and regulate slave property rights throughout the country. Your Grandfather Deaver believes this new law might make a difference and has been promoting that notion here in Haywood to anybody who will listen to him. And I would say, a majority of us feel the same way and have been just watching and waiting for the past year or so for something to settle out in Congress. If that happens—the law passes—then those few cotton states that have already seceded would likely as not return to the fold." Then turning his eyes away from the fire and looking directly toward Rufus, Basil checked for understanding. "Now is that about as clear as mud to you, son?"

Rufus was watching the dancing flames and listening closely. He nodded his head a couple of times, indicating that even at his youthful age he got the gist of the matter. Then, with a furrowed brow, he returned his father's stare and responded, "Yeah, reckon so. But if the government fails to agree on that there new law—Crittenden's Law—then what? Will North Carolina secede then? And if it does, will we have to go off and fight them Yankees? And what if they come here, to the Haywood mountains, to fight us? That sure would be something, don't you reckon? What then?"

"Wooaaah now, son—simmer down a little, and let's try not to get the cart before the horse. We're just going to have to carry on here and see what falls out of this fool act in South Carolina. Let them nullify, revolute, secede, and be damned. There's no need for us to follow South Carolina's lead. So far, North Carolina has voted to repeal secession. Let's hope that our fair state continues to do so. And don't you forget that your Great-Grandfather Edmunston fought the British to establish this country of ours. Far as I'm concerned, we're still way better off being a part of the United States. I reckon I'm still a Unionist at heart, until better reason than this South Carolina tiff turns me into a rebel."

That declaration gave the father and son both reason for pause and reflection. They turned and fixed their gazes on the orange blaze of the fire, as darkness slowly closed over the East Fork River Valley. Neither of them foresaw the dire consequences of the news brought by the letter carrier that day.

Chapter 2

Dream Girl

In a matter of only a few weeks, most of the Haywood County fence-sitters with a Unionist proclivity, like Basil Edmunston and his father-in-law, Colonel Joseph Deaver, shirked their loyalty to the Stars and Stripes and became full-fledged Rebels. President Lincoln's reaction to the rebellious foolery at Charleston Harbor was to call for 75,000 militiamen to squash the insurrection. North Carolinians, including those highlanders residing in remote Forks of Pigeon, were infuriated at this usurpation of power. They viewed the United States government's action as a violation of the laws of the country and an impingement on the liberties of its people. Soon thereafter, the State of North Carolina seceded and joined with the other alienated states in a confederation styled 'The Confederate States of America.'

War was on the horizon, and the incensed mountaineers in Haywood County were infected with a keen want to do battle with the infernal Yankees that were threatening to invade their homeland. The Rebels had begun to feel mighty Southern, one could say.

Summer's solstice on the East Fork River found the forests flushed with fresh green leaves and the high rocky ridges ablaze with flaming azalea blooms. Around the Den, matters were functioning common as usual. The bottom corn fields had been manured, plowed, and planted, and lush stalks of green were already poking through the rich soil. Rufus had recently endured several days of back-breaking work, with Jesse and the other slaves, reaping the winter wheat. And his Grandfather Deaver's horse-powered threshing machine was scheduled to arrive any day now to extract the valuable grain.

Winter losses of the various varieties of livestock on the farm had been polled. Cattle selected to fatten and breed had been pastured, and hogs so chosen had been released into the woods. The slaves were still wielding shears in their efforts to relieve the sheep of their winter wool coats. Those unfortunate domestic beasts destined for the butchers' blocks were penned and would soon be driven to the various mountain markets. Things did indeed give the outward appearance of normalcy, but inside the old Den, trouble was brewing.

"Basil, you don't have to accept just because they decided for you to be their captain, you crazy thing!" Julia nervously admonished in a raised voice. She was obviously distressed and upset about something. "Besides, you're getting too old for that sort of thing, and you're not fit, either, with that bad leg of yours." The bad leg being a carryover from Basil's dealings with Sam Beck and a near-fatal fall off Devil's Face Mountain fifteen years earlier. Basil still walked with a heavy limp favoring the right leg, but he never complained. The mere fact that he had survived was a miracle in itself. It had compelled him to thank his God every day for the wonderful fresh air he still breathed.

Basil knew he was on precarious ground and tread lightly with his atoning reply. "But, dear, my neighbors are determined to have a company from this section of the county. One has been formed at Waynesville, but these local men don't want to be a part of it. It's just that—well, I'm so peculiarly situated here, Julia, that I can't turn them down. It's my duty to accept, I believe, and no honorable man could think of declining under such conditions." Basil paused to assess the effect of his argument on Julia. But he quickly discovered that her armored stubbornness had not been dented in the slightest.

"Duty—how can you say that, Basil?" Julia began in a lower, slower, and more determined tone. "Your duty is to your family here. What are we going to do while you're off gallivantin' along the warpath? Why, you're now thirty-five years old! Do you believe that bad leg of yours and your poor constitution will tolerate living in the field on long military campaigns? Don't you think you can better serve your country by staying right here and making bread and meat for the soldiers?" Her eyes glared hard into his, and she shook her head slowly, from side to side, as large tears welled up and chased down her cheeks. No amount of debate or explanation on Basil's part was about to justify his acceptance of the high honor his neighbors had bestowed upon him that very morning. Precious few arguments had infected their marriage previously. However, this one was bitter, and left both parties depressed and hurt. Julia was heartbroken and scared, and Basil became infused with a nagging sense of doubt and disloyalty to his cherished family.

The election of officers had taken place that very morning down at Deaver's Store. Over the past several weeks, a hundred or more of Basil's neighbors had volunteered their services and signed their names—or made their marks—on the roster of the Haywood Highlanders. That was the brand they had given the local militia company they were forming; and farmers and farmers' sons, between the ages of seventeen and forty, had been urged to join up. It was these men, along with many other male members of the community, who had gathered by mid-morning at Deaver's. The volunteers were there to cast their votes for the company's leadership positions and to pledge their allegiance to the State and to the Confederacy.

After all the votes had been tallied, an esteemed gentleman named Columbus Hartgrove bellowed to the multitude waiting outside the store. He was the area's elected county commissioner and had been drafted to organize and oversee this election. "Listen up! Give me yer 'tention!" Hartgrove hailed at the top of his lungs. He was standing on the raised porch of the store, with his belly pressed against the pole railing. Slowly, the herd of people moved in closer and congregated in the store yard before him.

Finally seeing that his audience was placed advantageously, Hartgrove announced loudly, "Okay everybody, I have here the final tally counts fer the votes cast fer officers." He paused and looked out to make sure he could be heard above the commotion. As it happened, Hartgrove himself was hard of hearing. It had been his misfortune—those many years ago—to get one of his ears shot off when he fought at Basil's side against the vile Sam Beck and another henchman.

Convinced that he had everyone's undivided attention, Hartgrove began to pronounce the election results so everyone could hear. "Fer captain—ye're not going to believe this—Basil Edmunston received ninety-nine out of the hunderd and three votes. He's elected practically 'nanimous as yer captain."

The yard erupted with wild whooping, hollering, and spirited hoorahs directed squarely at the East Fork farmer. An embarrassed Basil stood back a ways, next to Colonel and Burton Deaver, and nonchalantly acknowledged the attention aimed in his direction. Rufus and Jesse were there observing the proceedings along with Hack Hartgrove, Columbus's son.

Besides Jesse, Hack was about as good a companion as Rufus had. The boys were excited and stood quietly under a nearby tree taking things in. A proud sensation arose inside Rufus, as he became attuned to his father's popularity and the high honor bestowed to him. But almost instantly, this feeling was snuffed out by an opposite emotional reaction, when it dawned on him that his father must surely go off to war soon—and might never come back.

"Listen up! Settle down now!" Columbus continued on. "Burton Deaver is elected first lieutenant, garnering some seventy-eight votes; and James Blalock wins second lieutenant with sixty-four votes." Although Burton was more than forty years old, he had volunteered his services anyway—he along with a few other older local mountaineers, whose blood boiled to send the Northern invaders back whence they had come. To the extreme disappointment of Rufus's companion, Hack Hartgrove, no men under seventeen years of age had been allowed to volunteer.

After the names of the elected sergeants, corporals, and color corporal were read and the oaths of allegiance sworn, the farmers headed back to their homesteads perched on the ridge tops or huddled close against the gurgling streams. Awaiting them there were anxious wives and children, who were nervous about the impending war—just as Julia and her daughters were.

Rufus and his two friends stuck around the store after the crowd had mostly dispersed. They sat on the ground in the shade with their backs against a huge oak tree and engaged in some youthful pondering. As dapples of sunlight pierced the overhead canopy and reflected off Hack's face, he boasted to his friends, "I sure wish my pa would let me go fight them Yankees. I've got a real hankering to show them what fer. What ye say, Rufe? Ye feel the same way?"

Jesse allowed Rufus no time to reply. "You mean you's wants to go an get youself killed, Hack? Why you's wants to go and do dat fo'? Them Yankees may be real mean. How you's know dey's not real mean, and not goin' shoot you's dead? How you's know dat? Huh?"

"Ah, Jess, there ain't nothing to be skeered of," Hack responded with a touch of sarcasm. "Pa showed me in the Asheville paper where one of them South Carolina fire-brand bigwigs says it will take ten of them Yankees to whip one of us Rebels. But then, he went on and tolt me not to believe sech foolishness. I reckon, though, there might be a touch of truth to the notion. What ye allow 'bout that, Rufe?"

But Jesse was not about to let go of the bone, and he gnawed away at Hack. "Don't take but one of dem lead balls to kill you's, Hack, the ways I sees it. Be no need fo' dem other nine Yanks to fool with you's den." And with that, Rufus and Jesse lit up with laughing and heehaws so boisterous they gained the attention of some of the patrons loafing over at the store.

Most of the folks thereabouts took a dim view of Rufus's slave friend following him around everywhere. The relatively insignificant population of bonded Africans in the mountain region of North Carolina did not lessen the prejudice held against the race by a majority of the mountaineers. Commonly referred to as 'darkeys' or 'niggers,' the sons of Africa were thought to be vastly inferior to the whites, barely reaching the social status of the farm stock. However, Rufus did not see it that way, not entirely—nor did the rest of his family for that matter. On more than one occasion, he had physically confronted and attempted to put older loud-mouthed bigots in their place. This habit, or want, to defend Jesse had led Rufus up a steep learning curve in the use of his fists, and by now he was more than able to hold his own in a brawl.

After the cackling died down, Rufus took pity on Hack and tried to bear him up. "Don't get yer feathers ruffled now, Hack. No disrespect intended.

However, I believe that I favor Jess's point of view regarding them Yankees. I know how nervous Father seems about the coming fight. He says the politicians have stirred up a hornet's nest. He's traveled up there in the North before and says they've got way more of everything than us—soldiers, trains, guns, ammunition—all that there stuff. If we do go to war, then he says it won't be no flare-up. If what he believes is true, then you and me both could end up testing those Yankees one day."

Hack looked suspiciously at Jesse and began to reply, "Yeah—well I'll take ten of them on, and ye can take ten of them on, and let's just see what ol' Jess here will have to laugh at then." Just as Hack finished his clever comeback, the boys' attentions were drawn toward the store front, where Colonel Deaver's miller was pulling up in a wagon laden with baskets of wheat.

"There she be's, Rufus. You's ever goin' to says somethings to her?" chided Jesse, as the boys gawked over at the wagon where the miller's daughter, Hazeltine, was seated.

She was 'a looker,' as the boys termed it, and about as fine-looking a girl as Forks of Pigeon had to offer and of an age that drew the boys' interest. Rufus suspected she was a year or so older than he was—about the same age as Hack. When school was not in session, she routinely helped her father, Horace, with the milling business or just keeping the place tidied up. Turns out, Hazeltine took great delight in the splashing sounds of water rushing through the millrace head-on against the huge water wheel. The low groaning of the circular mechanism, turning round and round and driving the mill's workings; the rhythmic clacking noise of wooden gears meshing in amazing concert; and the continuous hum of the millstones grating against each other were not only music to the miller's ears, but to his daughter's as well.

Ever since Rufus bumped into Hazeltine at the mill a few months back, she had affected his dreams and nocturnal musings on a regular basis. It had been such a freak encounter. He and Jess had hauled a few bushels of corn down to be milled, and the girl happened to be there at the time, assisting her father. As the boys hopped off the wagon and moved to fetch the baskets of corn, Hazeltine sallied out of the mill door to help the young customers with their load. However, the wooden steps leading from the loading porch to the parking area were still dampy-slick from the previous evening's rain. The unfortunate girl slipped down the short flight and suffered a hard tumble down every last step, all the way to the muddy ground. Of course, Rufus and Jesse immediately rushed to her aid and tried to help the poor girl to her feet, but they quickly discovered she could not stand. Unfortunately, Hazeltine's ankle had been broken. So in one quick instinctive swoop, Rufus picked up the injured girl in his strong arms, cradling her in front of him, and carried her up the steps and inside the mill.

The way she had felt and the way she had smelled must have been infectious; because every night since then, just before nodding off to sleep, his mind raced to appraise those pleasurable sensations, over and over again. Just the previous evening, he had dreamed of peering deep into the strange girl's mesmerizing green eyes. He had also remembered how her ample bosom had crushed against his own chest, sending surges of adrenalin and other hormonal substances charging through his body. Every night, he dreamed of her, and every night the thoughts of holding her once again lulled him to sleep.

But Rufus doubted Hazeltine even knew his name, as he looked on with his companions at the beautiful belle sitting in the wagon. A few tresses of auburn-colored hair spilled from under the white bonnet she was wearing. Her plain sky-blue dress covered her from just below the chin to the tops of her shoes. *A picture of sure loveliness*, Rufus thought, as he gaped in her direction. And then, of all things, Hazeltine spotted them and smiled and waved. The three of them, stunned at first, simply waved back like homesick sailors signaling to their eager girls waiting at the dock.

"You's not goin' over to says somethings to her, Rufus?" Jesse excitedly asked again.

"If you don't go, Rufe, then I might try it myself," Hack threatened.

The war talk must have inspired Rufus with a newfound courage. While still staring at Hazeltine, he responded to his pals, "Well, why not? Here goes nothin', boys. Let's see what trouble I can get myself into. Wish me luck!" And he raised himself up off the ground, brushed the dirt off his pants, and sauntered over to where the girl of his dreams sat in the seat of the wagon.

"Hello there, Hazeltine. How you doing? It's a pretty fair day, isn't it?" Rufus was nervous, and it showed. *Two questions at once—what am I thinking—idiot!* he admonished himself.

"Oh, hello, Rufus. Doing fine, and, yes, it is a pretty day. Haven't seen you about the mill recently. Thought you might have forgotten all about me—after having to carry me up those steps like you did." And then Hazeltine gave Rufus a teasing smile that sent shivers down his spine. *She does know my name! She remembers me!* He was thrilled.

"Oh, no—no! Of course, I haven't forgotten you, not atall. I—"

No sooner had their chat begun than it was interrupted, as Horace Mann strode up and vaulted into the wagon seat. Taking up the reins to the mule team, he took notice of the handsome young man who had been chatting with his daughter. The miller reached over to shake Rufus's hand and greeted, "Hello there, Rufus. Heared inside that your pa's going to captain our company. Won't you congratulate him fer me please, and tell him we'll be praying fer him and all his soldiers."

Damn it all to hell, Rufus thought. *Couldn't you have given us just a little more time?* Then he gave the miller a stout hand shake and replied, "Yes sir, Mr. Mann. I'll tell him. Sure will." Then he backed off from the wagon as it started to move.

"Oh, Rufus, it's 'Tine.' Call me 'Tine' the next time we meet, won't you? I hope it will be real soon. Don't be a stranger at the mill, hear?" And then Hazeltine turned away, as her father headed up the East Fork toward the mill.

Hack and Jesse rushed over to him, excited and puzzling over what the conversation had entailed. "Did she like you's, Rufus?" Jesse blurted out.

And Hack queried, "Well, what did she say to ye, Rufe?"

Dumbfounded and barely able to speak, Rufus answered with a brevity born of frustration, "Aww, nothing."

Chapter 3

The Bee Woman

It was a sweltering July 4th morning, and everyone who lived in the upper Pigeon River drainage basin had come out to give the boys a rousing send-off. The Edmunston clan was there, as well as most of their tenant families from the furthermost reaches of the East Fork River. They were joined at Deaver's Store by the good folk from the West Fork River Valley and all those hailing from the expansive bottomland surrounding the juncture of the two forks of the Pigeon River. The hundred or so volunteers calling themselves the Haywood Highlanders were about to head to far-off battlefields and unknown dangers. Before doing so, their families and neighbors aimed to say their proper goodbyes and send them on their way in style.

Long wooden tables were set up across the store yard, and spread on top of these was an astounding variety of lavish country fare: cornbread, biscuits, hoe cakes, cream corn, potato and squash and cucumber salads, hashed and mashed potatoes, gravy, green beans, jams, jellies, honey, bacon hams, fried chicken, cobblers, pies, cookies, and much more. The soldiers-to-be gobbled the food down, as their families, loved ones, and friends mingled around their boys—while eating heartily themselves. It was a going-away gathering, of course, and mixed with the pride and excitement was a good deal of anxiety and sadness. Heartfelt prayers were offered to the courageous Rebel soldiers, and storms of tears were shed. There were certainly no dry eyes at the table where the Edmunstons assembled.

Basil and Julia hugged each other, time and time again, while Mary and Emily clung to them tightly, sobbing and crying unashamedly. Rufus stood back and watched as the bottled-up sadness within him sought relief. But he was not about to succumb to such sentimental weakness. For goodness sakes, he was fifteen years old. Besides that, his father was counting on him to look after things and take care of the women. It took everything he had to conceal his sorrow and glistening eyes, but he somehow got away with it.

Rufus not only loved his father, but he admired the man. Basil had been only twenty years old in 1846, when he was relegated to the family's plantation in Haywood's wild mountains. He was sent there to fend for himself and manage the business affairs of the expansive farming enterprise, along with overseeing the band of slaves who worked the place. It was his *familial duty*, as his father put it to him at the time, and Basil did not shirk those duties. Now, the way Rufus saw things, the same familial responsibility was transferred to his broad young shoulders. In his father's absence, it was going to be up to him to run the place, and he meant to do his father proud, no matter what the tests and challenges.

"Oh, Basil, dear Basil, please look after yourself. Promise me that you will, and that you won't take any unnecessary risks," pled a shattered and pitiable Julia. "I don't think I will ever be able to go to sleep, knowing that you are in a dangerous way."

Mary and Emily heaved with distress as the teary wetness plastered their sweet smooth faces. "Come back to us soon, Father. Don't stay gone long," young Emily ordered.

And Mary insisted, "Watch out for those awful Yankees, Father. Please don't let them shoot you! And don't you forget, you promised to send us letters every other day."

Such sad last conversations were being repeated a hundredfold around Deaver's Store that late morning. When midday approached, the allotted time Captain Edmunston was to march his troops off to Asheville, a sudden loud and familiar voice boomed over the din. "Ever'body gather in close! Come on over here!" It was none other than Commissioner Hartgrove standing on the store porch and doing the speech-making again. "That's right, come on in a little closer now!" After a minute or two of shuffling and edging tighter and tighter together, Columbus Hartgrove saw that his audience was positioned well enough for him to proceed.

"Thank ye all, ladies and gentlemen, fer coming out today. And most of all, we want to give thanks to these here brave men who have volunteered their services to the State of North Carolina and, I reckon, to the Confederacy. There ain't no telling what hard duty awaits them or what battlefields, way yonder beyond these mountains, they may fight on. But I kin say one thing fer certain. These here men of our'en, ever last one of 'em, will do us all proud. Ain't no doubts atall about it. If them Northern Yankees set out to invade our state, then these men will stand at our border and send them back with their tails between their legs. Course, that be them Yanks that don't get shot first." He paused to assess the crowd's reaction to the artful dose of humor and was pleased with the loud outburst of applause and vocal agreement. When the commotion died down, Commissioner Hartgrove started up again.

"Now, I don't mean to give no speech here today. But before our Haywood Highlanders—that's the name they give to themselves—before these Haywood Highlanders marches off down the road towards Asheville, I thought it only right and proper that we should offer a good prayer to send them on their way. So with that being said, let's everyone, now, bow our heads so we can pray." Hartgrove paused to let the solemnity of the moment settle in. In mere seconds the silence was deafening, and he began the heavenly entreaty.

"Our Father, we bow down together here in humble recognition of Yer great goodness and wisdom and power. We stand before Ye today, as our brave men are about to set off on a great crusade against an evil that dares to stomp on our rights and independence. Our boys are likely to march into danger's way in the death's valley, and fight the Northern foe that seems bent on descending into this here state. Ye, who shines the light that guides us and offers the hope that kindles our inspiration, will certainly know at whose side righteousness resides. We humbly ask that Ye bless our boys, O heavenly Father, with the bodily strength and courage to crush the enemy who dares to invade our own homeland. Watch out fer 'em, dear Lord, we beseech Ye. We remain Yer servants, dear God, and intend to abide by Yer word and wishes, as tolt to us in the Bible—Amen."

The crowd of more than five hundred men, women, and children repeated Hartgrove's "Amen" and then moved in mass to break up. Uneasy soldiers behaving as proud crusaders began forming into files, just as they had been taught in the company drills over the past several weeks. After kissing Julia and the girls one final time, Basil pulled Rufus to the side and gave him some last-minute fatherly counsel.

"You be strong, boy. I don't have any doubts that you can oversee our farming business and take good care of your mother and sisters. Remember what I said about the Africans. They can be vexing at times, so don't let them have their way. Be firm with them, and, if need be, call up Columbus Hartgrove to help you with the hard-disciplining business. There's one more thing, Rufus. I don't want you holing up too closely to the Den. Get out and go to other places with your mother and sisters and enlarge your acquaintances. You need to hear the opinions and transactions of the neighbors, and then you can make your own decisions. That's what your Grandfather Edmunston told me once, and I found his advice to be sound."

Basil then moved closer to Rufus and wrapped his powerful arms around the boy, pulling him in close and hugging and kissing the side of the boy's face. "I love you, son." Then quickly the embrace was broken, and Basil hurried over to take charge of his company. Rufus's eyes followed his father's stride, as a slow stream of giant tear drops finally washed down his cheeks and a scary feeling of emptiness crept over him.

In the first weeks of his father's absence, Rufus kept extraordinarily busy. He thought it best to show some spunk and initiative, so as not to worry his mother nor leave any doubts in the minds of the Africans that a new master was in charge. So, he drove the slaves hard. When they were not out in the fields battling the weeds, he had them ditching and splitting rails for fencing. The female slaves had the gardens to tend to and were kept busy with their spinning and weaving work, as well. On rare occasions, one or more of the slaves were mandated to a tenant farm when a crisis arose or the farmers got themselves in some sort of fix. It was for this reason, today, that Rufus had escorted Jess and his father, Lark, up the river to help out old man Josiah Anderson, leaseholder of the Crab Orchard farm.

Deriving its name from the dense thickets of native flowering crabapple trees that grew on the hillsides, the Crab Orchard property was uncharacteristic of the East Fork land. It contained a wide expansive flood plain, spreading from the right bank of the river to the heavily forested, steep mountainsides. The Orchard's vast acreage of fertile alluvial soil held the most productive potential, by far, of any of the Edmunstons' tenant tracts. Of late, the elderly Anderson had found himself in a bind after his only son, Manson, came up with a broken leg. Josiah, whose years totaled well into the sixties, was not strong enough to plow and tend to the more than thirty acres of corn and wheat crops by himself.

The scarcity of male hands on the premises could be attributed to a contagion that had infected the family some ten years before. All four of Josiah's grandsons—and a granddaughter—had succumbed to an unusually virulent strain of measles. So, it was for good reason that Rufus endeavored to give the old man some much-needed assistance. And, after all, Anderson was his natural maternal grandfather.

"Here's some help fer you, Mr. Anderson. Brought up Jess and Lark to hoe that bottom cornfield fer you. It looks like the weeds have 'bout taken it over." Rufus cracked a grin to ensure the men his comment was only an attempt to inject some humor into the situation. Josiah had been right tardy in getting his crop planted, and it appeared to Rufus that it was not going to make much of anything if they did not hurry and get the weeds whacked down. "What you think, Lark? A couple of days or so to hoe all those rows?"

Surprised somewhat by the question directed his way, Lark was a little slow to answer, "I—I can't say fo' sure, Massa Rufus, but I believes dat be 'bout right. We's goin' to works hard and steady to gets it done fo' you's and Massa Anderson. Yessir, we's goin' to works real hard." Nodding his head up and down, Lark looked over toward Jesse for understanding and support. His son gave him a blank look and then turned his head toward the cornfield, dreading the toil ahead.

But then Josiah jumped in. "Don't ye worry yerselves none, boys. I'll lend ye a hand with the hoeing! Ain't nary too old and feeble to heft a hoe, don't reckon. Never going to be that old—no siree!" From the looks on their faces, neither Lark nor Jesse appeared impressed with the old man's gesture.

Rufus heard Josiah's words and could sense the slaves' doubtful sentiments that any real assistance would come from Anderson's quarter. But he let the thing hang, as his mind inexplicably flashed away from the present into a soulful musing about his Anderson heritage. Josiah Anderson was, in fact, his natural grandfather. Rufus had been born to Josiah's daughter, Altha, shortly after Basil had made his appearance on the East Fork—fifteen years ago. The story of Rufus's birth had long been ingrained into his being.

Basil had recounted to his son how, in the middle of the night, he had been summoned to the Andersons' cabin after Altha had gone into labor. Her unborn baby was breeched, he soon discovered, and consequently the young master was forced into a very nerve-racking, uncomfortable, and unpleasant midwifing duty. Somehow, though, he summoned the courage and gumption to reach inside Altha's birthing canal and miraculously extract the slimy but healthy baby boy—Rufus.

In doing so, Basil had unwittingly saved the lives of the mother and child, both of whom he came to adore. But promising plans to make a family with them unraveled upon the startling reemergence of Altha's estranged husband, who had deserted her months before. In a sudden and tragic turn of events, the demented husband, Sam Beck, stabbed Altha to death. Reacting with justifiable fury, Basil tracked down and killed the scamp. Afterward, the brokenhearted Basil contracted with Altha's father, Josiah, to adopt Rufus.

"You's not hears me, Rufus?" Jess impatiently asked, as he startled his master friend out of the stupor.

"No, I'm sorry, Jess—what did you say?" Rufus apologized.

"I axed if we's can start with da hoeing now. There be's a sight of hoeing needs be done." Jesse was annoyed at his friend's lack of attention. A solid two days of work was staring him right in the face, and he was anxious to get on with it.

"Oh, yeah, Jess, go on and get yerselves started. I've got to go over and see the Bee Woman. Reckon she's about, Mr. Anderson?" Rufus had never called the old man 'Grandfather.' He did not feel comfortable addressing him as such, although there were certainly no ill feelings harbored. Theirs was not a strained relationship atall, but truthfully, Josiah had never tried to get too close to the boy. The mere sight of Rufus manifested hurtful memories that the grandfather simply wished to remain buried.

Josiah furrowed his brow slightly and moved his head slowly, up and down. "'Spect so, son, lessen she's took off into the woods somers. Been right concerned 'bout Folsom lately—I sure 'nuff have. She jest don't seem right in the head no more, it seems to me. I do believe them critters she keeps 'bout her place has got more sense than she does. Don't doubt it none atall, if they've gone to sleeping with her." The old man acted genuinely concerned about the plight of his widowed daughter-in-law.

Folsom Anderson lived in a little log structure up the creek a short ways from Josiah. Known to the locals as the Bee Woman and to be the best healer in the county, she kept bees around her place. The Bee Woman was all by herself up there in the woods, except for her bees and a menagerie of wild animals that wandered in and out of her cabin at leisure: possums, coons, squirrels, a polecat, black snakes, and the like. Her dozen or so bee gums— short stubby sections of hollowed-out black gum tree trunks—were spotted a short piece off from her place, along the edge of a clearing. Thousands upon thousands of buzzing and humming honey bees occupied these hives, constantly working to convert nature's nectar into sweet delicious honey. In addition to sweetening her breads and puddings, the Bee Woman found this honey to be an essential ingredient for her potent healing concoctions.

She also was a childless widow, the Bee Woman was. Many years ago, her husband, Jesse Anderson, had been killed on an adventurous undertaking with Basil to round up two runaway slaves. Coincidently, these runaways turned out to be the future parents of Rufus's slave friend, who was later named after the Bee Woman's husband. Tragedy again fell upon Folsom's doorstep in just a few short years, when the measles disease struck down her and Jesse's only children—a boy and girl.

Upon Jesse Anderson's last dying breaths, Rufus's grief-stricken father had made a promise to look after the tenant's family, and he had made good on that promise. Rufus's business with the Bee Woman today was in that vein. He had a sack of corn meal strapped to his horse's back, and he aimed to deliver it to his Aunt Folsom.

Her place was downright creepy, and it gave Rufus an uneasy jittery feeling sometimes. The cabin had once been a crude stock shelter. After Jesse and Folsom married, they threw up some more logs and spiffed the place up a mite, and called it home. A decaying bear hide and two ragged wolf pelts—old conquests of Jesse's—were still tacked high to an outside wall. From the porch's low rafter poles hung racks of deer antlers, bunches of drying herbs and plants and flowers, strings of leather-britches beans, and several long clusters of box turtle shells strung together. When the breezes blew through the copse of woods where the cabin nestled, an eerie sound of rattling antlers and clapping tortoise shells gave fair warning to unsuspecting visitors. However, on this oppressively muggy day, the wind was calm, and Rufus was spared the haunting tolls.

"Aunt Folsom," Rufus called out, as he peeked inside the open doorway. "Hello! Are you in, Aunt Folsom?" As his eyes adjusted to the darkness of the cabin interior, he began to make things out. Hanging from pegs and covering the walls were even more small bundles of dried plants, many more. These, he knew to be her magic plants—the ones that would be ground up or simmered and ultimately mixed with honey to make the healing potions. A sudden movement on the dirt floor caught Rufus's attention. He shuddered when his eyes focused on a long black snake, slithering away from a patch of bright light on the floor where a sunbeam warmed the ground. The perturbed serpent slipped silently beneath the bedstead along the far wall, where it could lie low and monitor the intruder's movements.

After catching his breath again and regaining a semblance of composure, Rufus took note of the small rock hearth. There was no burning fire, only an iron cooking oven and skillet resting in a pile of cold ashes. A roughhewn mantle beam stretched across the fireplace opening. Placed on it were a single candle in a stand and various pieces of earthen flatware, mugs, and cups. Other than the bed, a crude table and chair, and some shelving along the side wall opposite the hearth, he detected no other items of creature comfort. As usual, Rufus was taken aback by the extremely primitive nature of his aunt's abode and her eccentric lifestyle.

The shelving fixed to one of the log walls—four long boards secured one above the other—was crammed full with jars and crocks. It was the honey stash, Basil knew for certain, and he stepped over to make a closer study, and maybe even get himself a taste. The ceramic vessels were of different sizes and shapes, but each one had been carefully sealed with a piece of cloth, stretched over the top and tightly secured with a string tied around the neck. "Hmmm," he mumbled, as he reached up to take one down.

"See something that interests ye, son?"

Almost startled out of his boots and on the verge of screaming, Basil instantly retracted his arm and turned about to face the Bee Woman.

"Oh, Aunt Folsom—whoo—you scared the living daylights out of me. I was jest looking at all the honey you've got stashed away. Has it been a good spring and summer fer it—fer making honey, I mean?"

The Bee Woman did not answer him directly. She just looked up at Rufus and grinned with snuff-stained teeth at him. Her hair, the color of wood ash with splashes of white and black mixed in, was combed neatly and fell loosely on her shoulders. Surprisingly, no bonnet or hat covered her head, even in the blistering heat of this mid-summer day. The effect of such careless abandon had left her skin bronzed and leathery, with faint creases lining the fine features of her face. Wrinkles crossed her brow and crinkled cups formed beneath her eyes. The simple homespun dress she wore, formless and stained with walnut dye, extended down to the tops of her toughened bare feet.

Folsom moved over closer to Rufus and wrapped him in her arms in a tight squeeze. "It's good to see ye agin, Rufus." Rufus was about the best friend the old woman had, other than her bees and wild critters, that is. He had developed a fondness for his eccentric aunt that could not be easily explained. And over time, Aunt Folsom had developed a special affinity for her nephew, too, relishing his frequent visits.

Folsom was comfortable with the seclusion and lonesomeness of her lifestyle in the woods at the Orchard, and she distanced herself from societal entanglements. Raised to be God-fearing, she was once as pleasant and as outgoing as any of God's creature persons on the East Fork River. But ever since the harsh stings of death were visited upon first her husband and then her children, she had lost all of her Godly fears and beliefs. It could fairly be said that she became godless, shunning any and all who tried to redeem her soul—including concerned kinfolk.

Taking the place of religion, Folsom had discovered a joy and satisfaction in keeping bees and in the healing work she provided to the community. It was the realization that her healing honey potions actually benefitted others that boosted her will to live and kept her going. Making the sickly feel better or warding off diseases gave authentic purpose to her life. She became convinced of the real good being rendered to her neighbors. It was not just some vague promise of a good to come in an afterlife. It was a service that was real and good and now. Folsom lived for one thing only—to offer her healing gifts to all those around her who needed and sought them.

Finally pulling out of the embrace, the Bee Woman reached up to one of the shelves. "Been a right good honey season, I reckon. Here, let's take down a couple of these fer ye to take back to yer mother. Tell her this here one in the brown jug is sourwood honey, and, let's see, I reckon this other one is mostly jest plain old clover honey. It be nearly as tasty as the sourwood though. Now, ye've got to let me know what ye allow 'bout it," insisted the Bee Woman, as she handed the jars over to Rufus.

"Thank you, Aunt Folsom. We're all much obliged to you fer yer honey. Since Father went off to the war, I've not bothered with our orchard gums. Think you might be able to see yer way clear to come down and help me harvest what honey there might be in them? Don't believe I'd want to risk it on my own."

Folsom visited her own bee gums daily, walking up to them and standing so near that she was able to clearly hear and see the busy worker bees flying to and fro, in and out of the hives. She habitually hummed an eerie Scotch-Irish chant that had a mysterious settling effect on the bees. So calming was her humming that the bees harbored no fear of the strange woman or sensed a threat to their queens or their special hidden world within the log gums. Even during those extreme occasions when Folsom carefully opened and scooped out the golden honey from the hives, her monotonous droning prevented serious assaults from her bee friends—except for the odd sting every now and again. And the Bee Woman had it in the back of her mind that, one day, she was going to pass along this magical knack to Rufus.

"Be glad to, son," Folsom eagerly replied to her nephew's request for assistance. "Don't reckon it's too late to be robbing the honey. And next week will bring on a new moon—the best time fer robbing, mind ye. Let that be a lesson to ye, Rufus. Only mess with your bees when the moon is on the rise. Come Tuesday be soon enough fer ye?"

"Yes, ma'am, that'll be fine. Say, I saw a snake crawl under yer bed. Do ye want me and Jesse to get rid of it fer you?" Even if he had to pull Jess out of the corn rows to do it, Rufus figured the two of them might be able to muster enough courage to catch the thing.

The Bee Woman nearly pitched a fit at the foolish notion. "What? Certainly not, Rufus! You'll do no such thing. That poor creature ain't going to hurt nary a soul. Why, if not for that snake, this place would be jest a crawling with rats and sech. And don't ye light in on my other critters 'round here, neither. They's as welcome as can be in my home. There's an ol' polecat that's been coming round right regular, and she's taken up to sleeping under the bed. She don't like that snake nary bit, neither. They keep their distance apart, they surely do."

Rufus was accustomed to hearing the Bee Woman speak about her animal friends, as if living amongst them was the most natural thing in the world. But it did not seem natural atall to him, and he would just as soon avoid the subject. "Oh, I almost forgot, Aunt Folsom. I've brought you a sack of cornmeal. It's fresh too. Jest had it milled." And that was all it took for the young man to lose his senses. Only the mere thought and mention of the mill illuminated Rufus's imagination and fantasies. A youthful longing for Hazeltine Mann—or Tine, as she had suggested he call her—flushed his insides with warmth and pleasurable sensations.

After concluding his short visit with the Bee Woman, Rufus carefully stowed the gifted jars of honey in his saddle bags and set off for the Den. Jesse and Lark could be seen in the distance, doing battle with the weeds in the corn rows. Stooped over slightly, the pair of slaves wielded the long-helved hoes expertly, as they attacked and chopped at the invasive plants choking the precious corn stalks. Spying Rufus riding by, both of them threw up their hands and waved at him. And their young master waved back.

The whole time Rufus was plodding down the river road, he could not get Tine out of his mind. He knew he must see her soon and get some bothersome things off his chest. Maybe he could just come right out and express his true feelings for her. That's what he wanted to do. *Anyway, what can I lose*, he wondered.

Well, for one thing, he figured, she might just laugh at him, call him silly, and, then send him packing. Yep, that was certainly a possibility—it was a very good possibility. But worse things had happened before, he realized. After all, at that very minute were there not Americans fighting against each other—that is, trying to kill one another? There sure were, and for no good reason atall that he could cipher. Some families had even been torn apart by their partisanship—one brother favoring the Union and another partial to the Rebels. Or maybe a father and son had chosen opposite sides to fight for. Their beliefs being so strong, they had actually gone off to a war so as to shoot at each other.

How bad is that? he reasoned to himself. *Well, a rejection from Tine could never be that bad, for sure*, Rufus figured. *But what if—say—she receives my sentiments and reacts somewhat favorably? Why, she might just come out and return the affections, and say she likes me, too. That would really be something. What then?*

Giving his horse a gentle kick to liven up the pace, Rufus figured it best to cross that bridge when he came to it—if he ever got to the bridge. And that was a mighty big 'if.'

Chapter 4

Ruckus at the Mill

Rufus was fretting around the Den, trying to locate his clean shirt before heading down to Forks of Pigeon. As was her custom in recent days, Julia was anxious about Basil—and no wonder. More than two months had passed since he marched the Haywood Highlanders out of Forks of Pigeon. The last the family had heard, he was still cooped up in an Asheville military camp awaiting orders to move out. His company and another one from Waynesville, one from Georgia, and seven more from the western Carolina mountains—ten in all—had been assembled into a regiment that would eventually be designated as the 25th North Carolina Infantry Troops. Thomas L. Clingman, a prominent politician from Asheville, had been elected colonel of the regiment, and for more than two months he and his field and staff had been drilling the mountain boys hard, as they learned the steps and maneuvers of a soldier.

Even though the posting at nearby Asheville was far removed from the battlefields and the news from northern Virginia in early September brought word of a great Confederate victory at Manassas, military life was not a bed of roses for Captain Edmunston. He wrote to the family about the tiring and exasperating daily trials he was forced to endure, describing his grueling schedule as follows:

I find the army business requires very close application by myself to make any progress. My time is more fully occupied than it ever was at school or college. We have to recite two hours per day to Colonel Clingman, be drilled by him one hour, and drill our companies for two hours. And then attend battalion drill one hour—making six hours work besides studying lessons, etc., etc.

Basil also wrote that many of the men in the regiment were not fit for army duty or could not adapt to the extreme disciplinary measures required of a soldier. Of particular interest was one account of an attempted revolt by a few disgruntled men, regarding which he wrote:

We had some trouble in the camp Friday night but I think the worst of it is past. Some of the men were trying to get up a rebellion alleging the reason to be that the discipline was such they would not submit to it. Thankfully none in my company were engaged in the revolt. The ring leaders were arrested, and the three of them are now in jail in Asheville. However, I have 3 or 4 in my company now that ought not to have been received. I wish they were out again and will henceforth examine recruits more closely.

Such writings from her dear husband caused Julia to worry frightfully. Although thankful that Basil was staying well out of harm's way, at least so far, she could not bear the thought that he might be exposed to undue duress. Ever hopeful that a postal missive from him might await them at her father's store, she insisted that Rufus go down and check.

"Now, Rufus, while Mr. Mann is grinding your corn, go on down and see if we have a letter from your father. Surely, we must have one. It's been more than a week now, since we've heard anything from him. Oh, how I worry about him so."

Rufus felt his mother's pain, and he also agonized for his father, although secretly. A captain's responsibilities were so immense. At least, it seemed to him they were, with all those soldiers' families counting on his father to lead their men properly and look after their welfare.

"Don't you worry, Mother. I'm sure he's doing as well as can be expected. I'll go and check fer mail. Do you want me to pick anything else up fer you or the girls?"

Mary overheard him and, sticking her head out the kitchen door, announced a special request, "A stick of licorice would suit me fine, Rufe."

And Emily chimed out excitedly from behind the wall, "Me too!"

Looking toward his mother who nodded her compliance, Rufus's reply produced shivers of pleasurable anxiousness within his young sisters. "Okay, girls, I'll take yer candy orders and see about getting them filled," he said as he finished dressing. "Now I'm off everyone. Be back in a few hours." And with that said, he hustled out the door toward the barn and the slaves' quarters.

Rufus found Jesse busily hitching up a team of mules to an ancient box-sided farm wagon. It was one whose utility had been demonstrated over a considerable span of years, extending way back to the era of Rufus's grandfather, Thomas Edmunston. He and his wife, Louisa, had in fact pioneered the East Fork wilderness. They settled there in the early 1800s on land endowed to them by Louisa's father as a wedding gift. For twenty years, they struggled to make a life and living for themselves in the dark mountainous country, before finally giving it up and removing back east to the Edmunston family plantation. But they held on to their vast Haywood landholdings and, over the years, had employed local overseers to manage the slaves and the farming operation, until Rufus's reluctant father was anointed overseer and master in 1846.

The two boys loaded a couple of baskets of fresh shelled corn into the back of the old wagon, along with another basket of wheat. It was just enough, in Rufus's estimation, to occupy miller Mann's time while the lovely daughter was sought out. That was his plan anyway—to talk to Tine and try to get more familiar. He reckoned if he was going to dream about her every night, then he ought to get to know her better and see what she allowed about him. And if she took to him atall, why who knows, maybe they could start courting and such. That was what was running through his mind, as he and Jesse started for Forks of Pigeon.

Rolling down the river road, Rufus and Jesse whiled away their time with idle conversation. It was a cool and pleasant Saturday morning with the feel of fall settling over the mountains. Although the forest trees were not yet fully awash with autumn's bright hues, the stately poplars flashed tints of golden butter and the maple leaves were just beginning to redden. These hints of the colorful show soon to come were everywhere but, if the boys noticed, they did not show it.

"Guess I'm going to have to send you and the others up to the Orchard to help Mr. Anderson get in that late corn crop," Rufus mumbled to Jesse. "Manson is back on his feet but still ain't much fit to work—don't reckon. I'll tell Lark to get up a crew Monday and head that way." Jesse offered no reaction, and the two of them just stared blankly at the road ahead.

Finally, these few words issued from the slave's mouth, as his attentions remained fully on the road and the team he was handling, "Okay, Rufus. We's goes and picks the corn if you says so. 'Spect some may be frostbited?"

"Surely do, after that early frost. Mother allowed it was the earliest frost she can remember. Tell yer father—no, I'll do it—I'll talk to Lark myself, and let him know that the Den's share of the crop should contain at least one third of the corn that's been bit bad."

The two friends carried on with such 'lively' prattle until they laid eyes on the mill in the distance. Just as Rufus had feared, there were several wagons and horses already lined up in front of the mill. Men and boys could be seen piddling outside, awaiting their turn-of-meal to get their grinding done. Jesse eased up behind the last wagon in line, and Rufus hopped out to greet a few of the waiting customers he recognized. A quick glance toward the open door of the mill revealed no sign of the miller's daughter anywhere.

Stepping inside the darkened interior of the massive timber frame building, his senses attuned to the unique pungent smells of the place. Grain dust, souring from age and dampness, coated the posts and overhead beams and clung to the rough-sawn siding boards. The smelly dank powder had penetrated deep into every dark crevice and corner. Also grabbing his attention were the distinctive sounds of the mill—rushing water, clattering iron and wooden mechanisms turning and meshing, and the constant humming of three pairs of burr stones. As his eyes slowly accustomed to the dimness,

Rufus spotted Mr. Mann adjusting the feed rate of corn dropping into the whirling eye of a set of running stones. But Tine was nowhere to be seen. *Where was she?* he fretted.

"Hello, Mr. Mann. Brought you a few bushels of grain to be ground. How long you reckon before you can get to me?" As Rufus queried the miller, a sinking feeling came over him. It appeared that Hazeltine was not there and that his trip was destined to be fruitless. The weighty burden of longing he had carried to the mill that morning was not going to be eased, for sure. There was no doubt in his mind, atall.

"Morning, son. Good to see ye down. Looks to be more than an hour or so, if'en ye don't mind waiting a short spell." As he spoke to Rufus, the miller gave a concerned glance through the open doorway at the growing mob outside. On such a busy morning, he was not only extremely conscious of the waiting patrons, but he worried that his milling equipment would break down under the heavy operational stresses. He was keeping his fingers crossed and praying there would be no interruptions.

"Suppose we'll wait then. Say, Mr. Mann, is Hazeltine around anywhere?" Rufus shyly asked, although he was convinced at that point she was nowhere to be found. But the miller surprised him.

"Yep—she is, son. Ye'll find her and Hack upstairs at the loading hoppers."

What in hell is Hack doing up there with her? Rufus instinctively worried. "Oh—okay. Would it be all right, then, to go up there to talk to them?"

"Guess it would. But best ye be kerful, son, ye hear? Can't have anyone getting themselves hurt in my mill."

"Yes, sir, I will! Thank you, Mr. Mann!" replied Rufus as he hustled toward the steps and proceeded to bound up the long flight to the upper floor.

Both Tine and Hack Hartgrove were surprised to see the handsome blond head rising up out of the stairwell. Rufus, being a full six feet and two inches tall and still growing, had to stoop to clear the lowest rafter beams, as he ambled over to speak to the obviously friendly couple. Hack bellowed out first to his best friend, "Rufe, good to see ye. Ye're jest in time to help me and Tine load up these here hoppers."

Rufus was obviously annoyed, but tried to bury it with a bit of sarcastic humor. "What you doing up here bothering this pretty girl fer, Hack? Surely you're not doing anything that might resemble work." He could see that both Hack and Hazeltine were covered in grain dust, and it was plainly obvious they had been toiling hard.

Hack hesitated to rebut, but not Hazeltine. She let out a hearty laugh and took up for Hartgrove. "He's helping me lift all these heavy baskets, Rufus. Did you come up to help me too?"

"I didn't know you needed any help, Tine," Rufus answered. "Looks like Hack has beat me to it though."

Hack explained, "I've been helping Mr. Mann fer the past week. During this heavy milling period, he allowed how he could use some help. So I took him up on it. 'Sides, I can use me some tobac'er money—sure can. How did ye find me up here?"

"Reckon I just got lucky," the sarcasm continued. And then Rufus turned to address the beautiful ghostlike girl whose dress and face were blanketed in grain dust. "I was actually looking for Tine here—not you, Hack. Your father told me where to find you. Didn't have anything special to discuss—just wanted to pass the time of day, is all." Deep down Rufus knew his romantic plans had run afoul, and it was destined to be yet another wasted day. Any sort of lonesome rendezvous with his dream girl was definitely out of the question now.

"Oh, how sweet of you, Rufus. But we have to keep feeding these hoppers, or else Father's not going to be too happy with us." Hazeltine's disappointment was manifest, but she came up with another suggestion. "I was telling Hack there's a corn shucking party this coming Wednesday afternoon down at Osbornes'. Why don't you meet us there? Should be plenty of food and fun to go around."

So Hack's going to be there too, Rufus thought. *What's he trying to do? Make a move on Tine?* While pondering Hack's purpose, he responded to the invitation. "Sure, Tine. That sounds real good to me. I'll jest plan on seeing the two of you there, I reckon." Well, after all, he had no other option the way he figured it. He could not just give up on the girl before he had a chance to express his heartfelt sentiments. Surely, at the corn-shucking lark he could steal some alone time with Tine and find a way to convey his true intentions toward her.

"Good!" an excited Tine replied, as she approached nearer to Rufus. Leaning over and kissing the side of his face, she whispered in his ear. "We can talk and have a grand time there." Then she was all business again as she pulled back and stated, "Now, Hack Hartgrove, we need to bring up some more baskets of corn, I believe. Want to walk down the stairs with us, Rufe—I hope I can call you that?"

Rufus's heart rate climbed dramatically with the touch of the ghostly Tine's lips to his face and her fragrance overpowering the sharp scents of the mill. As he cast a skeptical eye toward Hack, he responded, "Course you can call me that, Tine." Then he fell in behind the working couple as they descended the stairs and stepped outside onto the loading platform.

Automatically looking for his wagon, Rufus's eyes landed instead on a noisy gang of people encircling a scuffle of some sort. From his elevated perch he could easily make out that the only Negro there that day, Jesse, was at the center of attention. With no second thoughts, Rufus leaped off the porch in a flash and rushed into the crowd, pushing and shoving his way through. He found Jesse lying partially on his back and trying to right himself, with his face badly blooded and his shirt ripped to shreds.

Crack!! The terrible sound of a bull whip's braided leather thong tearing into Jesse's flesh resounded above the shouting voices. Instantly, Rufus turned to spot a brute of a man holding the butt-end of the whip. He was a rough-looking sort all right, with a head full of long white hair, a scruffy beard, and dressed head-to-toe in buckskin. The man was in the act of yanking the long leather strap high into the air and preparing to unleash yet another powerful cracking blow against Jesse's hide.

A mighty fury erupted inside Rufus, boiling his blood and steeling his muscles. He had no idea how Jesse could have gotten himself into such a fix, but he was confident it was not because of the slave's doings. Like a panther pouncing on its prey, Rufus gave out a loud guttural howl and charged at the whip-wielding brute, crashing heavily into him and bowling the two of them down hard onto the ground. The beastly man was about his father's age and a good bit heavier and stouter than Rufus, that was for sure.

Rufus moved deftly and quickly, leveraging himself on top of the ruffian and throwing a hard punch that was partially deflected. The man clasped both his enormous hands around Rufus's throat and began to strangle the life out of the wild stripling who had him penned down. At the same time Rufus was being choked to death, he was grabbed from behind by another participant in the brawl. This unseen person was attempting to jerk Rufus off of the brutish adversary, who still clutched Rufus's neck in a death grip. Whoever the mysterious attacker was—Rufus could not get a look at him—his grasp relaxed and, all of a sudden, broke completely loose. *Thank goodness for that!* Rufus was already fearful that he might have taken on a little more bear than he had powder and lead.

Lo and behold, Hack had interjected himself into the middle of the ruckus. Seeing that Rufus was at a disadvantage and being double-teamed, he had wildly tackled and bulled the other assailant off of his friend. The whole situation had become frantic and crazy now. It had grown into a full-blown, four-man, anything-goes contest. Fighting for their lives in front of Deaver's Mill, the pair of teenage boys had gone to battle against two much older and stronger men.

Crawling away from the fray to lick his wounds, poor Jesse could not believe the mess he had gotten himself and his master into. Certainly, he had not intended to stir up any trouble with these two men—a father and son named Bugg. While Rufus was inside the mill romancing, the Buggs had rudely bucked in front of Jesse in the long queue of wagons. All Jesse had done was to politely try to reclaim his rightful position in the line. Just that simple acknowledgment of his turn in the meal line—handled in the most civil manner possible—had set the two men off.

Spewing profanities and calling Jesse an arrogant black nigger, they both had rushed him and drug him out of the wagon. The older Bugg—Amos was his given name—had taken a coiled whip from his hip and immediately began delivering fierce stinging blows to Jesse's body. Concurrently, Bugg's son, Eli, was beating and kicking Jesse on the ground as the blows from the rawhide strap had continued, cutting deeply into the slave's hide. Excited onlookers had hurriedly crowded around to observe the brutal action—but not one of them had protested or made a move to help.

"What do ye say now, ye arrogant blackie—still want yer place in line?" Amos had hollered as he cocked his arm high, readying to serve another lash against the hapless slave.

Eli had taunted, "Going to learn ye a lesson, nigger, ye ain't never 'bout to ferget. Ain't right fer a nigger to talk to us white folk unless ye're tolt to." As another loud blow cracked across Jesse's body, Eli had screamed out, "How's that feel, nigger? God-damn yer black hide, ye son-of-a-bitch!"

Yes, Jesse had unwittingly got himself into a real scrape all right, but now he had Rufus and Hack fighting on his behalf. As the slave looked over at the action, Hack was shoving Eli Bugg away from Rufus and screaming, "Leave them alone. If ye want to fight somebody, then have at me." Hack was wiry and feisty, but Eli was the much stronger of the two. The younger Bugg puffed himself up and took up the challenge, throwing a colossal punch straight at Hack's face.

In the meantime, the battle between the elder Bugg and Rufus was very much in doubt. Amos Bugg was indeed a beast and even stronger and meaner than he looked. However, Rufus was taller than Bugg and what he gave up in physical strength, he made up for with cat-like quickness and youthful stamina. After fending off the choking attempt by biting deep into the strangler's forearm, Rufus was knocked over to the ground by a powerful backhanded slap to the face. Bugg instantly jumped on top of him and ferociously began trying to gouge out the meddling boy's eyes. But Rufus fought off the malicious scratching and gouging efforts and was able to wrestle his foe onto the ground for a brief instant. It was just long enough for him to rare back and deliver a firm close-fisted clout to Bugg's nose, severely breaking it, as it turned out. Bugg screamed in pain with blood gushing from his snout. What a lucky punch it was! But Rufus seized the advantage and let the mean bully have it again and again. Soon, the wretched man had had enough, writhing and whimpering on the ground in excruciating pain. He was through with his bullying ways—for this day at least.

Hack was not faring so well with Eli Bugg, though. They had equally exchanged slugs until a particularly effective one landed Hack on his back. Bugg had pounced on him and was trying to exploit weaknesses and openings to punch Hack into oblivion. As Rufus slowly raised himself off the ground and stretched out his tall frame, he recognized his buddy's dire predicament. *Time to return Hack's favor*, he thought to himself. Still in survival mode and digging deep for his last ounces of energy, Rufus took about three running steps and launched a mule-like kick with his boot to the side of the younger Bugg's head. The man never saw it coming and simply careened over limply on top of the struggling Hack.

Just like that, it was all over. The excited gawkers must have felt highly entertained and content to have witnessed a good fight. It had been such an unlikely bout, with the two fledglings pitted against the brutish and seasoned father-and-son duo. Rufus and Hack had been extremely fortunate on this day. Their David-and-Goliath encounter could easily have gone the other way, with the direst of consequences for both of them. But they were young and fearless and would soon shuck off this whole affair. Things happen, they reckoned, and sometimes there's nothing a body can do but to fight for what is right. And the both of them figured Jesse was worth fighting for.

"You all right?" an exhausted, hunched-over Rufus asked Hack, while gasping for air. Hack pushed Eli's body to the side and slowly got to his feet. Both boys were bloodied, and their bruised faces and ribcages were already turning black and blue.

"Guess so. He jest 'bout got the best of me though. Ye okay?"

"I reckon I am. Let's go see what Jess looks like."

Rufus gave a hasty glance around at the dispersing bystanders headed back to the queue, at the two Buggs lying prostrate on the ground, and finally over toward the mill. There, on the loading porch, his eyes found Tine staring directly at him. Standing beside her father, she had witnessed the awful fight from the elevated vantage point and had suffered every pain and hurt inflicted on both Rufus and Hack. Her face glistened with tears, as she struggled to control her breathing and regain her composure. Realizing she must do something to help her friends, Tine stepped down from the porch and hurried over to join them.

Chapter 5

SHUCKING FOR LOVE

Rufus was hunched over and busily staunching his slave friend's bloody wounds, when he felt a hand on his shoulder and heard a familiar voice.

"Here, son, let's have a good look at him."

He twisted around quickly to find his Grandfather Deaver stooping over to offer assistance. In no time, word of the altercation had reached the Colonel at his store, located a half mile down the river. The old man had lost little time getting up to the mill to check on his grandson and see what trouble the boy had gotten himself into.

"'Fraid he's going to need a doctor's care fer sure, Rufus," the Colonel allowed, after only a brief examination. He then stood up and prompted one of the onlookers to ride off for Doctor Allen, who lived down the river a ways at Flowery Garden. "Okay, men, let's git him in the wagon and over there out of the hot sun. See if ye kin find some fresh straw or a tick—something soft—yonder at the mill to lay him on. Need to git him comfortable while we wait fer the doctor." In scant minutes, the aged and revered Colonel Deaver had rendered some real organized assistance on Jesse's behalf and brought order to the confused madness at the mill.

As the Colonel interrogated Rufus and Hack concerning the incident, he looked them over real good too, feeling and probing their facial cuts and bruises. "Say he didn't provoke them nary bit?" Deaver queried.

"No, Grandfather. Jesse said them men were trying to take his turn-of-meal. He said he only told them he was in line and that started the whole blamed thing off."

Colonel Deaver gazed at the two Buggs, who by now had come to and had crawled over to the side of the road, away from the traffic. They were both lying with their backs propped up against an old rotten log. "Them men ain't no good, Rufus. Ye need to keep yer distance from them, ye hear me now. Let this thing be. They's been teched by the devil, I do believe they have. Yer father had to kick them off his land fer squatting a few years back. Besides, I'm holding debt notes of their'en for more than a hunderd dollars—been holding 'em fer a good long while now. Ain't no good, them two men ain't."

"I don't aim to cause them bullies any more trouble, Grandfather. It was their fault anyway. Fer sure, I didn't want to get into it with 'em. But they brought it on themselves as fer as I'm concerned. Me and Hack, we'll let it be. I promise you. What you say, Hack?" asked Rufus as he glanced over at his battered friend.

Although Hack was smarting a good deal from the blows he had absorbed, he still had a feisty look about him. Responding to the query, he allowed, "Yeah, I don't want no more trouble with 'em. They're meaner than them Yankees, I 'spect, and can sure fight a sight better. But I reckon we'll have to see if they're going to let this thing rest."

Colonel Deaver had his suspicions that the Buggs would not let it lie. So he strode over to where they sat against the log, shaking off their beatings. Looking down at the two Buggs the Colonel stated matter-of-factly, "Hope ye men have had enough. Got a good mind to send after the sheriff fer this trouble ye've caused."

Gingerly feeling his broken nose, Amos Bugg looked at the Colonel in surprise and growled, "What in hell ye mean, Deaver. Them boys 'tacked us. Ain't that right, Eli?"

"Sure 'nuff did!" replied the furious son. "All Pa aimed to do wus give that uppity nigger boy a right smart lesson. Had it coming to him fer yapping back at us like he did. Said we wus taking his place in line—hah! His place—who ever heard of a nigger having a place?" Eli spoke with a firm conviction that Jesse had the whipping coming to him and that Rufus had caused the fight. "Jest 'cause he be a Edmunston slave don't give him no right to talk back at white folks like us'ens. And then that Edmunston boy jumped Pa fer nary good reason atall."

"Them boys ain't grown yet, Bugg," continued Colonel Deaver. "I'm of a mind to law ye fer beating up on children, never mind that note I'm holding of yer'en that ye ain't never paid me back."

"What goddamned children, Deaver?" an incredulous Amos Bugg snapped back. "That Edmunston boy 'tacked me like a wildcat—ferocious he was. He ain't no children, not by a long sight. He's fitter than any other man I ever seen in these here parts."

"He ain't turned sixteen yet, Bugg, and the other one ain't much older. Fer as I'm concerned, ye've fer sure broken some law or nuther." The Colonel knew his heavy threat was founded on precarious legal ground, but he issued it sternly and resolutely anyhow. "Ye know something, Bugg, if ye and yer son are so keen to fight, ye might consider taking out yer ills on them infernal Yankees. Better to fight them than our own children, don't ye reckon? Ye should've joined up with our brave boys 'fore they marched off to Asheville. Ain't too late, don't 'spect, fer ye to show a little loyalty fer our cause." Deaver paused to let his words sink in and then proposed another option. "But I'm going to leave the thing be, if'en the two of ye drop this here matter—here and now. What ye say?"

Amos was still aching on both the inside and outside as blood trickled from his busted nose. But after Colonel Deaver's scolding, he boiled with an inner evil hatred—Eli too. These men were not going to bow down at the feet of rich folks like the Deavers and Edmunstons—no way were they. However, Amos was hurting so badly that he felt it prudent to shut the old-man Deaver up, so he reluctantly nodded his head, agreeing to drop the matter. Of course the Colonel, who was not known to suffer from naïvity, intuited that he had struck a deal with the devil. He suspected that neither of these Bugg men was likely to keep their promise. But for the time being, he could think of nothing else to do to simmer the heated tensions.

As the Colonel turned to walk away, he gave the Buggs one last fair warning. "Still need my money, Bugg. Going to turn the dunning business over to the sheriff and the court, if ye ain't paid up by year's end." The two Buggs just leered at the behind of the prosperous merchant as he ambled away. Such a cocky son-of-a-bitch, they thought. In their minds, there was still some reckoning to be done with the Edmunston clan, and old man Deaver, too. The Buggs were not done with that lot yet—not by a long shot were they.

During the final days of September, the Haywood Highlanders, or Company F as they were designated within their regiment, marched eastward out of Asheville toward the nearest railhead at Morganton, more than sixty miles distant. The men, wearing the same clothes on their backs as they had worn marching away from Forks of Pigeon, trudged along poor roads winding through the high mountain passes. Luckily, they were not yet burdened with weapons, which were in dire short supply in the Confederacy. The Highlanders simply tramped along in good humor, for the most part, and marveled with wide open eyes at the foreign country they were passing through.

As Captain Edmunston's company approached the rail station at last, his men began shouting loud 'Hoorahs' as a raucous chatter erupted throughout the entire regiment. Ahead of them could be seen a huffing and puffing iron monster, the likes of which most mountain men had never before laid eyes upon.

Private William Bonham, just barely seventeen years old, had the gumption to approach his captain and inquire, "Captain Edmunston, I reckon that there is a train, ain't it?"

"Sure is, Private. And that puffing monster at the head is a steam locomotive engine. Never seen one before?"

"No sir, I ain't, fer sure. Never seen such a sight as this here. It's bigger than big, I reckon. Is that steam belching out from that there high stack, sir?"

"No, that would be smoke, Private Bonham. All that white vapor spewing out from around the engine is steam, I expect. Now, it looks like they're about ready for us. Time to form up, Private." Then Captain Edmunston turned to Lieutenant Deaver and instructed him to prepare the men for boarding.

The rail cars were filled beyond capacity as the train steamed out of Morganton along the tracks to Raleigh, the capital city of North Carolina. Hooting and hollering Rebels hung their heads out of the windows to catch every sight whizzing by. Others, crammed tight against each other on hard wooden benches, had a lark of a time bouncing and jolting every inch of the way. Reaching Raleigh, the regiment disembarked and camped for a couple of days, waiting to receive their uniforms. When they finally drew them, one of the Highlanders declared in amazement that the new gray sack coats and pants were as fine as there ever was.

Adorned with shiny brass buttons upon the breast and a black stripe up the legs, the uniformed mountaineers strutted like peacocks as they took to the train again for the final passage to the Atlantic coast. Once at their coastal encampment in Wilmington, the 25th North Carolina Troops were at long last issued weapons and other accoutrements of war. Whereupon, Captain Basil Edmunston and his Haywood Highlanders drilled and trained in the use of their new armament, while eagerly awaiting the enemy's naval expedition—reportedly headed their way.

On this late Wednesday afternoon, a fair-sized crowd of young people were gathered at the Osborne's farm for the corn-shucking festivities. Rufus had not forgotten the personal invitation Tine had extended him the past Saturday, and when he got there, she and Hack were already shucking away. It was early evening—almost dusky dark—but Rufus could still make out the faces. An open fire burned nearby, and he could see upwards of twenty boys and girls, about his age, seated around a huge mountain of corn and stripping off husks to beat. He recognized a few of the laughing folks partying there, some of whom he had studied with at the Crab Orchard schoolhouse. They all acted friendly enough toward him, and more than one girl called out for Rufus to take a seat at her side, including Edith Osborne whose father owned the place.

"Over here, Rufus, next to me," Edie encouraged as she grinned enticingly at him and patted the ground next to her.

"No, Rufe, over here beside me and Hack. We've saved your place," Tine called out loudly and hurriedly, afraid that her evening might be ruined before it even got started good.

Rufus gazed sheepishly at Edie and explained, "Sorry, Edie, Tine invited me here tonight, and I guess it's only right fer me to crowd in over there next to her."

"Okay, be that way then." But as Rufus squeezed next to Tine the pretty goldilocked Edie plopped down and scrunched up against him. "We can all have fun together, can't we now?" she giggled, digging down into the pile for an ear of corn.

Tine looked closely at Rufus's face and gingerly probed one of the blackened bruises. "Oh, Rufe, what am I going to do with you and Hack? Does it still hurt?" Rufus could see that both of Hack's eyes were black, and he had an ugly cut under one of them.

"Don't I look like a coon or somethin', Rufe?" Hack interjected with a chuckle.

Before Rufus could respond, one of the boys on the other side of the corn pile hollered out, "A red ear, I got one! See!" And the lucky feller proceeded to bend over and plant a big kiss on the girl sitting next to him. That was what this whole corn-husking soiree was about. It was a competition to find the few red ears of Indian corn that Edie Osborne's father had planted within the mountain of corn. Anyone fortunate enough to discover a red ear could kiss the person of his or her choice. It was just a big ol' party, with laughing, frolicking, flirting, and romancing, while someone scratched off tunes from a fiddle, and Edie's mother served up baked sweet potatoes and other tasty nourishments. In this manner, the farmer Osborne got his mountain of corn shucked, and fun was had all around.

Rufus felt funny being sandwiched between two girls, the way he was. Tine looked ravishing, and it was not long before he got that longing inside for her. He wanted to talk to her, just the two of them, but any opportunity for that seemed mighty remote this evening. Ol' Raccoon Hartgrove and Edie Osborne were seeing to that.

Then before too long had passed, there came a scream from Edie at his side, yelling out loudly for everyone to hear, "Found one!" Holding up a red ear to prove her claim, she looked about teasingly at all the boys as she tried to decide who the lucky one was going to be—the one she would bestow her treasured kiss upon. Suddenly, she bounced to her feet and grabbed Rufus's hand, yanking him up off the ground. "Okay, Rufus, let's go."

Edie then led Rufus behind a nearby black walnut tree and clamped her arms tightly around him. "Are you ready for this, handsome?" she brazenly whispered, as she pressed her body against his. Edie was a flirt all right and was doing her upmost to arouse Rufus's romantic urges. She need not have worried. He was about as excited and stirred-up as he had ever been around a girl.

"Ready," came his nervous but anxious reply.

And then Edie pressed her moist hungry lips hard against his and held the kiss for what seemed like ages, Rufus reckoned. She pressed and pressed, and he tasted her deliciousness and felt the wetness of her delicate lips. Finally, she broke away and their lips separated.

"Whew—how was that?" Edie asked, as she gathered herself and tried to catch her breath.

Rufus had never experienced such a sensational feeling. He was queasy and his loins pulsed and ached with the increased rush of blood. "Not bad atall," he was barely able to utter.

Edie led Rufus from behind the tree and back to the circle. The couple maintained sheepish grins, while bearing up under their fellow huskers good-natured heckling. As they resumed their positions around the pile of corn, Rufus cast a glance in Tine's direction in order to gauge her reaction to what had just transpired. And her feigned laughing antics did not conceal the well-directed scowl that found him. She did not appear to be pleased atall with his innocent and harmless indiscretion. The blameless Rufus was beside himself, as he wondered what he might have done differently and worried about what he should do the next time. This corn-shucking business was turning out to be way more problematic than he had suspected.

The evening wore on as the shucking gaiety continued, and the mountain of corn gradually diminished to a mere hill. Visible vapors began to issue from the laughing mouths of the corn huskers as the night air grew crisper and colder. Red ears of corn became scarcer and harder to come by, as did the fortunes of Tine and Hack and Rufus. Neither of these unlucky shuckers so much as sniffed at a red ear of corn until the party drew pert near to a close. Taking up one of the last few ears scattered over the ground, the dejected Rufus tore away the stiff leafy outer wraps. Slowly and before his very eyes, the color of scarlet kernels showed from under the hairy silk covering. At last, Rufus had discovered his own red ear, and now he could relieve those pent-up affections of his. He would take Tine behind that black walnut tree and show her how he felt about her, and give away his heart. That is what he intended to do.

But, unfortunately, it was not to be. At that very moment, when the excited Rufus was about to announce his discovery, Mr. and Mrs. Osborne abruptly broke up the party without warning, thanking everyone for coming and calling it time to be heading home. "Thank ye, everyone! That was a sight of work ye done tonight, and we 'preciate yer efforts! Be careful going home now, ye hear!" With that being said, all of the gay shuckers parted, setting off in every direction as the romantic air of the evening drifted with them.

The hosts were obviously happy with this evening's labors, deeming the party a general success. Edie Osborne was pleased, and so were the several other sweethearts who had enjoyed loving busses. However, an irritated Rufus figured differently and, in frustration, hauled off and hurled his worthless red ear toward the log shuck pen.

Damn it all to hell, he thought to himself as he watched the ear of corn spiral into the darkness.

"Oh, Rufe, would you be so good as to walk me home?"

Shocked, Rufus turned and met Tine's eyes looking up hopefully into his. At the same time, Hack stuck out his hand and gave Rufus a stout shake, allowing, "'Spect I'll be heading down the other way, y'all. It's a fer piece, but don't ye worry none 'bout me. I'll be jest fine." He laughed at his two friends, as he pulled his floppy hat low over his blackened eyes and turned to walk away.

"We'll see ye, Hack. Good luck with that Berkshire sow tomorrow!" Then Rufus looked at Tine and gave her the answer she was expecting—one that he was so thankful to offer. "Sure, Tine. It's right on my way and won't be nary trouble atall."

The night had turned right cold and was faintly lit by the waning quarter moon. Although the stars shone brightly all around, the tinted autumn colors of the forest's trees were lost in gloomy masses of black and gray. Rufus led his horse behind him, as he and Tine walked side-by-side up the darkened river road.

"Father was hoping that either you or Hack would see me home in the dark," Tine explained, as they ambled along while being right careful not to step in mud holes.

Rufus could not believe that his fate had changed so quickly. One moment he thought the whole shucking evening had been a colossal waste of time and the next—well, he could not have hoped for a better opportunity, or venue, to reveal his true feelings to Tine. "Glad to do it, Tine," he replied stiffly. His brain was working furiously to come up with some way to delicately reveal his intimate affections. *How should I begin?*

"Say, Tine, you know that kiss Edie Osborne gave me was all her doing—not mine—don't you? It meant nothing atall to me." It was not the most brilliant start to a heartfelt confession, but at least he got the fire kindled.

With a keen skepticism, Tine replied, "Well, Rufus Edmunston, you sure could have fooled me. You and Edie were both flushed red as beets when you finally came out from hiding behind that tree."

Taken aback and somewhat off balance, Rufus parried that barb as best he could, "I was embarrassed is all. I wasn't expecting such a big kiss and—well—to tell you the truth, Tine, it was the first time I've ever been kissed by a girl, except by my mother and sisters and all."

Tine was still skeptical but demonstrated advanced levels of maturity and tolerance with her considered response, "Sure, Rufe—okay then, I believe you. Wish you could have used that last red ear on me."

What was that? Had he heard her correctly? *So, she knew I had found a red ear of corn.* "Well, I was going to, but Mr. Osborne broke things up right about that time. That's my luck fer you."

"Too bad—I was wishing I could have had a chance to show you the difference between my kiss and Edie's."

Rufus could not believe his ears! Maybe he was not the only one looking for an opportunity to lay things out in the open. Tine, also, seemed bent on revealing her true passions. This was his chance and he did not want to blow it, but how to start? He did not rightly know how, but went ahead anyway. "Tine—I've been meaning to get a chance to say something to you. Well—ever since that day at the mill when you fell and got hurt—'member when I picked you up and carried you inside?" Rufus paused as Tine affirmed with a nod. "Well, ever since I held you, I can't get you out of my mind. I think about you all the time, even in my sleep." There, the young East Forker had done it, and as his heart began to pound harder and harder, he watched anxiously to catch the reaction of the beautiful miller's daughter.

Tine looked closely at his still tender and bruised face and deep into his blue eyes. She then uttered with the upmost satisfaction, "Really?" Thinking there might be even more confessions, she wanted to hear them.

Nervous to get it all out there, Rufus continued, "That's right! I still remember how it felt to hold you against me, and I even 'member how ye smelled. Every night, before I go to bed, I dream about you, Tine. Don't ye make fun at me now—can you believe that? I hope you do 'cause I really like ye, Tine. I don't know what it all means, but I reckon it means I have right smart feelings fer you."

They had stopped and were standing close together, facing each other in the middle of the lonely lane. In the near distance, firelight could be spotted flickering through the only window of her father's small cabin. Tine had held her breath as she drunk in Rufus's every word, swallowing them whole and savoring their tasty implications. She remembered the instance of her injury as distinctly as Rufus did. His strength and sweetness had impressed her, never mind the handsome looks of a boy nearly a year her junior. She had taken notice of him then and had realized almost immediately he was something special. Now, she meant to tell him just what she thought about him, too.

"Oh, Rufe, you're so special. You're the dearest and sweetest boy there could ever be." Tine reached out with one hand and caressed Rufus's battered face. "And I want you to know that I have held feelings for you, ever since that day when you heaved me up into your arms and carried me up those steps. I've reserved my affections for you, Rufe—my sincerest, fondest feelings. Now, let me show you them."

Awkwardly perhaps, yet instinctively, the two solitary figures standing in the dark of the night linked as one into each other's clutches. Their arms wrapped around one another and squeezed tighter and tighter in a consuming embrace. Quickly and passionately, their faces touched, and their lips met in a crush. Their receptive mouths pressed together, forever it seemed, tasting and sensing the other's affections and love. Yes, that was what it was. It was young love they felt for each other that evening in the deserted lane. Theirs was a desperate love—desperate to be expressed and desperate to be returned.

When at long last their lips parted, they remained snugly in each other's clutches, with their noses still touching. Both of them breathed heavily, as their hungry eyes met, and their stares melted into one. In a profound understanding, they seemed able to peer into each other's minds and share the most secret, tender thoughts that lurked there. And they were good thoughts—loving thoughts. They were the pleasing and confusing thoughts of youthful dreams—dreams of a shared future.

Chapter 6

On Thin Ice

During that first winter of the Civil War, Hazeltine Mann and Rufus experienced few opportunities to cultivate their nascent romance. Schooling for Rufus had been supplanted by farming and slave-master responsibilities, which occupied inordinate amounts of his time. Bacon hams from the sixty or more hogs that were slaughtered at the Den were hung to dry in the smokehouse, with the surplus being sold or bartered at Deaver's Store for needed supplies. The corn crops from the Den's bottom fields, as well as those one-third portions from the tenant farms up and down the East Fork, were cribbed and the husk pens filled to overflowing. Several hundred additional bushels of corn were hauled and exchanged for precious Confederate dollars at a drover's stand on the Buncombe Turnpike near Asheville. Livestock was sold at Deaver's Store and to local farmers preparing to drive herds to Greenville, South Carolina, and Augusta, Georgia. The remaining cattle, sheep, and hogs had to be adequately quartered to survive the severe winter weather. All of these tasks, and many more, required Rufus's undivided attention to keep the slaves' backs bent and their minds fixed to the work. It was a full-time, vexing job for sure, with few moments spared for romancing.

Elsewhere on the war front, Captain Edmunston and his Haywood Highlanders, still posted at Wilmington, had passively and impatiently awaited the expected Union amphibious invasion of coastal North Carolina. However, the Yankees decided to bypass the Outer Banks region, and instead sailed for South Carolina's Atlantic coast. Confederate officials reacted immediately when the enemy's intentions became known. Troops were shuttled to South Carolina to defend against the incursion, and amongst these harried Rebel forces was the 25th North Carolina Infantry Regiment. As it turned out, Haywood's mountain boys arrived too late to either fight or prevent the Yankees' naval armada from capturing Hilton Head Island. But they remained stationed nearby in Grahamville, South Carolina, throughout the long winter—along with General Robert E. Lee, whose headquarters were in the vicinity—with orders to protect the vital Confederate railroad connecting the Southern port cities of Charleston, South Carolina, and Savannah, Georgia.

Winter's cold north wind howled outside the East Fork Den, whistling through the chinks in the log walls. Inside, a cozy fire crackled and burned, and the Edmunston family huddled around the hearth while Rufus read aloud from his father's most recent letter from the South Carolina front.

My Dearest Family,

I don't think it probable that the Yanks will attempt to march either on Charleston or Savannah, and if they do not we can't attack them under the cover of their fine guns. So it seems probable to me that if we do not die of disease we will be encamped in this vicinity for some time yet without a general fight, but probably with some skirmishing.

We've lost several men from the measles and last night one man from Cherokee County was shot. He was one of ten men sent several miles from camp to guard a railroad trestle and was shot through mistake by one of his friends who supposed he was an enemy.

You've heard I'm sure of the news from Roanoke Island. The Yanks have taken it also and seemed poised to move inland. This seems like a dark day for the Southern Confederacy, but I do not by any means despair. For I still believe that the Confederate States will yet be free and independent, and a great nation. But of course such defeats as we have lately sustained will prolong the struggle and increase the sum of missing and suffering.

    Don't you worry about me. I can look after myself, and when I get to feeling sick or sad I am accustomed to think of my Wee Bit Wife and fine children and soon thereafter become cheerful as usual.
Your affectionate Husband and Father,
Basil

Rufus lowered the letter to his lap and stared soulfully into the yellow flames. His mother fought to hold back tears as she gazed through cloudy eyes at her knitting work. Both Mary and Emily looked expectantly toward first Rufus and then their mother for additional commentary about their father's words. Finally, Emily could stand the silence no longer and sadly asked, "He didn't say when he was coming home, did he?"

Demonstrating a maturity beyond her years, Mary responded, "No, silly. He can't come home until all the Yankees are whipped and go back to their own homes in the North. But Father still seems sure that we will triumph—doesn't he, Mother?"

Julia let a slight smile grow across her face as she wiped away a stray tear. "Yes, dear, he sounds very confident. And just think, every night before he falls off to sleep, he thinks of us so that he can continue on. Just the mere thought of his family cheers your father up."

Rufus, watching the jumping blaze intently, felt compelled to add, "Sounds to me like the measles and our own men are a bigger threat to the Highlanders than the Yankees are. They have already lost three men from disease and—fer as I can tell—have fired nary shot at the enemy." These words were not spoken in sarcasm but as a result of his growing displeasure for the war, for his father's extended absence, for his own weighty responsibilities, for the growing general shortages of salt and other important domestic necessities, for the weighty Confederate tariffs that threatened to spoil the Edmunstons' very way of life, and for other things too. Although his friend Hack Hartgrove was still pining to join the army, Rufus was ready for the whole thing to be over. He wanted the old normalcy to return and, most of all, he wanted to spend more time with Tine—the thoughts of whom still warmed his passions and dreams.

Rufus hurried to buckle a pair of crude ice skates to the bottoms of his boots. February had brought freezing cold weather to the Forks, with temperatures hovering close to the zero mark. A few inches of ice had formed over the Pigeon River along Deaver's Mill, and he reckoned it to be sufficiently thick for skating. Word of the pending spectacle had spread quickly, and a small gathering crowded the banks to watch him put on a real skating exhibition. Importantly, Tine and her father were there along with his mother and sisters. Also showing up to witness the unusual event were Hack and Jesse—of course—as well as Columbus Hartgrove, Colonel Deaver and his wife, Maggie, and a few other friends and curious spectators.

This skating tradition had started years earlier with his father showing off for the locals. Though not a skater himself, Rufus was determined to carry on with the unique ritual. As far as he knew, he wore the only pair of skates that existed in the Forks of Pigeon community, and the novelty was not lost on the lookers who yelled their excited encouragement.

"Let's see what ye're made of, boy. See if ye kin slide on them there irons and not yer behind," someone called out from the top of the riverbank as a chorus of laughter ensued.

Hack Hartgrove cheered him on with even more support. "Ain't no way, Rufe, to stand on them things. Ye're going to bust yer ass bigger than Pete."

Tine called out loudly to him, "Careful now, Rufe. Don't get too rambunctious down there. Slowly does it best."

Rufus called back to the crowd, just loud enough to be heard, "Okay everybody—'member now, I make no claims of being an expert. Jest trying to put on a show fer you is all. Now hold yer applause so you don't disturb me," he requested with a laugh that was immediately rejoined with a roar from the onlookers, who appreciated the humor in his words.

Slowly, Rufus rose to his feet and stood unsteadily on the frozen surface. Irregularities abounded over the river's icy crust with large rocks protruding randomly from bank to bank. Not only did Rufus have to actually skate and maintain his balance on the slippery ice, but he had to negotiate the numerous obstacles that stood in his way. Gently and carefully he began to move, first taking baby steps on the skating irons to gain a little confidence. He was not sliding yet, just stepping slowly, very slowly–step…step…step. After moving just a few feet, he paused and turned to see how all of the witnesses were reacting.

"Ye're going so slow we ain't rightly seen ye move yet," came one observation.

"It's called skating, Rufe, not walking. Reckon ye kin pick it up a bit, and try to slide some on them infernal irons?" taunted another.

"Came a fer piece to see ye slide, Rufus. I believe I could top that what ye're doing. Don't disappoint us now," one particular discouraged fan hailed out.

The adulation was not overwhelming, nor was his confidence boosted with the outpouring of advice. Tine and his sisters were the exception, rooting him on with "Slowly but surely, Rufe," and "You can do it, Rufus," and "Careful now, don't fall!"

He started to move again, cautiously and determinedly–step…step…step and slide…slide…step…step…slide…slide. Wondrously, he began to slip over the ice, and then walk, and then slide again–step…step…slide…slide and step…step…slide…slide. He kept this pattern up and gradually gained momentum, moving further and further onto the ice. Once, he fell down onto the hard surface, as the well-wishers expressed an audible disappointment. But he got right back up and kept on going, until at last he reached the far side of the river. Turning not being his strong point yet, he came to an unsteady halt at the opposite bank, twisted back around, and began stepping and skating slowly again in the direction of the gawkers.

Believe it or not, Rufus was getting the hang of the thing! Within just a short time, he began to actually skate a little and swing his arms in a natural rhythm to assure his balance and maintain momentum.

Rock after rock he dodged, as he seemingly slid effortlessly back and forth across the Pigeon. Eventually, Rufus figured out how to skate in a wide curve, so that he did not have to stop when he reached the far shore. Sliding along confidently, but not expertly, he glided in big circles while his sharp iron skates etched traces in the frozen wake. Oh, how he relished the sound of the iron carving into the ice! Cheering praise and admiration flooded down from the pleased fans, and he basked in the glory. His admirers had come to see a true exhibition of ice sliding and he was certainly giving them one—one they would never forget.

Sliding gracefully to and fro, Rufus was emotionally carried away with the success of his fantastic ice spectacle. He glanced up at the dazzled onlookers and met their enthusiastic waves with his own. So completely distracted did he become in all the excitement, that one of his skates accidently glided into a protruding rock that had gone unnoticed in front of him. The dreadful collision caused him to stumble and lose his balance. Unfortunately, it was an awkward fall, and his head whiplashed and crashed hard against the unforgiving frozen surface. Almost instantly, Rufus was knocked out cold by the terrible impact—colder than the icy floor upon which he fell—and a simultaneous moan arose from the stunned bystanders.

Several of the men quickly gathered their wits about them, and after skidding down the river bank, began to cautiously make their way across the ice to aid Rufus. One of them—the oldest person attending the spectacle that day—had the extreme misfortune of treading over a singular fracture in the frozen crust. For that exact fragile point happened to be too weak to bear the Colonel's full body weight. Consequently, he punched through the shattering ice and almost instantaneously was submersed in the frigid water below.

In the several minutes it took for the rescuers to extract the struggling Colonel Deaver from the polar river water, his body temperature dropped dangerously low. Bodily functions were severely shocked and the Colonel's diminished cardiovascular vigor was taxed beyond its limit. At the advanced age of almost seventy years, his worn-out heart, the same dynamic engine that for ages had generated phenomenal energies, slowly and agonizingly arrested.

With Maggie, Julia, and the girls at his side, and a semiconscious Rufus propped up for a final view through blurred eyes, a most revered and useful man was taken from the Forks of Pigeon community. The family, and others who were gathered around, sadly watched as Colonel Joseph Deaver's heart beat its last beat. As quick as that, his soul was gone forever from this earth and likely in transit to the far-better afterlife of which he was such a firm believer and promoter.

In late March, Julia and her children found themselves again in front of a warm fire reading yet another of Basil's war epistles. Rufus was there too, but in body only. Still struggling with guilt over his grandfather's death, he just sat glaring woefully into the flames as his mother began to read the pages of the letter aloud. Naturally he blamed himself for the tragedy that had befallen the Colonel and always would. No justification or reasoning to the contrary could lessen the weighty burden of fault that he carried. He figured any news from his father could only make him feel worse about himself and his circumstances.

The news from the war front found Captain Edmunston and his Company F on the move again. Just as Basil had suspected, the Union's capture of North Carolina's Roanoke Island did indeed lead to an inland invasion. Northern forces easily routed a heavy contingent of Rebels defending New Bern; so in mid-March, the 25th North Carolina Troops boarded the trains for a railroad march to Kinston, North Carolina, to oppose further Yankee incursions. Julia's recitation of the captain's unfettered words captured the raw excitement of war.

My Dearest Family,

We are whirling along on our way to Wilmington and the cars are jolting but they are now beginning to stop. Don't know why just yet. In Charleston last night we were marched to a large depot and all ten of the companies slept in the same large room. That is more than a thousand men in one room—can you imagine? I wrote to you a couple of nights ago to direct your next letter to New Bern, but we heard by the down train today that New Bern is in the hands of the enemy. We suppose it to be so, but have no particulars. We also heard that Wilmington was threatened and we expect to be stopped there. So you must write to Wilmington first.

We have just had a melancholy accident and that is the reason for the stop. A man from another company, being intoxicated, got on top of the cars and attempted to step or jump from one to the others. He fell between and about half a dozen of the hindmost cars passed over him, cutting him almost entirely in two just below the hips. He still breathes but will certainly die very soon.

We spent last night in the cars—not passenger cars, mind you! Today we are all well except for the unfortunate man who fell under the cars. He died not long after. Other than that we are all in fine spirits. Will write again soon.

Your affectionate Husband and Father,
Basil

As her mother lowered the letter, Mary exclaimed, "Oooohh, how gruesome! That man got cut in two by the train."

It was indeed a horrendous story, Julia thought to herself. *Why, for heaven's sake, did Basil include that message about the terrible accident in a letter intended for the eyes and ears of the entire family?* "Okay, girls, please try to forget that part. War is frightful, and awful things happen. Now just forget it."

Rufus mused to himself that it surely was a terrible tragedy. But he was still fascinated by the fact that nine months had come and gone since his father led the Haywood Highlanders off to war. In that time, they had fired no shots at the enemy, and the Yanks apparently had returned the favor. The only deaths he had heard of in his father's regiment were caused either by disease, friendly fire, or accident—as in this instance of a train cutting a man in half. It was a different war that the Haywood Highlanders were fighting. There was no doubt about it.

Chapter 7

THE MUSIC OF WAR

In the spring of 1862, the Confederate Government enacted extreme measures to reinforce the strength of its army in the field. One of the provisions of a new impressment law required that all of the one-year volunteers, including almost every man in Captain Edmunston's company, sign up for an additional two years of service. It also mandated that all able-bodied men in the South between the ages of eighteen and thirty-five were liable for military service for a period of three years. That is to say, these men had to join the army and fight whether they wanted to or not. Needless to say, the Rebel soldiers from Forks of Pigeon were none too happy about this unexpected turn of events.

They had volunteered to fight for one year only, and their time was nigh up. These farmer soldiers had fields that needed plowing and crops to be planted, and they had expected this war to be over in plenty of time to get back home to perform these vital chores. Besides, to them volunteering to fight and being made to fight were two entirely different things. They had gone to war to preserve certain of their individual rights, and this 'press law,' as they called it, seemed to be a drastic usurpation of power by the new government, infringing on their liberties. And their ire was further raised by a special proviso in the new law that exempted slave owners from the fighting. For good reason, the mountain farmers began to view the struggle against the North as a rich man's war and a poor man's fight.

"Father says that the men don't cotton much to the new impressment law atall," Rufus informed a small group assembled outside of Deaver's Store. Hack and Jesse were there with him. Tine had shown up. Also present were the grieving widow, Maggie Deaver, and Columbus Hartgrove, who had taken over managerial responsibility of the Deaver enterprises. Hartgrove had assumed these new duties at the behest of the widow Deaver, agreeing to look after the business affairs until her son, Lieutenant Burton Deaver, returned home from the war.

They had all gathered there on a beautiful spring morning to send Hack off to the war in style. The willful youth had decided to join the Rebel army, against his parents' best counsel and severe admonitions. Although not yet eighteen, as the Confederate authorities believed he was, Hack had enlisted anyway in Captain Edmunston's company. He was told to expect to join up with the 25th North Carolina Troops at Kinston in less than three weeks. Columbus would accompany his son over to Asheville so he could bring his horse back.

Continuing on the stump, Rufus pulled a crumpled letter from his shirt pocket and proceeded to unfold and read it. "Now listen up to what Father wrote. He says here that there is a great deal of dissatisfaction in camp concerning the press law. And some say they're going home when their time is out, regardless of consequences." Looking up from the letter toward the Hartgroves, he added, "That's what he says."

Columbus felt he knew all the boys in the company pretty well and that desertion so soon was not very likely. "That's what they say to yer father, Rufus, 'cause they's agitated with the impressing business, and he's an authority figure they can grouse at without nary severe repercussions. But ain't none of them boys going to come home against the law. 'Sides, they still ain't been in nary fight as of yet, and if I know them men, they aim to get a Yank or two 'fore hightailing it fer home."

Hack was getting riled up over all this war talk and jumped in at this point, "That's what I signed up fer, and I tell you here and now them Yanks better look out. I aim to put a few of them to skidaddling—those I don't plant first."

Columbus did not dispute these foolish remarks, while silently containing his misgivings about his son's participation in the war. The elder Hartgrove knew that soon the Haywood Highlanders were bound to join the bloody fray and come in harm's way. And it was not going to be a pretty sight, either. For some reason, Hack was as jumpy as a horse with a cocklebur under its saddle to go off and shoot Yankees. Columbus could only fathom the Yankees doing all the shooting and feared terribly for his son's life. Watching the boy bid farewell to his friends, the elder Hartgrove tried desperately to extinguish morbid imaginations of his son lying stiff in a pine box, with both arms folded across his chest, his eyes closed, and lips set in a peculiar puckered expression.

Jesse still had his doubts too, but this time he chose to bolster his friend's spirits. "You's still aims to kill 'bout ten of dem Yanks, Hack?"

Hack chimed back, "Ye betcha I am, Jess, and a sight more'n that."

"You's be careful and takes real good care of youself. Keeps you's head down now," Jess cautioned with an encouraging tone.

Trying to pass along some advice, as if he knew what he was talking about, Rufus spoke up, "There's a right smart amount of disciplining to put up with, Hack. Don't let it get you down. Father will look after you, I'm sure. And I'm going to write him to expect you. Take good care of yerself, you hear?"

"'Preciate it, Rufe. I kin take orders, can't I, Pa?"

"That ye sure 'nuff can, son. Now I 'spect we better be getting off," Columbus replied.

All of them, including Maggie, gave Hack a huge hug and watched as the father and son mounted their steeds and began plodding down the Pigeon River road. They waved and remained vigilant until the Hartgroves were well out of sight.

"Say, Rufe, will you and Jesse please walk me back to the mill?" Tine requested sweetly.

Now, what a fine idea! Rufus figured. "You bet we will, Tine. Be more than glad to," he replied teasingly, while casting a smiling glance at Jesse and his grandmother.

Leading their horses behind them, Rufus and Jesse accompanied Tine on the short walk up the East Fork. Jesse was not only worried about Hack but he was fretting for Rufus as well. "Rufus, I hope you's never has to go to no war. You's 'spects one day you's might go off?"

Before Rufus could reply, Tine answered for him. "Of course he won't have to go! The war will be over before long now, and besides, you're only sixteen! You've got two more years, and everybody knows it's not going to take us that long to whip the Yankees."

"Well, that may be, Tine. But if they need me before that, I may have to go," Rufus replied, looking resolutely at Tine and then Jesse. "Say for instance, Father writes that he needs me, then I'll have to go off and fight beside him and Hack. But like Tine says, Jess, I don't expect the war will last long enough fer me to have to go."

"Den dat be's real good fo' us here. I hope you's can stay home and keeps on as our massa."

When they got to the mill, there were no customers around, and Mr. Mann happened to be on the lower floor with a millwright, replacing broken teeth in a gearing mechanism. Jesse remained outside, and as Rufus and Tine entered the dim building, they could hear the men hammering and talking below them. So the couple immediately seized on the lucky opportunity to be alone and slipped quickly into an even darker corner. These chances were precious and rare, and they tried to make the most of it. Lusting for each other, they instantly entangled themselves in a passionate embrace. For more than a minute, they kissed, tasted, felt, and sniffed as romantically as their youthful experience would allow. Fearing discovery by her miller father, however, Tine finally broke out of the cuddle, and the two of them strode back out onto the loading porch and into the sunshine.

Jesse eyed the couple closely, and their sheepish expressions and labored breathing did not escape him. No, the two sweethearts' nonchalant acting did not fool him one bit. He cracked a toothy grin at his Master, and without speaking a word, just sauntered over to the side of the mill to gaze out over the river. Rufus was appreciative of the gesture, realizing that Jesse was just offering him more space and time to prolong this tender encounter with Tine at the mill.

Having sated his amorous appetite, Rufus felt a relaxed ease come over him. Tine was temporarily satisfied as well. Their heavy longings would be suppressed for a few days now, but the dreams of being with each other and of exploring their feelings in a deeper and more meaningful way would return soon enough. And, importantly, Rufus temporarily snapped out of the melancholic disposition that had been dragging him down ever since his grandfather's passing.

Unquestionably, the blame still rested heavily on his shoulders, but he was discovering ways to compartmentalize his assorted feelings of love and anger and guilt and such. Rufus was learning the hard way that it was a mighty complicated world and that in order to survive, a person not only had to fight and to love but they had to cope. And he had discovered the best way to cope with the immense guilt he felt was to smother it with his growing feelings for Tine. That was what he aimed to do all right.

Private Hack Hartgrove arrived by train at the Kinston, North Carolina, station just in time for the hurried exodus of the Rebel troops to Richmond, Virginia—the capital of the Confederacy. It was mid-June 1862, and at the time Richmond was being threatened by a grand Union Army led by General George McClellan. Confederate General Robert E. Lee, being desperate for more troops to defend against McClellan's invaders, had issued an urgent summons to the North Carolina regiments then stationed at Kinston. Captain Edmunston was preparing his Haywood Highlanders to board the northbound train when, out of the blue, he heard his name being called.

"Hello there, Mr. Edmunston! How goes it?" The captain turned to see who had hailed him and was pleasantly surprised to spy young Hack Hartgrove waving like a mad man, prancing along the station platform toward him.

"Hack! Glad to see you, boy!" The captain approached the rushing boy and shoved his hand out for a shake. "Didn't expect to see you so soon, but damned if you didn't make it just in time." They had themselves a hearty handshake as the captain asked, "Where's your uniform?"

"Weren't none in Asheville. They tolt me I could git one from my company when I arrived here. Reckon there's an extra one 'bout?"

With a slight frown and chuckle, Captain Edmunston answered, "We'll get you one when we get to Virginia. Glad to have you with us, Private Hartgrove. Now let me get the sergeant over here to take care of you," and he called out to one of the excited men waiting on the platform.

"Sergeant Henson, this here is Private Hack Hartgrove straight from Forks of Pigeon, by way of the Asheville training camp. Private Hartgrove, meet your first sergeant, Garland Henson. He'll look out after you and help you round up a uniform and a gun and other accoutrements, and what not. Sergeant, why don't you introduce the private here to the officers and other men? I reckon he knows them all, but present him anyway." The sergeant was only a couple of years older than Hack, and the two young soldiers gripped each other's hands stoutly and shook.

"Good to meet ye," the sergeant greeted.

"Yeah, likewise here. Can't say why I don't know ye. Where 'bouts ye from, anyhow?" Hack ventured to ask.

"From the Crabtree area. Got folks over at the Flowery Gardens though—below the Forks," Sergeant Henson offered in way of explaining how a foreigner, such as himself from the other side of Haywood County, came to be in Company F.

"That so?" replied Private Hartgrove.

By that time, the other Haywood Highlanders had spotted Hack and were making their way over to greet him. The jubilation around the boarding platform was manifest, as the mountaineers enthusiastically welcomed the new recruit into the company. But Captain Edmunston's troops were also stimulated by something else—they were keenly aware of the genuine prospect of a looming battle. It seemed very probable that Private Hartgrove had entered the war just as the Haywood Highlanders were moving to the brink of actual combat. Maybe the private would get that chance at the Yankees he had been spoiling for.

The 25th North Carolina was one of several regiments making up Ransom's Brigade. Just south of Richmond, General Robert Ransom off-loaded his brigade from the train cars and encamped, awaiting further developments along the front and orders from General Lee. Turns out, the brigadier general did not have very long to wait. At daylight on June 25th, Ransom's Brigade was rushed eastward down the dusty Williamsburg Road to stop an unexpected advance by Union troops along the railroad leading into Richmond. The 25th North Carolina Troops, now led by Colonel Henry Middleton Rutledge—Colonel Clingman had recently been promoted to general and assigned a brigade of his own—hustled on the double-quick through clouds of dust to meet the Yankees. And, of course, Captain Edmunston's Haywood Highlanders, along with the new recruit Private Hack Hartgrove, were in the mix.

Hack, still without a uniform, was laboring mightily to keep up with the rest of his company. He wore only homespun britches and shirt with a pair of worn-out brogans covering his feet. Moreover, he was bogged down with a weighty Mississippi rifle and bayonet, a cartridge box on his belt, and a canteen full of water. But that was traveling light compared to the standards of the other boys. In addition to their weaponry and water containers, the veteran soldiers also toted a blanket over their shoulder, haversack full of essential personal items, and a frying pan and tin cup. Still, Hack felt the weighty discomfort of his partial load with every awkward stride he took.

Blood charged through Private Hartgrove's body, and the thrill of seeing a Yankee was almost palatable. He had hankered for this moment for a long time and was finally about to get his chance to strike a blow against the hated foe. But there was more than exhilaration coursing through his veins. He perceived that a touch of reluctance, or even fear, had come over him. It was a strange feeling—one he had not reckoned on. But it was certainly there. He was not scared to death, for sure, but he was definitely frightened for what might lie just beyond the dust storm stirred up by the double-quicking Rebels. Hack looked for Sergeant Henson and could see him just ahead. *Got to stay close to Sergeant*, he kept telling himself while struggling to catch up.

Hack had learned only a few rudiments of soldiering during the short time he had spent at Asheville. During his training, he had not drilled in groups larger than forty or fifty men. Now however, he was moving with his entire regiment into battle—more than a thousand men—and everyone in his company, he noticed, kept their eyes peeled toward the regimental flag. Wherever the flag—or the colors—went, so did the soldiers, as they pursued the road leading to the ever-increasing roar of cannon fire and the deafening sounds of war.

In less than half an hour, the Minié balls whistling through the air, artillery rounds exploding on the ground around them, and screaming grapeshot told Hack that the battle had been joined. Colonel Rutledge's 25th North Carolina Troops were hastily thrown into a line immediately to the left of the Williamsburg Road, within rifle range of the enemy, who was lodged firmly on a rise near a frame schoolhouse building. One company abreast another—ten in all—took up their positions behind the impressive mounted colonel and his color sergeant, who was standing and holding the regimental flag high. The courageous color bearer stood tall and hoisted the flag so the colors could be seen by every man in every company of the regiment. Company F formed up in two ranks—one row behind the other—near the center of the long line. Then the anxious Highlanders watched attentively to see where the colors would lead them.

"Hack, keep yer eyes on me and do what I do," Sergeant Henson screamed to be heard over the noise.

"Okay—ye jest show me what to do, Garland—I mean, Sergeant Henson!" Hack was terribly excited and fearful at the same time. But he kept his head about him. He gaped anxiously toward the enemy line, where flashes and spits of smoke spewed from countless muskets, and black clouds rose over the Union cannon emplacements. The loud explosions and shock waves, sharp claps from the rifle fire, and shrill cries from the soldiers were incessant and deafening.

It was the music of war that Hack heard, and just two or three men over from him—merely feet away—a different chord was struck. A distinctive thud and then a frightful cry of anguish caused him to glance to his side quickly. At once, he discerned a friend had been shot, and he witnessed the young mountaineer fall to the ground in dying agony. A dreadful cold shiver rippled through Private Hartgrove as he turned back and peered toward Sergeant Henson.

The sergeant and the entire front rank rose from their kneeling position, took aim at an enemy target before them, and upon Lieutenant Deaver's barking command, fired a tremendous broadside at the enemy—*Crack!* Hack sluggishly followed their lead by a second or two and launched his first hostile shot ever at a Yankee soldier. It was impossible for him to tell if he hit his target, as he had to quickly stoop down while the rear rank stood and fired in near unison over his head toward the Yankee line. Frantically, the men reloaded and repeatedly fired volley after volley toward the blue-coated enemy. Not being as skillful as the rest in reloading his weapon, Hack missed a few turns to shoot, and he chided himself for his incompetence.

The furious fight continued in this manner for nearly an hour's time. It appeared that the Union forces were content to simply defend their strong position and shoot it out with the Rebels. But the Confederates were not about to settle for the status quo. Finally, Captain Edmunston strode in front of the company with his sword in hand. The battle still raged and the shots flew dangerously close by him as he yelled out for his men to look to Colonel Rutledge on their left. "Look there at the colonel, boys! He wants to lead you forward! Are you brave enough to follow him?"

The captain was rejoined with a loud affirmative cry from his men, as their nervous stares turned toward Colonel Rutledge riding back and forth on his gray mount. Captain Edmunston then commanded, "Fix bayonets!" Within seconds, the sharp-edged spikes were affixed to the ends of every man's Mississippi rifle.

All eyes were again directed to Colonel Rutledge, whose sword reached toward the heavens. Then, as the sound of a bugle signaled for the charge to begin, a loud Rebel yell resounded up and down the Confederate line. If a hybrid mix of a panther's cry and wolf's howl can be imagined, then that was the exact sound that issued from the throats of the wild Rebel hordes lurching forward. It was a peculiar shriek that wrought terror in the hearts of the bluecoats and conversely infused courage into the souls of the Rebels, steeling their resolve. Slowly, the regiment—including Hack, who still hung close to his sergeant—began to move directly toward the enemy line.

Out of the corners of both eyes, Private Hartgrove could see and sense men falling at his sides. But he kept walking at a growing pace to keep up with Sergeant Henson. The private winced at the loud cracking rifle sounds and the whistling noise of lethal projectiles flying by his head, but he did not stop. Nor did he turn and run away. The seventeen-year-old boy kept advancing toward the Yankees, just like he told Jesse he would do. *There's ten Yanks somewhere out there who'd better watch out*, he kept thinking to himself.

The Rebel line closed to within seventy-five yards of the Yankee defensive position, while grape from the enemy cannons took a terrible deathly toll on the advancing troops. To Hack's surprise, the Rebels' forward progression was slowing dramatically. The men were looking behind them and from side-to-side at their slain and wounded brothers. Some of the boys were intentionally falling to the ground, in an effort to find cover from the storm of lead being thrown at them. Hack happened to glance toward the colonel where the regimental colors still flew in plain view. Just as his eyes shifted to the flag he bore witness to a most horrific scene. The brave color bearer suddenly collapsed—his head blown horrifically apart—and the flag he held drooped and then fluttered to the ground.

Private Hartgrove looked on in a stupor as Colonel Rutledge circled around and around on his horse. His colonel was furiously yelling encouragement to the men and demanding they follow him on ahead, while pointing the way with his sword. But to Hack's shock and dismay, the wavering line's forward movement stalled. Worse yet, no one had bothered to take up the fallen colors. The regimental flag just lay there on the ground beside the lifeless color bearer, as the center of the Confederate line began to slowly disintegrate.

Why don't they take it up? he fretted. *Pick it up somebody!* Nobody moved to pick up the colors, and Hack could not understand why. *Well this won't do*, he thought to himself. *It won't do atall!*

It was the instinctive decision of a green soldier in the heat of combat—one that not only surprised his comrades but would befuddle even Private Hartgrove upon reflection. Seeing the regimental colors fall to the ground and sensing that the attack was failing, the private innately rushed from his company's ranks and ran toward Colonel Rutledge and the downed flag. Sergeant Henson cried out for him to stop, and Captain Edmunston watched in dismay as Hack ran away—not to the rear, as might have been expected from someone so youthful and inexperienced, but toward the front. He ran as fast as his skinny legs could go, passing the colonel who was still on his horse beseeching his men to follow him. Finally reaching the standard, the private swiftly heaved the pole off the ground and began waving the regimental colors over the field again.

Colonel Rutledge was keen to the act of bravery and lauded loudly the young soldier, who did not even wear a Rebel uniform. "See that brave man with our flag! Let's follow him to our destiny! Follow the colors, men! Forward!"

And with Hack waving the flag as high as he could hold it and the colonel riding at his side, the two of them started moving slowly in the direction of the Yankee line. The other Rebels could finally see their familiar colors again, and they saw their courageous colonel proceeding forward against all hazards. Such a scene inspired the least heroic among the Confederate troops and budged them into motion once more toward the violent guns of the enemy. Up and down the Confederate line, the soldiers spied the flag at their center advancing again, and their resolve strengthened. In just minutes, the momentum of the battle abruptly shifted, and the 25th North Carolina Regiment resumed the attack, ultimately charging directly into the enemy line.

The Yankees did not have the heart or fight in them to resist the onslaught for long. They gave way to the Rebels, after bearing extreme losses of men and several of their artillery pieces. Throughout the rest of the day, the Yanks, using a heavy fire of musketry, tried on three separate occasions to regain their lines but failed. And just before nightfall, a heavy fire of grapeshot was opened on the 25th North Carolina, without demoralizing or displacing the regiment from the schoolhouse hill.

Eventually, darkness shrouded the battlefield and the roaring of gunnery subsided. Soldiers lay down on the ground and closed their eyes. With thoughts of home in their heads and the pitiful cries of the wounded piercing the night air, the Highlanders, one by one, drifted into fitful sleep. Captain Edmunston's Company F and the inexperienced Private Hack Hartgrove had given a good accounting of themselves that day. They had borne up tolerably well in their initial test and had shown an unwavering gallantry under tremendous fire from the enemy. But Hack could not say for sure whether he killed a Yank atall. Just before he dropped off to sleep, he was fretting about what he could report to his family and friends back home.

Chapter 8

THE HEART OF A LION

Over a period of several days following the skirmish at the schoolhouse, the 25th North Carolina Troops remained ever vigilant of the Union troops in their front. However, they saw very little action. Their fighting role in the Seven Days' Battle was over. Elsewhere, the bulk of the Confederate Army attacked McClellan's forces every day for the next six days, until the Yanks had been pushed clear across the Virginia Peninsula and hard against the north bank of the James River. The Army of the Potomac lingered there under the protection of their fleet of gunboats for several weeks, until General McClellan eventually gave up his notion of capturing Richmond. Then, he abruptly loaded his grand army into naval transports and sailed back to the North. The Confederate capital city had been saved—for the time being.

The duties for Captain Edmunston's Highlanders were mundane, while waiting and observing McClellan's activities on the James River. It was an idle period, you could say, but Private Hartgrove took full advantage of the lull and practiced loading and shooting his bulky Mississippi rifle. At the schoolhouse fight, he had been quick to notice his severe inefficiency in using the weapon. He had been able to fire only twice in the same time the other men had shot thrice. Realizing he was not near as nimble at the task as they, the private endeavored to remedy his deficiency.

In an isolated grove of woods, Private Hartgrove practiced the loading and firing steps over and over, with Sergeant Henson and friends offering instructions. Time after time, he tore open cartridges with his teeth and poured the black powder contents into the rifle barrel, rammed the paper wad and lead ball home to the bottom of the barrel, retrieved a percussion cap from his cartridge box and placed it in the gunlock, cocked the hammer, raised his weapon, aimed, and fired. The weary private practiced and fired so many times, he thought he was in real trouble one morning when Captain Edmunston sauntered out to confront him.

"Private Hartgrove, you about to get the hang of it?" the captain queried.

Thank goodness, Hack thought. *I'm not in for it.* "Yes sir, Captain Edmunston. It ain't as hard as I reckoned. Believe I kin 'bout keep up with the other boys now."

"Good! At this rate you're going to shoot us out of ammunition. Give your gun to the sergeant, and you come with me," the captain ordered, motioning to Sergeant Henson. "We've been called to the colonel's headquarters."

Hack's mouth fell open as he gave the captain a blank stare. *Had he heard Captain right?* He wondered what in the world the colonel would want to see him and the captain about, thinking he was in for it now—for sure! *The colonel must have gotten wind I was wasting ammunition.* As Hack's mind raced, he thought the trouble might possibly have something to do with his civilian clothes. He still had not been issued a uniform and, to be honest, he was embarrassed at his unsoldierly appearance.

When Hack and Captain Edmunston arrived at the colonel's tent, they were asked to wait outside until Colonel Rutledge finished some paperwork. While the captain spoke with the lieutenant colonel and major regarding his company's casualties at the schoolhouse, Hack stood by patiently, waiting and worrying about the trouble he was in. Finally, after a long few minutes, the colonel threw open the flaps of his tent and strode out to meet the group.

"Attenn—shunnn!" one of the officers barked, and Hack stiffened and saluted.

Aristocratic planter's blood ran through Colonel Rutledge's young veins. He was only twenty-three years old, lanky tall with dark wavy hair, and uncommonly handsome. He struck a fine military figure indeed that morning, dressed in his summer gray uniform, high black boots, and topped with a slouch officer's hat plumed with a hawk's feather. Hack was filled with awe and nervous trepidation as the colonel approached him.

Looking Private Hartgrove over good from head to toe, the colonel then commanded, "At ease, Private. I say 'Private,' but I see you are out of uniform. Explain yourself, sir!"

Hack cleared his throat and attempted to explain, "That's right, Colonel. I'm jest a private, but I ain't got no uniform. Ye see, they didn't give me one at Asheville, and they's ain't give me one here, neither, in Virginee." He hesitated to ascertain whether the colonel was following him.

"Go on, Private."

"Well, Colonel, there weren't no time to get me one in North Carolina before they shooed me up here to Virginee. And Sergeant Henson ain't been able to find me one in these here parts. Says he's been looking for a corpse 'bout my size to git me a uniform, but he ain't found the right dead corpse yet, sir. So, Colonel—sir—that's why I'm wearing this here homespun my ma made fer me." After such a thorough explanation, Private Hartgrove decided to leave it be, as he glanced over at his captain. It certainly appeared to him that Captain Edmunston understood everything and appreciated the extenuating circumstances. Why, the captain even cracked a confident smile toward the colonel.

Colonel Rutledge stiffened in front of Hack and looked down his nose at the private. "That's quite a story, Private. Don't you agree, Captain Edmunston?"

"Yes sir, Colonel. That's about the size of it. My sergeant is looking diligently for a uniform for Private Hartgrove."

"That so?" Colonel Rutledge turned back to Hack and stared down at him. By this time, the skinny private was sweating profusely and trembling in anticipation of what terrible consequences were about to rain down on him over this uniform flap.

The colonel started strongly, "Private Hartgrove—I must tell you something." Colonel Rutledge's demeanor and the tone of his voice then softened somewhat. "A damn uniform doesn't make the soldier—no, sir! It's what's in here that makes a good soldier." Then the colonel stuck his finger sharply against Hack's chest, directly over the heart. "A good soldier has to have the heart to fight. He must have courage and gumption, and he must have the will. Well, Private Hartgrove, I saw what you did at that battle we had with the Yanks. You've got everything it takes to be a good soldier, son. You've got the heart of a fighter and, by God, you're a damn good soldier—uniform or no uniform!"

Colonel Rutledge was not finished, but he had to pause and gather himself and compose his thoughts before going on. Captain Edmunston looked on with pride at his private, when it became obvious to him what this affair was all about.

"I observed you, Private Hartgrove, running across the field to hoist our fallen colors. It was an audacious act, and one that took the courage contained in a lion's heart to carry out. You, Private Hartgrove, have the heart of a lion—and the heart of a true warrior. These men here with us know it because they saw the same thing I did, didn't you, gentlemen?'"

The captain and the staff officers all acknowledged that they had seen Hack's brave deed by snapping out hearty and loud "Yes sirs." Private Hartgrove at last realized he was not in trouble and that the colonel was apparently not mad atall at him for not wearing a uniform. So Hack began to feel a little more settled, although embarrassed over some of the things the colonel was allowing about his heart.

"Private Hartgrove, I will unconditionally state, here and now, that you saved the day for our regiment. The 25th was faltering until the moment those colors were picked up and raised over the field again. We have you to congratulate for our victorious rout of the enemy, and I want to personally thank you for it, Private." The colonel reached his hand out, and Hack took it, and they had a vigorous shake.

Hack appreciated the colonel's kind words and attention and said so. "Thank ye, Colonel Rutledge!"

"Oh, and one more thing—we need to find you a uniform, don't we, Private? Major Francis, please see that Private Hartgrove receives a uniform today. Don't care where it comes from. And there's another thing. Captain Edmunston—make sure that uniform has a corporal's stripes on it. Understood?"

The captain understood, and with a smile on his face, replied, "Yes sir, Colonel Rutledge!"

But before dismissing the newly promoted Corporal Hartgrove, the colonel had one more thing on his mind. "Now, Corporal, as long as you are in my regiment, and hopefully you'll have a new uniform soon, you're going to need a hat—aren't you?" Without waiting for the private's response, Colonel Rutledge took off his own officer's slouch hat and placed it on top of Hack's unruly shock of light brown hair. "Accept this one as a token of my esteem for what you did on the battlefield, Corporal. I'll look for it the next time we take to the field, and I will be mighty proud to fight with the likes of you, sir."

The corn crops around Forks of Pigeon were laid by and the back-breaking wheat harvests were well underway. On this midsummer day, Rufus had broken away from the work at the Den and was down at Deaver's Store, where Columbus Hartgrove had summoned him to share some recent news from Hack. Jesse had tagged along, and the peculiar duo huddled in the post office as Columbus read from Hack's most recent letter. The enticing scents wafting through the air aroused the boys' senses, as they moved in closer to hear the words Hack had written. They were incredulous words—these ones Columbus was reeling off to them just now.

"A hat! Colonel Rutledge gave him his hat?" Rufus interrupted. He was not sure he had heard Columbus correctly.

"That's what he says right here," Columbus replied. "He says—let's see—let me read it again to ye. Here goes."

> *...me and Captain Edmunston was ordered to the colonel's headquarters and the colonel give me a good talking to. He was right pleased with the way I picked up the regiment's flag and toted it at the enemy lines during the schoolhouse battle. Them bullets was flying round me thicker than a bunch of bees but nary one stung me. I was saddened though to see Henry Thompson shot down at my side. He was a good friend. Please tell his father so for me. We have drove the enemy down to the river under the guns of their*

big boats and have done but little fighting since. Colonel says I have a lion's heart and he thanked me for saving the day for the 25th. And he give me his very own big fancy hat to wear. It's prettier than anything you ever saw before and the men have got to calling me Hat instead of Hack. Ain't that something? Got to go practice my musketry now. You all take care and I'll write again soon.

Your affectionate son,

Hat

p.s. – They give me a promotion to corporal and tell Rufus about the hat.

Jesse could not believe his ears. "Whew—eeee! Hack says so to us. He says dat he aims to get dem Yankees. Do it says how many he got?"

"No, it don't say nary thing 'bout that." Columbus replied patiently.

"Mr. Hartgrove, Father wrote about how proud he was of Hack and how he was a hero in the fight. He said that he got all teary-eyed when the colonel told Hack he had the heart of a lion—and that he was a fine soldier. That makes us all proud, too. Just wanted you to know that. Mother says so too. He didn't say anything 'bout the hat, though."

"Thank ye, son. Well, I'll be. Rufus, look who jest stuck their heads in the door. I do believe it be them two Buggs that ye and the boy tangled with. Let me jest go over and see what their business is." And Hartgrove then walked over and began speaking to Amos Bugg.

This was the first time since his run-in with them that Rufus had set eyes on either Bugg. Apparently Eli had not enlisted in the army, as of yet, although his age placed him well within the conscription limits. Very soon, the Confederate officials would come looking for him and impress his service for the army, Rufus figured. For sure, Jesse could never forget the Buggs. He still had long welts across his torso and a slight one on his face that reminded him every day of the two mean men who took a lash to him.

"Let's get going, Jess. 'Spect we need to get up to the Orchard and help the others."

"'Spect we do's," the worried Jesse replied. Directing his eyes toward the Buggs, he asked, "You's goin' says somethings to dem?"

"Don't plan on it."

Rufus had hoped not to make a stir, as he and Jessie sauntered by the Buggs on their way out. But Amos spotted them coming and seized on the opportunity to offer a salutation.

"Good to see ye agin, Edmunston. It's been a right long spell since we bumped into each other, ain't it?" the odious Bugg asked with a growing sneer.

Rufus stopped and turned to the elder Bugg. He noticed that the man's nose, which had been broken in their earlier tussle, had a slight crook in it now. But other than that, nothing had changed. He was still a hulk of a man and appeared to be spoiling for another fight. Rufus sure hoped he was mistaken.

"Yes sir—it's been a right smart time." Rufus just stared at the man with a polite smile, and then gazed at Eli for a second or two before focusing again on the elder Bugg. The sneer remained on Amos's face.

"Ain't fergot 'bout ye, boy. Reckon we've still got some settling up to do one of these days, ain't we?"

"If you say so, sir." Rufus politely responded.

"I know yer old man ain't here 'bouts and that grandfather of yers is planted now. Ain't nobody here to protect ye now, is they?"

Still grinning on the outside but seething with a mixture of hate and wrath and jitters on the inside, Rufus rejoined, "Don't believe I need any protection, sir, as long as it's a fair fight. But I don't reckon you know what fair is. That be why you carry that big old bullwhip of yers?" Rufus had noticed that Bugg still carried the coiled leather thong on his hip.

Columbus Hartgrove, who had been sidetracked elsewhere, noticed Bugg and Rufus having some words near the doorway. Fearing there might be an explosion of wills leading to another altercation, he quickly moved to intervene. "All right, men, ain't going be no trouble in this store. Rufus, ye and Jesse should be moving on 'bout now. We'll ketch ye 'nother time."

Rufus did not want to make any trouble for Mr. Hartgrove, nor was he looking for any trouble himself. He figured it might be for the best to forget these Buggs and mosey on. "Okay, sir," he said to Hartgrove. Rufus motioned to Jesse, and they started to exit the store when Amos called out.

"Kerful of yer back, boy. Best not let yer guard down none 'cause we'll be coming to see ye. Ye kin count on it!"

With a smile of confidence concealing inner unease, the teenager just nodded back to Bugg and coolly retorted, "Ketch ye next time, sir."

As usual that afternoon, Tine was lingering about at the mill trying to make herself useful. Being the only child of a widower, it was no wonder she spent so much time there. Two younger brothers had died years ago from the scarlet fever and, regrettably, Tine's mother had not been able to shake her remorse and the ensuing debilitating bouts of depression. One day while her miller husband was off to work, she gave a kiss to her ten-year-old daughter and walked out the cabin door toward the Pigeon River, never to return. Two days later, her drowned body was found, her apron pockets filled with heavy river rocks.

As the motherless girl grew out of those tragic adolescence years, her father, friends, and acquaintances could not help but observe Tine's wonderful metamorphosis. Her youthful tomboyish features evolved over time into those of a strikingly beautiful woman. A once-gangly frame filled out to ideal proportions—pleasing in every sense—and the color of her long flowing hair gradually ripened to its current chestnut tint. Appropriately though, she customarily wore her auburn locks fixed tightly behind her head and often covered with a bonnet, as she did on this day while working inside the dusty environs of the grist mill.

The sun was still high in the sky, and Tine was visiting with patrons on the loading porch, when she happened to spot Rufus and Jesse making their way up the river road. Immediately, she threw up her hand and waved, hoping to get their attention. Still stinging and irritated over the encounter with Amos Bugg at Deaver's Store, Rufus was in no mood to socialize or romance. But Tine had spied him, and he could not very well just ride on by. So he and Jesse reined their horses in the direction of the mill.

"Hello, Rufe! How are you boys doing on this fine hot day?" Tine greeted enthusiastically, while giving them a huge smile.

It was definitely a scorching day, with few clouds to screen the intense heat of the sun's harsh rays. However, 'fine' is not the word Rufus would have picked to describe it. The Bugg business worried him more than he dared disclose, but he feigned a good-natured response. "Tine, you're looking mighty sprite today. How goes it?"

"Kinda busy here. Folks have kept the flour burrs whining steady. Did ye get your threshing done yet?"

"No. Mr. Hartgrove promises to get the thresher up to the Den this coming week. The confounded machine's getting so old, it keeps breaking down, he says."

Rufus went on to relay the war news about Hack's heroic act and the bestowal of the colonel's hat to him. And Tine was as surprised and impressed as Rufus and Jesse. After a few minutes of bantering over their friend's brave feat and his perilous prospects, Tine changed the tenor of the conversation. She issued a special invitation to Rufus to spend the next day with her.

"Rufe, how would you like to go with us to church at the Crab Orchard schoolhouse tomorrow? Pa wants to go up and hear Preacher Poston one last time before his retirement."

Rufus's mother and sisters habitually attended the Methodist church at Forks of Pigeon. However, he had adopted his father's religious skepticism and routinely shied away from the church houses. But this was entirely different. He thought it might be a sight more interesting to worship, or at least observe, in the enchanting company of the girl of his dreams. Furthermore, had not his father's last bit of advice encouraged getting away from the Den and listening to the opinions of his neighbors? Well, Rufus's neighbor and tenant, Preacher Poston, would for certain give out a good dose of opinions, as related to his fire-and-brimstone Christian beliefs.

That's the least I can do—listen to Mr. Poston and see what he has to allow, Rufus figured.

So with a pleased look on his face, Rufus responded, "Be happy to, Tine, if they will let me into the place. Most of those East Fork folks know that Father and I don't visit the house of the Lord too frequently. Let's see if they shut me out, why don't we? If you and Mr. Mann will stop by the Den on the way up the river tomorrow, I reckon me and my horse can plod along and keep you some good company."

Tine beamed happiness, with her hazel green eyes glinting sparkles in the sunlight. "Okay then, it's a plan. And I might just pack some food and sweet-talk Pa into taking us berry-picking thereabouts. Do you know of any good berry patches in the vicinity?"

Rufus happened to know of a great spot near where the Bee Woman kept her bees. However, there was no telling what Tine and her father might allow about his reclusive aunt and the menagerie of critters she kept around her place. Fretting over this for only a split second or two, he reluctantly suggested, "Sure do, and maybe we can go by and visit with my Aunt Folsom fer a spell." Rufus had decided it was a risk well worth taking.

Chapter 9

STUCK IN EVERLASTING FIRE

For many years, lay-preacher Isaac Poston had led the weekly religious services at the schoolhouse on the Crab Orchard tenant farm. The crude log building was constructed many years ago by Rufus's grandfather, Thomas Edmunston, and was intended to serve as a learning center for the children up and down the East Fork River. Basil had continued the Edmunston's support of the school by funding the services of a teacher for the annual fall and winter sessions. In fact, Basil thought so highly of the tiny institution that he enrolled Rufus there to learn his letters and ciphers. But most every Sabbath, the house of learning was conveniently transformed into God's house, and many of the rural folk living along the East Fork flocked there to hear Preacher Poston's biblical recitations and Christian moral urgings.

On this blistering hot morning, some thirty worshippers were cooped up in the stifling structure, paying their undivided attention to Reverend Poston. Because only two small windows and a door were cut into the aging timber walls, the stagnant air inside was miserably oppressive. The uncomfortable congregants—men and boys sitting on the left side and the fairer sex on the right—squirmed on the hard benches and used either their hands or flimsy song sheets to fan their faces. Any movement of air atall brought some brief relief to these suffering souls.

Rufus looked across the narrow aisle at Tine, who was intensely focused on Poston's sermon. Watching her and the others open their hearts and spill their religious zeal that morning left him feeling a kind of spiritual emptiness. He was currently devoid of any sort of personal devotion to Christian beliefs. For the past couple of years, he had begun to seriously doubt the veracity of Biblical miracles and question the overarching concepts of Heaven and Hell and the enticement of an afterlife. Instead, he was starting to form his own personal notions of an all-powerful Creator of the complicated and cruel world he inhabited. But for Tine's sake this morning, Rufus was striving diligently to take in and comprehend his devout tenant's message of personal salvation and the Last Judgment.

Poston could not be blamed for holding an abbreviated service of just under two hours on such a sweltering morning. After all, he had reached an advanced age and, over the last few years, had even begun to tone down his rebukes of the sinners he customarily preached to. Alternatively, he was trying to offer his flock more promising prospects for salvation and was beginning to paint for them far brighter pictures of the afterlife. That was what they wanted to hear; and, finally, after several decades of lay preaching, he had belatedly come to realize it.

Interestingly, Preacher Poston had pioneered the East Fork with Thomas Edmunston in the early 1800's, and the good Reverend had lived on one of the Edmunston's tenant farms—the furthermost one up the East Fork River—for almost five decades. Poston now had sons, daughters, and grandchildren sharing a living on his tenant property. Actually, two of the grandsons and a great-grandson were off to the war fighting with the Haywood Highlanders. So for the past year or more, he had increasingly shared with his faithful followers a conviction that the Yankees were indeed devils and that God Himself was fighting with the Rebel regiments and Captain Edmunston's Haywood Highlanders. And he did so again today, as he wrapped up a particularly strong lesson on the Last Judgment.

"*For all of us will eventually appear before the judgment seat of Christ,*" Poston assured everyone, while reading from a tattered sheet of paper that fell limp in his hand. "*When the Son of God shall come in His glory and all the holy angels with Him, then He shall sit on the throne of His glory.*" A brief pause worked well to let the East Forkers grasp the magnitude of what he was reciting to them. Then continuing on, "*And before Him shall be gathered all nations and He shall separate them one from another, as a shepherd divideth his sheep from goats.*" Poston looked out amongst his exhausted but eager listeners and interjected, "Did ye get that bit? He shall gather all nations, it says in the Bible. And don't ye worry none. That will fer sure include the Yankee states and our Rebel nation. Remember—I tolt it to ye!"

But he was not finished by any means and proceeded to recite. "*And He shall set the sheep on His right hand and the goats will be set on the left.*" The good reverend abruptly halted his recital and sought understanding. "Hear that, brethren? It says the sheep will be put in the right hand. That would fer sure be all us Rebels. It means here, in these words, that the Confederate nation will be put in God's right hand—that's the best one, the right hand. And it's for certain the Yanks—or goats—will sit in His left hand. Now here comes the important part. Listen up good now. *Then shall the King say unto them on His right hand, come ye blessed of My Father, inherit the kingdom prepared for you from the foundation of the world.*" Silence pervaded the church house as Poston let these weighty words sink in.

It could not get any better or clearer than this, the preacher and his listeners believed. They were, of course, on God's right hand and would be saved. It said so right there on that tattered piece of paper Preacher Poston grasped in his hand. Then the preacher started up again, slowly, "The kingdom! We will inherit the kingdom it says. All ye sinners out there—ever one of ye—must profess yer sins, amend yer wicked ways, and accept the Lord as yer Savior, if ye want to go to the kingdom. That's what all these here complicated words mean. I'm here to tell ye, that's what it means! Tell Him in yer prayers ye have sinned! Tell Him ye're sorry fer it, and ye don't aim to do it nary more again! Fer if ye do confess yer sins, then ye can jump right off God's right hand into His kingdom. And our Confederate Rebels will jump off that right hand with ye.

"Almost finished now. This here is real important too. Listen up close to these words. *Then shall He say also unto them on the left hand, depart from Me, ye cursed, into everlasting fire prepared for the devil and his angels.*" There could be no misunderstanding of this profound revelation, but the preacher wanted to be sure. "Ye know what that means, don't ye? Well, fer those out there—those of ye who don't rightly understand—them words 'everlasting fire' is infernal Hell! That's what it means—Hell! All them goats sitting in God's left hand—well, that be the sinners amongst us who ain't yet professed and ain't never intending to. And that, also, be all them wicked nations like the Yankee land. They's going to be given over to the devil to live in hell forever. That be the everlasting fire, mind ye. I'm a'feared that's what it means. It says so! It's right clear to me that none amongst us should endeavor to be a goat and that the Yanks ain't got a chance in hell of avoiding everlasting fire. Now please, if ye'ens will bow with me fer the benediction."

Rufus and Tine sprawled leisurely on the shady bank of the East Fork River as the cold, gurgling water gushed by. Miller Mann was within earshot a respectable distance away, considerately allowing the young couple some time to themselves. Wolfing down piece after piece of cornbread smeared with honey from the basket of food Tine had prepared, Rufus thought nothing could be better than this. Those damn Buggs and his heavy burden of guilt were temporarily shunted aside during these sweet moments, as he shared delicious eatings with the most beautiful girl in the world. All of a sudden, life was good again. If only it could always be like this.

"That was a mighty powerful sermon on the Last Judgment, wasn't it—talking about sheep and goats and stuff?" Rufus asked, trying to introduce some substantive banter into their pleasant diversion.

The two of them discussed the merits of Poston's message for a few minutes, and then Tine thoughtfully observed, "You know something, Rufe, did you ever stop to think that in New York and Pennsylvania and Connecticut—up there in the North—that they figure us to be the goats and that they are surely the Lord's sheep? Who's to say who's right? You know what I mean?"

Rufus deliberated about what she allowed for a few moments and came back, "No—can't say I thought of it like that, Tine. You know, fer the life of me I can't get my head 'round the notion of a fiery Hell where the Devil resides. It don't seem right that God would do that to His own creatures—send people He created to such a terrible fate. That notion doesn't appeal to me, atall. But hey, what do I know? We don't care, do we? We're going berry-picking, ain't that right?"

Tine instantly cheered up and replied, "That's right! You said you knew a good spot around here. Where is it?"

"It's right up there above the schoolhouse, at my Aunt Folsom's," he replied pointing toward a high ridge above them. "You 'bout ready to go?"

The Bee Woman was outside piddling around on her porch when the berry-picking party came within sight. Rufus let out a loud hail as Tine and her father gazed suspiciously toward the woman. "Hello, Aunt Folsom! See you're at it."

The three church-goers climbed a single stepping stone onto the weathered floorboards where Folsom was working. Tine and the miller Mann could not be faulted for nervously looking around for the black snake Rufus had warned them about or warily observing the myriad animal pelts, stag horns, and turtle shells on display. But their mysterious host soon put them at ease.

"Well, I'll say! This is certainly a surprise, Rufus. Weren't expecting company on such a hot day as this one." Turning her smile toward Tine and the miller, she went on. "Glad to see ye'ens. I'm sure this boy has tolt ye heaps 'bout me. But I ain't half as bad as all that," the Bee Woman declared with a chuckle.

The miller chimed up, "No, ma'am. Rufus has spoke mighty high 'bout ye, Folsom—uhh—sorry, Mrs. Anderson. Says ye keep a bunch of bees 'round here somers."

"Now, sir, ye and this purty young girl here can call me Folsom if ye like. Won't have no more of that 'Mrs. Anderson' nonsense, ye hear me?" the Bee Woman insisted, and the miller and daughter readily agreed.

Folsom had seen Mr. Mann a time or two at the store but had never met his daughter. The girl's stunning looks had her musing whether this might possibly be the one Rufus had been carrying on about. But her nephew quickly cleared things up.

"Aunt Folsom, this is my good friend Hazeltine and her father. And I'm sure she won't mind you calling her Tine, like we all do. Will you now, Tine?"

"No—of course not—not at all! I'm very glad to finally get to meet you, Folsom."

Following the introductions, they visited a brief spell on the porch and talked niceties and such. Rufus was favorably impressed with his aunt's sociable reception and the excellent manners she was displaying. Although unusually abrupt and straightforward, she heartily welcomed the Manns to her cabin porch and treated them with the utmost dignity and politeness. Why, she even offered them a cup of peach cider to drink. But her guests declined and got straight to the point of their visit.

"Aunt Folsom, we aim to do some berry-picking, and I know you usually have bunches growing about in the woods and in that old field where you've got yer gums. Reckon you could direct us to some?" Rufus had no doubts that he would receive good guidance.

The Bee Woman did not disappoint. "Well, I 'spect there might be some about somers. The black berries are 'bout eaten up I 'spect. All them sweet-toothed varmints have laid into them hard by now. But ye might still find a few in the brambles over there in the bee field, Rufus. Now them bear berries are coming in right nice like, and ye might see some of them on the fringes of that old planting field where my gums are plopped."

The huckleberries were apparently plentiful that year, and the black bears were absolutely on the rampage feasting on them. So the Bee Woman gave the party fair warning. "Cover yer heads up good now fer the sun, and best ye keep on the lookout fer bears. Been seeing 'em most days browsing 'bout fer something to eat. And look out fer the snakes too. They's always around somers, so I'd be extra kerful if I was ye."

Fair warning indeed she gave them. So good was her warning that most sane folks would have opted out of the berry hunt. But that did not apply to Rufus and Tine. Sane they were not on this hot afternoon. They were in love, or at least thought they were in love. And nothing, not even the very real threat of black bears, snakes, and sun burn, would prevent or distract them from being together on this fine day.

Taking his chaperoning duties seriously, the miller stayed within a reasonable distance of the couple, just to make things proper. But to be frank about the matter, there were a host of other things he would rather have been doing, besides wading around in brambles and thickets in the scorching heat picking tiny berries. Tine was all he had though, and he knew this berry hunt was awfully important to her. So he meant to do this thing for the girl, while making every effort to remain in either eye or ear shot of Rufus and Tine—to keep them out of trouble, of course.

The merry berry-pickers were having a lark, talking sweet nothings with each other and joking around. Cautioned by the Bee Woman, they each wore protection on their heads against the sun's dangerous rays. Tine shielded her auburn tresses and face with a light blue bonnet, and Rufus donned his floppy felt hat. Both carried a handled basket and were making reasonable progress in filling them with mostly black berries. Every now and again, when they perceived a lapse in the miller's vigilance and the moment was just right, the sweethearts joined in an affectionate hug and kiss. There was obviously no time for passionate expressions of love, but the frequent quick kisses seemed to do them nicely.

Yellow Black-eyed Susans grew profusely on the fringes of the woods and across the bramble-covered field near the bee gums. The ubiquitous clover blooms and pretty milkweed blossoms washed the landscape with white and blushing pink specs. Poking out of the ground like tall sentinels, the pale-green rabbit tobacco plants kept watch over nature's rite of summer, as Rufus and Tine waded through the field. The berry-pickers could not help but notice the numerous honey bees buzzing around the blooming flowers and making their way to and from Folsom's stubby bee gums. It was such a pleasant afternoon, and the teenagers reveled in their natural surroundings, enjoying the precious time with each other. At that moment, life was gooder than ary angel.

Miller Mann had spotted a bear rambling around on a higher ridge, quite a distance off, and was keeping a wary eye out for it. Rufus and Tine were certainly not concerned about bears, nor did they have any other fears. Aunt Folsom's warnings had fallen on deaf ears, it seems, and gone mostly unheeded. They had spotted another good-sized patch of berry-bearing plants and were moving in that direction to reach them. Rufus headed for one side, while Tine moved toward the opposite end.

The route the girl chose turned out to be the more challenging by far. Barring her way was a dense briar thicket and a slightly raised outcropping of rocks. One or the other could not be avoided, so she thought it prudent to dodge the briars. Her thin summer dress, long sleeved and covering her body from neck to shoe top, could not withstand nor protect her from a prickly entanglement with those thorny bushes. Besides that, the pile of exposed rocks did not, on first appearance, seem to be a formidable obstacle. Tine figured she could easily clamber over the mass of boulders that were not over six or eight feet high.

Selecting and stepping on one rough jagged rock at a time, she began to mount the stony cropping. Just as she started climbing, Rufus called out without taking notice of his sweetheart's dilemma, "Oh, Tine, you should see all the berries over here. We can fill our baskets fer sure. Hurry—come see!"

Stimulated by the announcement, she hurried just a touch more and reached the high point of the mound. Here, though, Tine paused for a moment to gauge the best route downward. Although not bothering to check her footing, it felt wobbly and precarious for some reason. Choosing what looked to be the best descending path, she raised a single foot to step down onto the next lower ledge. But suddenly, and terribly, the round wobbly stone under her other foot rolled and gave way, causing the foot to slip off into an unseen crevice. The crevice, or fissure, was just wide enough, and deep enough, that Tine's entire leg poked into it and buried up to the thigh. Poor thing—she fell heavily and hard on her butt in an awkward split, with the one leg trapped in the cranny, and the other sliding free down the side of the rock pile.

Although she could not see her buried leg, she knew it must be scraped badly because it hurt dreadfully. But that was not the worst of Tine's problems, nor what horrified her so much that she began screaming to high heaven. She felt movements around her shoe top and ankle. And that was not all. She began to hear the loud terrifying rattling sound of the most-feared reptile that she could ever imagine—a rattlesnake.

Rufus had heard many a panther scream from the Cold Mountain rising above the Den, but nothing to compare with this. Tine's screech topped them all. And he would have no way of recollecting so long ago, when a similar scream rang out across the Crab Orchard and through this same valley. He had been no more than nine months old at the time, when his natural mother, Altha, had issued another bawling screech just before being stabbed to death by Rufus's natural father. It was good that he would never remember that awful sound, but this cry of Tine's, just now, was a memorable one that he would surely never forget.

In an instant, Rufus bounded to the top of the rock pile, and began pulling Tine's arms in an effort to extract her leg from the chamber of horrors it had squeezed into. The leg was not budging, and the hostile loud rattling sound of the dreaded viper was multiplying. Now Rufus himself became horrified. It was clear from the ominous singing sounds that it was not a lone snake they were dealing with. *There has to be heaps of snakes crawling over Tine's captured foot and leg*, he thought. Worse still he spotted one slithering out from under a rock—and then another—and yet another. Of all things to happen, Tine had gotten her leg stuck in a den of rattlesnakes, and she had riled them into an awful frenzied state.

Rufus kicked with his boots at the serpents crawling out through the cracks. One, then two, and three of them he booted off the pile. Others struck at his boots and legs, but somehow he warded off the venomous bites with his furious kicking and dancing. Then, he heard Tine cry out again, this time in awful pain, and he turned to see her tortured face.

"I've been bit, Rufe! Ohhh—help me! Help me!"

By this time, Tine's father had arrived at the scene and was wielding a heavy stick, whacking away wildly at the slithering creatures. One after another rattling serpent he struck with powerful crushing and glancing blows. While Rufus continued to exert every ounce of strength he could muster to pull Tine's leg out of the snakes' den, the miller battled the rattlesnakes and beat them off one after another. Finally, Rufus perceived Tine's leg budge ever so slightly out of the fissure.

"Hold on, Tine! Here goes—," and Rufus bent down and reached with both strong hands to grasp her waist stoutly. Then with all the might he could muster, he yanked and pulled, letting out a loud bellowing sound that must have given Tine still another fright. But it worked! At last, the leg broke free!

The few short minutes trapped in the serpents' den must have seemed as interminable and awful as the everlasting fire Preacher Poston had warned about scant hours earlier. Snakes were at once everywhere, and the entire rock mass appeared to be alive and moving, as Tine's father continued to bash away at the perturbed reptiles. Rufus could see the leg was bleeding profusely, and he suspected she had been bitten at least once. For sure, Tine had felt a set of sharp fangs pierce her lower leg, and she was certain the deadly venom had been injected into her—and was already coursing through her body! There could be no doubt about it. Time was of the essence now.

Rufus was desperately concerned for Tine's life. In one incredulous feat of brute strength and athleticism, he pulled the trembling girl to her feet, ducked down, and threw her over his shoulders. Abandoning his innate fear of snakes, at least temporarily, he bounded off the rock outcropping and started running with his sweetheart dangling over his back. He ran through the brambles and bushes. He ran through the high grasses and briars. He dodged the tall rabbit tobacco plants. Tine's life was in jeopardy, and Rufus knew of only one person who might be able to save her.

Chapter 10

Undoing the Intent

The Bee Woman, barefooted as usual, was messing about the porch when her exhausted nephew trudged up carrying Tine. It did not take much intuition on her part to realize something dreadful had befallen the girl and that her own healing skills were about to be put to the test. Rufus was so excited and out of breath he could barely talk.

"Snake—snakebite!" he stammered between heaving gulps of air. In a few seconds he revealed more. "She's been bitten—by a rattler! Help her, Aunt Folsom! Please!"

Miller Mann, who had hurried along beside the pair, added between deep breaths, "Please, Mrs. Anders—Folsom, help my daughter! She's gotten bit by a rattlesnake. Ain't nary doubt about it atall. I surely believe she's bit."

The Bee Woman's senses were instantly aroused as she eyed the girl's blood-smeared dress. Then her instincts kicked in. "On the bed, boy. Take her in and put her on the bedstead and take them shoes off her. You, sir," Folsom continued, as she directed her orders at the miller, "get some water and a rag, and warsh the blood off that leg so's we can see if'en she's been bit. The well bucket is there," she barked pointing to it.

Miller Mann stepped quickly to retrieve the water bucket but backed off when he was surprised by a coiled black snake, lying low in the corner next to it. The Bee Woman noticed his hesitancy and barked again, "Don't be shy 'bout that critter. It won't bite ye. Hurry now!"

The father obeyed her stern orders and began cleaning his daughter's leg in earnest. At least one set of dual fang marks could not be missed. On the side of Tine's right leg, just above shoe-top height, two puncture wounds about an inch apart were obvious and already festering. Miller Mann and then the Bee Woman gave Tine a good going-over. Thank the Lord, there were no other ghastly penetrations. A sizeable patch of skin had been scraped off her leg by the jagged rocks, but there were no other snakebites. That was good—real good! But one bite was bad enough, and the healer lit into her work.

She rushed about the place, inside and outside, gathering the different ingredients to be used in a healing poultice. At her table in the tiny cabin, she chopped up an onion, and then beat and ground the choppings in order to extract the strong liquid contents. To the juice of the onion she added salt, apple-cider vinegar, and the powder of a ground-up rattlesnake's rattle that she kept for just such occasions. Although scarce due to the war, she maintained a small medicinal supply of snuff in her inventory and added a tiny pinch to her mix. Rufus was then directed to snatch a jar of sourwood honey from the shelf and spoon out a glob into the mixing. That was it. The potion was all done except for another full minute or two of beating and blending into the desired consistency of a sticky paste.

The Bee Woman fell to her knees beside Tine and stared uneasily at the ever-reddening and swelling wound. But she had seen worse.

"Okay, Rufus, now I want ye to holt this bowl close to me here," and the nephew obeyed his aunt without a quibble.

"This may hurt a mite, dear, but won't be long," the words spoken in a soft whisper. Using her sharpest knife, the Bee Woman made a cut in Tine's leg, joining the two ugly fang wounds. The girl jumped slightly, making a short muffled cry. Poor Tine, her suffering was awful. Not only was the pain excruciating, but her foot, ankle, and lower leg had puffed to a fearful size around the snakebite.

The Bee Woman was undaunted. "Sorry, dear. Won't be no more of that. I promise ye." And then she hurried to wipe away blood and staunch the bleeding. Satisfied after a minute or two that the blood flow was checked, she looked around quickly—first to her patient, then to the miller, and finally to Rufus, who was still holding the magic honey mix. "Okay—here goes, Rufus."

The Bee Woman dipped her fingers into the gooey poultice that she had concocted and then applied a generous portion to the snakebite. Pressing her fingers against the wound, she moved them in a circular motion, round and round, and always rubbing precisely in a counterclockwise direction. For several minutes she massaged the area around the bite with this calculated motion, pressing the healing mixture deep into the wound, just as her grandmother had taught her. That was the way of the Cherokee, she had been instructed. The native Indians held that rubbing a snakebite in the same direction a serpent uncoils serves to undo the intent. The Bee Woman was very careful about this, as she strived to undo the rattlesnake's intent.

Directly, the Bee Woman stopped her rubbing and added a thick extra layer of honey directly over the wound to protect against further infection. Then realizing that everything in her power to help the girl had been done, she rose to her feet and declared, "Can't do no more fer her. We'll jest have to wait now and see how she gets along."

All three of them were standing and gazing down at the scared patient lying in the crude bed with one leg propped on a folded coverlet. By now, Tine's pain was unrelenting, and she moved fitfully to discover a more comfortable reclining position. Also, the pitiful girl was tormented with a frightful fever and a touch of nausea as well. It was obvious that she was in a bad way, and Rufus probed his aunt directly to know her prospects.

"She'll live—won't she, Aunt Folsom?"

The Bee Woman, anticipating such a question, did not hesitate. "We'll have to see, son. Most do, less'n there be complications. Lucky fer her and us'ens, she only got hit the once."

Miller Mann wondered to himself if his daughter needed a real doctor but did not know how best to ask this strange woman. "Ye reckon we'll be able to take her home this evening, Folsom?"

"No—don't believe I'd try to move her fer a few days. What she needs is rest and peaceable quiet. Rufus, I want ye to hop down to Josiah's and git us some ardent spirits. A spoonful of that ever now and again will help settle her."

"Will do!" and Rufus was off and out the door in a jiffy.

Miller Mann was still anxious and further queried, "Ye reckon—should we send after—"

The Bee Woman felt his unease and cut him off quickly, "If ye ker to fetch a doctor up here, sir, more power to ye. Ain't nary more one can do, but I understand how ye might feel the need fer one."

"Yes ma'am—thank ye. I reckon I'll shoot down the river to talk it over good with Doctor Allen, if ye don't mind none?"

"Don't mind atall, sir. Me and Rufus will look after this purty daughter of yer'en. Oh—might ye stop by the Edmunston's long enough to give Julia the news. She's going be fretting soon if Rufus don't get back 'fore night time."

"Yes, ma'am, Folsom, I'll do that!"

Before hopping into his wagon and heading off, the miller stooped to kiss Tine and whisper that he would be back soon. Deep down, he felt his daughter was in good hands with this mysterious Bee Woman, and there were surely no doubts in his mind that she sat securely in the right hand of God.

But something else had begun to subconsciously gnaw away at him. It was the Bee Woman herself. He was intrigued with the unusual barefooted woman who kept bees and critters; something about her caused a little stirring inside him. It was hard to figure exactly what it was, but he did not have time to reflect on it much, just now.

Another world away on the Virginia war front, rattlesnakes were the least of the Rebel soldiers' worries. After their skirmish at the schoolhouse and the conclusion of the Seven Days' Battle, the Haywood Highlanders and their regiment had remained in the Richmond area. For a couple of months, they were kept busy either monitoring General McClellan's stymied army or constructing fortifications to protect the important rail and industrial infrastructure at nearby Petersburg. During this lull in the fighting, the soldier boys from Forks of Pigeon swapped their Mississippi rifles for shovels and fell in with the local slaves digging trenches and toiling at various varieties of back-breaking earth work.

General Robert E. Lee could not tolerate watching his fine Army of Northern Virginia dawdling and digging defenses. While the weather was still suitable for maneuvering and fighting, he and his chief commanders, including General Thomas 'Stonewall' Jackson, designed to invade the North. For reasons both strategic and political, they intended to carry the war to the Yankees instead of waiting for their invading armies to attack and despoil the South. So the audacious Lee gave the appropriate orders to his troops, and during the stifling dog days of late August and early September, the 25th North Carolina Troops marched through northern Virginia, first by train and then by foot, toward the Potomac River—the watery demarcation separating the warring Northern and Southern states.

After a short train ride and a week of hoofing it over dusty northern Virginia roads, Captain Basil Edmunston's band of foot soldiers finally tramped up to the majestic river's edge. The wide and imposing Potomac flowed in their front, and beyond were the Yankee states of Maryland and Pennsylvania, with their unspoiled and essentially defenseless countryside—a veritable food basket ripe for easy taking. The Confederate Army's considerable number of horses required forage, and the troops could stand more nutritious foodstuffs than the Virginia countryside could continue to provide. So General Lee calculated to eat from the Yankee's table rather than from his own countrymen's.

Many of the Haywood Highlanders, including Corporal Hack Hartgrove, had literally walked out of their worn-out shoes and hobbled barefooted much of the way. They were tired, foot-worn, sore, and hungry. When word spread that the Potomac was to be crossed and the Yankee land beyond was to be overrun, the grumbling started. That night, around the disgruntled Rebels' campfires, murmurs of anger and disappointment spread like wildfire.

At the fireside where Corporal Hartgrove and a few buddies were sharing what little bacon and cornbread there was, one unhappy soldier weighed in. "Ain't right, I say—them sending us into the Yanks' kingdom. It's the very reason I joined up fer this here fight—to keep them nigger lovers from taking over our own land. Now, come to find out, General Lee and Ransom and that bunch aim fer us to do the same to them slave abolishers. It ain't right, and I don't like it nary atall, nary atall I say!"

Another like-minded discontent, a private by the name of Francis Christopher, added, "Reckon I feel the same, Jeremy. First they make us stay in longer than we ought—longer than we signed up fer—and now there's this here invasion foolishness. They ought to know better. I have a good notion to light out tonight and head back fer the hills. I do, I tell ye! What ye think, Hat—ye in with me?"

Hat, of course, was Corporal Hack Hartgrove, who by now had become accustomed to his new name. Turns out that Hat held a contrary view of this new situation they found themselves in. "Damn it to hell, Chris! Ye know ye don't aim to do it. Ye ain't never going to desert this army, no way in hell. What? Ye plan on jest leaving all us'ens here to do yer fighting fer ye? Ye'll never do that. Ye've got my back, and I've got yer'en. That's the way I see it! 'Sides, them Yanks is over there cross the river somers, and we'ens got to go get 'em."

Chris replied, "I've a right good mind to do it, I tell ye. Ain't jest babbling 'bout it, Hat! Hell no, I ain't."

One of the other boys jumped in about then. "'Peers to me to be a stupid thing to do—invading Maryland. Don't reckon our genius officers stopped to cipher long enough to figger it'll jest increase the Northern Army. Why, they ain't gonna like it no better than we did, and it'll jest serve to light a fire under their tails. Now, them Yanks are gonna start joining up bigger than Pete! Jest ye wait and see!"

Sergeant Garland Henson figured the boys had some right good points they were making, but he could not see the profits in debating the matter. "Ain't no use arguing 'bout it, boys. Captain has given down orders that 'morrow we're going to wade that big river—the 'Tomac is its name—and it ain't but 'bout waist deep, don't look like. And no more sech talk about desertion, Chris. Don't 'spect ye got it in ye, nor any of our mountain boys, I reckon. Now then, let's get us some rest 'fore swimming that there 'Tomac River tomorrow."

The following morning, the 7th day of September, found all of Captain Edmunston's Highlanders up to their waist belts in water, as they slowly waded across the Potomac River. Nary man in the company had actually made good on threats to desert. However, many others in the invading army did, in fact, throw down their arms and head for home. After fording the Potomac, the Haywood Highlanders, along with the nine other companies of the 25th North Carolina and several additional regiments that made up Ransom's Brigade, marched directly into Frederick, Maryland. Whereupon, General Ransom received immediate orders to backtrack, re-cross the river, and move on the Union-held river town of Harper's Ferry, about twenty miles away.

Several days later, the Highlanders participated in a brief siege that resulted in the capture of Harper's Ferry, including its bounty of thousands of prisoners, a veritable arsenal of military equipment and weapons, and, best of all, hoards of food. Unfortunately for Captain Edmunston's boys, before they had a chance to share the plunder, Ransom's Brigade received new orders to rush back to Maryland, where General Lee desperately required them. He had gotten his Army of Northern Virginia into a real fix.

While approximately one-half of Lee's army was cleaning out the Union forces in the region around Harper's Ferry; he had maintained the rest of the army on the north side of the Potomac River, operating in the Yankee country of Maryland and Pennsylvania. Essentially, he had divided his very strong army into two much weaker ones. And when Union General McClellan fortuitously discovered this ill-advised blunder, he launched his powerful Northern Army against Lee's much weaker forces north of the Potomac. The belligerents met up near the town of Sharpsburg, Maryland, on opposing sides of a small stream called Antietam Run. Nervously bracing for the forthcoming conflict, General Lee had sent urgent orders for his detached army at Harper's Ferry to come join him at once.

Captain Edmunston hurried his harried troops onto the battleground in the wee morning hours of September 17th. They had crossed the Potomac River for a third time and marched on the double-quick from Harper's Ferry to get there. The 25th North Carolina was thrown into a position at the extreme right side of the Confederate line. From there they were ordered to oppose the Federals at all costs in any attempt to cross either the bridge or the fording spot that spanned the meandering Antietam Run in their front.

Corporal Hat Hartgrove and the rest of the Haywood Highlanders sought the protection of trees and rail fences from which to fight. They threw themselves behind these makeshift defenses and waited, as the frantic sounds of great armies preparing to engage in battle could be heard up and down the lines, on both sides of the small stream. The Rebel Highlanders, peering out anxiously from their hiding places in the morning grayness, could sense that something big was up. Little did they anticipate the enormity of the looming battle or the critical role they eventually would play in it.

Chapter 11

Oceans of Bluecoats

The Bee Woman's healing power was proven once again with Tine's terrible snakebite incident. As expected, the girl endured terrible pain and agony for the first few days, but gradually, the torment subsided and the mending process kicked in. Her leg not only swelled to a grotesque size and shape but, over time, took on integrated shades of red, blue, and black. It was so ugly that for several weeks Tine could not stand to look at it, preferring to keep it covered and out of her sight. When the miller Mann had queried the good Doctor Allen whether his services should be employed, he received an emphatic endorsement of the eccentric healer's skills and was told in no uncertain terms that Tine was in good hands. Therefore, the girl remained under the Bee Woman's unconventional care at her Crab Orchard hovel for more than a week.

Believe it or not, Tine became accustomed to the covey of critters running about the place, although the coon was overly friendly at times. And strangely enough, given her recent experience, she came to accept the black snakes' presence and refrained from flinching or shivering upon sighting one slithering across the packed earth floor. The Bee Woman took to Tine like her precious bees do to sourwood blossoms, and the girl developed a fond affection of her own for the strange woman who gave her such tender and undivided attention. Even the miller, who faithfully rode up the river every evening to look in on Tine, began to harbor a special appreciation for the queer woman as well. Given his peculiar demeanor around Folsom during Tine's confinement at the Crab Orchard, one might allow that the miller Mann had become bewitched by his daughter's eccentric host. Or then again, it might have been something else entirely.

Rufus spent the better part of his days with Tine, during the trying times following the snakebite emergency. With the corn harvest in full swing, he left Lark in complete charge at the Den, with detailed instructions of what needed to be done. Without fail however, each evening when Rufus arrived back home, he was greeted with a different sort of troubles. This night was no exception. When the young master found Lark nervously waiting in the dark, he prepared himself for a new vexation.

"How you's be's doing, Massa?" Lark greeted, as he took the horse's reins.

"Oh—'spect I'm doing 'bout as good as usual, Lark. How 'bout you? Everything work out just right up at Preacher Poston's?" It was an innocent query. Rufus had instructed Lark to take a few of the boys and the wagon up to Poston's and to bring back the Den's share of the corn crop. It was not an unusual request—nothing out of the ordinary atall. Each tenant was required by their contract with the Edmunstons to give over a third of their corn as partial payment for living on the property. Lark had done it many times before, and it had seemed to Rufus to be a fairly straightforward chore. Well, complications had arisen.

"We has us problems up at Poston's, Massa Rufus. Sure do's."

Not overly surprised, the young master casually replied, "Oh? What kind of problems?"

"Well, soon's we gets to Poston's, he goes and says to us dat he's done fixed our corn pile fo' us—and den he shows us da Den's pile."

Nothing unusual there, Rufus thought, and with his patience dwindling he prodded his slave on, "So?"

"You's says before, Massa Rufus, dat alls us shares the frostbite corn. Dat not what you's says to us?"

"Right, Lark. We don't take just the good corn. We have to take some of his frostbitten corn as part of our share too. That's what Father always does. It's fair and that's what we aim to do." Should not be any misunderstanding on this point, Rufus thought as he finished his explanation.

"Dat's right, Massa Rufus. That be's what I says to Poston. But den he says da Den's pile has got good corn and frostbite corn—both dem corns." Lark paused and looked at Rufus to see if his master understood what he had just said. It was important. Rufus nodded for him to continue. "Well, Massa Rufus, we all looks real good at da Den's pile and sees dat it be all frostbite corn. And we looks at Poston's corn, and most of it be's all good corn."

By now Rufus was getting the gist of Lark's crisis and wanted to hear more. "So? What did you do, Lark?"

"Well, Massa Rufus, I says to Poston dat he be giving da Den all frostbite corn—and he gets real mad and talks mean to us. He says God chose da corn fo' him to give da Den, and dat be's what he puts in da Den's pile—God's corn."

It seemed strange to Rufus that a man of God like Poston would attempt to cheat his landlord. He did not recollect his father ever having trouble like this before. But he could not, by any means, slough off Lark's grievance. He had confidence in his slave's integrity and good sense, and felt there must be something to this gripe Lark was raising. "So, you're saying that Poston gave us all his frostbitten corn, huh, Lark?"

"Yessa, Massa Rufus. That be's 'bout it. We loaded da Den's corn in the wagon and brings it here jest like you's says. But we's not unloads it yet—not until you's has a good look at it."

"Good, Lark! That's good you didn't unload the corn. I'll take a look first thing in the morning. If it all appears to be frostbitten, like you say, then we'll take it right back up to Preacher Poston and compare it with what God allowed to be his corn. Okay?"

A smile lit up briefly on Lark's face and then went away as quickly as it had come. "Yessa, Massa. Uhh, Massa Rufus—dare be's one more thing I want to speaks to you's 'bout."

Rufus was hungry and definitely starting to lose his patience. "Okay, Lark, what is it then, and tell me quick? I'm starving fer a morsel to eat."

"Dare wus two mean men stops us on da road today. Dey says mean things to us. Jesse says it be da same mean men who whips him."

Those damn Buggs, Rufus thought instantly. *They're never going away.* "What else did they say, Lark?"

"The old mean man—da one wif hair dat be white like the snow—he says fo' you's not to forget 'bout him. He says one of dese days he will sees us here at da Den. Dat be's 'bout it, Massa Rufus. He says he will see's you. Dat be all he says to says to you's."

Rufus forgot about the hunger pains as the temperature of his blood soared. He was going to have to deal with those two Buggs sooner or later, and he was nervous about it. Not a nervousness born out of fear, mind you, but from his inexperience with such things. He had not mentioned anything to his mother about the continuing bad business between himself and the Buggs. And, of course, he had not bothered his father with such trivial matters, in the letters they had posted to the war front. This was his own doing, and he was going to have to take care of it himself—one of these days.

At the break of dawn on September 17th, Federal and Confederate cannon fire rang out across the valley of Antietam Run near Sharpsburg, Maryland. Captain Edmunston and his company of Highlanders from Haywood County watched the furious puffing of the enemy artillery and heard the escalating explosions on the far side of the battlefield. Lee's Confederate Army, comprised of a meager 35,000 troops, faced off against McClellan's powerful Union forces, almost 100,000 strong. Unaware of this great disparity, the Haywood Highlanders waited anxiously for the bluecoats to rush toward the small Antietam Run, flowing steadily by in front of them. But the Yankees never came.

The main Union attacking thrusts were occurring on the Confederate's left flank. From their vantage point, Captain Edmunston and his boys could clearly see the Federal gunners on the opposite bank loading and firing at the left wing of the Confederate Army. Above the distant roar of battle, the patter of rifle fire could easily be distinguished along with an occasional yell or cheer of infantry, as some advantage was gained by either side. After more than an hour of witnessing and listening to the raging battle being fought some two to three miles away, Colonel Rutledge received pressing orders to rush his 25th North Carolina regiment to the Confederate left, where General Stonewall Jackson was directing the defensive action.

The 25th and the other regiments comprising Ransom's Brigade moved out on the double-quick and rushed through the outskirts of the village of Sharpsburg toward the fighting. The Haywood Highlanders, a very small unit of the brigade, hurried along behind the main battle line, passing constant files of wounded soldiers coming out of the fray. The sounds of war became louder and louder until the popping of musketry, booming of the cannons, and whistling of shells became almost deafening. It was a significantly bigger fight than the Richmond schoolhouse skirmish, and Captain Edmunston wondered if he and his boys would have the mettle to stand up to the task.

Ransom's Brigade was deployed in a woody spot near a small brick church that was painted white, of all things. The action here was especially fierce and brutal, as the Federals had just broken the Confederate line and were pouring into the breach. *Such miraculous timing*, Stonewall Jackson thought, as he watched the fine brigade of North Carolina regiments swiftly and skillfully wheel into position and plug the hole in his defenses. Five minutes more, he mused, and the Confederate Army would have ceased to exist.

With their eerie Rebel yells resounding through the woods, the fresh Confederate troops struck the oncoming bluecoats with a thundering crash and drove them clear to the furthest edge of the woodlands. Over the entire morning, these same woods had been fought over, and the carnage veritably littered the forest floor. Captain Edmunston's Highlanders had to step over the bodies of dead and wounded soldiers, as they carried their relentless charge forward. For the entirety of that very long morning, the Haywood Highlanders stood their ground in those woods near the little white church and beat back repeated Federal efforts to retake the precious ground.

During a rare calm in the action, General Stonewall Jackson rode to where Colonel Rutledge was standing, giving Corporal Hack Hartgrove and all of the Highlanders a good look at the revered man. He sported a scruffy beard and wore an old worn uniform, with a slouch hat pulled low over his eyes. Most of the men, including Hack, figured him to be a right sorry sight for a general. But Stonewall cared little for how he looked. He was all business and had witnessed an earlier failed attempt by the 25th North Carolina to take a particularly bothersome battery of cannon emplacements. So he had come over to urge the colonel to try it once more.

"Colonel, I witnessed your brave attempt at yon battery. Why don't you try again? I believe you can take it." Stonewall was not as sure of himself as he let on, but he desperately wanted the regiment to have another go at the enemy cannons.

Colonel Rutledge thought differently, though, and respectfully replied, "I will attack if you order me to, General Jackson. But if I do, I believe I will fail again. I already lost more than thirty men trying it, and when we got to the top of that hill, I saw vast hordes of bluecoats on the other side."

"You did, huh?" But General Jackson was not about to give up on his objective. He needed some solid verification of what he had just been told. He could not let some whipper-snapper young colonel feed him a bunch of horseshit. "Colonel, have you a good climber in your command?"

"Sorry, sir, I don't understand," the colonel came back.

The general repeated himself. "Have you got a good climber in your regiment? I want a man to climb up yon hickory tree and take a gander at that battery."

Colonel Rutledge turned to Captain Edmunston, whose company happened to be holding the center of the regiment's position. "Captain, get us a volunteer that can climb trees."

The captain turned to his officers and put out the call for a volunteer. The first to tout his climbing skills was selected, and the skinny young soldier instantly threw down his rifle and various other accoutrements, tossed his fancy hat to a buddy, and hustled toward the sorry-looking General Jackson. Standing at attention, bareheaded and barefooted, Corporal Hack Hartgrove gave the general a salute and barked out confidently, "Yes sir!" Although Colonel Rutledge recognized the youthful lion-hearted volunteer, he remained stone-faced and unenthused with General Jackson's reconnaissance initiative.

Pointing to a tall hickory tree nearby, the general himself ordered, "Son, I want you to climb that tree as high as you can and tell me what you see beyond that pesky battery. Understand?"

"Yes sir, General!" And with that reply the corporal was soon shinnying up the tree quicker than a squirrel after an acorn delight.

When Hack got to the top, General Jackson hollered up to him, "How many troops are there behind the battery?"

Hack squirmed to get a good look. The Yankee sharpshooters' missiles whizzed by his head and cracked hard into the tree trunk his arms were wrapped around. It was a dangerous mission he had volunteered for, and the officers and men below recognized it as such.

Captain Edmunston was extremely fearful that Hack would be hit and called up to him. "Careful, Corporal!"

Hack did not reply and paid the lethal Minié balls no nevermind. He was looking for bluecoats, and when he had them in his view, he yelled down his answer, "There be oceans of them, General!"

That piece of intelligence gathering was not precise enough for General Jackson's liking. Colonel Rutledge had given him a similar assessment of the situation, but the general had refused to believe it. He shouted back, "Count the flags, Corporal! Tell me how many flags you see!"

"Yes sir!" And Corporal Hartgrove then began counting out loud—one, two, three, four, five—and on and on until he reached a count of thirty-nine flags, at which point General Jackson called up to him.

"That will do, sir! Come back down!" General Jackson then turned to Colonel Rutledge and offered, "Had to know for sure, Colonel. I want that battery silenced because it will be difficult to hold this position under the constant duress of accurate cannon fire. Hold off on any more attempts to take the battery, until I order different."

As the day wore on, General McClellan successively shifted the concentrated Federal attacks to the center of the Confederate line and, lastly, toward the vulnerable Rebel right flank. The 25th North Carolina and the Haywood Highlanders stayed put on the left flank near the little white church, while the exploding shells and lethal cannon balls rained upon their position. The troops simply hunkered down the best they could to withstand the murderous barrage and tried not to get themselves killed.

Over the course of the long afternoon, Yankee artillerists, manning the annoying battery that General Jackson had wanted quieted, began to close in on their Rebel targets by constantly refining their aims and trajectories. Although most of the men hid themselves well enough to survive the bombardment unscathed, one soldier was not so fortunate.

Noticing that a small squad of his men were unduly exposed, an irate captain made a rash judgment to give them a talking to. So he leaped up and left the safety of his cover—a large tree that had not yet been blasted to kingdom come—and ran toward the squad. Hunched over and moving fast toward his boys, he had taken no more than four or five running gaits when he felt some kind of blow—or something—to his trailing leg, and a simultaneous stinging sensation. The sheer force of that blow had launched the captain into the air, twisting and somersaulting and finally landing hard onto the ground.

Gulping and heaving deeply to draw air into his lungs, the captain—Captain Edmunston—struggled mightily to get his breath. He simply could not breathe and fell into a state of dizziness, followed by several minutes of semi-consciousness. Upon regaining his senses, he sluggishly recognized Sergeant Henson and Corporal Hartgrove and realized they were dragging him back to safe cover. The pain he felt was like nothing he had ever experienced before. Bolts of the most awful, acute hurting raced through his body. His right leg—he could not see it—throbbed as if it was on fire one second, and the next, felt as cold as an icicle. When the men laid the captain down, he knew something bad had happened to him—that something was terribly wrong. What was it?

I've been hit! That's got to be it. He knew he had been hit and desperately wanted to know how badly he was wounded. Not looking at his saviors but trying to see his leg, he gave frantic orders to his men. "Help raise me up, boys. Let me take a look at my—my leg. I believe it's hurt—" And then Captain Edmunston abruptly fell silent, as he stared open-mouthed at the bloody remains of what was once his leg.

Chapter 12

A Regrettable Task

The Edmunston family was rolling happily down the river road toward Forks of Pigeon on a cool Saturday morning. A brilliant blue sky shone over them, and puffy white clouds drifted across the magnificent azure backdrop. Forest canopies scorched with glorious shades of orange, yellow, and red crowded the rutted trace. It was a spectacular fall extravaganza that most East Forkers, being accustomed to such natural beauty, were somewhat callous to. However, on this day Rufus and his mother and sisters basked in the splendor of their rugged native countryside, as they made their way to Deaver's Store for a visit with Maggie Deaver.

Rufus was on horseback, as usual, serving as escort for the troupe, which also included Jesse, who was handling the wagon's pulling mule team. When the mill was reached, Rufus begged his mother's permission to abandon them for a brief spell, so that he could ride over and check on Tine. Of course, Julia had no objections.

"Okay, then, I'll catch up with you at the store," Rufus called back, as he broke away from the pack and headed toward the ponderous building hugging the edge of the East Fork River.

More than two months had elapsed since Tine's run-in with the rattlesnake, and in that time her leg had healed rather nicely. The swelling had gone down, and only a small discoloration lingered around the telltale scar from the fang wound. One would never have guessed that the fortunate girl had recently survived a dangerous tussle with death by only a hair's breadth.

Tine and the miller Mann attributed her miraculous survival to the Bee Woman's healing powers, and they continued to pay regular visits to her little shack up at the Orchard to show their gratitude.

Now that Tine was rehabilitated and walking normally again, she had returned to her father's side at the mill. The harvest season was winding down, and with the milling business ramping up, the miller was very much in need of her valuable services. When Rufus got there, he found Tine on the upper floor loading some corn into one of the hoppers. Breathing heavily after bounding up the long flight of stairs, he huffed out a fond greeting, "Hello there, my pretty little ghost."

The poor girl, as usual, was covered from head to toe in grain dust and did indeed present a pale ghostly appearance. Startled and raring back in surprise at the unexpected intrusion, she almost screamed. "Ohh! Oh, for heaven's sake, you almost scared me to death, Rufus!"

"Sorry 'bout that, Tine. Didn't mean to skeer ye none. How goes it?"

"Not bad—just working steady." She leaned over close to Rufus and delighted him with a big buss. Then, as Rufus was savoring the kiss, Tine backed away, giving him a delicious smile and commenting, "Okay, Rufe, help me finish this order and then we can visit a spell. Have I got something interesting to share with you—and right juicy news it is."

In the meantime, a short distance down river at Deaver's Store, Mary and Emily were romping up and down the aisles trying to discover some wonderful hidden delight that might possibly have escaped their attention in the past. Even these young girls were not insensible to the drastic diminution of merchandise on the store's mostly empty shelves.

After one and a half years of war, the Confederacy was suffering dire shortages of not only weaponry and war supplies but also vital domestic necessities such as salt, sugar, coffee, textiles, tinware, and metal fabrications. Agricultural crops and manufactured goods produced in the South were almost wholly dedicated to sustaining the army in the field. In addition, the strangling Yankee naval blockade was successfully shutting out most imported materials—those for military as well as domestic consumption. In short, the South's civilian markets were starved for foods and products that had been in abundant supply only eighteen months earlier.

It was no wonder there were few frivolous or girlie items on the store shelves drawing Mary's and Emily's attention. After a short prowl and coming up empty, they bounced outside to continue their explorations. Directly, they found the smith working steady at his blazing forge and one of the Deaver's slaves sitting at the shoe last, hammering and pecking away. Welcome or not, these busy craftsmen were blessed with the lively presence and friendly company of two young girls peppering them with chatter and questions.

Inside the store, Julia visited with her mother, as Columbus Hartgrove minded the business. As might be expected, Maggie's grieving process had continued without abate, and she was still struggling to cope with her lonesome state of widowhood. With God's help and blessings, the support of her extended family, and Hartgrove's dedicated assistance, she was managing to get by—barely. These frequent and healing visits from Julia and the grandchildren were extremely helpful and highly savored.

The mother and daughter were sitting in rockers near the fireplace chatting blithely and rocking away, when suddenly the elderly matron remembered something. "Oh, for heaven's sake, I completely forgot, dear. Yesterday's post had a letter for you from your brother. How nice of him to think of you and write," she said, as they both got up and strolled over to the letter office.

"Anything from Basil?" Julia asked, hoping her luck would further extend to two letters.

"Don't believe so—nope, nothing," Maggie replied while shuffling through a stack of mail. Here's your brother's letter. Looks like it's postmarked from Winchester, Virginia."

As Julia held the letter and studied it before breaking the seal, she muttered excitedly to her mother, "Don't know where Winchester, Virginia is. Wonder if it's close to Sharpsburg? I haven't heard from Basil since before that big battle near there."

She carefully opened the letter and began to read it with relish. In a matter of mere moments, however, she let loose with a high-pitched scream of "No! No!" and then was overcome with hysterical wailing. The commotion roused Hartgrove's interest, and he stepped over to see what was the matter. After learning the nature and contents of the message, Columbus hurried out outside and sent Jesse running up to the mill to fetch Rufus.

By the time Rufus arrived, gasping and out of breath, Julia had partially regained her composure and was sitting with Maggie next to the fire. His mother appeared to be extremely nervous, and it was obvious she had been crying. In her lap he could see a letter, but other than that, he had no notion of the circumstances of his mother's distress. Jesse had been clueless about the emergency, and Hartgrove, usually a reliable source of information, was with a customer at the far end of the store. So, Rufus just gave his mother a blank look and simply asked, "What? What's this all about? What's wrong, Mother?"

Julia sniffed real big and handed the letter over to him, "It's your father, dear. I'm afraid something dreadful has happened to him."

Rufus's heart skipped several beats, and his mouth fell open and froze. Instantly, he thought the worst. *Father has been killed fer sure—that's got to be it. Why else would Mother be so upset?* Hesitant and nervous, he began to read the tear-stained missive his mother handed him.

Winchester, Va – Oct. 2, 1862

Dear Sister,

I have the regrettable task of writing to inform you of some real bad news about Basil. At the Battle with the Yanks near Sharpsburg, Maryland on 17th Sept. he got hit in the leg with a cannon shot. It was his right leg that got blown off. But I believe he may yet be saved. The boys carried him behind the lines where the surgeon doctors were working and they give him to them. I looked in on him quick as I could before our army moved back to Virginia and I seen they had amputated his leg just below the knee. He lost a considerable amount of blood and was in right smart pain but doing tolerable well considering all things. The doctor allowed he might live if a bad infection don't set in. I feel terrible Julia that we didn't bring him with us. Colonel said to leave the badly wounded. He reckoned they would slow us down. And the doctor told me the wagon ride would kill Basil for sure. So we left him back there in Maryland, Julia. Please don't think too harshly of me. I would have carried him with us but had no real say in the matter. I hope you will believe me and forgive me for leaving Basil in the Yankee country.

Sadly we had 3 boys killed in the fighting and several others wounded. The ones killed were A. Crawford, F. Henson, and J. Meece. Please tell C. Hartgrove to inform their families as easy as he can. These men were planted in a field behind the lines.

We are now camped in the Shenandoah Mountains in north Virginia and waiting for further orders. These mountains here remind me a lot of home. Its been right cool and we have been sleeping under the stars with no tents. The men elected me captain in place of Basil and I hope to fill his shoes proper like. Give my regards to Rufus, Mary & Emily.
Your affectionate loving brother,
Burton

With watery eyes, Rufus read the letter two more times before finally putting it down. A dumb-founded expression aimed at his mother was the only reaction he had at first. Then he bluntly asked, "I wonder if he's dead by now?"

This being such a delicate and traumatic time for Julia, her son's insensitive query was not what she needed just at that moment. At once, she broke into crying heaves and muffled bawls. But Rufus, saddened and hurt by these bad tidings as well, did not rush to comfort his mother. He was distracted and lost in his own troubled thoughts about the tragedy. There was a fleeting instant, while perusing the letter for the third time, when he was struck with an overwhelming inspiration.

He was possessed with the sudden powerful conviction that he had to go rescue his father. His father was alive—he knew it, somehow—and he was convinced that the tortured man was, at that very moment, barely clinging to the cusp of life. Time was of the essence, Rufus figured, and someone must go and save his father from the Yankees. That is what had to be done, and that is precisely what Rufus decided he would do.

Over the coming day or two, while Rufus and Jesse were flying around making preparations for the long ride north, it dawned on at least one of the boys that they did not have a plan. Neither had ever been to Virginia, let alone Maryland. They had no earthly idea which roads to take to get up there, or how far they had to travel. So, they turned to the best remaining resource in the area, now that Basil was away at the war—and possibly dead—and the Colonel was among the angels. They rode down to Deaver's Store to confer with Columbus Hartgrove.

Neither Hartgrove nor Rufus's mother was very keen on this rescue notion. The very proposal of the idea had launched Julia into another tantrum of despair. Hartgrove had judged the boys were simply not up to such a long and arduous journey into a strange war-torn land, never mind the extreme odds against finding Basil. But Rufus would not be disabused of his intentions, and Columbus was finally persuaded to lend his support.

He and the boys gathered around a large map of the Southern states tacked on the store wall and began studying it. Using this reference, they traced out a route northward from Asheville up the Buncombe Turnpike and penetrating into east Tennessee. The map indicated the various roads leading from there into Virginia and then up through the Shenandoah Valley. Although they could not pinpoint the exact location of Sharpsburg, Maryland, because the geographic features of the map did not extend beyond Virginia, the cities of Martinsburg and Harper's Ferry, hugging the Potomac River, were prominently defined. Hartgrove advised Rufus to make inquiries along the way for directions to either of these two places. If they got that far, then they should be able to learn the way to Sharpsburg with little problems. It was somewhere in Maryland—that they knew for sure.

As Hartgrove was pointing out some of the key towns and other features on the route, his finger lingered at a place named 'New Market,' situated deep within Virginia's Shenandoah Valley. Then, as his mind assimilated the town's name, the irony suddenly struck him. "Well, I'll be. Ain't that something?" he asked to no one in particular. "See this here town here, Rufus? That's New Market. Did yer pa ever tell ye 'bout that there town—either one of ye?" Hartgrove looked at Rufus and then Jesse and could see the blank looks on their faces. The boys shook their heads to confirm they had no previous knowledge of the strange place.

Columbus just grinned at them before setting in to spin the wildest tale about the time when Jesse's father and mother—Lark and Delia—escaped their Haywood County masters and fled north, so they could marry and find their freedom. The runaways were apprehended near New Market, and Basil and the Bee Woman's husband journeyed up there to claim the slaves. It was an enticing story and the boys hung on to every word out of Hartgrove's mouth. He spoke of how Lark had been shot and almost killed, how the Bee Woman's husband had tragically been murdered by bandits, and how Basil had eventually acquired Delia from her master and allowed the two slaves to finally marry.

When Hartgrove returned to his analysis of the best travel options, Rufus was so distracted he could not give the important matter his undivided attention. *Why had Father not shared the slave runaway story with me?* he fretted. *It would have been thoughtful of my old man to relate the circumstances of Aunt Folsom's widowhood.* Rufus could not fathom a reason, and as he mulled it over, he was jarred back to the business at hand by Hartgrove.

"Did ye hear that, Rufus? Ye seem to be lost somers," Columbus stated, somewhat miffed that his valuable time was not being fully appreciated. "I said the trip ciphers out to be pert near five hundred miles long. Course it 'pends on how hard ye'ens ride, but it might take ye 'tween two and three weeks to reach Maryland, I reckon."

Their meeting with Hartgrove lasted for almost two hours, counting the time that the busy man broke away to tend to customers. But when it was concluded, Rufus and Jesse at least had a working plan for the journey and better understood the formidable challenges ahead. And before finally breaking up, Hartgrove gave one last piece of friendly advice. "Take yerself a firearm, Rufus. Ye're liable to need it."

Chapter 13

Under the Good Dunkers' Care

After Captain Edmunston was carried from the battlefield, the South's forces continued to fight furiously against a Yankee army double its size. They beat back one furious charge after another, until darkness closed over the field and the troops on both sides could not find or see an enemy target to shoot at. Then all fell silent along the banks of Antietam Run, except for the monotonous songs of the crickets and cicadas and the frogs' continuous honking croaks. And everywhere, it seemed, there were the piercing, haunting wails of wounded soldiers lying on the field, crying out for water and pleading for someone—anyone—to help them.

Thousands upon thousands of soldiers donned in blue and gray uniforms had fallen on the field, making it the single bloodiest day in the Civil War. Union General McClellan's thirst for fighting was apparently sated by the red rivers of blood that washed over the cornfields and through woody thickets into the clear waters of the Antietam. The reluctant Federal general wanted no more such sanguinary days, and on the morning following the battle, he refused to throw the powerful forces at his disposal against the poised Confederate defenders. General Lee, his army smarting and licking its wounds, fully expected another all-out Yankee attack—but there was none. So under the cover of darkness and pelting rain, he led his army out of the blood-stained valley of the Antietam and retreated across the Potomac River into the Shenandoah Mountains of Virginia.

It was from a Confederate encampment in these mountains that Captain Deaver wrote to Julia with the regrettable news about Basil. Deaver had led Julia to believe that Basil might yet be alive and, in fact, Captain Edmunston had miraculously survived, thanks to the compassion of a local farmer and his family.

The Rebel surgeons and their ambulatory patients had retreated with the rest of the army, leaving Lee's most severely wounded and immobile soldiers behind. These unfortunate men, including the captain, were left either to die or to be taken as prisoners of war. In Basil's case, a local farmer by the name of Andrew Shook and his young son discovered him before the Yankees did. Luckily, the Shooks were members of a minor religious sect in the community known as the Dunkers, after their tradition of fully immersing—or dunking—baptismal candidates into a river or stream. Fighting and war was not condoned by the Dunkers. However, providing aid to a fellow man, destined almost certainly to die otherwise, was apparently not considered a blasphemous act. When the Shooks stumbled upon Basil, they did not shrink from the opportunity to provide him assistance.

They had found the wounded Highlander lying in a pool of his own blood next to a barn—one the Confederates had used for a field hospital. He was sprawled on the ground beside a festering pile of amputated limbs more than six feet high. Almost certainly, one of these gruesome appendages had been his own. When farmer Shook and his son came across Basil, he was crying out in anguish and mumbling to be set free from the torturous, insufferable suffering. Unfortunately, the Shooks could not relieve him of the unbearable pain. But with the aid of another merciful citizen and an old tattered blanket, they carried the pitiful soldier to their farmhouse just outside of Sharpsburg and attended to him with remarkable devotion.

Basil awoke in the middle of the night, after many hours of unconsciousness and fitful sleep. All was quiet around him. The embers of the spent fire still gave off a dim red glow. He found himself covered with a blanket and resting on a blood-stained straw tick on the puncheon floor. His stump—for that was all that was left of the lower right leg—burned intensely, as if it was in flames. Steady, throbbing, agonizing pains shot through his entire body from the raw bleeding stub that extended only a few inches below his knee. Trying to raise his head to see around him, he moaned, "Where—where am I?" Then spotting his strange hosts, who were trying to get some well-deserved sleep, he raised his voice slightly to awaken them, "Hello over there—where am I? Who are you?"

Roused from their sleep on a small bedstead against a stone wall, the Shooks were at once relieved to learn their patient had come to his senses. He had been with them for more than two days now, and it was the first intelligible thing they had heard him utter. In her night dress, Mrs. Shook hurried to Basil's side and kneeled down next to him. She spoke softly, "You're going to be all right now, sir. We're the Shooks—Andrew and Eloise Shook. And we mean to help you get better. Now let me see about getting you some water."

Day after long day, the boys trudged along the rutted turnpikes on their way to rescue Basil. Both Rufus and Jesse rode pretty fair mounts and led a tethered pack mule behind them. Rufus had a sheathed hunting knife and his father's old cap-and-ball pistol tucked uncomfortably under his belt. However, Columbus Hartgrove had advised against Jesse's carrying weapons. He had allowed the drovers, soldiers, and other folks encountered along the way would not tolerate an armed slave riding a saddled horse in broad daylight. The reason being that white Southerners harbored an innate fear of slave insurrections, and, besides that, it was just not right for them to possess guns. He feared that Jesse might get himself taken up and carted off to a runaway jail. Or worse, the Yankees would carry him back up North where the niggers were being recruited to fight against their white masters. And that was not all Hartgrove had counseled them about.

He especially cautioned the boys to stay out of sight of army men, both Rebels and Yankees. "They will steal your fine horses before you know it," he had warned them. Hartgrove was dead set against this thieving impressment practice for the greater cause of the military. Having lost several mules and a horse to the Southern cause, he thought it to be nothing shy of armed robbery.

The intrepid East Forkers rode from daylight until dusk, in rain or shine. They were vigilant and careful to avoid attracting the attention of soldiers. When passing drovers or travelers, they did not linger to talk, unless specific directions or information were needed. At campsites off the roadways, they scoffed down the food they had carried with them from the Den, this being bacon for the most part that was heated in a skillet over an open fire. Apple orchards abounded along the way but, regrettably, the fruit had already been picked. However, their niggling pains of hunger often moved them to sample the rotting apples littering the ground under the trees. At night when sleep was so badly needed, they took uncommon measures not to relax their guard. Remembering Hartgrove's runaway tale about Jesse's mother and father and the part about the Bee Woman's husband being murdered in the middle of the night by highway bandits, they slept in shifts with the loaded pistol at hand.

Finally, after sixteen grueling, uneventful days of turnpikes and river crossings, they reached Martinsburg, Virginia. Come to find out, they were less than a day's ride from Sharpsburg. The next day—the first Saturday in November—Rufus and Jesse forded the Potomac River at the same place the Confederate Army crossed to escape McClellan's forces, and in very little time, they covered the short distance to Sharpsburg.

Immediately upon their arrival in the war-ravaged little town, they started panning from shop to shop and house to house seeking information on the whereabouts of a wounded Confederate captain by the name of Edmunston. In each case, they were met with blank stares, shaking doubtful heads, and annoyed expressions that led them nowhere. All afternoon, they queried and bothered the citizens of Sharpsburg, sometimes asking the same person twice, either from forgetfulness or overzealousness. By nighttime, it became manifest to the searchers that this rescue quest was not going to be as straightforward or as easy as imagined. Truthfully, Rufus was already out of ideas and had no notion atall where to resume the morrow's quest.

The next morning was the Sabbath, and it dawned clear with a gleaming sunrise spreading over the Sharpsburg countryside. It was plenty cool—

cool enough that the boys scrunched closer to the fire as they warmed their pork meat. With the blaze popping and the fat sizzling, they chatted about home and other mundane things. Eventually though, they got around to the matter at hand and started bouncing tactical ideas off of each other for resuming their search. While engaged in this thoughtful exercise, it occurred to Rufus that they were very near to an actual battleground—one where the Haywood Highlanders had fought and his father had been either wounded or killed—he was not sure which. Naturally, the notion came over him to go out and have a gander at it, and an excited Jesse wholeheartedly concurred. So in little time, the two young men were blithely riding northward up the Hagerstown Turnpike, eager to learn what an actual battlefield might look like.

They certainly did not have long to wonder about it. Almost immediately, they began running into scenes of indescribable devastation. Broken and shattered and burned-out remains of wagons and caissons and other unrecognizable military debris cluttered both sides of the turnpike. The smelly decaying corpses of draft animals and cavalry horses were yet to be buried and dotted the destroyed landscape. Trees were blown to splintered pieces, and great craters pocked the fields where artillery shells had landed and exploded.

In a small wooded copse off the road a short distance, a grouping of makeshift stick crosses could be seen poking out of raised earthen mounds. Rufus believed this to be evidence of hurried burials of dead soldiers, and he contemplated whether one of them might possibly be his father's. But he very quickly purged that woeful thought from his mind. His father was alive, he tried to reassure himself. He had to be alive, and Rufus figured he was going to find him—somehow.

A mile or so outside of town, they spotted a small white structure in the distance, and Rufus could plainly hear the faint singing sounds of Christian verse emanating from the far-off spot. He intuited—correctly as it turned out—that it must be a church. A few horses tied up near the place, as well as a couple of teams with wagons, helped to confirm his suspicion. Then a thought flashed through his mind. With very little deliberation atall, he whirled around in a blur toward Jesse, while pronouncing at the same time,

"Let's go there, Jess!" Pointing at the church with one arm, Rufus reined his horse with the other, gave the steed a good kick, and hurriedly lit off, with Jesse and the pack mule on his heels.

They rode through a field of corn stubble rows and noticed upon approaching the little church building that it had obviously been badly battered during the battle. Two yawning holes had been blasted in the white brick walls, and through these they could see inside where the worshippers were singing to high heaven. Rufus had not entirely worked out in his mind what he intended to do, as he hopped down from his horse and handed the reins to Jesse.

"Wait out here, Jess. I'm going inside to make some inquiries."

Rufus pulled easily at the wooden entrance door, and it opened slowly as the hinges creaked and screeched loudly. The preacher, standing up front in a raised pulpit, was the first to lay eyes on the reluctant visitor. He abruptly ceased chanting and held both hands up high in a signal to the congregation. The plain-dressed folk immediately halted their singing in mid-verse and turned to have a look at the young man who had so impudently interrupted their holy service.

"Come on up front, son. Now don't be shy about it," the agitated pastor ordered.

Holding his floppy hat in one hand, the lanky towhead strode between the rows of worshippers to the front of the little church, as every head in the house turned to follow him.

"What would be your business with us here today, son? Don't believe I recognize you, do I?" the elderly pastor asked, wishing to get on with his service sooner than later. Such an invasion of God's time was uncalled for and unacceptable.

Rufus summoned up the courage to reply. "No sir, I don't reckon you do." He paused for just a second or two and then blundered ahead, speaking loud enough for all inside to hear. "I'm searching fer my father, sir. And I'm mighty sorry to barge in like this here, but I was wanting to ask if anybody might know something 'bout him—where he might be."

Then Rufus bashfully turned around to face the congregants and continued in a more emphatic fashion. "His name is Edmunston—Captain Basil

Edmunston. He fought in the battle here with the 25th North Carolina—in the Rebel army. Have any of you heard of him or know whereabouts he could be?" He paused and perused the audience to see if there was an interested reaction. Not noticing anything promising, he finished, "They say he got his leg blown off." And that was all Rufus knew to say, as he just stood there looking hopefully at the sympathetic faces.

Then toward the back of the room—actually in the very last pew—a man slowly raised his hand up over his head and announced, "I may know something about him, son. Let's me and you go outside and talk."

Upon exiting the church, this man turned to Rufus and shook his hand. "My name is Andrew Shook, and I'd venture to say you're Rufus, aren't you?"

Rufus just stood there motionless for a few seconds, with a bewildered expression on his face. At last, he was able to answer, "Yes sir—I'm Rufus. How do you know my name? Do—do you have any news of my father?"

"Yes I do, son. He's alive, and he's quartered at my place. Give me a minute and I'll gather up the family, and we'll take you to him." And the man then turned and disappeared back inside the church—the church of the Dunkers, as Rufus would soon find out.

Ducking through the doorway of the Shooks' stone farmhouse, Rufus's eyes were almost instantly drawn to the familiar figure sitting at the dining table. His father looked up from the letter he was writing to see who was coming in. He reckoned it was a little early for the Shooks to be returning from church. Upon spotting his son, a great smile spread across Basil's entire face, and he cried out, "Rufus! Hello, son!"

Rufus did not reply but rushed to his father's side, stooped over, and gave him a huge hug. "Hello, Father! We found you, didn't we? How in the world are you? How are you feeling?" For several minutes, pent-up and heartfelt sentiments were exchanged, until Basil finally asked for Rufus's assistance.

"Give me a hand, son, and let's get up from here." Shook moved to retrieve a crude crutch propped against the wall, as Rufus helped his father onto the good leg and foot. Taking the crutch and clenching it between his right arm and side, Basil hobbled energetically around the room for his son to see how well he could get about. The throbbing pain in his stump was still there, but not nearly so intense. It was bearable and, given more time, would continue to ease. Above all, perhaps, this ability to hop from one place to another, though only with the aid of a stick, sustained a veiled hope within Basil that he could possibly overcome his terrible misfortune. Now here was his son at his side, cheering and praising his measly shambling feat. Why, it was not inconceivable that he might become a whole man again, after all! That impossible possibility definitely began to flicker inside the captain's mind.

"Well, what do you think about that, son?" Basil asked while breathing heavily and grinning.

Rufus was overjoyed to see the pride his beaming father demonstrated on being able to limp around the room with the aid of the stick crutch. And it made him happy for his father. But it was still hard for him to absorb all this at once—and so soon. He had yet to come to grips with the fact that his father was so extremely disabled. Not only would the rest of Basil's life be dramatically changed for it, but the entire family would be required to adapt to the patriarch's diminished capacities and provide him with constant and never-ending support. But his father was alive, and that was plenty to be thankful for just now, Rufus reasoned to himself.

In response to his father's query, Rufus offered back, "I think it's amazing, Father. You're going to be good as new before you know it. Why, I can jest see you now plodding around in the mud and manure with those old wooden pumps you made. Reckon you'll have to figger out a way to attach one to that there crutch though, won't ye?"

"Oh no, son—not going to need a crutch soon's I can get me a new wooden leg made. Prosthetic leg—that's what I heard them called in Richmond. I saw men—wounded men like me, whose stumps are shorter than mine—walking on wood legs along the streets of Richmond, just like it was nothing atall. When we get back home, I'm going to look into getting one made." Basil stated all this with an assured optimism that even raised Rufus's spirits and hopes. The son probed for more details concerning the artificial leg, and they chatted for a while about the possibility of finding someone with the specialized skills to fabricate such a contraption. And then their attentions turned to getting back home.

Within a couple of days after the happy reunion, the East Forkers embarked on the return trip to Haywood. In parting with the Shook family, Basil had assured his saviors they would forever possess a special place in his mind and heart. Offers of monetary compensation for the Shooks' significant troubles and expenses had fallen on deaf ears. But they had insisted that, when the abominable war came to a close, Basil and Rufus should return with Julia and the girls for an extended visit. Their invitation had been gratefully accepted.

The ragged travelers were slowly making their way southward, with Rufus riding point. They were fully expectant of a long and miserable ride of three weeks' duration, more or less, not to mention the pain and discomfort Basil was having to endure. Transportation arrangements were relatively straightforward. Basil was laid on a thick layer of straw in a rickety wagon, and Jesse was handling the pulling mule team with a great deal of difficulty, to say the least.

Rufus had traded with a man for the wagon and team, giving him in exchange Jesse's horse and saddle, with the pack mule and old pistol thrown in to boot. He admitted to his father that the rolling assemblage was not much to look at, but if it could make it all the way back to the East Fork Valley in one piece, then he figured the swap to be a right good one. Basil was not as proud of the horse trade as his son was, but he kept that opinion to himself. He was more worried about the long ride home and whether he could survive the eternal jolting and jostling in Rufus's wagon.

Chapter 14

Glimmer in the Basement

It was going on six weeks since Rufus embarked on the mission to find his father. Tine missed him badly, and she longed to see his handsome face and feel the warmth and strength of his arms wrapped securely around her. Not long after Rufus's departure for the North, his mother had received a letter from Basil, informing her that he was alive and was being cared for by a family of Dunkers in Sharpsburg. Of course, Julia immediately shared the good news with the rest of the community, and day after day the anxious Tine kept expecting to see Rufe's smiling face riding up.

In the meantime, she continued to keep herself fully occupied and useful around the mill. Late November brought cold weather to the Forks, and winter's somber gray shroud already cloaked the mountains. The milling activity had slowed substantially from just a month earlier, but the miller Mann was not completely caught up. He could always find chores that needed doing, and he had come to depend on Tine to get them done with little complaint and few directions. Today, while her father was dressing a runner stone, she worked below at the lower-level cleaning up.

It was a dark, dank space down there where she labored. Stone foundation walls enclosed the basement, and very little daylight shone through the two small window openings. An overhead lantern dangling from a floor joist was unlit, so the lighting was murky at best. Timber posts, heavy beams, and clattering power-transfer mechanisms surrounded Tine. There were also three large wooden grain boxes located in the basement, collecting cornmeal that spilled through chutes from the pairs of running stones on the floor above. From time to time, miller Mann came down to sack the grist in these boxes and carry it back upstairs for the customers to claim. Often times, this job—bagging and lugging the heavy grain sacks up the steps—fell to Tine, but not today. Her father had specifically requested that she clean up all the powdery dust and piles of damp soured grain that literally coated the flooring, walls, and equipment at the basement level.

It was a thankless job but one that had to be done regularly, without fail. Only recently had her father begun entrusting Tine to do this dirty work. His hesitance was not necessarily due to the work being filthy drudgery—which it was. The miller's reluctance was based on his keen knowledge of the dangers that lurked around the powerful moving machinery located in the mill's basement. He cautioned Tine to stay away from the rotating shafts and gears, and he insisted that she always keep her hair pulled back and tucked tightly under her bonnet. It required little imagination to envision the effects of an entanglement of her locks in the unforgiving mechanisms.

But Tine was not scared atall. As a matter of fact, she enjoyed working in the basement, where the fascinating sounds of rotating, whirring, and spinning devices originated. Clicking, clacking, creaking, and cracking—all of these unique noises associated with the mill's mechanized powertrain blended into a melodious rhythm that soothed her and inspired ruminations.

On the river side of the building, Tine's acute senses could distinguish the measured sounds of water rushing, splashing, and dripping, as the great revolving water wheel generated enormous torsional forces powering the machinery. Its incessant circular movement drove a huge timber shaft that pierced a mason's hole in the foundation wall, transmitting the water's energy to the interior workings of the mill. This giant turning shaft caused one after another smaller shafts and cogged gears to rotate and mesh in synchronous unison, this way and that way and every which way. Inevitably, the twirling of the last gear that spun the final drive shaft caused the runner stones to whirl and grind the farmer's vital grains. To most, this cacophony of manmade mechanical sounds was uninteresting or, dare say, annoying. But for the miller's daughter, the discordant noises served to dampen worries and yearnings for her delinquent boyfriend.

Tine launched into her work with enthusiasm and attacked the smelly old grain piles with abandon. The layers that coated the floor could not be easily swept, so she scooped up the caked material by the shovelful and pitched the stuff out one of the window openings. As she toiled, her thoughts turned to Rufus, wondering if he was safe and whether he had found his father. She remembered that day he was summoned down to the store to receive the terrible news from the war front. There had been something very important she had wanted to tell him, but he had left the mill in such haste she had been unable to share the juicy gossip with him.

Tine had intended to divulge an unusual turn of events that would have surely pleased Rufus—at least, she thought so. She, herself, had been pleasantly surprised to learn that her father had grown sweet on the Bee Woman. Out of the blue one day, the miller revealed to her that he had romantic feelings for Folsom Anderson. Of all things, who could have dreamed that Tine's horrific rattlesnake bite would lead to her father's getting bit himself by a sweet-toothed love bug? The miller had not shared his amorous feelings with the Bee Woman as of yet, but he aimed to do so at the first good opportunity. Tine wanted Rufus to go up and talk to his aunt to feel her out, to see if she might possibly be amenable to entertaining such a notion. *If only Rufus would ever get back*, she fretted.

Around this same time, the East Fork sojourners were less than a week away from making it home. The journey south was just as they thought it would be—arduous and boring. For the wounded captain, lying on the straw bed in the wagon, the jolting ride was not only painful but it was a downright, never-ending, hellish agony. If Basil had been privy to Preacher Poston's farewell sermon, he would have likened his continuous torment and jostling torture to the reception of the everlasting fire the good reverend had warned about. For three long weeks, the captain had endured the rough roads, as Jesse prodded and whipped the mule team onward at a glacial pace.

Day after day, all day long, the slave whistled at the pair of mules, jawed at them, and even cussed the poor things to goad them onward.

"Dam you's, Jenny! Get on up! Haw, Jean, haw! Get on over to da left—no, not you's, Jenny! Gee, Jenny, gee! You's goes on ahead now! Haw, haw, Jean!"

And Jesse carried on like this from dusk 'til dawn talking to his mules, Jenny and Jean, and forever urging them forward. Basil simply lay in agony in the back and tolerated Jesse's wrangling and fussing, while Rufus rode ahead, ignoring the ruckus behind him. His thoughts were usually far away—on Tine and on how happy he would be to see her beautiful face again.

After finally making their way through the Shenandoah Valley and out of Virginia into eastern Tennessee, Rufus spotted a large river ahead of them and called for Jesse to halt. Pulling over to the side of the turnpike, they recognized it to be the same ferry crossing over the Nolichucky River that they had used on the up trip. Basil raised himself in the back to see, curious about the stop and whether there was trouble brewing.

"What's wrong, boys? Why have we stopped?"

"It's nothing, Father. We've got to take a ferry across this big river. It's called the Nolichucky. Ever hear of it?" Rufus innocently queried.

"What's that, you say? The Nolichucky? We're going to take a ferry across the ol' Chucky River?" Basil asked and then broke into a loud cackling laugh. "Have I ever heard of it? Well, I'll say I've heard of it! Come on around here, and let me tell you boys a story. Why, I forgot all about the ol' 'Chucky River."

And he proceeded to tell them another story out of the Lark and Delia runaway saga—one that even Hartgrove likely had not heard. "Jess, I don't know if your folks ever told you about the time they ran away to get married," and Basil paused and looked at Jesse to confirm if he had heard or not.

"Can't says I ever hears of it, Massa Basil. Just da other day I hears from Hartgrove 'bout dem running fo' it. Dat be's all I hears 'bout it."

So Basil launched into the tale and told the boys about Lark and Delia running away. He explained how they fell in love with each other and how neither Basil nor Delia's master, Edie Osborne's grandfather, would allow them to get married and live together. So the two slaves ran for it and headed north, where they had heard the Africans were allowed to be free and the white people were not mean to the niggers. Traveling always at night directed by the North Star, the Nolichucky was their first real obstacle to freedom. The river was too wide for a substantial bridge to span and too deep to wade. Needless to say, neither slave could swim. Thus, they hid in the bramble bushes along the river's edge while cogitating on the river crossing.

All day long while hiding in the thickets at the river's edge, Lark studied the operation of the ponderous rope ferry. He watched how the operator adjusted attachment ropes to an overhead cable that spanned the river. Finally figuring out the secret to the ferry's motive power, he convinced Delia he could operate the blasted thing. So during the night when the owner-operator was asleep, they stole down the river bank and onto the ferry and embarked.

Lark had gotten them just about half way across the river when the shooting started. The operator, who was not a sound sleeper, discovered that his ferry had been snatched, and he started furiously cussing and shooting at the snatchers. But his aim was off due to the darkness, and the two slaves survived the voyage across the Nolichucky River. Basil laughingly explained how they jumped off the ferry boat and ran away like scared guinea hens, along this very same stretch of turnpike where the East Forkers were parked.

"Well, that's about it, boys. I can recall on the trip back home with Lark and Delia how that operator gave them both a good looking over. We were fearful he was going to recognize them and might try to make a big fuss about their snatching his ferry. Didn't happen though. We crossed peacefully." Upon finally recanting the last of the tale, he studied the big-eyed boys and discerned their intense interest. Feeling a tinge of guilt for not having shared this rich history long ago, Basil offered, "Remind me tonight, and I'll tell you the rest of the runaway tale at the fire."

Tine had worked all day long on the basement clean-up job. Using a stiff brush and some water, she had scrubbed the interior sides of the stone walls that could be safely reached. She had shoveled and swept the floors clean. Sizable oatmeal-colored drifts had piled up high under the windows outside, where she had tossed all of the debris and residue. Any curious wharf rats, looking on at her activities from the mill's dark corners, might have noticed more than a goodly amount of rank white powder covering the poor girl, all the way from her bonnet to her shoes. Thank goodness, Tine's work was almost done.

Two sets of millstones had continued to run throughout most of the day. Heeding her father's cautions, Tine had been extra careful not to work near the moving shafts and gear sets—until just before quitting time, that is. The worn-out girl was about to call it quits when, by chance, she happened to spot something shiny in a recessed cranny behind a noisy piece of equipment. It was late afternoon and the light was so poor that she was surprised to even have seen the glinting object. How she could ever have noticed it was beyond her, but certainly the chance sighting had piqued her curiosity and stirred a want to investigate further.

There did not appear to be a good way of getting to the thing though. It was apparently lodged in a crevice between a floor board and the stone wall. As luck would have it, the confounded thing was behind a set of whirling gears. Studying her few options for getting to it, she calculated that a horizontal rotating shaft would also be blocking her way. Whatever that shiny thing was, it sure looked to be out of her reach.

But the more Tine pondered on it, the more confident she became that she might actually be able to get to it. Could she not simply worm herself under that spinning shaft, and use a long stick or helve to reach the mysterious object? That would be one way she could retrieve it. *What could the thing be?* she wondered, as she crept nearer and nearer to the machinery and leaned over to get a better look.

The dingy lighting and shadows were such that the closer Tine got, the worse she could see. She had to back off a ways to discern the tiny gleaming object once again. *What in the world is it?* she asked herself. *Could it be an old coin or piece of jewelry that might have fallen through a crack in the overhead floor? That was likely it—had to be.*

Then a notion flashed into her head. It was actually an epiphanic manifestation, where a hidden memory had finally edged and wiggled and squeezed its way around in her mind until she could finally recall it. Tine remembered that years ago, when she was barely more than a toddler, her mother had lost a valuable treasure somewhere in the mill. It was an old broach—an heirloom—that had been passed down through several family generations. She was able to recollect how utterly devastated her mother had been over the loss. There had been such a to-do over the lost piece of jewelry that the experience had been seared into Tine's youthful head. The entire family had scoured the mill from its foundations to the rafters but had failed to locate it.

Could this be mother's long-lost broach? It must be! she speculated. Tine was now more determined than ever to find a way to recover the shiny object.

"About closing time, Tine! Going to be shutting down soon. Better be finishing up down there!" her father yelled out from the floor above. He had been impressed with her tireless efforts that day and aimed to reward her in some way for it. But just how he was going to demonstrate his appreciation was yet to be determined. He was still mulling on some sort of surprise for his daughter.

"Okay, Father. Be up in just a few minutes."

There was not much time, so she began hurrying to find a way to get in behind the hazardous mechanical equipment that still spun and whirred relentlessly. The light was getting poorer too. Everything taken together, including her state of extreme exhaustion from the long day's work, seemed to be working against a successful recovery. But sweet Tine knew she could get to the thing—that enticing shiny object. So, she stooped down to business. Having found an old broken broom handle, she held it in one hand and crawled on all fours in her long dress, worming herself under the large rotating shaft. The girl was determined to get close enough to poke at the glimmering thing behind the gear set, in order to see what in the world it was. Lower and lower she crouched, thinking she was well below the hefty rotating timber. She was under it for sure—but just barely.

The shining object was almost within her reach, and Tine probed and gouged at it with the broom stick—again and again. But she was unsuccessful in prying it loose from the tight crack. Frustrated that she was not quite close enough to budge it out from the hiding place, she scooted on hands and knees ever so slightly toward the thing, not even realizing that the bonnet she wore on her head was actually brushing against the revolving beam above. Tine could certainly not sense anything. She was dead set on retrieving the puzzling object that was almost within her grasp now. Just a little closer she inched, and with one lurching poke of the broom handle the glimmering treasure bounced out of the crack onto the flooring. Tine was ecstatic! She could in fact see it clearly now. She could definitely make out that it was—

And then it happened! The most unimaginable horror that could ever happen, happened. In an instant, Tine's bonnet, which was tied snugly underneath her chin, became entangled and hopelessly wrapped around the whirling shaft. Then, quicker than her brain could comprehend anything awry, her hair was undone and snarled and twisted tightly round and round the spinning beam. Instantaneously, her head and then her whole body were yanked with tremendous force and slammed around the terrible revolving shaft. In just mere seconds, Tine's hair and entire scalp were savagely ripped off her head, and the rest of her lifeless body was thrown hard against the clean floor. Thank goodness that she had felt only a momentary shock of pain. As quick as that, it was all over. There had not even been time to scream out in alarm and anguish.

Throughout that dark basement the sounds continued unchanged, as the splendid equipment clicked and clacked in perfect union with the rushing and splashing water. Then the miller's anxious voice pierced the din, ringing out from above, "Still waiting on ye, Tine! Got a good surprise planned fer ye tonight!"

Chapter 15

GLIMPSE INTO A YANK'S SOUL

It came as a crushing shock to Rufus when Columbus Hartgrove broke the tragic news at the store. He, his father, and Jesse had just rolled into Forks of Pigeon, and had stopped off for a brief reunion with Maggie Deaver before heading up to the Den. Basil had struggled out of the wagon in the rain and hobbled around in the mud to demonstrate his improving mobility to the storekeeper and the few customers who happened to be there. And Maggie, of course, had cried in happiness for her son-in-law, as well as in sympathy for the trials yet to come for him and his family. It was just after this joyful business that Hartgrove had pulled Rufus aside and related the puzzling circumstances surrounding Tine's death.

Upon hearing the terrible tidings, Rufus was overcome with hesitancy at first, then disbelief, and finally utter devastation—all in a matter of brief moments. The proud elation he felt for the successful rescue of his father was shattered. In its place rushed harder emotions—sorrow, grief, helplessness, and anger—which would pervade his soul for many months to come. Interestingly, the unbelieving Rufus's reaction was to ride straight away to the cemetery near the Methodist church and have a look for himself. And sure enough, Hartgrove had not been joshing him.

Rufus stood there alone with the cold rain pelting down on his bare head. His soaked woolen clothes were hanging heavy on his weary body. While he clutched his old floppy hat in one hand, the other worked steadily to wipe away gushing tears and rainfall from his emotion-wracked face. The crying came in heaving bursts, as he peered through the wetness at the pile of damp dirt and struggled to breathe. Confined for all time underneath this reddish earthen mound was his sweet, lifeless Tine, lying alone inside a coffin box. Never again would he gaze upon her beautiful and enchanting face. Nor could he ever hold her in his arms and sense the girl's cheerful energy, and feel with peculiar delight her wonderful bosoms pressing against him. Tine's scent and the taste of her delicate lips were lost to him for all time. For some inexplicable reason, God had seen fit to take the beautiful creature from him, thus shattering their ardent dreams of a promising and fruitful life together.

Why—why has God done this? Rufus kept asking himself, as he looked down at the soggy grave and fought to contain the immense love he still held for Tine. He suspected his love for her would eventually ebb and shadow her to wherever she had gone. But he wanted to hang on to his passionate feelings for as long as possible. Somewhere, he had read or heard tell that the kind of love he felt for Tine was undying love. But surely that could not be—undying love—love that never died or ever went away. He knew better than that. One day, the fond feelings he possessed for Tine would be reduced to only hurtful memories, concealed in a deep, secret well in his heart. From time to time, he likely would be able to reflect back on her sweetness before harsh reality smothered those recollections. However, for these sorrowful moments at the graveyard and the trying days and months to come, Rufus desperately wanted to hold on to Tine and the special young love and passion he possessed for her.

Three weeks had passed since that unforgettable homecoming. Even now that Christmas time was upon the Den and his one-legged father was assimilated back into the family, Rufus could not be cheered. He moped around, dejected and aimless, pitying himself and daring anyone to try making him feel better. Even the girls, in all their enthusiasm for the expected visit that very night from Saint Nicholas, knew better than to share the spirits of the season with Rufus. While they and Julia hummed

Christmas carols in the kitchen and piddled around making tree ornaments, Rufus and Basil warmed their feet in front of a roaring fire.

"Son, after these holidays I want you and Jesse to carry me over to Asheville. Got to find someone to make a wooden leg for this stump." Basil was getting around the cabin on his own fairly well by now, and with Julia's help was learning how to minimize the severity of his handicap. His lovely wife had, in fact, perked him up and brought him back to life in no time after his arrival home. They had even been able to resurrect some private passions and amorous joys that both had worried might be extinguished for good.

In the worst way, Basil wanted one of those legs like he had seen in Richmond so he could get about without a confounded crutch. "Reckon I'll start with the doctors there to see if that sort of know-how resides atall in these God-forsaken mountains. If not, then maybe they can point me towards someone who does possess the expertise; though I hate to think I might have to go all the way to Charleston or Savannah to get one."

Believing that this wild goose chase might give him a worthwhile purpose, Rufus replied in the most upbeat manner he could manage, although still somewhat sour, "Be glad to go over there with ye. Ye don't reckon—" and he stopped suddenly, interrupted by a loud knock at the door. "Well, I'll say. Now who could that be?" he said, as he looked toward his father with a puzzled look.

Quickly jumping up and opening the door, Rufus stared into the waning afternoon light at a gathering of friendly Christmas visitors on the doorstep. The cold air rushed in around them as Basil hailed from his rocking chair, "Well, hello there, folks! Come on in, please! Come in!" And Rufus welcomed Columbus Hartgrove and his clan along with Maggie Deaver and Horace Mann into the Den. Julia and the girls rushed out to hug their grandmother, and the cabin was spontaneously infused with lively conversation and a gaiety that had been in very short supply that Christmas. Even Rufus was inclined to budge from his stoic demeanor and demonstrate a little pleasantry and good humor.

"Merry Christmas, dear girls," Maggie uttered as she offered a sack of presents for Rufus to take and then wrapped her granddaughters in her arms.

"We jest wanted to be neighborly and see ye'ens, being Christmas Eve and all," Hartgrove heartily explained.

His wife, Nannie, added, "It's been a coon's age, I reckon, since I've been up here last, Julia." Excitedly handing over a couple of cold apple pies, she added, "Here, dear—we brung ye some sweets I made this morning."

Miller Mann was still grieving mightily, and the prominent black band he wore around his shirt sleeve could easily be seen as he shed his outerwear. "Hello, everyone. Thought I would jest duck in to say Merry Christmas to ye, too. I overtook Maggie and the Hartgroves on the way up the river."

The entire community was still heartbroken for the miller after his tragic loss. During his brief visit with them that Christmas Eve, the Edmunstons tried their best to bring some joy into his life. And come to find out, the Den was just a way-stop for him this evening. The miller hosted intentions of venturing further up the river.

"Rufus, I've got me some cornmeal strapped to the horse and was taking it up to Mrs. Anderson. Reckon ye could ride on up the river with me fer a short spell?" the miller pressed, as his sorrowful yet hopeful gaze landed square on Rufus. It was a look that could not very well be rejected. As bad as Rufus felt over losing Tine, he knew that the miller must feel a sight worse. The man had lost his entire family due to one tragedy after another. And now, for some reason, he was set on visiting up at the Bee Woman's on Christmas Eve. Little did Rufus realize that Mr. Mann was smitten with his aunt. Poor Tine had not had a chance to reveal that juicy little tidbit to him.

"Sure can, Mr. Mann. I'll go up with you. I jest saw her a couple days ago, and she seemed to be in rare spirits."

"Thank ye, Rufus. Then we'll go up there in a spell. Won't stay too long," the miller gratefully replied. In fact, he was afraid of popping in all by himself on the unsuspecting woman. It would not seem natural, he had thought, and thus had connived to get Rufus to go along to tidy up the visit—make it seem respectable. He was still nervous about it, though, and was fearful of what the Bee Woman would allow about his forwardness.

"Afore ye go off, Rufus, I brung ye the boy's last letter fer ye to read—jest got it yestidy. They had a time of it up there about Fredericksburg in Virginia. Here, ye can read it fer yerself." Hartgrove was a proud father, and it showed, as he handed over a wrinkled and much-perused note from Hack.

Rufus missed Hack more than ever now that Tine was gone. He thought of his friend often and was actually beginning to entertain a rash notion of joining up to fight the Yankees himself. Having nearly lost his spirit to live, he figured he may as well die on the war front fighting the men who had shot his father's leg off, rather than die of heartbreak at home. That was exactly how he felt as he unfolded Hack's letter and began to read it.

Corporal Hack Hartgrove and the Haywood Highlanders found themselves embroiled in another heated affair some two months after the Battle of Sharpsburg, Maryland. He and tens of thousands of other Rebel troops were arrayed on a high ground overlooking the old colonial town of Fredericksburg, Virginia, spreading out under them. They could easily see the quaint red-brick houses and store buildings and, just beyond them, the narrow, deep-flowing Rappahannock River. On the other side of the stream blue hordes of Federal army troops could be detected massing and teeming in anxious excitement, while waiting for pontoon bridges to be thrown across the wet obstacle blocking their advance. Their aim was to cross the river and destroy the Rebels lodged on the imposing heights commanding Fredericksburg, who were effectively blocking the path to the Confederate capital city, Richmond.

This current strategy to capture Richmond by assault from the north was the brainchild of General Ambrose Burnside, President Lincoln's choice of successor to the reluctant general he had just fired, George McClellan. Lincoln had been most unhappy when McClellan failed to use his powerful army to finish off Lee's Army of Northern Virginia at Sharpsburg. It had been a grand opportunity to destroy the Rebel forces, but McClellan had thought otherwise—so Lincoln sacked him. The President's orders to General Burnside were to take the fight to the enemy, and the Union commander was intent on doing that—right here at Fredericksburg.

Captain Deaver's boys were resting in a spot beside a stately mansion with the rest of the 25th North Carolina Troops and Ransom's Brigade. Designated as reserve regiments, they could see the battleground and the Rebel's first line of defense behind a stone wall far below them. When the Yanks at last began to stream across their bridges and assemble in rows, preparing for the offensive, Hack looked down at them in nervousness and wonder.

"Looky at all that blue, Sergeant. They're swarming like a big bunch of mad hornets and can't wait to 'tack us," observed Corporal Hartgrove. "Reckon they's jest going to march straight across them fields at our boys behind that rock wall?" Such a foolish thing did not seem possible to this veteran soldier, who was almost eighteen years old now and had one battle and a skirmish under his belt.

"Believe so," allowed Sergeant Henson, who was also in disbelief. "They—well I'll be damned, here they come. Here they come! Look, they're coming at us!" he hollered in excitement, as the Confederate cannons surrounding them on the heights began firing at the long blue lines of attackers. And from the other side of the river, countless puffs of white smoke could be seen, as the Union batteries opened up in support of their brave infantry troops, walking steadily and bravely into the face of death.

Captain Deaver and the officers screamed for the men to lie down on the ground, as numerous deadly artillery rounds exploded loudly nearby. Soon, the faint cracking of rifle fire could be heard above the horrific blasts, and the clamor of soldiers' yells and 'Hurrahs' became ever louder. Over the heads of the Haywood Highlanders whizzed a profusion of lead balls, and they hugged their Mother Earth tighter than they had ever done before.

"Get down—everybody down!" an officer screamed, as a round crashed into a neighboring regiment with mortal consequences.

Hack watched the brave Federal boys walking hunched over toward the Southern sharpshooters, who were firing from behind the cover of a low stone wall. First one line of defenders would rise up, take aim over the top of the rocks, and fire their single-shot muskets. Then as they ducked down to reload, another bunch of Rebs would peek over the rocks, aim, and release a deadly volley at the easy targets scant yards away. Line after line of determined Union troops marched toward the lethal Rebel fire, and each was met by a devastating sheet of lead and death. Wave upon vast wave of Yankees walked and crawled and tripped over the corn stubbles and bodies in the fields, and the murderous Confederate barrages found them. Like sheaves before the sickle, the courageous soldiers in blue fell.

For more than an hour, Corporal Hartgrove watched in astonishment as the Union officers fed their brave soldiers into the Rebel thresher. And he saw the wailing, bloody bits and pieces being spit back out onto the ground. Finally, Hack was aroused from his shocked state by hurried orders from the company and regimental officers. Lieutenant Blalock informed them that a regiment behind the stone wall was running short on ammunition, and they must move to its relief as quickly as possible.

The corporal cast his eye first to one side and then the other, as his regiment formed in a long line at the crest of the hill facing toward the Union cannons and rifle fire. One, two, then scores, it seemed, of his fellow North Carolinians fell to the ground, victims of the enemy's well-aimed cannon shots and musket fire. On the double-quick, the 25th North Carolina rushed down the hill to take its place behind the stone wall just in time to meet an especially resolute Federal charge. Hack had no time even to think. Stepping over a dead gray-coated soldier, he stood up at the wall, picked out a blue-coat rushing toward him, aimed, and fired. Immediately upon the loud crack of his rifle, he watched the Yankee lurch backward and crumple to the ground in horrible agony.

Even though he had bragged to Rufus and Jesse about how he would relish killing Yankees, he did not feel particularly good after actually doing the deed. Hack kneeled down and began furiously reloading his Mississippi rifle, thinking how it was just a young boy he had shot, probably not much older than he was. He had no real grievance against that boy. He was just fighting them Yankees because, because—well, he could not rightly think of why he might have shot that boy, but he did shoot him.

He was sure of it. And he could not mull about it for long, because he was reloaded and it was time to do it all over again.

Raising himself to a standing position, he looked out to where that boy he killed still lay, saw another one coming toward him, aimed, and fired. Down went another Yankee and down went Hack again to reload. He kept this up for the better part of an hour, until the Union generals were eventually convinced of the futility of the foolhardy attacks.

That night, Hack's North Carolina regiment lay behind the protective cover of the low stone wall that some Virginia farmers had so fortuitously stacked long ago. The Rebel troops had made good use of it during the day, and they were now trying to put it to further utility by sleeping behind it. But Hack couldn't sleep a lick. He kept thinking about all the Yankees he had killed and listening to the wounded ones crying out in anguish from the field in front of him. He must have got all ten of those Yanks he had bragged to Rufus and Jesse that he would get—and many more. Probably one of those men moaning out in pain for water was one that he had nicked but not killed. He could not stand to hear those sorrowful cries and could not sleep because of them.

"Sergeant Henson," Hack whispered, trying to wake up his dozing sergeant a ways off from him. "Sergeant Henson," he tried again.

Finally a man lying next to the sergeant rousted him, and the irritated Henson groused back, "What? What is it, Corporal?"

"Okay if I go out and give them men some water?"

"No! Hell, no! Ye'll git yerself shot, Hat. Ye stay put right here. Got that?" The sergeant was most emphatic about it.

"Can't sleep with 'em crying out like that, Sergeant."

"Ye ain't going out there, Hat! Go to sleep!" Sergeant Henson barked as forcefully as he could without waking the entire company. He then turned over to go back to sleep.

Damn it all, Hack thought to himself, as he watched the sergeant turn his back to him. *How can they be so hard and not want to help those men out there?* Again he tried his best to get some shut-eye, but to no avail. He was too overcome with emotion from the day's fighting, and the haunting sounds of the wounded on the field wracked his conscience. Peeping over the wall did no good either. It was too dark to get a good look and see who was alive and moving. All he could think of was those poor soldiers out there who were suffering and dying in the freezing cold night air, a few pleading urgently for someone to help them.

Rolling back under his blanket, Hack listened and brooded as he twisted and turned and attempted in vain to doze off. But there was no way that he could just lie there all night long and listen to those boys die without so much as lifting a hand in their favor. So he made up his mind what he was going to do, and if the sergeant did not like it—well then—to hell with him.

Hack left his gun and ammunition on his blanket, along with his haversack and various other accoutrements, but grabbed his canteen before he crawled over the low rock wall. Immediately, he began encountering and bumping into dead men lying all over the ground in grotesque contortions. Their mouths and eyes were gaping open or closed shut or somewhere in between, and stiff tongues lapped out of more than a few of the mouths. Hack had to crawl around the bodies, heaped one on top of another, while smelling the decaying tissue and the blood and spilled guts—the gory carnage of war.

As he made his way through a labyrinth of corpses toward a muffled moaning sound, he wondered which of these boys were his doing—were his victims. He was certain that he had killed more than a few of them. And it was a sobering feeling to peer through the darkness into their faces at close range to see what they actually looked like. They did not look mean atall, and because of him those boys he had shot dead would never see their loving families again. These were depressing sentiments that rushed through young Corporal Hartgrove's mind as he strived to reach a man crying out in the distance.

The boy was gut-shot and lying on top of another dead soldier. Although still lucid, he was in great pain and was likely dying a slow death. He held one hand against his bleeding abdominal wound while the other was stretched out to get Hack's attention. "Here—over here. Water—water—please—give me some water," he grunted between gasps.

When Hack reached the poor soldier boy, he could readily see how young he was. No more than twenty he reckoned, as he looked into the Yank's eyes and stroked a hand over his brow and long dark hair trying to comfort him. *Is he one that I shot?* Hack wondered to himself, as he looked into the young Yankee's soul and reached for the canteen.

"Okay—here's ye some water. Drink it slow now—slow. There ye go." Hack cradled the young soldier's head with one arm and held the canteen up to the boy's mouth, allowing him to drink until his dying thirst was satisfied.

"Thanks—I appreciate that—best water I ever tasted. Say, you're a Rebel, aren't you?" the Yankee asked in a weak gasping voice, as he looked directly into Hack's wide-open brown eyes.

"Reckon so. I'm from North Carolina—in the mountain part."

"Never been that far south. My name is Elliot—Elliot Ames—from Wayland, Massachusetts. Can you give me a little more water—please?"

Hack was still cradling Elliot's head and fed him some more water. A contented expression passed swiftly across the boy's face, before being replaced once again with the twisted scowl of anguish

"Thanks! That sure is good—what's your name?" the Yankee asked with extreme difficulty.

"Hack—Hack Hartgrove. I'm a corporal."

"Then you outrank me, sir. That's my father underneath me—he was our sergeant. I believe he's dead—can you check him for me, corporal?" Elliot did not have many breaths left in him and struggled mightily to talk.

Hack let go of Elliot and moved around to where he could take a good look at the father, who was face down in the dirt. Picking the head up slightly, he saw right away that a portion of the man's face had been blown off, and he was definitely a goner. Then Hack moved back quickly to regain a position to comfort Elliot, and he shared the bad news.

"Sorry, Elliot—he's dead fer sure. Been shot in the head," Hack confirmed as delicately as he knew how to the enemy soldier.

Elliot did not reply but just closed his eyes. After a moment or two he whispered, "Don't believe I'm too long for this world either—oohhh—this hole in my belly hurts terrible. Corporal—Hack, will you stay with me here until I'm gone? Don't leave me, Hack. Please don't leave me alone."

"Don't ye worry none, Elliot. I'll stay right here with ye."

"In my coat pocket—in my coat—my wife's name and address—please write to her and tell her that I love her. Tell her those were my dying words, Hack—that I love her—"

Hack stayed with Elliot for the rest of the night, and he even fell asleep with the dead Yankee's head in his arms. At sunup he was awakened by shouting and the sound of his own name. After the few seconds it took to come to his senses, he definitely heard men calling out to him.

"Hat! Hat! Get yer dumb ass back over here, right now!"

"Careful, Hack! They're still shooting at us—stay low!"

Hack could for certain make out Sergeant Henson's directive, and one of the Christopher brothers was cautioning him about the snipers who were still active. The sporadic cracking of rifle fire was proof of it, as was the lead ball that whizzed by his head just then. Hack slumped down low into the corpses of the father and son and then began to crawl toward the rock wall and his company. But suddenly he stopped. The wife's name and address—he had forgotten to get it out of Elliot's coat!

So Hack backtracked against a storm of Minié balls toward where the young Yank lay. The foolish Rebel, crawling around in no-man's land, had attracted the undivided attention of the bluecoats, who shot at his every movement. Figuring Hack was out there robbing their brethren's corpses, their ire was heightened and their determination to put an end to this thief's days was manifest.

Finally, with lead balls peppering the Ames' bodies, Hack found the piece of paper with the wife's information, tucked it safely away, and turned toward the cover of the stone wall. For more than fifty yards he slithered and crawled and hid behind one dead Yankee after another. Somehow, though, Hack miraculously remained unscathed, as the bullets zinged through the air and chased his every move, all the way to his cover. Jumping friskily over the wall, he landed in the waiting arms of the stupefied Christopher brothers and was immediately subjected to the volcanic ire of the raging Sergeant Henson.

"Ye're in fer it now, Corporal!"

Chapter 16

A Mite Partial to Her

The green locust log that Mary had just tossed on the fire began popping and hissing, spitting burning embers at the Christmas revelers. No one noticed. The inhabitants of the old Den were having a grand time, now that Maggie Deaver and Columbus Hartgrove and his wife and family had dropped in to share their holiday cheer. The miller Mann was there as well, and even his melancholic spirits had seemed to brighten after downing a cup of the Edmunstons' special cider. Rufus was sequestered by himself in a corner of the cabin, next to the Christmas tree, reading the last letter that Hack had sent home from the war front.

> ...and them bullets were flying thicker than bumble bees round my head but nary one hit me thank the Lord. My sergeant lit in to me bad for going over that wall to give water to them dying Yanks but it don't skeer me none. I figgered it was right to do it so I did it. The Yank that I fed water to give me a name and address for his wife and asked me to write to her. He allowed I ought to tell her that he loved her and those be his dying words to her. Her name is Harriet Ames and she lives in Wayland, Massachusetts way up there in the North. Lieutenant tells me that it ain't possible for me to send a letter to Harriet. Says there is a mail blockade that don't allow sending our letters to Yankees. But I told Elliot I would do it and I will have to find a way to send Harriet a letter. I'll write her anyway just as soon as I finish up this here letter and I hope I can find the right words to tell her easy about Elliot.

Well folks this here Fredicksberg battle was something else to behold I tell you that. We whupped them something awful and I don't reckon old General Burnside will try us again soon. Least wise I hope he don't try it. Figure I've killed all the Yanks I want for quite some time. We are still camped here guarding so they don't try it again. They must be 6 inches of snow on the ground and them socks you sent me keep my feet right warm. Tell Rufe and Jesse for me that it ain't as fun to kill Yanks as I thought. It feels right bad matter of fact.

Your affectionate son,

Hack

p.s. – If you get this letter before Christmas then Merry Christmas to all of you!

An amazed Rufus folded up the letter and became lost in his thoughts about Hack and his war experience. "Killing Yanks"–Hack *wrote that. He said that he was killing Yanks, and it was not as fun as he thought it would be.* Rufus rehashed the words over and over again. He could not imagine the experience that Hack Hartgrove was having while fighting in the war. Every day was a new adventure for the Rebel corporal, while here was Rufus, with a dead girlfriend in the ground and relegated to back-up master duty at the Den.

On this Christmas Eve night, Rufus did not yet realize he was looking for alternatives to the aimless direction of his still young, but floundering, life. In some sort of mental balancing mechanism, he was weighing his own current predicament with the sensational tales Hack was writing home about. Whether unwittingly or by purpose, Rufus did not think long or hard enough to remember the carnage he had recently witnessed on the battlefields of Sharpsburg, nor did he make an allowance for his own father's tragic experience. It was no wonder, then, that Rufus's fantasy balance was teetering heavily in favor of his going to war.

Foremost in his mind at this time was joining Hack Hartgrove in General Robert E. Lee's victorious Army of Northern Virginia. He was becoming keener and keener on the idea of participating in some of the greatest battles the world had ever known. That was the fool notion flashing through his head as he mulled over Hack's interesting letter. But just about that time, the miller Mann approached Rufus and asked if he was ready to head up to the Bee Woman's, and Rufus allowed that he was.

With the gloaming hour upon them, the miller and Rufus rode side by side up the East Fork toward the Crab Orchard. Little was said until Mr. Mann suddenly offered, "Rufus, I reckon I've figgered it out. I know what happened to Tine now—why she got caught up in that goddamned spinning shaft."

"That so! What you figger happened, Mr. Mann?" Rufus was all ears. It had been a mystery to everyone what might have caused Tine's carelessness in getting too close to the dangerous milling equipment. Rufus had been so distraught and torn up that he had not spent a lot of time pondering about it though. His dear Tine was gone, and there was nothing much he could do to bring her back.

"It was her mother's broach. She found her mother's lost broach and must have been trying to get to it. I knowed there had to be something. It kept eating at me how she got wrapped up in that shaft. Then yestidy when the mill was down, I took a good look again behind them gears and, sure 'nuff, I found the damned thing. She seen it fer sure, too. Ain't no doubt in my mind." As the miller finished his revelation his voice broke, and he struggled to maintain control over his emotions.

Rufus sensed the miller's state and did not really know how to reply. "Had to be something like that to lure her in. She was too sensible otherwise. Say, Mr. Mann, I know you miss Tine a sight. But I reckon you oughta know I miss her almost as much as you do. Anyway, I don't know how anybody could miss her worse. I believe I loved her for sure and still can't get her out of my mind."

They rode on in silence for a while longer, until the Bee Woman's cottage came into sight. In a somewhat edgy tone, it seemed to Rufus, the miller hastily instructed him, "Now, Rufus, ye help me along with the conversing with Mrs. Anderson, ye hear. I don't know her none too good yet, although I hope to get to know her a sight better. And if ye sense a lack of words on my part, then ye jest jump in with both them big feet of yer'en. Understand?"

Rufus did not know if he understood atall. *Why is Mr. Mann suddenly becoming so anxious about this visit?* he wondered to himself. He seems all nervous and excited about it for some reason. "Reckon so, sir. I can find all kinds of things to talk to Aunt Folsom about. And don't you worry none 'bout them snakes. They must all be hibernating 'bout now."

The startled Bee Woman welcomed the Christmas visitors into her cabin with a hearty greeting. "Well, well, well—if this ain't a real surprise. Come in, come on in before all this warmth escapes." She motioned for Rufus and the miller to hurry into the cozy confines. "If it had been ol' Saint Nicholas hisself, I don't reckon I would have been more shocked."

"Merry Christmas, Aunt Folsom!" Rufus said with a level of joy and enthusiasm that surprised him a little. Now that he found himself up the river with his aunt, he felt more comfortable and free of the worries and grieving that burdened him so at the Den. His eccentric aunt had a settling effect on him, and he liked being in her company in these strange surroundings.

"Good evening, Folsom, and merry Christmas to ye," stated the miller as he took off his felt hat and wrestled to keep hold of the sack of meal he was toting. "Brung ye some meal fer a Christmas present." With a grin gradually forming over his dour face, he continued, "Thought ye might be able to use it."

"Why, thank'ee, sir! That's mighty kind of ye. Would ye mind putting it over there on the table fer me?" Although the Bee Woman had quickly formed a tight bond with the miller's daughter, she had not become overly familiar with the father. When she learned of the tragedy that befell Tine, some days after it happened, she walked all the way down to the Forks to pay her respects to the miller and to visit the girl's grave. It was not that the miller was cold to her—or she to him—but he seemed a little backward or shy around her for some reason. The Bee Woman simply did not know what to allow about that. Consequently, she just maintained a polite friendship with him.

"Will do, Folsom, and if ye wouldn't mind—it would be right friendly of ye to jest call me Horace. 'Sides, I don't cotton much to being called 'sir.' Jest don't seem right fer some reason."

The Bee Woman allowed she had no problems with that request, as the miller lugged the weighty sack over to the table. So far, he had only spotted a coon and possum hiding in the dark corners, but he had no doubts there were other critters lurking about somewhere.

The Bee Woman's cabin, all splashed with evergreen boughs adorning the walls, was kept tolerably warm with a hot fire burning in the fireplace. Rufus and the slaves had helped his aunt get plenty of wood in during the summer—enough to easily last through the harsh mountain winter. To augment the light given off by the flaming logs, there was a candle stub burning on the mantel. It was a cozy and inviting hearth, and the pair of visitors gravitated there to sit a brief spell with their host, socialize, and make Christmas cheer.

The Bee Woman talked about her latest patient's chronic cough and the honey tonic she brewed up for the sick child. Rufus told them about his father's progress and the various things Basil had learned to do with the aid of a crutch. He also spoke of his father's ambition to get a wooden leg and how they would be going over to Asheville soon to see about it. Horace, poor man, could only talk of his poor departed Tine. For sure, none of these topics was particularly appropriate for this special evening. It was Christmas Eve, for heaven's sake. Holiday merriment was in order. But it seemed to be in very short supply that night at the Orchard.

The miller revealed that he had wanted to quit the mill, but Columbus Hartgrove had talked him out of it. Hartgrove had explained that the miller's work was all Horace had, now that Tine was gone. Without it, Hartgrove had reasoned, the miller would go crazy without anything to do, and in his sorrowful condition, there was no telling what state he might fall into. Although Columbus had not directly mentioned it, Horace was certainly able to grasp his neighbor's meaning—alluding to a parallel between the miller's circumstances and those that had driven his wife to take her life. So, he had heeded Hartgrove's advice and continued on at Deaver's Mill. It was not an especially joyful revelation, but it was a meaningful one that Rufus and his Aunt Folsom could appreciate.

After an hour or more of such discussion and sipping of hard cider from a gourd dipper, Rufus started fidgeting around and cutting his eyes toward the miller. He was ready to get on back down to the Den, and Horace could tell that the boy was becoming a little squirrelly. Duly prompted and enlivened with a dose of fortitude gained from the ardent spirits, Miller Mann abruptly changed the tone of his conversation with the host.

"Folsom, I reckon we'll need to be going soon, so Rufus can get back to his family. But I jest want ye to know that I enjoyed this here little visit tonight—I enjoyed it a sight. And I was wanting to ask ye—well, I was wondering if'en I might be able to come back from time to time—jest me by my lonesome and visit with ye?" It was an awfully hard thing to get these words out of his mouth—out in the open for everyone to hear. But the sips of cider had encouraged the miller to open his heart and spill out his feelings to the Bee Woman. Now he stiffened in the hard chair and fretted what her answer would be.

Folsom was understandably taken aback by the confounding question, and she puzzled over the ramifications and the miller's intent. *Why, the idea of such a thing!* Unabashedly, she stared at him hard and direct-like in the eyes, and replied, "Horace, I don't rightly know what ye might be up to with sech a question as that there to a widow like me. So spit it out, mister—tell me straight out what it is that ye've got on yer mind."

Rufus was simply aghast at this sudden turn of events. He had no idea why Mr. Mann had said what he had, nor did he know whether or not his Aunt Folsom was going to kick the miller out the door. So he did the prudent thing and just sat there and watched and listened.

"Why, Folsom, I'm sorry—I don't mean nothing untoward by it atall, I can assure ye of that. What's on my mind is—well, it's you! That's all." Horace stopped and tried to regain his composure and decide what to say next, without getting his face slapped. He was definitely flustered, and the cider he had imbibed was by no means helping him think clearly. Gathering up all his courage, he fixed his eyes on the Bee Woman and then unleased his passionate sentiments. "All's I'm saying is that I'm jest a mite partial to ye, Folsom. I reckon I've got special feelings fer ye, and I jest wanted to be 'round ye more. That's all in the world I'm saying."

Folsom could not believe her ears. It had been a long spell since she had felt anything for a man in that way. But here was one in front of her professing that he was partial to her, and this one surely knew her strange manners. She was shocked, to say the least. Quickly ciphering on the notion, the strange woman's heart opened just a tad. She entertained a suspicion that it might not be bad atall to have real company ever now and again—other than the critter company. Male companionship might even be acceptable occasionally, she reckoned. And this man was respectable and a hard worker, she knew that for a fact. And he was not so bad to look at either. So, she softened her defensive shell somewhat and offered up this reply to the miller.

"That so? Well, I reckon that's different then, ain't it? If'en ye want to be 'round me more, then—then I reckon that will be jest fine with me. I'd 'preciate the company, Horace. Yessir, I reckon I'd enjoy yer company right much."

"Well then, that's jest fine and dandy, Folsom. I'll be coming up to visit ye more often then," said the relieved miller. He was genuinely elated that his proposal had been accepted, although his face didn't show it so much.

"And, Horace, I 'preciate ye being partial to me. I do indeed 'preciate it."

Given Horace Mann's emotional state, the Bee Woman's consent for future visits and her appreciation of his feelings towards her was probably the biggest and best Christmas gift anyone on the East Fork—or in the whole of Haywood County for that matter—received that holiday season.

Chapter 17

SNEAK ATTACK AT GUM SWAMP

The Christmas season of 1862 had come and gone, and another long hard mountain winter was at its end. Rufus had whiled away a good deal of time with Jesse, hunting deer and bear with his grandfather's old long rifle. Other than that, he had continued to struggle through the slow grieving process and, mostly, had done nothing, except mope around and feel sorry for himself. Ice-skating exhibitions for his local fans were forgone, and the care of livestock across the immense farm acreage had been relegated solely to the slaves and tenants. Rufus had lost all interest in the business affairs of the Den and instead contemplated a headfirst plunge into the war. Any mention of the crazy plan to join up with the Haywood Highlanders was discouraged by his father and, of course, strongly rebuked by Julia.

However, the Confederate Army was desperate for manpower at this time. Staggering numbers of men had either died of disease or had been wounded or killed in battle. Many more had simply laid down their guns and deserted from their companies. For these reasons, the Confederate government increased its efforts to round up deserters as well as to find and forcefully impress the services of all eligible men.

In the fall of 1862, the age limits for mandatory service in the army had been further broadened to include every man between the ages of eighteen and forty-five years. Although Rufus still remained outside this range, he was almost old enough. In fact, there were many boys younger than himself who were currently fighting and dying for the South. The increasing military and political pressures, a desire to join Hack Hartgrove, who had gone off to the war at age seventeen, and a lost sense of worth and purpose accentuated by depressing bouts with grief were all influencing factors that would eventually force Rufus's hand.

Back in January, Basil and Rufus had journeyed to Asheville in search of someone to fashion a wooden leg for the elder Edmunston. Their inquiries had turned up a prospective craftsman in Wilmington, and subsequent correspondence with the man verified that he had experience with an amputee case very similar to Basil's. So in mid-April, not long after Rufus celebrated his seventeenth birthday, the father and son made their way east to Morganton, where they embarked on a train to the coastal city of Wilmington, the furthest point in the state. There they found the craftsman and for an entire week stayed with the man while he measured and fabricated a prosthetic leg for Basil.

The design was simple enough. It was basically an extension—or wooden stilt—that attached to his shortened leg. The stilt was forked at the top, and designed such that the two sides of the fork could be strapped tightly to Basil's thigh, in order to hold the contraption in place. His knee rested in a cushioned ring at the top of the stilt, with the stump poking through the ring. This allowed for the knee to fully support his body weight. For three days, he trained and walked around on the artificial leg, as modifications were made to improve its comfort, stability, and utility. It was a frustratingly painful process for Basil, as his stump still remained extremely raw and sensitive. But he bore up, and by the end of the week he was highly satisfied with his new wooden prosthesis.

At a stop in Kinston on the long train trip back home, the Edmunstons encountered, of all people, Captain Burton Deaver at the rail station. It was truly a happenstance meeting, and the captain was overwhelmed with joy to see his brother-in-law alive and actually able to amble around impressively on the new prosthetic leg.

"That's jest great, Captain. Look at ye! It's so good to see ye again. Who'd a thunk it?" asked Deaver to no one in particular, as vivid images of his fallen friend on the Sharpsburg battlefield crept into his mind.

And Basil was just as pleased to see Deaver. "Not too bad for an old amputee Haywood Highlander, huh, Captain?"

The three of them caught up quickly, and, come to find out, the company was camped only a few miles away. On a whim, Deaver invited them over to see the boys, and the Edmunstons readily took him up on the offer.

While Basil visited with the company officers and called on the regimental field and staff, Rufus was entertained by Corporal Hartgrove and some of his buddies.

"Been missing ye, Rufe. Pa wrote to me 'bout Tine. Sorry 'bout that. It must've been hard on ye," said the empathetic corporal.

"Yea, it's been right hard all right. Still not over it, don't reckon," replied Rufus. And then he looked at the fancy hat Hack was wearing, and a big grin came over his face. "So that's the famous hat the colonel gave you, huh Hat?" he asked with feigned curiosity and sarcasm, and the crowd that had gathered broke out in hysterical laughter.

One of the Christopher brothers—Francis—then blurted out, "Better not say nuthin bad 'bout his hat, Rufus. Ol' Hat don't take too kindly to funning him 'bout it. Do ye, Hat?" And then another round of hysterics ensued.

They carried on like this for an hour or more, while Rufus visited with old friends and new acquaintances that Hack introduced him to. Almost every one of the Reb soldiers, without exception, encouraged Rufus to join them in the fight against the damned Yankees. Sergeant Garland Henson was one of the more adamant recruiters.

"We sure 'nuff need some new blood, Rufus. There ain't but forty-some of us left in the company. Ever since we come back here after that big fight at Fredericksburg, the boys have been deserting and lighting out fer the mountains. And they're doing it knowing they'll be shot soon's they get caught! If that don't beat a hen-a-rooting, I don't know what does."

The sergeant's earnest attempt to convince Rufus to join up prompted the rest to do the same. They set in to pestering and begging him to become a Rebel—one of them—until he did not rightly know what he was going to do, or how to say "no."

"We could use ye, Rufe, but I ain't going to lie to ye. Soldiering ain't easy nary bit," Corporal Hartgrove advised. "It's a hard thing to see a body get killed. And them Yanks I killed in Fred'icksburg, I ain't proud of it nary bit—nary bit, I say."

By the time his father hobbled over to collect him, Rufus had resolved his dilemma and knew exactly what he must do. The loyal Highlanders had convinced him that he was direly needed—needed to fight along beside them in the terrible battles that were sure to come. So he pulled his father to the side, out of earshot from the others, and stood as tall as he could so as to speak his mind. "Father, I hope you won't mind, but I'm going to stay here and join-up with the company. Been giving it a lot of thought lately, and it's what I want to do. I reckon it's my duty to fight with all these friends of mine here, who are making sech a big sacrifice. Don't know any other way of saying it, I reckon."

This was a message that Basil had dreaded hearing but had been expecting for the past months. The first thought that he had, while Rufus was breaking this news, was that it had been a damn fool thing to take up Captain Deaver's invite to visit the company in camp. But it was too late to reconsider that snap decision. Another thing he considered almost instantly was his own situation at the beginning of the war. When elected captain, he had thought it his duty to serve, and there had seemed to be no other options. Well, Rufus was in a similar tough spot just now, and Basil recognized it. *What in hell will I tell Julia?* he worried.

"So you've made your mind up, have you?" Basil asked while buying more time to mull over a reply to his son. "You see what war has done to me, don't you, Rufus?" Without a pause for an answer he went on. "But I was one of the lucky ones. I came back alive. If you stay here with Hack and all those other boys, there's a real good chance you won't make it back home to see your mother and sisters. You've thought that through, I hope? It's not a pretty thing—war—but I reckon you're old enough now to make up your own mind. Now, you're sure that's what you want to do and not just what they want you to do?" he finished, nodding towards Hack and a bunch of the boys gathered around a boiling pot of coffee.

"Thought long and hard 'bout it, Father. I've ciphered on all those things, and it's what I want to do. I figure it's my duty, and I want to do it fer sure."

With a sigh, Basil relented, "Okay, son. If that's your decision, then I'll support you. But heaven help me when I tell your mother."

Since being rushed back to North Carolina from Virginia in early 1863, the Haywood Highlanders and the rest of Ransom's Brigade had been shuffled from one coastal town to another. Governor Zebulon Vance had demanded that General Lee send these native troops back to the state to protect against the continuing Yankee atrocities in the coastal regions. Although rumors of another naval invasion were rampant, when Rufus joined up with the Haywood Highlanders they had seen very little action in the Tarheel State, besides a considerable amount of marching to and fro through the sandy pine forests and swamps.

In the month or so since becoming a Rebel, Rufus was subjected to tiring and repetitive drills to learn the rudiments of soldiering. Captain Deaver insisted that the lieutenant and sergeants push him to—and beyond—his physical limits. He figured this to be the best way to indoctrinate his nephew, so that he might have a slight chance of surviving the war.

In a short time, Rufus developed a tolerable competency in reloading and firing the rifle he was issued. He learned by study, rote, and drill the infantry tactics that guided the movements of army groups in the field. Shadowing Hack and Sergeant Henson everywhere they went, he ate what they ate, slept where and when they slept, and literally shit when they shit. Eventually, he was entrusted with picket duties, and on this very evening he was fighting off mosquitoes and a bout of drowsiness, while guarding against a sneak Yankee attack.

Rufus and Hack, along with a detail of about thirty-five other men, were posted a good hundred yards out from the circular earthworks that the 25th North Carolina Troops and another regiment were holding in the Gum Swamp. The considerable earthen fortifications were thrown up by the Rebels to protect the railroad leading from the Union-held port at New Bern to the Confederate rail center of Goldsboro, located about sixty miles inland. Most of the train transports—commercial and passenger—from the South's important Atlantic seaboard region were routed through Goldsboro to reach Richmond. It was absolutely vital that the town's rail facilities not fall into enemy hands, and the two Haywood soldiers were being exceptionally vigilant this evening to ensure it did not happen.

The night was warm and humid, and Rufus and Hack were fighting off a vast array of nocturnal insects, while keeping their eyes and ears peeled for Yanks and snakes. The ubiquitous cottonmouth water moccasins thrived in the swampy environs, and Hack had already killed one of the lethal critters. Before going out to their posts, Lieutenant Blalock had warned them that the Yanks were overdue for another attempt at Goldsboro. "Stay awake and keep your eyes open," he had told them. They were doing their best to stay awake.

"Ye getting sleepy, Rufe?" Hack whispered.

"Can't hardly keep my eyes open," was the hushed reply.

Hidden behind some dead trees, they stood on a rotten log in order to keep their feet dry in the boggy wetness. The other men were spread out a good distance away on higher ground. As the waning moon moved lower and lower in the sky, it became especially dark out and felt downright lonely and eerie to the young lookouts.

"Ye ain't a'skeered of snakes, are ye?"

"I wouldn't say skeered. Let's jest say I'm a little uneasy 'bout 'em," Rufus lied. "'Spect we'll put these bayonets to good use again tonight, fending more of them things off."

"'Spect so." But the corporal was thinking about more than snakes, and threw Rufus off with his next comment. "Sometimes, Rufe, I think 'bout her and wonder if she ever received my letter?"

"What's that, Hack? What letter you talking 'bout?" Rufus responded in a low quizzical voice.

"You 'member me talking 'bout that dead Yank at Fred'icksburg—'member? Elliot was his name—Elliot Ames. He asked me to write to his wife. And I did it, jest like I tolt him I would."

"Oh—her—yep, I 'member you saying something 'bout it. Fact, I read 'bout it in a letter you sent your folks. But you never sent it to her though, did you—the letter? Weren't no way to."

"I sure did send it! Ye're not going to believe this, Rufe. Couple of days after the battle, the generals called fer a cease fire—a truce with a white flag and all that—to scoop up all the dead men and bury them. I came tolerable close to a live Yank—close 'nuff to touch him—and the idee suddenly came to me. I spoke up to that Yank and right out asked him if he would post the letter fer me."

Rufus could not believe the fantastic yarn he was hearing. "You're joshing me, ain't ye, Hack?"

"No, I ain't joshing. Why would I josh ye 'bout that? Well, I pulled the letter out of my pocket, give it to the Yank along with a good-sized hunk of 'bacco, and he tolt me he aimed to put it in the post fer me. By the way, her name is Harriet—pretty name, don't ye think?"

"Yep, it's right nice," Rufus acknowledged in a low whisper, as he pondered this business of Hack's and whether or not Harriet might have actually received his letter.

"Don't let me fall asleep, okay?"

"I'll try not to. Same here," replied Rufus as he continued his lone musings.

About an hour later, sometime around two o'clock, Rufus's head nodded hard against a stiff limb, and he awoke with a start. It took a second or two for him to regain his awareness and realize where he was. Hack had fallen asleep, too, and Rufus reached out and shook him awake.

"Shhhh," Rufus shushed with a finger up to his mouth as Hack awoke. He had heard something out of the ordinary just at that moment. His ears were attuned to pick-up the routine riot of night-time sounds that usually wafted through the swamp, courtesy of the crickets, flying insects, frogs, bats, owls, and other nighttime noisemakers. But he had heard something else—something curiously distinguishable from these common noises. Now they both strained to listen for something different—something peculiar or extraordinary.

Then, in a moment or two, they both picked it up—a barely audible metal clanking sound that could be heard over the croaking frogs' love songs. "You hear that?" Rufus asked excitedly looking at Hack.

Hack nodded, and they continued to listen intently. In a moment or two, a short series of slight metallic clinks could again be detected, and then the clinking suddenly stopped. It was definitely not a natural noise they had heard, and their acute senses were heightened to full alert.

"What ye reckon?" Hack murmured.

"It's got to be Yanks. You stay here. I'm going to see Sergeant," Rufus answered excitedly, as he began wading through the water to tell his sergeant what they had heard.

When he got there, he was astonished to find Sergeant Henson sound asleep, and the rest of the men in the same state. "Sergeant, wake up—wake up," Rufus whispered, as he gave Garland Henson a sharp nudge. The sergeant lifted his head slightly and opened his eyes, as if they had only been closed for a brief resting spell.

"What is it?" he whispered.

"We heard something out there. I think it's Yanks on the move."

Sergeant Henson looked around him and saw that all the other men were napping, as he had been, against strict orders, of course. He stared at Rufus, and they both froze still and attentive to listen for the Yankees. But there were no clanking sounds to be heard above the men's snoring and nightly noises, nothing odd or abnormal atall. For several minutes, they stretched their necks and cupped their hands around their ears to better catch the stray sounds, but to no avail. There were no Yankees to be heard.

"Go back and stay at it. Let me know if ye hear it again," the sergeant directed, and the befuddled Rufus moved quietly back through the swamp to his hide, as the sergeant rousted the other men out of their slumber.

"You still hearing 'em, Hack?"

"Ever now and again," he whispered as he turned to help Rufus up onto the decaying log. "What did Sergeant allow?"

"Said to keep at it, and let him know if we heard anything else."

Hack just looked at him oddly and then turned to stare into the dark swamp. For the next five or ten minutes they kept making out the same distinct sounds, until finally Rufus's patience ran out.

"Damn it—I'm going out there closer. Maybe I can see something," he said as he looked toward Hack for a confirmation that it might be a reasonable notion.

"Ye're crazy, Rufe!" his unbelieving buddy whispered in amazement. "What 'bout them snakes ye can't even see good? 'Sides, it's so dark ye ain't going to be able to spot nary thing out there."

"We'll see," Rufus said, as he stripped off his belt with cartridge and cap boxes, pulled off his shirt, and handed Hack his rifle. With only the bayonet to ward off the venomous reptiles, he stepped off the log and began wading through knee-deep wet murkiness into the gloomy darkness. Glancing back at Hack, he whispered, "If I'm not back in a half hour, go tell the sergeant."

Even in broad daylight, taking off across the swamp, like Rufus was doing, would be a daunting experience, and certainly not one for the fainthearted. Like most normal folks, he had an aversion to snakes, especially poisonous ones. Through the deeper pools, when the water level rose up high on his chest, he worried more about getting struck in the face by a swimming cottonmouth than getting shot by a Yankee. Somehow though, he overcame his innate fears and as quietly as possible waded and trudged toward the sounds they had heard, stopping frequently to listen after advancing a few yards.

The sporadic clinks and clanks became more and more perceptible, and the distinct shuffling noises of moving troops could now be discerned. There were no doubts atall. The infernal chinking and clomping was coming from a relatively short distance off—just ahead.

Figuring that he had slogged more than two hundred yards from where Hack waited, Rufus came upon some higher and drier ground. He stopped, concealed himself within a dense thicket, and then listened intently. Up ahead of him, he detected movement and finally was able to spot, through the trees, a continuous line of hushed soldiers stealing discreetly and almost noiselessly along a trail through the swamp. *They were Yanks!* he instantly recognized. Unknown to him at the time, or any of the other Rebels for that matter, the Yankees had employed a local native to lead them through the marshy wilderness. Immediately, Rufus sensed that the enemy troops were sneaking up on them. Even with his inexperience and dearth of military knowledge, he realized that this troop movement was important and posed an extreme danger to his regiment back at the fort.

The damn Yankees are trying to get behind our defenses, he reckoned—no—he was sure of it. *I'll bet they're planning to launch a surprise attack against our unprotected rear.*

Rufus stayed put for several more minutes as the troops continued to steadily pour by in an unbroken line. *There must be more than one regiment on the move*, he estimated as he sneaked away and began backtracking through the mire, ever mindful of the reptilian dangers plying the waters.

Reaching Hack at long last, they hurried over to alert Sergeant Henson, who immediately sent them back to the fort to report their newly gained intelligence. Breathlessly, Rufus related his actions and what he had seen to Lieutenant Blalock, and in scant minutes, Colonel Rutledge had both regiments hustling about the fort to prepare its own surprise for the anticipated Federal attack.

When the sun broke over the cypress trees along the eastern horizon, the Union forces drove in the Confederate pickets and launched an all-out frontal attack—just as suspected. The 49th North Carolina was poised in a strongly fortified position and ready for the assailants. Two Yankee regiments in succession attacked, and each assault was staunchly repulsed by the resolute defenders.

Calculating that the Confederates must be fully occupied with the frontal thrusts, a Union bugle signaled for the surprise attack to be made against the rear of the Rebel fort. Surely, the Confederates would not be anticipating an attack from that direction, the Union general in charge had theorized. Besides, their stealthy troop movement in the dead of night could never have been detected out in the middle of that miserable black swamp. But unbeknownst to the Yankees, the 25th North Carolina had received advance warning of their intentions—thanks to the vigilance of one seventeen-year-old soldier. The regiment was waiting and fully ready for the Federal surprise attack.

Rufus had guessed there was more than one Union regiment on the move, and his judgment was proven accurate. There were actually two that assailed their flank positions, but the Haywood Highlanders and the nine other companies, along with excellent work from the artillerists manning their well-placed guns, turned back wave after wave of stiff Yankee attacks.

Rufus lined up next to Hack and Sergeant Henson and helped the Haywood Highlanders throw up a wall of lead to hold back the rushing tide of Yankee boys. Hack could not help but think of Elliot Ames, when he aimed and fired at the blue-coated, kepi-capped soldiers storming at them in straight lines. Rufus got his first bloody taste of battle and without a doubt dispatched his first Yank. There could be no qualms about it, because it was an especially valiant blue-coated assailant who had eluded the storm of lead shot but had been unable to escape the thrust of Rufus's bayonet.

Eventually, the Federals grew tired of the fruitless and costly assaults on the stubborn Rebel outpost, and by ten o'clock that morning, they were retreating through the Gum Swamp back to New Bern. While Rufus and Hack and some of the other men were resting and quenching their thirsts, a jubilant Captain Deaver came over to have a word.

"Good job today, men. Ye showed them Yanks this morning what us Highlanders are made of. That not right?"

Although worn out, the men cried out together in raspy voices, "Right, Captain!"

"You too, Rufus! That was a hell of a thing ye did—discovering them sneaking around behind us through that nasty-ass swamp. A hell of a thing! Ain't that right, boys?" Rufus was still queasy over bayoneting the one Yank and shooting a few others and elected not to reply. But his companions sure did.

"Right, Captain!" They all looked at the novice private with knowing expressions that he had rendered an invaluable service to their regiment. And they were almost as proud of him as his Uncle Deaver was.

"Keep that up, Private Edmunston, and ye might get yerself a fancy hat like this here one of the corporal's," kidded Captain Deaver as he pulled Hack's hat down over his eyes.

Everyone got a big kick out of the funning, including Hat. Rufus glanced over at Corporal Hartgrove, appreciative of the special friendship they enjoyed. Putting aside his queasiness and unease following the battle, he allowed, "I figure I ain't earned no hat yet, like Hat did. But one of these days I might get me one, too. Can't let you beat me, now—can I, Hat?" And the two youthful Rebs just smiled at one another, glad to be alive and glad to have each other's backs in such a perilous, God-awful war.

Chapter 18

AN IRRITATING ITCH

At the same time as Rufus and his regiment were stranded in the marshy wilderness of the Gum Swamp, squashing pesky mosquitoes and Yank attacks, the Army of Northern Virginia was warring again. In early May, General Lee and his veteran Rebel troops scored a decisive victory in a thick wilderness area near Chancellorsville, Virginia, just a few miles north of Fredericksburg. Replete with confidence from his recent overwhelming successes, Lee again decided to venture across the Potomac River and invade Northern territory. However, his luck was about to change. In early July, the Confederate Army ran up against a well-led Federal force at Gettysburg, Pennsylvania. After three days of hard fighting, the Yankees turned back the Southern invaders and sent them fleeing in retreat back to Virginia. Unbeknownst to General Lee and every other Confederate Rebel at the time, the Southern tide of battlefield superiority had crested and, with this defeat at Gettysburg, the slow ebb began.

Southern morale, already low in the North Carolina mountains, plummeted with news of the disaster at Gettysburg. Deserters from the army, men evading conscription, and Union sympathizers flocked to the hinterlands of western North Carolina to hide from the Confederate government. Some of these men even formed themselves into gangs and began prowling the rural countryside, preying on the hapless families whose menfolk had been lost in the war or were still off fighting in the horrible conflict. Haywood County was not exempt from their heinous acts of depredation.

Rufus first heard about the marauding gangs of outlaws in a letter he received from his mother. As he sat near a campfire one night in coastal North Carolina, he read with great interest her account of a local raid. So troubled was he with the deteriorating state of affairs in Haywood, he read aloud parts of the letter to Hack and Francis Christopher, who were sharing his fire.

> *There is a terrible state of things upon these mountains particularly here in Haywood. A band of robbers and villains are constantly plundering the people in the night. Sometimes they can be driven off if a especially resolute defense is made but more times than not someone is killed. Two weeks ago they attacked a house in Cataloochee. The family resisted and fired at them from the house. A neighbor, Jonathan Woody, heard the shooting and hurried over with his gun. The bandits discovered him first and fired upon him with a ball passing through his heart. They say this band of bad men number about 12 or 14 and conceal their faces under black hoods. This same party robbed a Smathers family down in Dutch Cove taking some 150 dollars Confederate, several pieces of silver service, and a load of bacon hams. The Smathers man is serving in Company C of your regiment, I believe, and they tied up his wife and several children and put them under guard while rummaging through their things.*
>
> *I tell you, Rufus, I have terrible forebodings about these things and these times. Not only can the whole strength of the country not be got out but desertion is rife and the money is nigh worthless. They say there are a bunch of your and your father's Haywood Highlanders lying out in the mountains around here, holed up in caves etc. and that their wives and children sustain them, taking them food. I do not doubt it atall. Mother says that a man give her 10 dollars for a watermelon the other day. Did you ever hear of such a thing?*

Upon finishing the reading, he put the letter down and looked toward his buddies to get their reaction. "That's 'bout it, boys. The rest is sort of personal. Thought you might be interested to hear of the terrible state there is in ol' Haywood."

"Who ye reckon them raiders are?" Hack brooded out loud.

Francis Christopher had an idea. "They ought to send a bunch of us back to them hills to round that gang up and hang ever last one of 'em, leastwise the ones we don't shoot."

"I'm with you there, Francis. Instead of helping us fight the Yanks, like they ought to, they're out robbing and killing our womenfolk and children. They're sure 'nuff a bad bunch and need to be dealt with. Wonder if any Haywood Highlanders that's deserted us have joined that bunch?" mused Rufus. "If they have, then they ought to be hung or shot, too."

Amos Bugg and his son, Eli, had made themselves scarce around the Forks of Pigeon community for a year or more, ever since the latest revision of the conscription law had obliged their service to the Confederate Army. They had jointly determined it would be plain foolish to risk their lives for a cause that meant nothing atall to them. Neither Confederate nor Union sympathies filled a place in their hearts. The shameless Buggs became convinced they could lie low in the mountains and remain invulnerable to the pathetic attempts of local Home Guardsmen to round up draft evaders like themselves and the numerous army deserters. Their confidence did not stop there, either.

With a great majority of the Haywood men manning the far-away battle lines and given the seemingly ineffectual law enforcement capability in the region, Amos Bugg looked upon the countryside with hungry eyes. What he saw were lonely cabins where mothers and wives and children, aching for their men to come home, struggled to make crops and livings on their tiny farms. These were truly pitiful situations, but Bugg did not view them through compassionate lenses. He saw only promising conditions and ripe opportunities for exploitation and plunder.

On this late summer night, Bugg was planning a raid that would satisfy even his ravenous appetite for pillage and thievery. Way up in the wilderness of the West Fork River, underneath the high Shining Rock and approximately ten miles upriver from Forks of Pigeon, Amos Bugg and his scraggly band of bad men prepared for the night's ride.

There were thirteen of them in all, including Eli and Amos. About half of the gang were army deserters, and the rest were draft dodgers like the two Buggs. All of the members of this marauding band appreciated their inherent strength in numbers; and with each successful plundering raid, they were able to funnel shares of the stolen food and other loot to their own needful families.

One of the deserters, Pinkney Queen, had actually served with the Haywood Highlanders. After Fredericksburg, though, when the 25th North Carolina returned back to its home state, he—along with two other Haywood men—ran for it. Even the penalty of death by firing squad had failed to deter them. They had stomached all the war they could stand, and besides, their families were in a bad way and desperately needed them back home.

"Ever'body got them guns loaded?" snapped Amos as the men gathered tightly around him on their mounts. Bugg still wore his white mane long and his nose still had a decided crook in it, ever since the altercation with Rufus. All of the men confirmed they were loaded up and ready to go.

"Ye men with revolvers, careful now how much ye shoot 'em off. Need to try and save them cartridges, scarce as they's getting." A few of the bandits carried multi-shot Colt revolvers, and the rest were armed with single-shot percussion pistols and rifles. Such a heavilyarmed group could have their way with any farmer, merchant, or Home Guard unit likely to be encountered in Haywood.

"'Member now, when we get in sight of that first cabin down yonder, put yer hoods on fer the rest of the ride to the Forks. Don't want nobodies getting a good look at us'ens and recognizing who we are." Bugg was referring to the black hoods that each of them wore over their heads during the raids. Fashioned from rough-woven sackcloth with holes cut out for the eyes and mouth, these sinister black-dyed disguises made the bandits appear unusually egregious and evil.

"When we get to the Forks, ye'ens allow me to do all the talking and do jest like we talked 'bout—ye hear?" finished Bugg, as his eyes scanned around and he aimed a sinister scowl at each one of the outlaws. They all nodded in obedience, affirming that the night's plan was committed to memory.

"Okay, let's git!" ordered Bugg, as he spurred his horse and bulled his way out of the throng, taking the lead down the narrow road along the West Fork River. He pushed his men hard as they rode in silence toward Forks of Pigeon, where the waters of the East and West Forks are joined. There he meant to settle a long overdue score with the uppity Deavers.

Maggie Deaver was asleep in one of the four upstairs bedrooms when Bugg's bandits broke into her house at half past one o'clock in the morning. Nestled in their comfortable beds in the other small bedrooms were Burton Deaver's wife and her four children. Several of the bad men stormed into the bedrooms at once, overpowering their victims and rapidly hog-tying each and every one of them. The rest of the thieves prowled the grounds around the house, securing their unsuspecting sleepy targets. There were no other homes within shouting distance, so there was little chance their clandestine actions might be heard or observed by neighbors. Inside a tiny room attached to the forge shed, the snoozing blacksmith—reputed to be the stoutest man living in the area—was surprised and knocked over the head, rendering him senseless. Bugg's outlaws, also, proceeded to efficiently and mercilessly round up the several Deaver slaves and lock them in the smoke house, where one of the desperados stood guard.

At the sight of the black-hooded bandits, the Africans trembled with a terror usually reserved for the wicked white overseers, who wrought so much pain and misery with their evil lashes. Of course, the Deavers employed no such harsh overseers; but men of this ilk were known to be in Haywood, and the Deavers' slaves feared the likes of them—and the likes of these scary, black-hooded men now rounding them up.

Back inside the house, Amos Bugg barked while pointing to Maggie, "Keep an eye on them and bring the old woman downstairs!" He then bounded down the stairway and helped the men shove her into a chair at the dining room table. "Now put a blind over her—bind her up good and tight too—quick about it!"

"What is this? What are ye men doing to me?" Maggie wailed as she was forcefully blindfolded and strapped to the wooden chair.

"One of ye stand outside on the porch and keep an eye out fer trouble—and watch the road real good!"

Amos Bugg looked all around him and immediately spotted a tall buffet loaded with pewter and sterling silverware. "Over there—yender! Get yer sacks and start loading them things up men—quick!" Bugg barked, pointing to the silver. And then he turned his attentions to Maggie.

"So, ye're curious 'bout us, ere ye? What ere we doing, ye say? Well, I'll tell ye this here, ma'am. That man of yer'en—yer dead husband—he never treated us no good atall." Bugg was no fool, and he knew enough that he ought not say too much, less this Deaver woman be able to identify him. Unless, that is, she was not going to be around to do so. Bugg had not yet made up his mind about Maggie's fate. It was still up in the air, so to speak.

"Ye don't know what ye're saying, sir. The Colonel never treated nobody bad. Ain't nobody, sir, going to make me believe contrary. Ye hold them scandalous words to yerself!" Maggie was crying and she was fearful of the invaders' intentions, but she was defiant nevertheless. "He was a better man than ye'll ever be—a hundred-fold better!"

Her words riled the burly man. "Deaver treated me like I was no better than a goddamned nigger—especially after that run-in with the Edmunston boy—yer grandson, I reckon he is." Reflecting for just a second or two on what he had allowed about the Edmunston boy, Bugg damned himself for his stupidity. *Damn it to hell! Why did I mention Edmunston? If the old woman's not completely scared out of her wits, she might figure out who I am—can't help but know!*

The very thought of this sparked such pent-up ire in Amos Bugg that he had to find a relief. He could not help himself. Raring one strong arm up high in the air, Bugg then cast it at Maggie, smacking her violently across the side of the face with his huge open hand. Her eyes were blindfolded, and she had not seen the blow coming. Instantly, the elderly woman's head snapped to one side at the horrendous impact, and a rush of terrible stinging pain exploded inside her skull. *What—what in the world is happening?* she dreamed. Upon regaining her senses, she screamed out loudly from fright and surprise. For that, Bugg let her have it again!

"Keep on doing it, ma'am, and ye'll get more of the same. Ye hear me good?"

Maggie, in all her living years, had never been treated like this. Certainly, the Colonel had never struck her in a fit of anger. Why, he had never struck her atall—ever. Whimpering and trying to catch her breath, she obediently nodded that she understood him.

"Now tell me, whur do ye keep all that money of yer'en?" asked the annoyed Bugg. He was getting anxious and had no more time for her foolishness. The longer his crew lingered in the house, the more likely they were to be discovered. When Maggie hesitated, Bugg lit in on her again. This time he slapped the other side of her face, harder than before and almost knocking the poor woman unconscious. "There—that help ye 'member where ye stashed it?"

Maggie simply could not take any more of the cruel punishment. She had endured her fill and just wanted the nightmare to end. Struggling to lift up her hanging head, she murmured, "My bed—under the bed."

Bugg looked over to one of his henchmen and yelled, "Go check! Quick!"

In less than a minute, the man leaped up the steps, found a good-sized wooden box under the bed, and hurtled back down the steep flight with it.

"Now let's take a look-see at this here box." As Bugg broke into it and eagerly peered at the contents, his eyes glistened bright through the holes in the hood. Even the few stained teeth remaining in his head shone some specks of whiteness through a breathing slit. "Well, well, well—now looky here, boys! There must be a couple hunderd of them Rebel dollars, and looky, won't ye, at all them gold and silver coins. I'd say that this here is a good night's plunder. Yessir, it's worth our time sure 'nuff. What ye men allow?"

The two thieves assisting with his interrogation of Maggie agreed that it was a good take, but one of them nervously asked, "Ye want me to set it now, Amos?"

"Goddamned it! What did ye say my name fer!" Bugg snapped back at the man, as he looked over toward poor Maggie to see if she might have caught the slip. For certain, he could not afford leaving a living witness who could identify him. There was no way he could be sure if she had heard his name or not. Turning back around quickly he directed his henchman, "Guess it's 'bout time. Set them fires!"

And with that terse order, the men jumped into action, kindling small fires in the downstairs rooms. Bugg hollered out to the men on guard upstairs, "Lock 'em up, and make damn sure they can't get out them windows."

Having made up his mind about the old Deaver woman and her kin, Amos Bugg then coldly pulled a pistol from under his belt, aimed it, and shot a bullet into the side of Maggie's sagging head. The evil Bugg took this drastic measure with the upmost satisfaction, although his smug expression went unseen behind the disguise. She had likely heard his name called out; either that or the old woman had inferred he was a Bugg, after the reckless mention of the run-in with her grandson. No matter, he could not afford to chance the Deaver woman escaping the burning inferno that was about to utterly consume the house in flames.

Maggie had not suspected that she would be summarily executed. Thus, she did not realize or feel a thing, thank God. Her battered dead body remained strapped and slumped over in the chair at her dining room table, as the firestorm began to envelop the house. Upstairs, the bound and wailing Deavers were not so fortunate. They were left to struggle helplessly as the blazes began to lick at their feet and horrifically consume each and every one of them, along with their dreams and promising prospects. In short order, the fine house and Deaver occupants became nothing more than a smoking pile of ruins and charred bones.

Bugg's murdering bandits quickly and expertly gathered the sacks of loot, including a good many bacon hams from the smokehouse and rode off in several directions. It was their preferred method of escape—each thief fleeing to a favorite cave or shelter deep in the dark mountainous forests. Later, after allowing things to cool off a spell, they would slink back to the hideout at the head of the West Fork River; whereupon the bounty from the raid would be spread on the ground and equitably distributed among the robbers.

The Deaver raid was spectacularly rewarding to Bugg's bandits and especially gratifying for him. An old irritating itch he had suffered for a good while was satisfied on this evening. And one of these days, he planned to pay a similar nocturnal visit to those nigger-loving Edmunstons, so as to relieve himself of yet another annoying itch.

Chapter 19

Ten Muskets—Five Balls

Clear across the state in coastal North Carolina, things did not change much for the Haywood Highlanders as the dreary winter war months of 1863-1864 wore on with minimal military action. However, back in Haywood, all-out manhunts for the murderers of Captain Burton Deaver's beloved mother and loving wife and children were undertaken throughout the county. Old men and young boys teamed up with the sheriff and rode high and low, endeavoring to flush out the thieving killers. And even Basil, though hobbled by his extreme handicap, rode with several posses, spending long grueling days in the saddle, scouring the wilderness areas for the killers of Julia's mother and family.

Finally, just after the New Year was rung in, a single murdering thief was apprehended by one of the search parties. Captain Edmunston was able to identify the man as Pinkney Queen, who had been one of his former Haywood Highlanders. The Rebel deserter was discovered in possession of incriminating evidence in the form of a sterling silver goblet bearing the letter "D" engraved with fancy curlicues. It was, undoubtedly, a prized piece from the Deavers' dinner service taken by the damned Bugg gang. Although claiming to have found the valuable item, Queen was not believed for a minute by his captors and was carted off to Waynesville and incarcerated in the Haywood County jail.

In February, Captain Burton Deaver, who had been at home on an extended furlough from the army to take care of family and estate affairs, agreed to escort Queen back to the army for an expeditious court-martial proceeding. The captain and a couple of local Home Guardsmen accompanied the prisoner to the vicinity of Tarboro in eastern North Carolina, where the greater part of Ransom's Brigade was stationed. A court-martial board was rapidly convened, and it subsequently found Pinkney Queen guilty of desertion beyond any reasonable doubt. For this manifest dereliction of duty in the extreme, he was condemned to death by firing squad.

The night before the execution was scheduled, Captain Deaver summoned Lieutenant Blalock and Sergeant Henson to his tent. As the men entered, they found their captain buried in a mountain of paperwork under the gloomy light of a dim candle. After exchanging formal salutes, the captain ordered the soldiers to take their ease, and they got down to business.

"Men, got orders all the way from General Ransom that Company F is to do the executing tomorrow. Couldn't happen to a worse man, I don't reckon. Queen's a deserter and a murderer too, as we all know. I'd do the shooting myself if it was allowed, but it ain't." Of course, it was not for desertion that the captain was so eager for the young man to be shot. It was for killing his mother and his wife and children, or at least for having, doubtlessly, played a role in those reprehensible acts.

"How many men, Captain?" Lieutenant Blalock asked.

"Going to need ten of 'em, Lieutenant. Ye can ask fer volunteers or pick 'em yerself. Makes no matter to me. Now here's how I want ye to do it. Load five muskets with a ball and five without a ball. When ye give them men the guns, don't let on which ones ere which. Them men ain't to know which'en shot a ball into Pinkney Queen. Understood?"

"Yes sir! Leave it to us, Captain," replied the lieutenant, acknowledging his understanding of the orders.

Upon exiting the captain's tent, Lieutenant Blaylock immediately mustered the company near their campfires. There were only thirty-one Highlanders left at this point in the war, and they all stood at ease in files, soberly waiting to hear why they had been roused at this time of night. Some suspected it might have something or other to do with Pinkney Queen's capital punishment.

Sergeant Henson addressed the soldiers. "They want us to do the shooting tomorrow. All of ye know Pink's history—know what he's done back home. 'Spect not many of ye feel sorry fer him, and I can't blame ye none. Here's the detail of ten men we've selected to carry out the sentence," and he proceeded to read the names from a list he held. Corporal Hartgrove was one of the men chosen and, significantly, Private Edmunston's name was the last one to be recited. Captain Deaver had made it known to the lieutenant that he wanted Rufus on the detail.

Relaxing near their fire before going to bed, Rufus and his close buddies exchanged somber thoughts about the serious job to be performed the next morning.

"You can be sure my aim ain't goin' be off nary inch," Rufus allowed. "Hope my grandmother is watching over me and steadies my musket. Believe I'm going to aim fer his heart."

Francis Christopher had a different perspective. "I 'member Pink real good. It was different back in the beginning. At that there schoolhouse fight, he shot a Yankee off me—sure did! Never will forget that. He was a right good soldier 'fore he went up."

Corporal Hartgrove jumped in, "Ye've got that right, Francis. He was just like one of us'ens. Can't figure out how he went bad so quick-like. Pa says they still don't have any idee who else rode in that outlaw gang. And they say Pink ain't let on, neither, who he rode with."

"Can't figure why he would take that to the grave with him. If he aims to be forgiven, he ought to give up that information, seems to me," Rufus added, while not putting much stock atall in the 'forgiven' part.

"Maybe if he makes a last appeal to the Almighty tomorrow, he'll say the names of them other men before we shoot him," opined Hack.

"Hope so—but I seriously doubt he'll do that," Rufus rejoined. "He'll be too skeered. I would be!"

At ten o'clock the next morning, in a large open field normally used as a drilling and parade ground, the several regiments of Ransom's Brigade were formed up for the execution. They were positioned on three sides of an extensive square, and at the open end a rough post had been set in the ground where Pinkney Queen was to be shot. Captain Deaver aligned his company—the smallest one in all the regiments—where the men would be sure to get a good view of the proceedings.

When the troops were finally arranged in their proper places, General Ransom and Colonel Rutledge led the prisoner and the firing squad escort to the lone wooden post. Following close behind in the small somber procession, was the brigade band tooting out and beating the solemn notes of the *Death March*. Other than the music, the quietness and soberness of the occasion was absolute; and the gravity of the formal affair was not lost on the mass of hardened soldiers gathered there to witness the execution.

For a few of the Haywood Highlanders, however, including Captain Deaver and Private Edmunston, the punishment was for something much more horrific than desertion. This prisoner, who was being tied to the stake with his arms pinioned behind his back, was responsible for grave criminal acts against their precious loved ones. It was only right, in their way of reckoning, that the man be put to death for what he had done. 'A life for a life' is how they figured it. No matter that Queen was only twenty-two years old, with a wife and two young children starving back in the mountains. His family would likely get by somehow, as would all the other civilians who were suffering from the ravaging and destructive effects of the terrible war. As plain as could be said, Captain Deaver and Private Edmunston harbored no sympathies atall for the condemned man.

Sergeant Garland Henson's firing squad finished securing the prisoner to the post and then marched to their positions about ten paces away. Colonel Rutledge, the officer of the day, read aloud Pinkney Queen's offense and the sentence that was to be carried out. Then the regimental chaplain approached Queen to lead him in a prayer and help the condemned man set things right with his Maker. But after only a few moments of private consultation, the preacher turned to Colonel Rutledge and informed him of a dying request from the prisoner.

"Colonel, the prisoner asks to speak to one of the men. He has something to say to a—Hack Hartgrove."

The colonel was not at all happy at this turn of events, and his only interest was to get this execution carried out without any hitches. But he was human and thought he might be able to bend to the request and grant a brief delay—for just a minute or two. Receiving an affirmative nod from General Ransom, Colonel Rutledge barked back at the chaplain, "Okay, but you've only got two minutes." He looked over at his lieutenant colonel and ordered, "Find me this Hartgrove man—Hack Hartgrove!"

But before the officer could turn to the task, Corporal Hartgrove took a step out of the firing squad lineup and spoke up toward the colonel, "Here, sir! I'm Hack Hartgrove!" Standing only a few paces from the prisoner and not much farther from Colonel Rutledge, Hack had heard the whole thing.

"Good! Go see what the prisoner wants with you, Hartgrove!" the colonel ordered, as he stared hard at the corporal. He thought he recognized the young soldier, and the fancy hat on his head definitely looked familiar. Then, as Hack advanced toward Pinkney Queen, it finally dawned on the colonel who this Hartgrove boy was. It was the young soldier who had picked up the regimental colors and saved the day at the Richmond skirmish. *Surely won't forget that boy again*, the colonel chided himself.

"What ye need, Pink?" Hack asked, not trying to get overly friendly with the doomed man.

Pinkney Queen was obviously nervous and terrified of what was about to happen to him. And he was very much aware of the distinct possibility that a hot place in the caverns of everlasting fire was reserved for his immediate arrival. First, though, he needed to get something off his chest. "Bugg—it was Amos Bugg that killed them Deavers, Hack. And please, give my love to my wife and children fer me." After that Pinkney broke down in bawling tears.

"That's enough time, Corporal Hartgrove! Get back to your place now!" snapped the colonel.

Hack did not have much time to reply to Queen. He just nodded his head and confirmed, "Will do, Pink," before pivoting around and returning to Sergeant Henson's detail. As he took up his position, he glanced over at Captain Deaver, who was keenly interested in what Queen might have said. Corporal Hartgrove gave the captain a reassuring look, as he did to Rufus, who also brandished a quizzical expression on his face.

A blindfold was placed over Queen's eyes, so he could not see the muzzles about to be leveled at him. Then Colonel Rutledge nodded at Sergeant Henson, who instantly called out the order, "Ready!"

The squad of ten Haywood Highlanders stiffened and prepared themselves. The clicking of their guns' locks broke the prevailing silence, and nary one of the executioners knew if his gun was loaded with a ball or not. At least one of them, though—Rufus—hoped to hell his was.

"Aim!" shouted the sergeant, and ten muskets were instantly raised and leveled at the breast of the scared, trembling prisoner. The breathing of some two thousand soldiers, arrayed in a broad square around the lonely man, hushed in intense anticipation of what was to come. Rufus sighted down the barrel of his rifle directly at Queen's heart. But he was not as steady as usual. His hands tremored, his heart beat furiously, and his eyes began to blur.

"Fire!" The thunder of ten rifles going off as one cracked loudly across the field. Every man watched as Pinkney Queen's body instantly lurched backward and then slumped in the horrible relaxation of death, hanging by the tethers to the stake. Rufus gazed at the corpse of the perished mountaineer who had betrayed his country and its people and who had been responsible in some way for the murders of his beloved kin folk. He was completely satisfied that he had done his duty for the Confederacy and for his mother and Burton Deaver.

After the grisly business was over, the regiments filed past the lifeless corpse, getting a good look at it as they marched off the field. These Rebel soldiers could now turn their attentions away from their own and back to the damned Yankees.

"Amos Bugg—he said Amos Bugg was the killer?" interrogated Captain Deaver. He had called Hack and Rufus to his tent to learn what Pinkney Queen had allowed before being shot. The captain recognized the name for sure, remembering the wretched scoundrel for what he was—a low-life deadbeat who was unfailingly slow to pay his notes at the store.

"That's what he tolt me, Captain. He said Amos Bugg kilt the Deavers. That's what he sure 'nuff tolt me," Hack replied. Then he and Rufus elaborated and related all the facts about their brawl at the mill with the two Buggs. Captain Deaver was duly impressed and, immediately upon the dismissal of the two young soldiers, composed and sent a letter to the sheriff of Haywood County, relating this new information.

For the next several months in Haywood County, more posses were formed to search for Bugg and his band of bad men. Basil participated in many of these futile efforts, which penetrated the roughest country imaginable to flush out the murderers. But neither hide nor hair of the Buggs could be found, and eventually the enthusiasm to discover the outlaw band diminished—until the next plundering depredation.

During this period, it was more of the same for the Haywood Highlanders in coastal North Carolina. In February, after the execution of Pinkney Queen, the 25th North Carolina participated in a Confederate assailment of New Bern to recapture that important port town. It was a bungled attempt from the start and met with absolute failure. Following that fiasco, the regiment marched to southeast Virginia and moved on the enemy-held Suffolk. The Rebels handily drove off the Federal forces occupying the town, and, for the first time ever, the Highlanders fought against black Union soldiers. It would not be the last time, either.

After that successful operation, the 25th North Carolina marched back to the vicinity of Tarboro, where General Robert F. Hoke was assembling a small division of troops to recapture another vital port town—Plymouth. Most of Ransom's Brigade, including the 25th North Carolina Infantry Regiment, was thrown in with Hoke's other forces just prior to marching off toward Plymouth in mid-April of 1864. It was to be yet another audacious Confederate attempt to take a strong Yankee position. And the prospects that Rufus and Hack and the Haywood Highlanders would enter into another ferocious battle appeared very promising indeed.

Chapter 20

A Hollow Victory

In the wee hours of an April morning, Rufus, Hack, and the rest of the Haywood Highlanders finally were able to spread their wet blankets on the marshy ground, lie down, and sleep for an hour or so. It had been a difficult slog over the past two days, participating in one failed attack after another against the heavily fortified town of Plymouth. General Hoke had been unable to crack the hard defensive shell the resourceful Yankees had built-up around the port town.

Forts, redoubts, and hefty breastworks protecting some two hundred well-placed siege guns rang the town's outer perimeter—except on one side, where the languid waters of the Roanoke River flowed. Plying this wide body of water were several Yankee naval gunboats, whose firepower had been especially effective in keeping the Rebels at bay. However, it was rumored that the recently-constructed Confederate ram *C.S.S. Albemarle* was, on this very night, steaming down the river to give battle to the Union Navy and reinforce General Hoke's forces.

Just prior to lying down for the much-needed rest, Ransom's Brigade of Rebels had been able to cross Conaby Creek over a hastily constructed pontoon bridge. They were presently situated on the enemy's flank at the edge of town, hard against the Roanoke River. The men's sleep was short-lived, however. In no time it seemed to the Haywood Highlanders, the coarse voice of Colonel Rutledge blared out, "Attention, regiment!" These unwelcome words interrupted many a dream and were soon followed by the company officers' harassing calls, stirring the weary men from their brief slumber. Private Edmunston and his buddies were on their feet instantly, rolling up and adjusting their twisted blankets across their left shoulders and through the belts on the right hip. They fidgeted and hurried to gather up their guns and myriad accoutrements and then rushed to fall in line with the rest of their company.

Captain Deaver waited impatiently for the men to form up. Rufus pulled on his slouch hat, and Hat adjusted his fancy headdress, which now sported two turkey feathers—he had lost the original hawk's feather. When they were at last ready, the captain addressed the company briefly. "Okay, men, it's 'bout time fer us to go in. They give the 25th this river flank to take. Colonel says we'll advance up along the riverfront and sweep away whatever gets in the way. Them's his very words he used. General Hoke's going to attack from the other side of town. And don't ye worry none 'bout them Yank boats. A Confederate boat's coming—Colonel allowed—and it's jest 'bove the town now. It's supposed to chase them other boats off. I reckon we'll see 'bout that," the captain explained, not sounding totally convinced of the naval strategy.

"Now, are y'all ready?" he asked, trying to rouse the men's spirits.

"Yes sir!" rejoined the entire company, save one or two faint hearts.

"Going to show 'em what us Highlanders are made from?" prodded the captain, as he continued to fire up the boys.

"Yes sir!" responded the men of Company F, just as a deafening Confederate artillery barrage opened up on the entrenched enemy.

The other mountain companies in the 25th were ready as well, and every man looked anxiously toward Colonel Rutledge. The colonel's voice soon rang out loudly again, "This is it, men!—Fix bayonets!—Trail arms!—Forward, march!"

At first the five regiments of Ransom's Brigade moved forward in a wave, with their colors held high to guide the assault. However, as the enemy's land and naval cannon fire began raining death and destruction upon the Rebel troops and when the defensive breastworks and strongholds were encountered, the regimental attacks grew more independent and piecemeal. Not only that, but in less than thirty minutes, the Haywood Highlanders had gotten separated—somehow—from all the other companies in its own regiment. Now the men were fighting alone along the Roanoke River waterfront.

As the Yankee naval cutters trained their guns on the Highlanders working their way along the river, Rufus, Hack, Sergeant Henson, the Christopher brothers, and the others struggled to find cover. A canal had blocked their way initially, but they had been able to wade across that without spoiling their ammunition. Soaking wet, these men crawled out and crept for another fifty yards or so, as the shells exploded almost on top of them and lead balls whistled dangerously near.

"That's getting mighty close," an out-of-breath Hack said, as he fell on the ground next to Rufus. "We've got to find some cover." There was none. A swampy wetlands area was on their left flank and the river on the other side. Directly in front was a cattle pen, where a bunch of frightened cattle were nervously bawling and jumping at every exploding sound.

"There," Rufus pointed, "Let's get behind them beef cows." And before his companions could challenge his sanity, he was running hunched over toward the cows.

A few of the boys either jumped through or leaped over a split rail fence and got right in the middle of the herd with him. As the crazed Rebels settled and paused to think about their next move, they could hear and feel the awful thudding sounds of the sharpshooters' bullets impacting against the flesh of the poor beasts surrounding them. Thank God, the cannon fire from the river seemed to be dwindling. With the cows bawling in pain, Francis Christopher looked out over the water and noticed a large gunboat arriving on the scene. Incredibly, it was flying a Confederate flag!

"There it is," he yelled excitedly. "A Rebel ship! It must be the *Albemarle* the captain tolt us 'bout!" Hiding between the dead and dying cows, the Highlanders watched in awe as the strange-looking vessel slowly approached the Yankee boats.

It was the first naval battle the mountaineers had ever witnessed, and it was something to behold. Galvanized toward the action, the astounded Haywood Highlanders could hear the loud booming shots from the enemy ships' guns. They also discerned the metallic ringing sounds of the heavy cannon balls clanking harmlessly off the sloping iron sides of the C.S.S.

Albemarle. Shot after shot was fired at the *Albemarle*, but the monstrous vessel kept on steaming steadily toward one of the cutters—directly at it.

Looking on from the cover of the jittery beef cows, the Rebels saw the *Albemarle* plow head on into the side of the enemy boat, its heavily reinforced bow impaling and penetrating deep inside the hapless craft. Then, before their very eyes, the Confederate gunboat miraculously reversed itself and backed away, as the stricken Federal cutter sank quickly to the river bottom and out of view.

"Looky—them other Yank boats are skidaddling!" an amazed Hack cried out. The mountain boys observed the other three Yankee gunboats speeding furiously down the river, beneath huge clouds of black smoke spewing from their stacks. As quick as that, the naval battle was over. In less than half an hour, the *Albemarle* had dispatched the Union Navy and now turned its fine guns landward on the enemy forts.

Rufus and his bunch had not remained cowering behind the animals through the whole of the exciting naval scene. They had spotted a shed and moved to that crude wooden shelter for protection. But they could not stay there for long. Their orders were to sweep away the enemy, and so far they had not done much sweeping. The naval actions had distracted them, and now they had to catch up with the rest of their company. A dirt street stretched in front of them, running by the wharves with storefronts and houses on both sides. Yankee soldiers holed up in the buildings lining the street were at that very moment aggressively sniping at the Highlanders.

"Rufe, we're going have to take 'em one at a time, I reckon," Hack said. "Let's get them there ones," he said, pointing to the closest structure where a few Yankees could be seen popping up and firing. At this same time, the exploding cannon shells became more pronounced and heavier than ever—much too close for comfort. A dangerous enemy redoubt on the banks of the river had aimed its guns toward the 25th North Carolina's soldiers, tenaciously pushing their way into the town.

"Okay, Hack," Rufus replied and then passed the word along to eight or nine of the other men sheltering close by. In concert, all of these Haywood Highlanders leveled their muskets at a store building where some Yankees were hiding. When the first Yank popped up in a window to shoot, he was greeted with a salvo of musketry fire and a corresponding storm of bullets. That unfortunate bluecoat fell to the floor with a gushing hole in his head. His three partners, who themselves were fixing to shoot at the Rebels, hesitated upon seeing their writhing soon-to-be-dead comrade only a few feet away. Instead of firing back, the Yanks fled out a rear doorway, and the Highlanders quickly advanced to occupy the vacant store. These organized tactics proved so effective that the men continued to employ them thereafter, in varying schemes, and one by one they proceeded to help clear the houses and stores along the riverfront.

Throughout that morning, as General Hoke's attack developed on the opposite side of town and the *Albemarle* and Rebel artillerists directed a withering barrage at the Yankee defenses, the Haywood Highlanders kept moving from one building to another. A couple of the company's men had fallen from Yankee rifle fire while advancing up the street along the river. An exploding cannon shell had killed another and wounded several more. Fortunately, Rufus and Hack remained unscathed so far, but they were absolutely exhausted.

In one of the vacant river houses, Sergeant Henson and a few of his men sprawled on the floor for a short breather. Like most of the other residences, it was just a small wooden structure built on timber piling above the water, with a simple pier located in back. The fishermen and their families who normally occupied these simple utilitarian dwellings had wisely fled for the safety of the countryside, some even leaving their precious fishing crafts behind.

"Wish we had something to eat. I'm starved," Hack allowed, while he sipped from his canteen.

"Aren't we all?" Rufus quipped, his long body stretched out on the floor for a quick rest.

"Rufus, go check out that boat back yender. 'Bout two houses back, I reckon it was. See if you can find something inside it fer us to eat," directed Sergeant Henson, whose appetite was whetted by the eating talk. He remembered seeing a fishing boat earlier, behind one of the houses they had stormed.

Suddenly, the distinctive whistling sound of a speedy cannon shell could be heard as it fell to earth, and the boys flinched in anticipation of the explosion. Almost instantly, they felt a percussive shock wave, and then the deafening boom resounded so close and so loud that the men feared for a split second they must have been hit. Fortunately, they escaped this one, and as if nothing had just happened, Rufus complained back to his sergeant.

"Ah, there ain't nothing back there, Sergeant. They ain't left nary a thing in these houses fer us to eat."

"Yep, that's a fact, but we ain't looked in nary boat yet. There's a big 'un back there a ways. Go out and take a look," the sergeant ordered again.

Still grumbling, Rufus made a show of slowly raising himself up off the plank floor before ducking outside. Leaving his gun and all his stuff behind, he backtracked along the river about four houses down, to where a faded white fishing boat was bobbing in the water. The Yankee cannon fire was thickening, and shells were exploding with alarming suddenness and intensity behind and in front of him. Rufus tried to ignore these dangers, as he studied how best to board the good-sized craft and check it for stores.

It had a single tall mast and the sail was stowed, but that was about the extent of what he could tell about the sailing vessel—his knowledge of nautical things being greatly limited. Then suddenly, as he was awkwardly making his way over the gunwale to board the boat, he heard another incoming ordnance round. Balancing on top of the bulwark, he froze in place and waited with his eyes closed for the flying bomb to harmlessly explode somewhere close by—as they always had done before. But this time, Rufus was not quite so lucky.

The shell impacted directly into the wharf adjacent to where he was perched on the gunwale. As his ears were receiving the thunderous sound of the explosion, his body was already in midair, having been lifted by the blast's powerful forces. At the same time his mind was sorting out the horrendous burst of noise and the strange flying sensation, it processed another feeling as well. Shards of cast iron, or shrapnel, projected by the exploding shell had struck him on the head and elsewhere on his body, somewhere. The pain from these serious wounds, although immediate and acute, was only fleeting. For Rufus was rendered insensible from the severe head injury, and as he tumbled hard into the bottom of the boat, he literally did not know what had hit him. His state of conscious thought had been snuffed out like a candle flame before a strong gust of wind.

Just as this terrible event was unfolding, Sergeant Henson and the others were being summoned to what was then perceived to be an extreme emergency. A strong force of Union troops had reorganized and initiated a resolute counterattack against the 25th North Carolina. Colonel Rutledge direly needed all the men he could get to repulse the onslaught, and the few squads of Haywood Highlanders were ordered on the double-quick to get in the street and form up.

"What about Rufe, Sergeant?" asked Hack as they were hustling toward the action.

"Don't worry none 'bout him, Hat. He'll find us." Sergeant Henson knew Rufus had enough sense to catch up with them. As a matter of fact, he had a high opinion of the private and had no doubts he would figure out what to do. "Now, let's get a move on. We're in fer another fight, sure 'nuff!"

The Haywood Highlanders finally were able to help turn back that final Yankee thrust, and General Hoke's Rebel army eventually conquered the Union forces at Plymouth. By late afternoon, the Yanks had raised a white flag over the fort where they had retreated to make their last stand. Plymouth was surrendered, and the port was soon opened to Confederate commerce and the swift blockade runners.

In actuality, this great Southern victory at Plymouth would be the last one of the war for the South. At the very moment the Yankees were surrendering to General Hoke, two strong armies under the overall leadership of General Ulysses S. Grant were again threatening Richmond and the all-important rail center of Petersburg, just to the south of the Confederate capital. Thus, only two days after winning back the strategic port town of Plymouth, General Hoke and his victorious soldiers found themselves riding the trains to Virginia to stop Grant.

Captain Deaver and his company never found a trace of Rufus. They searched all night long after the Union surrender and into the next day but failed to turn up a body or any clues as to his whereabouts. Interestingly, because the pier had been blown to pieces and the boat had drifted away into the marshes, Hack and the rest of the company had not looked for Rufus in the boat—they had not even found the boat. For men like Captain Deaver, Corporal Hartgrove, Sergeant Garland Henson, and the Christopher brothers, the Battle of Plymouth was rendered a hollow victory by the loss of their compatriot. They left for Virginia with heavy hearts and were genuinely perplexed by the tragic disappearance of their good friend and brother-in-arms, Private Edmunston.

Chapter 21

Reb's Angel

"There she is, Harmon—just like I told you—sitting pretty and almost good as new." The two men were in a small skiff and had rowed through thick marsh grass to get to Harmon Davenport's fugitive fishing boat. Working from the smaller craft, it was not an easy matter to rig a line to the boat's bow and extract if from its reedy snare. But they managed to do it, and then both men manned the oars of the rescue vessel and rowed for more than two hours, tugging the broken boat back to Davenport's riverside house at Plymouth, two miles upstream.

"Appreciate your good help, neighbor. I'm indebted to you now," offered the grateful fisherman, Davenport, when they at last docked behind his house. "We'll get that big net of yours mended right away. You get it stretched out, and I'll be over directly to give you a hand with it." Davenport meant to pay back the favor to his neighbor right away. Then he heard his wife clopping out the back door.

"Harmon, you found the *Hester*! Where was it?" came her excited voice as she walked from the house out onto the remnants of their pier.

"James here spotted her down the river a ways—caught up in some grass. See the hole in her side there? Must have been hit by the same cannon shot that busted up our dock. Suppose, though, she can be fixed back good as new without too much trouble—I think."

The Davenport's two sons sauntered out to check on things about then. Although it was their family's livelihood—fishing—the boys were not quite as happy as their mother and father over the boat's discovery. Both had spent many a long day in the *Hester* out in the Albemarle Sound, manning the nets and hauling in catches of shad, herring, and striped bass, depending on the season of the year. The return of the weathered old fishing craft that bore their mother's name meant only one thing—the resumption of their family's toilsome fishing business.

Yes, it appeared things were going to get back to normal soon, or so they thought, not fully grasping the significance of their hometown falling back under Confederate control. In a matter of days, sleek and speedy blockade runners would resume their nightly voyages, slipping through the waters of the Roanoke with their vital offshore cargoes. Not only that, but the Davenport menfolk—true-blue Unionists—were going to be hard-pressed to dodge service in the Confederate Army.

Bounding like a cat from the river bank into the *Hester*, the youngest son thought he would give her a good look-see. A sizable portion of the port bulwark had been blown away, well above the waterline. Jagged pieces and splinters of wood were strewn across the boat's narrow deck. Quickly inspecting the flooring, the boy could see way more clutter about than these broken remnants. A net, oars, pieces of sail cloth, a fish trap, lines, anchors, bait containers, and many other fishing necessaries littered the bottom of the boat, just like he always remembered and expected. *Wait a minute!*

There was something very peculiar about the tattered, drabby-colored old sail cloth that caught his eye. *Were those large red-stained blotches? What the hell?* he wondered, as he bent over for a closer inspection. Grabbing hold of a corner of the coarse cloth, he yanked it up for a closer inspection.

"Ahhhh!" the boy shrieked as he fell backward in alarm. "What the hell?"

It was a stunning frightful sight that he looked down at. A man's bloodied face with closed eyes turned up to the sky, as motionless as sculpted stone.

At first he thought it was a dead corpse he had uncovered. It lay so perfectly inert. But then, quite unexpectedly, he glimpsed a slight facial quiver. First one eyelid and then another slowly fluttered and opened—just barely. And lo and behold, he noticed the lips tremor ever so delicately, and from them came a faint groan of agony. The boy figured it was a living dead man, and he abruptly pulled back and screamed frantically, "A man! There's a man in here!"

With extreme difficulty, the men and boys extracted the wounded Rebel from the bottom of the boat and moved him into the Davenport's river house. They were thoughtful enough to lay him out on a bed that could accommodate most of his lengthy frame before sending for the doctor. The Davenport's daughter, Emma—twin sister to the oldest son—helped her mother clean the man's face as best they could, without touching the ugly gash on his forehead. They could also see that he had a bad wound in his side, where blood was still seeping from a sizeable coagulation. While cleaning his face, the women noticed their patient frantically licking at the wetness of their small washcloths. Instantly realizing what this meant, Emma started dripping small amounts of water into his mouth to begin the rehydration process.

An elderly doctor arrived in short order and began urgently tending to the wounded soldier in an effort to save his life. Both of the women assisted as best they could, supplying hot water and linen cloths and helping move the patient so that the doc could get at the injuries.

"Well, Hester, Emma, I believe that's all I can do for him for the time being," the doctor said. He had done his best for the patient, and now the young man's fate was in the hands of God. "Unless that hole in his side gets infected, I do believe he has a chance to live. You saw the hunks of iron I fished out of him. Well, I hope that was all there was; and I didn't suture the wound completely closed, either. Left a drain hole, so keep your eye on it, and keep it clean and open so the pus can discharge. Oh, and that gouge on the side of his head—ain't much to worry about there, I don't believe. It must have been a real hard glancing blow, though. He sure did get lucky."

Hester's concern for the patient and her good sense were manifest when she asked, "Shouldn't we move this poor boy to the Confederate hospital, Doctor Phelps?"

"Hah! Wish you could, Hester—sure do. But there's no hospital now, to speak of. All the army's doctors left out with the troops for Virginia. The wounded and sick men that remained here, Yankees included, are over at Fort Williams under my care. They're dying right and left, I'm afraid, and there's not much we can do about it."

"Does that mean he ought to be left here? Do you think we can take care of him?" Emma asked in quick succession. Although she was nineteen years old and perfectly willing to take on the responsibility of caring for the patient, in reality Emma was not at all confident that she—or her mother for that matter—was competent to do so.

"His best chances of making it are right here, Emma. You and your mother should be able to care for his needs as well as anyone, I suspect. Besides, if you need me, you know where I live." And with that considered opinion and bit of expert advice, Doctor Phelps packed his implements and things into his black bag and bid the Davenport women goodbye.

Over the next several days, the Davenports—primarily Emma—doted over their Rebel patient and cared for his every need and whim. After repairs were completed on the *Hester*, the men returned to the Sound's fisheries while trying their damnedest to keep a low profile and evade the Confederates' attention. They were Unionists at heart. For the past two years of Yankee control at Plymouth, Harmon and his sons had not fretted atall about the Confederate draft laws. They had been out of the reach of the Rebel authorities and had stayed extremely busy supplying the Union soldiers in the area with fresh fish to eat. For sure, they did not want to advertise to the victorious Confederate officials that there was a wounded Rebel soldier convalescing under their roof.

The patient was beginning to move around more and more in the bed and was eating and drinking everything put in front of him. Emma made sure the drain in his side stayed clear, and she kept a clean bandage fixed over the wound to prevent infection. He had become lucid and talkative and even laughed with his caregivers as if nothing had happened. But there was one thing very unusual and bothersome about the wounded soldier's condition. He could not remember his name or anything else about himself. Although fortunate that the shrapnel blow to his head was not a penetrating wound, it had apparently been sufficiently forceful and traumatic to cause a memory loss.

"I'm mighty sorry, Emma. I don't know why I can't remember my name or even where my home is. They jest ain't nothing in there—no memories atall."

"Well, I'm certain of one thing, Reb. You're not from around here, that's for sure. With that heavy accent and dialect, why, you might even be from Scotland for all we know," Emma said with a chuckle. She and her mother had begun calling their patient 'Reb' for lack of a real name. And Reb did not seem to mind his new moniker. He took to it easily.

Within about a week or so, the spry Reb began to feel his oats again. One morning he surprised his pretty nurse with a suggestion. "Say, Emma, I want to try and get up off this bed. Believe it's 'bout time. Don't you reckon? Can you give me a hand?"

"Are you sure you're ready, Reb? Maybe it's a little too soon, don't you think?" Emma was none too certain of her patient's ability to leave his bed already, nor did she think it was a wise thing to do.

"Reckon I'm sure as sure can be," replied Reb. "Let's give it a go, why don't we?"

So with the reluctant Emma pulling and holding and supporting the best she could, the shirtless Reb moved slowly and painfully to a sitting position in the bed.

"Ahhh—that hurts so bad," Reb complained, as he favored the side wound. "Don't know if I can do this or not, Emma," he allowed, now doubting himself and his strength. But in a few moments the pain lessened a bit, stiffening his resolve once again. Then he braced himself to rise to his feet.

"Wait a second, Reb. Let me first take a look at your side to make sure the wound's not tearing. It's been healing so nicely," Emma said as she lifted the bandage to check. "No, thank goodness. It still looks fine."

"Okay then—here goes nothing."

Slowly Reb twisted and placed his bare feet on the floor boards. *Such a good feeling*, he thought as Emma clutched and held onto him as firmly as she could. He straightened his legs ever so deliberately, little by little. And then, as he began unbending from his midsection, his shoulders and head started moving upward, higher and higher. There—finally—Reb had done it! He stood erect and stiff while stretching upright to his full height.

"Ohhh—heaven forbid! That hurt something awful, Emma," Reb announced in triumphant agony.

The admiring nurse gazed up at the handsome figure, thinking that he was much taller than she had realized. Then with her steadying support by his side, Reb began gradually walking around the tiny back room that overlooked the Roanoke River. In the coming days, the patient doggedly kept at it. Soon he was able to rise up from bed and get around on his own without any help from his nurse atall. Emma was extremely proud of her patient, and he, in turn, was mighty grateful for what his pretty nurse had done for him. And that was not the extent of his feelings for her, it seemed. Over time, as he talked with Emma and looked at her and felt her caring hands touching him, he had gradually developed a fondness and infatuation for the girl. Not only that, but Emma had become enthralled with her handsome flaxen-haired patient as well.

By no means had these attentions gone unnoticed by the mother. Hester had even warned Emma not to get too close to Reb. She did not want her daughter getting hurt again. Two years earlier, Emma's beau—a local boy she had known for years—had been killed fighting with the Southern troops defending Roanoke Island from Burnside's Yankee invaders. The tragedy had devastated Emma, and she had pretty much withdrawn from all societal doings. During the turmoil of the cruel war, she had been a drowning soul in search of firm footing—that is, until Reb fell into their boat. The pathetic, good-looking, injured soldier made her forget her woes and think of nothing else but him. He was her lifeline, and she was trying to grasp hold. That was what frightened Hester so. The mother had assured Emma that as soon as Reb was fit, he would take off and be gone from her life forever. *Then what?* Hester had asked. But Emma did not heed her mother's well-intentioned warnings.

A few days after Reb became genuinely mobile again, Emma took him on a short walk and picnic. There was a nice peaceful spot she knew down near where the waters of Conaby Creek mingled with those of the Roanoke. It was a perfect place, where Reb could get some fresh air and delight in nature's beauty. To get there, they crossed over the deep creek by using the same pontoon bridge the Rebel army had built.

As Reb tread over the crude bridge timbers, memories began to flash through his mind. This bridge—he had helped build this very bridge. He was sure of it. It was a vivid memory, and he could even recollect men with familiar faces by his side, heaving planks into place to construct the confounded span. These were all faces that made him feel comfortable and good. But he could not associate names or anything else with these memories—not atall! Frustrated for sure, Reb did not let it get him down. At least he had remembered something. *My mind must be awakening a little*, he thought to himself. For some reason though, he decided not to tell Emma about the perplexing recollections—not yet anyway.

Along the edge of a small meadow, spotted with blue butterwort flowers and blooming yellow dandelions, they spread out a quilt under a large weeping-willow tree. Although the day had already become stifling hot, the willow's dangling, fully leaved branches offered the picnickers a shady patch to sprawl in. Flopping down on the coverlet, Emma removed her shoes and socks while Reb kicked off his pitiful army boots. Both of them had a good laugh at the ridiculous footwear with the loose, flapping soles.

"Don't know if the army will take me back, Emma. A man with shoes like that and can't even remember his own name won't be worth much to 'em, don't reckon."

"Now, now, Reb, you know what the doctor said. This spell of forgetfulness is just temporary. He told us it's nothing to worry about right now." Emma did not speak from conviction or hope, since she was not quite sure if she wanted Reb to regain his memory right away. As soon as that happened, he would either be off for home or trotting back to the war. Certainly, she wanted neither of those things, at least not until after she got to know him better.

A quite interlude beset the outing, as the nurse and patient basked in the fresh air and sun and enjoyed a picturesque view of the lethargic opaque creek. Reb used this time to study his angel closely. He had not asked Emma her age but guessed she might have a year or two on him. Her silky hair, glistening in the sunlight, was as dark as brown could be without being black. And it was pulled back and fixed tightly in a bun at the nape of her neck, as it was on most days. Reb remembered that night when he caught Emma unawares at the house. He had spied her beautiful dangling locks released from the confinement of pins and ribbons. Unexpectedly, he had been aroused at the wonderful sight of the streaming tresses tumbling well below her shoulders. Gazing upon Emma today, he imagined her hair loose, tossed and blown about in the gentle spring breezes.

Reb simply lay there on his good side, propped on an elbow, staring at Emma and thinking she was absolutely gorgeous. For a girl, she was taller than most—and thin, but not skinny. Her body proportions and sculpted facial features were exceptionally pleasing, he thought. So were her beautifully shaped lips and eyes. *And the color of those eyes—what was the color?* he mused. *Hazel, maybe? Yes, that was the color—*

"Hazel! Hazel! Yer eyes are hazel, ain't they, Emma?" But Reb did not allow time for her to answer, as he rushed on. "Hazel means something to me. I remember now. I remember hazel—hazel—what is it?" And then suddenly it hit him. He remembered what 'hazel' meant. It meant 'Hazeltine' to him. *Hazeltine—Tine—Tine!* He could clearly recall the name Tine, and he was able to make associations with the name. And in this case, the name Tine revived awful and painful memories.

"Tine! Tine! I remember her now, Emma. She was a girl. Tine was a girl I knew! She was killed back—back home, 'bout a year or so ago, seems like." Then it dawned on him that recollections of home were coming into focus. He suddenly remembered the East Fork and Forks of Pigeon—and his family. It was all flooding back to Reb now. His identity was gradually being revealed—even his name.

Emma naturally got caught up in the enthusiasm as well. "What's your name, Reb? Do you remember your name?" she elatedly asked.

"Yes! Yes, I do! My name is—Rufus! I'm Rufus Edmunston! And I'm from the mountains, Emma. I'm from Haywood County! You were right. I ain't from 'round here. I'm a mountain boy! Yahoooo! I can't hardly believe it's true! I've got my memory back bigger than Pete!" And with that announcement the two suddenly fell into each other's arms and began hugging excitedly.

Even though his sensitive side wound had a lot more healing to do, they continued to embrace as they fell onto the ground in happiness. Rufus could feel Emma real good, and he even went so far as to kiss her. And Emma kissed him back, and then he kissed her, and soon the whole thing got completely out of control. Before either one knew what was happening, they were groping and feeling one another in heated passion. It did not stop there, either. They started pulling at each other's clothes to find a way to feel freer—freer to express themselves, so that more opportunities and options might become available to them. Soon, Rufus had shucked his pants, and Emma's dress had been removed, and they were rolling in the grass under the willow tree, stark-naked and feeling as alive and excited and heated as either had ever felt in their entire lives.

In a snug embrace, their mouths and tongues tasted and explored. With one hand, Emma felt for Rufus and discovered his engorged manhood. Rufus sensed her hand grabbing him and squeezing him, and it almost drove him wild. He reacted by pressing his mouth harder against Emma's and jerking the blasted devices out of her hair, so that he could run his hands through her beautiful tresses. *There—free at last!* His fingers caressed her long loose locks that were so silky and smelled so deliciously inviting. God, how he loved Emma! He wanted her so bad, but he did not know how to love her.

Emma lacked actual loving experience as well. Even with her old boyfriend—the one that had got himself killed—she had never approached this level of intimacy. But having gone this far and knowing that she loved Rufus and would likely lose him to the war very soon, she decided to make the extreme sacrifice—her virginal purity. Emma wanted him badly, and she was going to find a way to have him.

Her animal juices were flowing, and the more savagely Rufus kissed her mouth and fondled her breasts and stroked her hair, the harder she squeezed and held onto his throbbing and unmistakably erect manhood. She opened her long slender legs and wiggled herself under Rufus, so she could receive him. He intuited what was going on and squirmed a mite to facilitate Emma's efforts. Using her hand, Emma guided Rufus's hardened appendage into her warm wet opening, and she felt it growing even larger and being pushed deeper and deeper inside. For Emma there was the discomfort of internal resistance at first, and then a sharp pain, and then—almost instantly—there was bliss!

They thrusted and humped, pushed and pulled, and eventually found a rhythm where they moved in a seemingly perfect cadence—a short synchronous symphony of physical movements where they each felt the maximum possible joy and fulfillment. After only a minute or so of these agitated innate exertions, Emma suddenly released her orgasmic tensions with a tremor and a scream of pure ecstasy. As if a signal to him, Rufus emitted a rivaling primal grunt, with his ejaculation exploding inside of the wonderful girl.

Over the course of the coming weeks, Emma continued to give her undivided attentions to her Rebel guest. Their relationship grew from the infatuations of a nurse and patient into true love and devotion to one another. There were other extended picnics with opportunities to share their fullest expressions of affection. And Rufus's memory recovered in full. Family recollections were most prominent in all of the returning memories. He could also recall his good army buddies—Hack, Garland, Francis, and the other Haywood Highlanders—who, he had learned, were fighting with General Lee in Virginia. The hard experiences of war along with the accompanying fears and terrors and cruelty were not lost either. These lucid sobering thoughts were back, and instinctively he comprehended that he must return to the sides of his fellow soldiers in the field—and soon. Of course he never forgot about Tine—poor Tine—nor would he ever forget her. However, the place in his heart that was once filled entirely with love for the miller's daughter was now crowded with similar loving affections for the daughter of a Unionist fisherman—his angel, Emma.

Not quite as tall as her blond boyfriend, but tall anyway, Emma held Rufus's hand as they roamed and savored the blooming countryside that surrounded war-torn Plymouth. One Sabbath, when Harmon was giving the *Hester* a rest, Emma persuaded her younger brother to take them out sailing. Needless to say, it was a unique experience for the mountaineer, who it could not be said had an affinity for water. He barely knew how to paddle like a dog and keep his head above the water.

Sailing before the wind down the Roanoke into the grand Albemarle Sound almost convinced Rufus he had gained the Atlantic Ocean and was clearly on his way across the sea to the Old World. He did not actually think that, but the expansiveness and grandeur of the sound was indeed impressive and not lost on him. He tried his hand at the tiller and steered the craft to and fro in the steady breezes. When given an opportunity, he trimmed the sheet and manned the boom as Emma's brother gave curt directions.

Late in the day, while beating homeward toward the setting sun, Rufus and Emma stood side by side, holding hands at the bow. Turning their faces away from the brisk wind, they stared adoringly at one another while struggling to maintain their balance in the pitching boat. Oblivious to the helmsman's attentive gaze, the couple moved closer and tighter together and met each other in a long and affectionate hug. Such tender moments capped a fantastic day on the water—one that was truly an exhilarating and fulfilling experience for Rufus. So much so, that he proclaimed to his hosts that sailing was one of the most enjoyable experiences of his young life. He allowed it was right up there with riding a fine horse.

For seven weeks, Emma nursed and cuddled and romanced Rufus, until it was finally time for him to return to the front. His side wound, still sore to the touch, had healed. There was a raw scar over the side of his brow, but it was not an open sore and would eventually become less conspicuous. And, of course, his memory had returned. He knew his name and the infantry regiment he belonged to. And that was all it took for the Confederate Army officials at Plymouth to welcome him back and immediately direct him northward. In mid-June of 1864, Rufus boarded a train in Weldon, North Carolina, and soon was on his way to the beleaguered Rebel troops in front of Petersburg, Virginia.

Chapter 22

Big Ol' Yankee Moles

It was a hot afternoon, and Private Edmunston was making his way through the supply depots and field hospitals outside of Petersburg, Virginia, toward the front lines. He could hear in the distance sporadic cannon and mortar fire along with exploding ordnance, and it was becoming more and more intense as he moved forward. The makeshift cobbling on his footwear was not holding up very well, and he was literally walking out of his boots. The soles had again come loose from the uppers. This minor inconvenience hindered his steps in a way that required him to lift his feet, pronouncedly and embarrassingly, as he walked. But Rufus was not alone. As he approached the front defenses, he took notice of the other Rebel infantry men going about their duties in bare feet. Such was the state of General Lee's Southern Army at that time, and any discomfiture Rufus may have felt about his boots soon vanished.

"Rufe! It's you! Damn if ye ain't alive!" Corporal Hartgrove yelled out, upon seeing his best buddy making awkward giant steps toward where he and the few remaining Highlanders were working. When the other men saw Rufus approaching, they halted in mid-swing of whatever digging implement they were using and simply gawked at him. It was as if they were looking at an apparition.

"Hello, Hack! Thought I'd never get here. It's good to see you!" Rufus hollered back. "Hello, boys!" Then he was stopped in his tracks by the onrush of all of his friends moving to greet him, and for the ensuing moments the scene was a huddle of confused happiness and embraces. They visited and funned with one another for the next little while, until at last the officers moved in and broke things up, putting the men back to work.

"It's real good to have ye back, Private. Better go and check in with Captain Deaver," Lieutenant Blalock instructed, pointing toward the captain's bombproof quarters a ways off. Turning to the work crew, he gave more lively orders. "Let's get back to it, men. Got to get this trenching done by nightfall, lest we have to work all night."

"Yes sir, Lieutenant. It's good to see you too," Rufus replied, and he headed off to see his uncle some hundred yards or so behind the front lines.

The captain could not believe his eyes and listened for an hour or so while his nephew recounted being blown into the fishing boat and eventually rescued by the fishermen. Captain Deaver was incredulous of the far-fetched tale and wrung every last detail from the private, including those about the superlative nurse. He was also apologetic. "Rufus, we searched fer ye all night long in that there whole town. Sergeant Henson tolt us 'bout the boat, but we ain't never found the damn thing. When we got orders to move on and give up the search, it hurt us terrible-like. Did ye write to yer folks?"

"Yep, wrote them a couple of weeks ago—soon's I finally remembered who I was. It was a real strange experience, Captain, not knowing my name or whur I come from."

"Well, I tolt them ye're likely as not dead, and I ain't heard nothing else from them 'bout it. Sure 'nuff, Rufus, we figgered ye fer dead—fer sure. Glad ye ain't dead though, Private. Now, let me tell ye what we've been up to all this time."

In May, when Ransom's Brigade was hurried away from Plymouth to Virginia, the North Carolinians helped turn back several Federal thrusts against Petersburg. During this same timeframe, General Lee's main Army of Northern Virginia was fighting north of Richmond and holding off another powerful Union Army led by General Ulysses S. Grant. Lee and Grant's forces clashed time after time, again and again, with both armies suffering staggering losses. Over the course of a couple of months, that battlefront shifted from north of Richmond around to the east and eventually southeast of the capital to the Petersburg battle lines—precisely where the Haywood Highlanders were now helping man the defenses. Grant's futile headlong bloody assaults to capture Richmond by direct force had compelled him to conceive and attempt another tactical course. Thus, he endeavored to besiege Petersburg, where Lee's army had shifted and was holed up now. President Lincoln fully supported this new approach, eagerly expressing to his new lieutenant general "to hold on with a bulldog grip, chew and choke as much as possible, and strangle the lifeblood out of the South."

This siege of the critical railroad hub and commercial center of Petersburg, where Lee's army was cornered, and Union General William Tecumseh Sherman's thrust into Georgia toward Atlanta was essentially what the Civil War had boiled down to in the summer of 1864. When Private Edmunston arrived at Petersburg, he found his fellow Highlanders digging defensive trenches from which to fight and hide. The Rebel troops worked diligently around the clock, excavating enormous quantities of red dirt. These trenches they were digging allowed them to sharpshoot at the Yankees, less than a hundred yards away, while sheltering from the Yank snipers and the lethal mortar shells that incessantly rained down from the sky. For additional protection from the incoming rounds of falling death, they constructed underground bombproof shelters and burrowed 'gopher' holes into the sides of their trenches to take cover in. Accordingly, the Yankee troops just opposite them were mirroring this entrenchment work with earth diggings and fortifications of their own.

Rufus fell in with the work crews, digging trenches and traverses and constructing the fortifications that the Confederate engineers had laid out for them. It reminded him of his slaves' ditching work at the Den and all those frustrating times when he had constantly badgered the Africans to keep at it. But he and Hack and the other Haywood Highlanders did not slack at all and toiled into the darkness of the night, when their efforts were better concealed from the Yankee sharpshooters. As it happened, on this particular evening, Private Edmunston and Corporal Hartgrove were building another important feature of the Rebel defenses—an elaborate breastwork in front of their trenches to afford additional protection from massed Yankee attacks.

"Rufe, Sergeant says these here sharpened tree poles are called 'abatis' in France—or something other." As Hack and Rufus struggled to set the lengthy slender poles in the ground and align them to point toward the Yanks, the corporal further allowed, "Them sharp spike tips ought to discourage them blue-bellies from charging us. Don't ye reckon, Rufe?"

"Reckon so," a huffing and puffing Rufus replied, as he heaved and lined up another one in a row, while Hack scotched it in place. "Ain't told you this yet, Hack, but I met me a girl in Plymouth. Emma's her name, and she sure is right pretty. Yeah, she's a beauty, sure 'nuff."

Hack, who was backfilling dirt over the butt ends of the poles Rufus was setting, was so surprised by the revelation that he momentarily stopped his work. "A girl! Ye're joshing me, feller. Ain't ye?"

"Nope, ain't joshing none atall. Emma Davenport's her name. She was my purty angel that nursed me back to the living. When I left her, she said she would wait for me until after the war. We aim to get married up soon's the shooting stops." Rufus paused and reflected a spell, while Hack waited for him to continue. Then with a hint of guilt in his voice, he felt his friend out, "What you think, Hack? Reckon Tine would care much for me taking up with Emma?"

Truthfully, Hack was somewhat surprised and taken aback that his friend would have these apparent shameful feelings. "Well, no! I don't reckon Tine would mind ye taking up with this here new Emma girl. Fact, I figger she would be right happy ye found some'ens else. Ain't no use fer ye to fret more 'bout that, Rufe. Tine won't ker nary bit, I'm right sure of it."

Getting back to their work they continued to chat about Emma, as Hack was real curious about what she was like. He had also been keenly interested in the sailing excursion that Rufus carried on about, allowing that one day he would like to try it, if he ever got the chance and did not get himself killed first. Then Hack completely turned the table on Rufus and unloaded a revelation of his own. "I wrote another letter to Harriet, Rufe."

Rufus was not sure he had heard correctly. "What? That dead Yank's wife?"

"Yep, that be her—Harriet Ames. Jest tolt her I've been thinking 'bout her and hope she's getting along tolerable well, considering Elliott's getting kilt and all. Never mentioned to her, though, that I might have been the one that kilt him. Ye can't never tell how she might react."

"What did you go and do that fer, Hack? So, how you plan on getting this letter to her?" asked an incredulous Rufus.

"Already took ker of it. Give it to another Yank on burial duty after that big flare-up we had at Drewry's Bluff. He said he'd be happy to mail it. Matter of fact, he went one better fer another chaw of 'bacco. Said he'd write his address fer Harriet to reply to, if she cares to. He's a hunderd-day man, though—ye know what they are, don't ye?"

The unbelieving Rufus could barely speak but managed this, "No, don't believe I do."

"Well, they're them Yank soldiers who only signed up to fight fer a hunderd days. After that, they can go home, I reckon. Sure wish we were hunderd-day men. Anyhow, he says if she replies to my letter and he ain't gone home by then, he'll find a way to smuggle her letter across the lines. Not bad, huh? What ye think 'bout that?"

Unbelievable was what Rufus thought about it. "I reckon you know more Yankee postmen than I know Rebels, Hack. What gives—are you hoping she's going write you something back?"

Hack stopped his shoveling and in a thoughtful and serious tone replied, "Reckon I'm hoping she will. I don't have me a girl like you do now. And when I see all these boys cuddling them letters from home and reading nice words from their wives and girlfriends, I get to feeling a mite lonely and left out—I do, I tell ye. Harriet's lost Elliot, and she might be feeling lonesome, too. That's the way I figger it, anyhows. So maybe we can jest be friends and write nice words back and forth to each other. That's all that I was thinking." After sharing these innermost tender thoughts, he glanced toward his best friend for understanding and then turned back to his dirt work again.

Rufus was moved by the sincerity of Hack's comments. Surprisingly, it all made sense to him—what Hack said—and he offered his approving support. "Well then, I hope she writes you back a nice letter with purty words in it, Hack. Long as you don't tell her 'bout killing her husband and long's that there Yankee postal service of yours don't fail, then you may jest find yerself a female friend—and a Yankee one to boot. That ain't so bad neither, don't reckon. Why, Emma's folks are pure-blue Unionists."

After a month of perilous and back-breaking labor, the Confederate defenses circling the eastern perimeter of Petersburg were finally adjudged to be strong enough to repulse a determined enemy attack. Throughout the blistering hot summer days of July, Private Edmunston and Corporal Hartgrove and the rest of the mountaineers peered at the Yankees through narrow slits in sand bags stacked along the tops of the trenches.

A shortage of ammunition put them at a distinct disadvantage with the blue-coated sharpshooters across the way, who were constantly firing at them. On average, for every ten lead rifle balls expended by the Yanks, the Haywood Highlanders and the rest of the Confederate forces shot only once. It was a source of frustration for the Rebels to see their own boys being picked off right and left and not being allowed to return the fire.

Captain Deaver was none too happy about these circumstances either. He complained to the colonel that whilst the men husbanded their ammunition, the enemy was thinning the Rebel ranks with embarrassing impunity. The captain allowed that the morale effect alone on his men would defeat them before long. However, his grievances about the want of ammunition fell mostly upon deaf ears of the higher-ups in the Confederate command. The fact of the matter was that the Confederacy simply did not have sufficient shooting powder and bullets to fight a sustained war.

On the next to last night of July, Rufus and Hack and the rest of the 25th North Carolina Troops were posted on the immediate left of one of the Confederate forts—or salients—that protruded out from the trench lines. These exposed fortified positions were important tactically because they enabled the Rebels to aim their big guns down the defensive lines and affect a devastating enfilading fire against attacking Yankee troops. The salient next to the 25th North Carolina was manned on this particular night by a regiment of South Carolina troops, along with an artillery company.

Lying on their blankets in the bottom of a trench, Rufus and Hack were having a customary chat before going to sleep. "What ye think about them underground digging sounds they been hearing next to us?" asked Corporal Hartgrove, who did not seem too concerned, just curious. "Them South Carolina boys allow they've been hearing 'em right regular lately."

"I spoke to one of the engineers who come to investigate, and they ain't found nothing yet," replied Rufus. "He showed me an augering tool on a long pole they've been using to investigate them strange noises. That thing can core a hole almost ten feet down, but he allowed there ain't nothing much down there to worry 'bout."

"Them boys over there think different though. They believe the Yanks have sappers tunneling underneath to blow up their works. I went over and couldn't hear nary thing atall though," Hack allowed. He was not convinced one way or the other.

"Jest their imaginations, I reckon. Now if we had bullets to shoot at them Yanks, them South Carolina boys wouldn't be jest sitting round all day long imagining strange noises in the ground. Maybe they just grow big ol' moles up here in this Virginia red-dirt country. Reckon?"

"Maybe—and I suppose this here war's going to end tomorrow too" rejoined Hack, giving back a dose of sarcasm of his own.

"I wish."

"Me too. Is that letter ye got today from Emma?" queried Hack changing the subject.

"Nope—from the folks. They say Mr. Hartgrove ain't got much to look after at the store. Ain't no supplies or merchandise can be got in from the low country, they say. Our Africans are slacking to beat and giving Father fits too. They're getting word somehow, can't say where from, of this emancipation business and believe Lincoln himself is on his way to the Forks to set them free. One of 'em—Harry—got so insolent Father had to have him whipped. Paid a man from Waynesville to come over and do it."

A mortar shell whistled in right about then and exploded with a thundering boom nearby. Looking up at the stars from the narrow confines of the red embankments, the boys fell silent while listening to the frantic calls of men checking to see if anyone was hurt. The Yanks were not about to let the Rebels sleep peacefully in their holes, and it was their habit to keep lobbing lethal exploding ordnance all night long into the Confederate lines. In addition to depriving the Reb rats of their sleep, they figured to kill a few of them every night, if they got lucky.

"Pa tolt me there weren't anything to carry in the store," Hack replied, as the two resumed their pillow talk a minute or two later. "Says that folks all over Haywood is suffering real bad shortages of food—and pert near everything else, fer that matter. I can't believe they still ain't caught that Bugg gang that killed yer and Captain's—uhh—sorry, Rufe. Ought not have raised that sore subject with ye. Sorry 'bout that."

"It's okay," Rufus said, as he began to yawn real big. "If they don't get him, then Burton and I will, soon as this bloody war ends. Ye aim to join us?"

"Damn right I aim to! Pa says they're still at their plundering business too."

"Sons of bitches! Then we'll have to have another go at them," the sleepy Rufus commented hatefully. "Don't want to think 'bout that now. It's too disturbing. Need to get me some sleep."

"Yep, me too. Night, Rufe."

"Good night, Hat."

Visions of an evil rampaging Amos Bugg visited Rufus that night, as he slept intermittently between the unrelenting explosions of mortar fire. Satanic horns sprouted from under Bugg's white mane, and his skin was tinted the color of a freshly sliced beet. With an image of flames in the background and Bugg's oversized musket and bayonet aimed dead at him, Rufus awoke suddenly to a thunderous explosion—one so strong that it launched him upward off of his blanket.

In the first split second of awareness, he verified that Bugg had not blown his head off. And in the ensuing seconds, he and Hack and the other Haywood Highlanders were scrambling to their feet and looking in shock at an enormous cloud of smoke, dirt, and debris spewing heavenward over the Confederate line immediately to their right. *What in the hell had just happened?* they each and every one wondered.

As they gazed toward the conflagration, backlit by the first glints of the rising sun, clods of earth began to rain down all around Rufus and his buddies. They were forced to shield their heads with their hands or jump into the nearest gopher holes. And that was not all that was falling out of the sky. Arms, legs, and other body parts—even whole bodies—thumped onto the ground around them, sending the Rebs ducking into their saps for fear of being hit. It soon became abundantly clear to Private Edmunston and Corporal Hartgrove what was transpiring in front of their very eyes. Apparently those noises the South Carolina boys had heard were indeed tunneling noises, and the damn Yanks had sure enough sprung a mine right underneath them. All those arms and legs and what-not falling down out of the sky like a hailstorm from Hades were bloody remnants of the unlucky South Carolinians who were blown up.

Rufus, Hack, and the rest of their regiment were damning the tricky Yankees for what they had done to those poor boys, as they pulled themselves together and prepared to make a fight. Erupting inside each of them was a renewed hatred for their scheming foes, and they were now more determined than ever to teach the Yanks a lesson.

Chapter 23

THE BLOODY CAULDRON

The Petersburg sunrise explosion had blasted a huge hole in the ground where once an entire South Carolina infantry regiment and artillerists had stood guard. In mere seconds, a critical fortified salient protecting the Rebel defensive line was reduced to a vast pocked rupture in the Confederate defenses—two hundred feet long, eighty feet wide, and thirty feet deep. That was the Yanks' purpose for springing the mine—to blast out the enormous crater and create a gaping hole in the Rebel cordon. And the Union strategists immediately sought to exploit the successful detonation. General Grant's officers began to send wave after wave of bluecoats into the crater to widen the rift and overwhelm the startled and disorganized Rebels.

Within minutes of the blast, even before the smoke and dust had settled, the Confederate troops began reacting and moving to defend against the surprise Union onslaught. Captain Deaver and his small clan of Haywood Highlanders were hurriedly marched with the 25th North Carolina to a ridge in the rear of the defenses, overlooking the giant crater. The few South Carolina boys who had not perished joined them at that position, and they began preparing to receive the expected enemy thrust. A quick look around was all it took for Private Edmunston and his Rebel brethren to recognize the obvious—their regiment was all that stood between the oceans of frenzied bluecoats and Petersburg. It was left to these scant North Carolina troops—and only them—to protect the town and its railroads and preserve the Confederacy.

"Okay, men, wait 'til ye see the whites of their eyes and give it to 'em," came the calm directive from Captain Deaver. His men anxiously watched the enemy's frothing regimental flags fill the crater and then spill over the rim in their direction. All the while, desperate Confederate forces up and down the lines were beginning to squeeze in at the sides of the Yank-infested cauldron, in an all-out effort to prevent the breech from growing.

"Look out, Rufe. Here they come!" cried out Hack, as he leveled his rifle and fired at the ominous blue line heading toward them.

Private Edmunston needed no coaching or coaxing. He was fully aware of the charging danger and likewise lowered down on a bluecoat and shot him square in the middle of the chest. It was not a pretty sight, but this was war, and after that sneaky Yankee mine trick Rufus yearned to kill Yanks. He instantly knelt down and began to reload his musket, while a man behind him stepped forward to fire a shot over his head at another Yankee.

For two long hours, the bluecoats kept boiling up out of that cauldron and coming at the 25th, and the North Carolinians presented as stubborn a defense as any offered before. More than once, Rufus used his bayonet to finish off a Yankee. Hack bloodied his rifle spike as well.

On one occasion when Corporal Hartgrove had his rifle knocked out of his hands, he instantly pounced on the pugnacious bluecoat and wrestled him to the ground. Unwittingly, Hack picked up a loose cartridge box from the ground and began beating the stunned soldier over the head with it. Fortunately, Rufus happened to catch a glance of the incredible scuffle and witness Hack's frantic struggle to best the much larger opponent. Instinctively, the private sprung to his friend's side and buried his blood-smeared bayonet into the stomach of the enemy soldier. Pulling it out of the wriggling dying man, he quickly looked down at Hack and their understanding eyes met for a brief moment.

"Thanks, Rufe! He was a tough 'en!"

"Hurry—get up from there and grab yer gun!" and then the two of them jumped back into position and resumed shooting at the enemy.

Several of the men at their sides had gone down, but neither Hack nor Rufus were grazed yet, thank the Lord. The lead rifle balls were flying thicker than a storm of locusts, and it was a sanctified miracle that every last

Haywood Highlander did not meet his doom then and there at the Petersburg crater. But most of the mountaineers were able to dodge the lethal bullets, and they kept up a steady fire and fought the enemy with a fury heretofore unleased. Shooting, bayoneting, and clubbing the Yanks, they clung to their position with the unwavering tenacity of Lincoln's fanciful bulldog, chewing and choking the lives out of the bluecoats.

Throughout the chaotic ordeal, Captain Deaver and Lieutenant Blalock stood firm at their positions on the flanks of the company, directing and encouraging their men. "Ye're gaining on 'em, boys! I can see they're slowing up! Keep throwing the lead at 'em!" the captain hollered.

His perception was correct. The steady stream of bluecoats was actually beginning to thin out considerably. But to the astonishment of the Rebels, the faces of the Yank soldiers oozing out of the crater began to take on an entirely different hue. Incredibly, these faces were dark—dark as a chunk of Virginia coal, and they were lit up with shining white eyes and snarling teeth. These were the unmistakable faces of Negro soldiers!

The former slaves proudly wore the blue uniforms of the Union, having waited their whole lives for such an opportunity to strike back at those who had so cruelly and ruthlessly shackled their entire race. With a pent-up ferocity long reserved for their wicked oppressors, the black troops charged at the waiting Rebels with vengeful rage, crying out so all could hear, "No quarter to the Rebels!" This development incensed the North Carolinians to no end, and they fought even harder, dispensing death more eagerly and hatefully to the damned uppity nigger Yankees.

A mile-long battle line of countless Federal regiments relentlessly attacked the Confederate works—on both sides of the crater—but General Lee's steadfast defenses held. As the furious battle wore on, the Rebel cannons were increasingly directed at the confused mass of bluecoats packing into the earthen cauldron. Every bursting shell and screaming iron projectile effectively wrought more carnage within the blue sea of writhing humanity. Those poor souls entering the crater—black and white—could barely move. With every regiment thrown into the fray, they were squashed tighter and tighter together. So much so, that they could not easily scale the steep walls trapping them—nor take aim with their rifles and shoot at the Rebels approaching the lip of the crater.

Throughout the morning, the 25th North Carolina and surviving South Carolinians resisted the main Federal attempts to break through their tentative stopgap position. Corporal Hartgrove and Private Edmunston were right there in the thick of things, barely holding the line and preventing the bluecoats from swarming into Petersburg. Toward mid-day, a reinforcing Georgia brigade along with the rest of Ransom's Brigade finally hurried to the scene to join them. Soon thereafter, a Rebel counterattack was launched to take back the original exploded works.

The troops of the 25th North Carolina were in the van, leading this attack and dashing down the ridge that they had tenaciously held all morning. Reaching the bottom, they did not stop there but continued to hustle on the double-quick up a short rise to the very brink of the deep crater. From the precarious vantage point along the rim, the North Carolinians gazed down at the huddled and confused masses of Yanks crowded into the hole. Rufus and Hack, extremely tired from the morning's fighting, yet pumped full of adrenaline, could not believe the scene stretched before their eyes. Both were nervous and excited, as they cast reassuring glances at one another before turning back to the business at hand—taking back the crater.

"Fire," shouted Captain Deaver, as he stood among his Haywood Highlanders at the edge of the abyss. Almost instantly, the simultaneous roar of cracking rifles sounded out, as the Rebels blasted away Yankee lives at near point-blank range. The devastation was beyond comprehension. It was a sight that might have brought much satisfaction to Private Edmunston had he not also witnessed another most distressing scene. While stooping to reload, he saw out of the corner of his eye the captain collapsing onto the ground. Unsure and unbelieving, he hurriedly turned to look and, at once, saw that his fallen uncle's head had been partially blown away. There was no doubt about it. Burton Deaver was very conspicuously dead, and there was nothing Rufus could do about it—or could he?

Staring fiercely at his uncle's bloody remains for a few moments, Rufus was suddenly unable to contain his furious rage. He simply erupted and pointed his gun downward at another young Negro Yank and blew the boy's brains out. Then looking over toward Hack and some of the other mountaineers, he waved his arm and cried out, "Come on! Let's go in and get them sons of bitches!"

Following that fanatical entreaty, Private Edmunston lunged into the crater and slid down its sloping earthen walls. Swinging the butt of his gun wildly, he crushed the heads of Negroes with every blow. Hack was right beside him, plunging his bayonet into any coat with a blue tint he could find. Sergeant Henson and the rest of the Haywood Highlanders, not to be outdone, were hot on their heels seeking revenge for their captain's killing. And they had still more company. Taking notice of the brave mountain men descending into the depths of the crater, a good many other Confederate attackers followed suit, screaming their eerie Rebel yells as they rushed into the cauldron to join their brave brethren in battle.

Close-quarters fighting ensued within the hellish pock, and it raged on and on—forever, it seemed. Finally, the shrill notes of a Union bugle could be discerned through the frantic cries and noisy mayhem of men killing each other. It was the signal to retreat, and, at last, the bluecoats began hastily backtracking out of the bloody cauldron of death. But the Rebels did not quit. They were obliged to shoot at the backs of the fleeing Yanks—damn them tricky sons-of-bitches. When all that remained of the enemy were the heaps of dead scattered everywhere across the floor of the crater, the Confederate forces moved swiftly to re-establish the old defenses. A Southern catastrophe had been averted by the narrowest of margins, and Petersburg was saved, at least for the time being.

"Captain Blalock says that Captain's body has finally been shipped back to the Forks." Hack thought he would pass along this bit of news to a few of the Haywood Highlanders bunched up in the trench with him. A few days had elapsed since the Yankee mine had set off the battle of the crater. In that time, Lieutenant Blalock had been promoted to captain of the company to replace the fallen Burton Deaver. His men were still recovering both physically and mentally. As a matter of fact, it was a painful struggle for Corporal Hartgrove to talk due to the severe bayonet stab wound he had received. His entire upper torso was wrapped with a large dirty linen bandage, covering the deep gash.

A despondent Francis Christopher, still grieving for his brother Luther, who was lost in the fighting, responded to the news from Hack, "They wouldn't allow it fer Luther. Captain said them rail cars are scarcer than hen's teeth these days, and weren't no way the army could ship ever dead man back home."

"Reckon that don't pertain to officers though," Sergeant Henson noted, as he adjusted a sling cradling his shot-up arm.

"Well, I'll tell you what, Francis, when this here war's over, we'll jest have to come back here and get Luther," chimed in Private Edmunston. "We'll dig him up out of that hospital cemetery and take him home for a proper planting in the hills. That's what we'll have to do," Rufus offered, as if there were no qualms about it. He had been injured himself and reached up to adjust the wrapping around his head. It was not a serious wound to his forehead, but it peculiarly mirrored the one he had received at Plymouth. "Reckon this Petersburg gouge will balance out the Plymouth one right nicely," he observed out loud and to no one in particular, while gingerly patting the bandaging. "I'm going to look real purty when this here war's over." Then he thought for a moment or two about what he had just said and quickly added, "Can't complain none, don't reckon. I'm a sight better off than Burton and Luther and you boys."

That night as he and Hack were stretching out their blankets in the bottom of the trench and getting ready to bed down, Hack reached into his haversack and pulled out an envelope. "Looky here, Rufe!" he said coyly.

"Gotcha a letter, did ye?" Rufus replied, as he eyed the small envelope.

"Ain't jest any letter. Guess who it's from."

Looking into Hack's eyes, Rufus ciphered for a moment or two. As the improbable notion came to him, he reacted in disbelief, "No! It ain't so! Is it from that Yank's wife?"

A huge grin grew across Hack's face as he nodded his head up and down. "Sure 'nuff is. Harriet wrote me back to that hunderd-day man—'member?"

Rufus could not believe his ears. "How'd ye get the letter then?"

"That hunderd-day Yank passed it to one of our men on picket duty—one of the 49th boys—and he come over and looked me up today and give it to me. Ain't that something?"

It truly was something—Hack's Yankee postal service was. And Rufus was duly impressed with his friend's initiative and resourcefulness. "You're really something else, Hartgrove, you really are. So what did she allow? Did she write you some purty words?"

"Purty 'nuff, I reckon. Want me to read ye some?"

Rufus was extremely curious about what the dead Yank's wife might have written to his friend, and he eagerly answered, "You bet I do! Lay them purty words on me, Hat."

"Okay, then, I'll read ye what she said." And Hack opened up the letter and began to read aloud.

Dear Mr. Hack Hartgrove,

Your kind letter is in hand and you cannot imagine my surprise and pleasure at receiving another letter from you. Elizabeth and I are getting along about as well as possible considering our Christmas tragedy more than twenty months past now. Elizabeth, or Beth as we have grown accustomed to calling her, is my daughter. She's not quite two years old yet and regrettably Elliot never had the opportunity to meet her. Just when I went into confinement he and his regiment were rushed off to the war. He would be so proud of Beth.

We have moved back in with my family and I'm doing seamstress work to help support us. Father is a wheelwright and our family is so large that it's difficult for us to get by during this awful war. Everything is so scarce and expensive here in Massachusetts that I don't know what we will do if it continues like this much longer. But enough about that. When you write to me next time, if you feel so inclined, you must tell me more about yourself. Please give me your particulars so that I will have a better knowledge of who my mysterious Reb correspondent is.

I do feel lonely, Hack. You asked if I am lonely, and the fact that Elliot is gone has left me feeling very lonely. I don't know what I would do if it were not for Beth. So if you would like to befriend me and Beth then we would consider it an honor to have you as our correspondent friend. You were so kind and comforting to Elliot in his last moments that I'm confident you must be a good person. One of these days if circumstances and God allow it, maybe you could even venture up into 'Yankee land' and pay us a visit.

Thank you for writing to me again and I very much look forward to another letter from you, Hack Hartgrove. For now however I must close and hope that somehow, someway this letter will find its way through the war front in Virginia and into your kind and considerate hands.
I am affectionately yours,
Harriet Ames

As Hack read the last "affectionately yours" part, he looked up at Rufus, who was lost in intense reflection on Harriet's words and message. Rufus was astounded and told Hack so. "Them's right purty words all right. Harriet seems to be a good person, even if she is a Yank. She's got a daughter, huh?"

"Appears so. She's almost two years old. Harriet wants to hear my particulars, whatever that means. I was thinking about going into Petersburg and getting one of them tintype likenesses made, so I can send it to her. That should be particular enough, wouldn't ye think, Rufe?"

Rufus thought it would. "Yep, I'd think after she sees that likeness of yours, she ought to be skeered off real good and not care fer any more particulars." With that point made, he broke out into boisterous laughing, as Hack grabbed Rufus's blanket and threw it at him.

"Real funny—ye're a real jack-ass, Edmunston!"

They talked some more about what particulars should be revealed to Harriet and about Hack's efficient Yankee postal courier service. Hack reckoned the odds were still pretty good that he could get another letter through to her, once he had his likeness made. However, just before dropping off to sleep, the tone of their conversation turned to an even more complicated matter.

"Hack, I can't get them Yanks' faces out of my mind—the ones I kilt. It's like they're trying to haunt me or something," Rufus suddenly confessed.

"What—them darkeys' faces?"

"Reckon it's them—and the regular boys too. I can still see the looks in their eyes jest before they died. They were skeered to death. Hell, I was too!"

"You were skeered? Well, I was sure skeered, but I didn't figger you fer being skeered." Hack felt a bit of relief come over him. Terror had racked his soul as he began to fight for his life during the recent crater fighting. But all sense of fear and danger had vanished with the sights and sounds and smells of war—men killing each other and trying to kill him. Instead, an inner fortitude and blind obsession had taken over, and he had battled like a savage warrior, resolved to kill anyone or anything in his path that moved.

"Yep—sure 'nuff was," Rufus responded. "But then, you jest forget 'bout everything and try not to get yourself killed. Leastwise, I forget and seems like I turn into someone else. Or, I ain't the same person, don't seem like. I become possessed with—with a fierceness, say—or with the soul of a crusading knight—or a Roman gladiator. Ahhh, hell, I don't know how to explain it. You understand what I'm saying, don't you, Hack? I jest lose my skeerdness, I reckon."

"Same here. I'm jest happy to know I ain't the only one with cowardly feelings sometimes. Them faces that's haunting ye, I 'spect they'll go away with time. Reckon?"

"I sure 'nuff hope so, 'cause I ain't been sleeping too good. 'Sides that, I still ain't heard a word from Emma. Here you are sending and receiving letters right and left from Yankee land, to a girl you don't even know, and I don't get nary one atall from Emma at Plymouth. I've mailed her three letters and ain't got nothing back. I can't figger it out."

Hack tried to console him. "She's probably writ to ye a dozen times, Rufe, but the letters got miscarried somehows. It's only been what—two months since ye left her?"

"'Bout that. I ought to use yer Yankee postal service. It's a damn-sight more reliable than our Confederate mail, and faster too! Hat's Yankee Express is what I'm going to use next time. Yessir, I reckon I will." Rufus stopped at that point and cast a quirky smile at his companion. Hack flashed one back at him, just as another Yank mortar round could be heard incoming.

Chapter 24

Yankee Eggnog

At Petersburg, the trench warfare settled into a routine that would endure the remaining five months of the year and extend into the early spring of 1865. Without respite, the Yankee mortars and cannons fired hundreds of rounds daily into the Confederate defensive trenches. Most of these shots were extremely effective in producing the intended carnage and terror within the Rebel defenses. Also, sharpshooters on each side continued to exchange deadly rifle fire across the narrow no-man's land between the lines. And Lincoln's bulldog general, Grant, constantly launched random attacks against the Rebel lines and relentlessly worked to break the crucial railroads servicing Petersburg.

As the months wore on, the number of Confederate troops in the trenches dwindled at an increasing and alarming rate. This harsh reality was attributable to several factors outside the many men killed and wounded by the Union artillery bombardments and Yankee sharpshooters. The living conditions were so horrific in the burrowed ditches and food so scarce the men were increasingly perishing from disease, hunger, and exposure to the elements. And, alarmingly, desertion from the ranks was still rife and growing. Taken all together, this overall attrition rate was bringing ruin to the Confederate Army.

Those poor souls living in the Petersburg saps—whether dressed in blue Federal uniforms or drab-colored Rebel rags—somehow found the will and way to survive. They resisted the temptations to flee to their homes and learned how to keep their heads down and stay out of harm's way when the war storms hit. Amazingly, between the blue and gray soldiers at the forward picket positions, a camaraderie of sorts developed at certain times. The pickets would occasionally agree to an informal truce at night and meet in the no-man's land to exchange stories, swap personal treasures, share tobacco, play games, and, on rare occasions, even exchange letters to be posted. Of course, fraternizing with the enemy was contradictory to the strict regulations and orders on both sides, but the men did it anyway. There was not a whole lot to lose at this point in the war.

The blistering hot summer days passed slowly for the miserable Rebels holed up in front of Petersburg. Eventually though, the cool crispness of autumn enveloped the scarred red earthworks, and then this comfortable coolness ultimately gave way to frigid winter temperatures, accompanied by freezing rain, snow, and ice. By Christmas, the number of Haywood Highlanders who manned the trenches had plummeted to a mere eighteen, as compared to the one hundred and few names that filled the roster at the beginning of the war.

Private Edmunston and Corporal Hartgrove were still among those loyal, pitiful souls serving, and on the night before Christmas they had been ordered to the picket line for hazardous guard duty, along with several other men from their regiment. Posted out in advance of the main defenses, the pair of buddies stood a lonely vigil for any tricky Yankee incursions that might be hatched.

"You hear anything from Harriet lately?" Rufus asked Hack as they peered over the trench walls into the dark night.

"Not in the last month or so. I tolt you, didn't I, she tacked my likeness over her and Beth's bed. She said they look at it every night and talk about their correspondent friend as they go to sleep."

"Yep, I believe I heard that before. She still looking fer you to come up there and visit her after the war is over, is she?" Rufus could not get over the fact that his friend was still planning this venture.

"Reckon so. She's invited me to do it in all four letters from her. Wonder what she and Beth are doing right now?"

"Reckon they'd be waiting for Saint Nicholas, like we used to. I'll bet Mother and the girls have the Den all spruced up with greenery and such. Sure would like to see 'em—Father, too. Hope they'll all have a merry Christmas—everybody at the ol' Den." As Rufus expressed this wish for his family, a strong longing for home came over him. Then his thoughts made a sudden detour from the western mountains to the watery eastern shores of North Carolina. "Emma, too—I hope she has a happy Christmas," he said as his eyes began to tear up.

"Something strange 'bout her going on, Rufe. She tolt ye she would be waiting on ye after the war and all. But she ain't even writ to you a single time. I don't know what to think 'bout that atall."

"I still love her, Hack, and it ain't right fer you to get all suspicious-like 'bout it," Rufus retorted strongly, after taking offense at Hack's innocent comments. "She told me she would wait fer me, and I believe her. Jest you wait and see!"

"Sorry, Rufe—I didn't mean to get ye all riled up—sure didn't mean anything bad about Emma. Jest can't figger out why she ain't writ to you is all I meant."

"There's a good reason fer it. You'll see. That's all I can say 'bout it. She'll be there fer me. I know she will."

In an effort to lighten the mood, Hack mused, "Looks like, after this here war, ye'll be heading off to Plymouth to get yer girl, and I'll be off to Yankee land to see Harriet. That is, if we make it out alive."

Then all of a sudden, they were surprised by a hushed voice intruding from the other side of the no-man's land, "Pssst—hey—sesh—are you there?" "Sesh" was short for secessionist and was a term the Yankees commonly used when referring to their Rebel foes, oft-times derisively.

Rufus and Hack looked at each other in silence, worried that the Yankees were up to something. After that mine trick, nothing could be put past the conniving bastards.

"Are you there, sesh? Merry Christmas!"

Finally Hack lobbed a reply back, "Yep, we're over here! Merry Christmas to you and yours, Yank!"

Again there was quietness for a minute or two and then, "When you going to give up, sesh? My hundred days is up in a week. Get to go back to Wisconsin to my wife."

Hack hesitated and then replied, "Good fer you, Yank! Too bad we didn't get ye first. May even get ye yet—ain't no giving up on this side, ye can count on it!"

The hidden Union soldier was quiet again for a few long moments, and then rejoined, "Doubt you'll get me, sesh. Ain't going to give you a chance. Say, we've got some eggnog over here. Want some?"

Suddenly, Hack and Rufus's suspicions were raised even higher. Assured that it was some kind of underhanded ruse, they remained alert and quiet. After a minute or two, the enemy soldier piped up again.

"What's the matter, sesh? Don't like eggnog? They do have eggnog down there in sesh country, don't they?"

Hack could not resist replying. "Yep, I've heared of eggnog. What kind of trick ye got up yer sleeve this time, Yank?"

"Ain't no trick, sesh! Just feeling the Christmas spirit is all. Wanted to share some eggnog with you and the other pickets holed up over there."

Hack and Rufus were still leery of this Yankee and his seemingly good intentions. But eventually Hack's curiosity got the best of him and he decided to take the risk. *Hell, what do I have to lose?* he ciphered. *Probably going to get killed before this damn war's over, anyhow.* Speaking up just loud enough so the enemy picket could hear him, Hack answered back, "I'll meet ye between the lines, Yank. I've got something fer you, too!"

"Okay, sesh. I'm coming. No guns—understood?"

"Understood."

"Are you crazy, you fool? Yer going to get yerself killed fer sure. Don't go out there, Hack!" Rufus admonished.

"Naahh, I'll be okay. Don't sound like a tricky Yank to me, no how," Hack assured his worried friend.

"Damn it, Hartgrove—now you be careful, you hear. He's a Yankee and could be laying fer you. I won't be able to see you atall, so holler if you need some help."

"Right—I will, Rufe." And then without further forethought or consideration, Hack crawled out of the trench and slowly worked his way through a gap in the snarled timber abatis to meet the Yank.

"Hello, Yank. Merry Christmas," Hack allowed after a lengthy crawl and finally meeting up with the bluecoat, brimming with the Christmas spirit.

"Merry Christmas, sesh," the Yankee replied with a big grin. He offered his hand and Hack grasped it, and they had a stout shake.

"Brung ye this twist of 'bacco ye might like," Hack said handing it over to the young Yankee. He was just a boy, probably no older than Hack. But he was good-sized, and his bare head revealed a shock of lengthy dark hair. Unlike Hack though, who was barefooted and whose ill-fitting pants and coat were in tatters, the Union soldier's uniform and heavy woolen coat were immaculate. Plus he had on a fine pair of shiny black boots.

"Thanks, sesh! Here—take a swig of this eggnog from my canteen and tell me if you like it."

Hack took the canteen, un-stoppered it, and guzzled down a mouthful of the holiday concoction. It was absolutely delicious, given Hack's reaction. "Ummm—that's good—gooder than good! Much obliged, Yank!"

"John—you can call me John."

"Okay, thanks, John. And ye can call me Hack. 'Preciate yer friendliness and the drink."

"It's nothing, Hack. It's Christmas, ain't it? Here—take the whole damn canteen back with you and share it with the others, why don't you. There's still a good bit in there."

"Well, ain't that mighty neighborly of ye?" said the surprised Hack. And with that, the two new acquaintances proceeded to chat for the next fifteen minutes or so in the no-man's land. All the while, Rufus was worried sick about Hack. Finally, the corporal slithered back over the rim of their hole, breathing heavily and clinging to the canteen the Yank had given him. He at once held the container up to his best friend and made him an offering of eggnog.

"Looky, Rufe! I brought us some eggnog. And looky here," he said, as he pointed down to the fine pair of over-sized black boots on his feet. "John jest up and give 'em to me! Said he could get another pair where these come from."

It is very likely that Hack and Rufus, out of the thousands upon thousands of miserable Rebel soldiers on the front lines defending Petersburg, were the only two to partake in a round of eggnog drink that Christmas. As they swilled down the contents of the canteen, the young men gave each other satisfied looks. They were thankful for the treat and, most of all, thankful to be alive.

"Merry Christmas, Hat!"

"Merry Christmas yerself, Rufe!"

That same Christmas Eve's night, the Edmunston family, less Rufus, was gathered around the burning Yule log, laughing and singing and relishing each other's company. Rufus had surmised correctly that the Den would be decked to the hilt in evergreen decorations. Julia and her teenage daughters, Mary and Emily, had seen to it. Hemlock cuttings dangled from every nook and knob that a piece of yarn could be lashed to. And with Lark and Jesse's help, Basil had chopped down a jack pine and propped it up for their Christmas tree.

As usual, the girls had fashioned a vast variety of bows and ornaments, and these were hung expertly on the drooping, scraggly boughs. Their father, standing wobbly on his wooden leg as both giggling girls and Julia steadied him, had fixed a burning candle just under the large paper-mache star that topped the tree. In the dim darkness of the cabin, lit only by the hearth fire and the illuminated Star of Bethlehem, the Edmunstons sang joyfully from a book of carols while Emily rang a little bell. Undoubtedly, there were visions of Saint Nicholas and gifts running through the teen girls' heads as they rung in Christmas on the East Fork River. Not so for the elder Edmunstons however, whose somber thoughts were of Rufus and the perils and hardships he surely must be enduring. Perhaps this symbolic star they had so prominently displayed might guide their son back to them.

Master Basil had given the slaves two days off for the Christmas holiday, as was his custom. So earlier that day, the entire band had congregated at Lark and Delia's tiny cabin to enjoy a Christmas Eve feast. A couple of wild turkeys had been roasted and gobbled up, along with a large bacon ham. Although vegetables were commonly in short supply during the mountain winters, large batches of sweet potatoes and leather-britches beans had been cooked up and devoured with great pleasure. Borrowing from their precious dried stashes, Delia had baked apple and peach pies that were barely cooled before filling the slaves' engorged stomachs. This fare was by far the grandest and most delicious of the year.

Later that evening, Jesse sat with his parents and several younger siblings before their burning Yule log, savoring the fine meal they had enjoyed earlier and exchanging holiday notions.

"Not a gooder time to celebrate da birth of baby Jesus den tonight is," Lark offered between puffs on the corncob pipe he held in his mouth. "Massa Basil says da baby Jesus was born in a manger, jest like we has in da barn. Dat is something—don't you's thinks? Baby Jesus be's born in a manger—Lordy, oh Lordy!"

Delia was not too sure she understood about this manger or where it was located at the Den. "What you's mean by 'manger,' Lark? Where 'bouts is dey a manger?"

"Over dare where da barn be's, Delia," a patient Lark explained. "Dare where we feed hay and shucks to da cows and horses. That be's da manger."

"So you's says da baby Jesus be's born in da barn, dat what you's says?" Delia asked.

"Dat be's it—dat be's what I says, Delia," replied an exceedingly contented Lark, satisfied to have clarified the important matter for his wife. Then he went a step further with the story. "Jesus wus jest uh baby when He be's born in dat manger. And Massa Basil says to me, dare be's three kings comes visiting with Jesus in dat manger. Jest uh baby and dare be's three kings comes round visiting. Dat is something—Lordy me!"

One of the younger girls chimed in, "Emily says dat a giant star 'bove the manger showed the kings whur'bouts to find da baby Jesus."

With that additional information, Lark's eyes widened and lit up. He looked over toward Delia and reminded her of a star they once had followed. "Hear dat, Delia? 'Member dat North Star we follows dat time? We follows it all da way to Virginee to get our freedom—'member how we's gots caught up by da mean men and dogs?"

Certainly Delia remembered. It was almost twenty years ago when they ran away from their masters in hopes of getting married. That adventure was permanently seared into her mind. How could she not remember? "I 'member fo' sure," she responded to her husband.

Jesse had heard enough of the story about the baby Jesus. His father's mention of freedom stirred him to ask, "Pa, this here war be 'bouts over with, I hear, and those Yankees be winning. What do Massa Basil says 'bouts us being free slaves?"

Basil had just recently discussed the issue with Lark, so he was able to shine some light on the subject for his son. "Massa says he will 'mancipates us just as President Lincoln says to do's. He says it will be up's to us if we stays here at da Den, or moves to some other place else to live."

Jesse knew what he would do but was not sure about his father's intentions. "You's wants to stay here or go on?"

Lark looked at the other children, who were not paying much attention, and then to Delia, "We not decides 'bout dat yet, Jesse. Massa Basil, he be's real good to us—he saves my life and takes us back after we's runs away. We's will see."

Jesse, who figured to stay on at the Den himself, offered, "I want to stay here and work with Rufus—if you's will allows me to—and Massa Basil." He missed Rufus—and Hack too, for that matter. On this special evening, when the story of Jesus's birth was being shared and his family's freedom discussed, Jesse's thoughts turned to his good friend. He had not heard from Rufus in some while, and hoped that his master friend was alive and well, and enjoying as fine a Christmas as they were having here at the Den. One day, things would get back to normal again. Then the two of them would inevitably take on the East Fork farming burdens—and deal with the likes of Amos Bugg.

Further up the East Fork River on the Crab Orchard property, a less spirited and smaller holiday gathering was underway. The Bee Woman was sitting in front of the fire, pulling on her own corncob pipe and humming the catchy new holiday tune *One-Horse Open Sleigh*. There was no Christmas tree crowding the cabin's sparse confines, but a garland of greenery hung from the mantle and a few sprigs of mistletoe dangled from overhead rafter poles. When the door opened abruptly, she looked up from her knitting work at the miller Mann, lugging in a load of firewood.

"Wheww—it's sure 'nuff cold out, Folsom!"

"Ye need some help, Horace?" said the Bee Woman, as she jumped up from her rocker and moved to close the door.

"Thank'ee fer that," said the freezing miller, hurriedly dropping the wood on the dirt floor next to the fireplace. Then, while breathing heavily and brushing the residue and splinters off his clothes, he continued, "That ought to last us a spell. Don't ye reckon?"

"Well, I reckon it might, Mister Miller," replied the Bee Woman mischievously. She then walked over to him and offered, "Seeing how ye're working so hard fer us and that ye're standing plumb under that there clump of mistletoe, I might jest give ye a kiss. What ye allow 'bout that, Horace?"

"I reckon I might jest take ye up on that there offer, Folsom!" And with the miller's wholehearted approval, they met in a tender embrace, as if a couple of decades had mysteriously gone missing from both of their lives. Not counting the Christmas before last—the one that Rufus had chaperoned—this was their second Christmas together and the first as man and wife. They had just been married the previous fall, during the crush in milling work, and had not yet sorted out their personal living arrangements. For the time being, both seemed content with being together at the Orchard on the Sabbaths when the mill was shut down.

A possum hid out in a dark corner and warily eyed the kissing couple. Oblivious to the passion and joy these two humans were sharing, it simply backed clean behind the butter churn to hide from all the commotion. Admittedly, the love and fond feelings these two humans had discovered and slowly nurtured had been unexpected. Neighbors were incredulous that the Bee Woman would have anybody atall in her life—except for her bees and varmints, that is. And certainly no one could have expected the miller, a respected and sound man suffering yet another terrible personal tragedy in his life, to succumb to the strange allure of the Bee Woman. It was an extraordinary partnership indeed, but it was authentic, and it was one they both were now entirely committed to.

After a brief spell, the Bee Woman and the miller slowly broke out of the passionate hug beneath the mistletoe and found their eyes fixed and staring into each other's inner souls. It went unsaid that they were glad to be together on this hallowed evening, one infused with the spirit of the Lord's birth and the specter of a bearded saint delivering gifts in the middle of the night. Breaking the trance at last, the miller was the first to speak.

"Merry Christmas, my dear Folsom."

"Happy Christmas, Horace. I'm mighty partial to ye, sir."

Chapter 25

Drama on Hare's Hill

The Petersburg stalemate drug on into the New Year of 1865, as another great Union Army marched through the deep South and ravaged the countryside at will. General Sherman's troops, after seizing and burning Atlanta, had turned toward the Atlantic Coast and plundered and pillaged the Southern farms and towns in a large swath to the sea. After capturing the coveted Confederate port city of Savannah, Georgia, Sherman had boastfully presented the city, via telegram, to President Lincoln as a Christmas present. Afterward, he continued to wage his scorched-earth campaign, directing it into the Carolinas. The able general speedily drove his troops northward with the strategic objective of uniting with General Grant in Virginia. When that happened— and it was only a matter of time—the combined Federal armies would destroy Lee's deteriorating, yet still dangerous, Army of Northern Virginia once and for all.

It was plain to the fighting soldiers and civilians alike—in the North and South—that a link-up of Sherman and Grant was inevitable. Whenever that came about, the fire of rebellion would undoubtedly be extinguished, and the so-called Southern Cause lost forever. Many thousands of once-loyal Rebel soldiers now perceived hopelessness in their purpose and deemed a continuation of the fight against such vastly superior Yankee forces as utterly senseless. So vast hordes of worn-out Rebels simply threw down their weapons and fled from the front lines. The secluded North Carolina mountains remained a haven for the worst sort of men evading the Confederate authorities, and gangs of these outlaws—like the Bugg gang—remained at large, roaming the countryside and preying on the weak.

Amos Bugg and his clan of ruthless foragers had lain low for several months after the raid on the Deaver homestead. Killing Maggie Deaver and her son Burton's family had not been a notion of genius, Bugg had concluded. His name had been tied to the Deaver murders by the last-minute confession of the condemned deserter Pinckney Queen. Consequently, there were months on end when posses of lawmen, civilians, and Confederate Home Guard troops combed the Haywood mountains searching for Bugg and his band. The Haywood country literally crawled with Bugg hunters, becoming so hot and dangerous that Bugg absconded to neighboring counties, where pillaging opportunities still abounded. In the relatively safe and fertile counties of Henderson and Transylvania, the scoundrels continued their nocturnal raiding and robbing ways, while always seeking safe refuge in the wilds along the Green River at the South Carolina border. It seemed no one was immune to the Bugg atrocities. Rich and poor alike found themselves targets of the plundering and murdering gang of thieves.

At Forks of Pigeon, a particularly harsh winter was coming to an end. Although the March blasts of cold air still howled out of the mountains, spring was only a week away. Mountain dogwoods and wild crabapple trees would soon light up the leafless forests with their refreshing blooms. But this particular day was dreary and cold, and the Edmunston family had journeyed down to pay their respects at the community cemetery, located just across the river opposite Deaver's Store. Basil and Julia, along with their two lovely daughters, Mary and Emily, stood in silence in front of a long row of new tombstones, all bearing the name "Deaver" etched boldly into the hard rock.

Patriarch Colonel Deaver rested under one grave marker, he being the victim of heart failure after falling through the river ice during Rufus's skating exhibition. Lying at his side was the matriarch, Maggie, who had been brutally murdered by Amos Bugg. Interred next to his parents, Burton Deaver, killed by the Yankees at Petersburg, lay in honorable peace. And next to him were buried the remains of his wife and four children, all horribly burned to death by the Bugg gang. Julia gazed at the graves and reflected on the lives of these deceased loved ones who had meant so much to her.

Certainly the war had been hard on everyone, but she carried an unusually large and heavy burden. Standing next to her was additional proof of that truth. The one-legged Basil, his severe handicap also courtesy of the war, reverently stared down at the markers and then to the cold mountains in the distance. He wondered how Rufus was doing and, of all things, whether one day they would be standing over his cold grave. Good thing Julia distracted Basil from such sober rumination and brought him back to the world of the living.

"Basil, why don't they just surrender and get it over with? There's no need to continue all the suffering and dying," an exasperated Julia vented, as she continued to look upon the graves of her family members and Emily clung close at her side.

"Going have to soon, I expect. Those boys up there in Petersburg, where Rufus is holed up, can't hold out much longer. Grant's cut the railroads and has General Lee bottled up. Won't be very long before he just up and corks the bottle."

Basil knew this because both he and Columbus Hartgrove stayed fairly well abreast of the war news, especially from the Virginia front where their sons were yet fighting it out. Columbus, who continued to manage the store and mill businesses for Julia and her remaining siblings, was privy to the latest newspaper reports, news out of Asheville, and plain old hearsay from his customers. Whenever a rare letter was received at the store from one of the remaining Haywood Highlanders still fighting—only nine were left in the Petersburg trenches, he was customarily enlightened as to its contents. And Basil was usually the first to hear the pertinent tidbits related to the war and their sons' welfare.

"Then they should surrender before Rufus or anybody else gets killed, shouldn't they?" Julia asked in frustration.

"You'd think they would, dear," Basil answered patiently before going on. "The South has shot its wad, and there's not one Confederate port left open to get in war supplies. I truly don't believe it will be long before we see Rufus trotting up the river road, coming home."

"That would be a sight for sore eyes!"

They stood over the graves a while longer before Mary broke the quiet. "That old mean Bugg man—why don't they catch him and hang him for what he did?" She looked at her mother and then father and waited for either of their responses. Then after an extended spell of quietness with nary a word offered in reply, she asked again, "Hello! Did you not hear me? That old mean Bugg man is still on the loose, right?"

Since the sore subject was not about to go away, Basil was compelled to reply, "He's still out there somewhere, Mary. But he's not been marauding in Haywood in the last year or so—maybe longer—since your grandmother... well, it's probably too hot for him around this country, and he's moved on for good. We won't be seeing him hereabouts again."

At least, Basil figured Bugg would not show his hide nor white hair in Haywood again. He would sure be a fool if he did. It pained him to think that if he only had been a whole man—had two good legs—then he would never have let up riding and searching for Bugg until the outlaw was apprehended. But it had been so terribly difficult on him, riding all day long, for days on end, with the prosthetic leg. He still bore the shame of having to explain to Julia that he was not fit or able to continue riding with the search posses. Although Julia had certainly been sympathetic and understanding, it still had been a bitter and humiliating thing for him to confess.

"Okay now, who wants to go see Mr. Hartgrove?" Julia teased, as she turned and headed toward the buggy.

A laughing cheer broke out across the solemn graveyard, as the girls raced by their mother toward the wagon, eager to visit the store. And their father limped along behind, doing his best to keep up.

By late March, General Lee's situation was grave indeed. He was well aware of Grant and Sherman's intentions of joining their armies to destroy his own. At that time, he counted about 25,000 Rebels at his disposal, who were reasonably capable of putting up a fight. That hardly matched the

100,000 blue-coated, well-armed, and well-fed Yankees that opposed him. It was a desperate time for the Confederacy, and the beleaguered General Lee finally decided it was time for desperate measures. Recognizing that Petersburg was already lost, he devised a scheme that could potentially throw the Yanks off balance and give his Army of Northern Virginia—what little there was left of it—a chance to escape from Petersburg and Grant's bulldog clutches. On this very evening, his officers were disseminating the details and various aspects of the audacious plan to the troops.

"Okay, come on in here and listen up, men," ordered Captain Blalock to his tiny company of Haywood Highlanders. Besides the captain, there were only eight of them left, including Rufus, Hack, Sergeant Henson, and Francis Christopher. "Tonight at one o'clock, our regiment's going to participate in a big attack. Ransom's Brigade is going to attack that hill over yonder—Hare's Hill," he said pointing in the direction of an enemy fortification directly in front of them. The captain paused for a moment to let the seriousness of the matter settle in on his boys before continuing. "I need a couple of volunteers to go in with Colonel Rutledge and capture them Yanks' fort—understood?"

Displaying no emotions, his sullen, barefooted warriors—their feet were wrapped in strips of woolen and linen cloth scraps, with the exception of Hat who still wore the fancy Christmas boots—just looked at him with wary eyes. They wondered whose stupid, grandiose idea this one could be. There was no way the Rebels were going to break up those strong enemy works and capture them. They knew it. So why did their generals not acknowledge such an obvious truth? But they listened anyway.

"Colonel aims on taking the fort, not attacking it. He needs a couple of volunteers fer a special unit he's assembling to sneak in and surprise the Yanks in that there fort. Now, which of ye'ens is up fer it?"

The eight soldiers looked around at each other, and nobody spoke up. They realized this war was almost over, and they had enough sense to appreciate a dangerous assignment whenever one showed its ugly head. They rightly figured if it looked like a skunk and stunk like a skunk, then it sure enough must be one. This plan had a bad smell about it, and the men wanted no part of it. In their way of ciphering, there was no need to go to extra trouble to get themselves killed. After all, this war was in its last throes, so what was the use?

Seeing that no one was going to outright volunteer for the job, the captain was left with no other choice. "So, ye want to leave it to me, do ye? Okay then—Corporal Hartgrove, you and Private Edmunston get yer gear, and let's go."

At midnight, an hour before the main Confederate attack was to be launched, Rufus and Hack found themselves crawling in the darkness between the lines through no-man's land. They were members of a special fifty-man team that Colonel Rutledge had tasked with taking and occupying the fort on Hare's Hill. On hands and knees, they sneaked and crept up to the tangles of timber abatis protecting the enemy breastworks. A rabbit might have been able to scamper through the thick woody barrier but not the skinny Rebel soldiers. So they waited for the pioneers, or ax men, to hack out paths for them to squeeze between.

"Don't ker much atall fer the colonel's plan," Hack whispered to Rufus, as they hunkered down and waited for the pioneers to finish their work.

"Me neither. Those Yank pickets are going to know we're up to something. I ain't any good at feigning, leastwise don't think I am."

"What ye going to say to 'em to make believe ye're a deserter?" queried Hack.

Rufus thought for a brief spell before responding, "Let's see now—I'll act out and tell 'em something like this, 'I give up, Yank. Take me prisoner. I can't take no more of this damn war.'" Not so sure of himself or his invented lines, he sought Hack's opinion, "So, what you think?"

"Ain't bad, Rufe. If'en I were a Yank, I reckon I'd believe ye," the corporal came back with a grin.

The pioneers worked swiftly and within just a few minutes had chopped out narrow pathways in the thickets for the men to slip through. Hurriedly, the Rebel soldiers worked their way through the clearings and stopped just short of the enemy's picket positions. As expected, the pioneers' work had been noisy and had aroused the wary Yankee pickets.

"Who's out there? We hear you! Come any closer and you're dead, sesh!" challenged one of the bluecoats.

The nervous Rebels just lay on the ground, breathing heavily. Then, one by one, they started giving themselves up, just like Rufus and Hack had practiced.

Rufus called out to a sparse group of Yank pickets in his front, "Don't shoot, Yank! I give up! I want you to take me prisoner and get me away from here."

Then Hack chimed in, "There's a bunch of us'ens want to go over to yer side. Can ye take all us'ens, Yank? We give up! Don't shoot!"

The Union pickets could hardly believe their ears. "Okay, all you seshes—drop your guns and come on out so we can see you!" hollered one of the incredulous Yanks. Immediately, twenty or more Rebel soldiers, acting like disloyal deserters, rose up off the ground and began straggling toward the enemy picket line.

"What? All of you are giving up?" asked one astonished bluecoat.

"Ain't no use going on. We all give up, Yank," one of the sly Rebels answered back.

"Watch them good, boys, and search all of them!" directed a Yankee sergeant.

There were as many Rebel deserters as there were Yank pickets. The bluecoats, convinced that this horde of sesh soldiers was actually deserting, let the entire passel of them come right into their entrenchments. While they were distracted and attempting to deal with the huge mass of traitors, the other thirty-odd Rebels—the ones that had not given up or shown themselves—swooped in and overpowered the entire Yankee corps in scant seconds. No shots were fired, and the Federal pickets were quickly disarmed and escorted back through the abatis to the Confederate lines.

With little time left before the commencement of the main attack, the lieutenant in charge of the stealthy operation quickly led his force of Rebel actors up Hare's Hill to the Union fort. In the darkness, it was a surprisingly easy matter to gain entry to the earthen citadel by posing as

Union pickets. Since no warnings or alarms had been sounded, most of the garrison manning the strong fortress were still sound asleep, including the officers. In less than twenty minutes, the entire enemy contingent was surprised, rounded up, and imprisoned in an underground shelter. And just as Colonel Rutledge had ordered, the fort had been captured—not attacked—and, amazingly, no shots had been fired. As Rufus and Hack helped move the fort's artillery pieces and redirect the big guns to the rear, they could distinctly hear the Confederate cannons beginning to roar. General Lee had obviously launched his major offensive, and on the flanks of Hare's Hill, the Rebel yells rung out, as the attacking Southern forces struck hard against the Union's fortified battle lines.

Corporal Hartgrove and Private Edmunston had never fired a cannon before, but on this night they became quick learners. Directed by one of the few artillerists the Confederate planners had thought to include in the mission, the two Highlanders loaded powder and shell into the barrel and stood back, covering their ears while the big gun exploded in fiery fury. Over and over that night, they labored at the cannon as the artillerist aimed and shot round after round in the direction of the Yankee troops. The enemy could not be seen atall, and it was unknown what effect their fire was having, but they stayed at it, anyway, until the first rays of sun broke over the horizon behind the swarming Yankee troops.

In the dawn's early light, Rufus and Hack could barely make out, through the thick haze of smoke hanging over the field, that the Confederate attack was stalled. And they soon realized that the several other forts up and down the Union line had not been captured as planned. The bluecoats still occupied those critical fortifications, as was readily apparent when the enfilading cannon and mortar fire began exploding all around their own position. But they swallowed their fears and sucked up every ounce of courage left in them to remain at their huge gun. The two Highlanders continued to service the weapon as the Confederate gunner took more careful aim and fired back at the now visible throngs of oncoming bluecoats.

But the Rebels were hopelessly outmanned and outgunned, and General Lee had no more reserve forces to stem the vast blue tide of counterattacking Yankees. Soon the streams of enemy troops began to mass all over the battlefield and push the Confederates backwards. The powerful Union guns wreaked death and destruction upon the retreating soldiers in gray. At last, Rufus and Hack tossed aside their artillery tools and made their way out of the fort with their fellow conspirators, as the shells increasingly burst all around them.

To make matters worse, the two Haywood Highlanders became separated from one another in short order, and Rufus was obliged to stop and go back to search for Hack. Thank goodness, he soon picked out his buddy amongst the confused mob. But just as he began screaming at the corporal, he witnessed the most terrible, frightening sight imaginable. A shell from a monstrous siege gun burst dangerously close to Corporal Hartgrove, and Rufus watched in horror as his best friend was hurled violently through the air by the blast's shock waves.

"Hack! Hack!" Rufus screamed. He was sure his friend was blasted to kingdom come, and he hustled back amidst the dead men and splintered timbers on the ground to see what might be left of the young corporal. Miraculously finding him in one piece, Rufus instantly dropped to his knees beside his fallen brother-in-arms, yelling out over the roars of battle, "Hack! Are ye okay?" Corporal Hartgrove was not moving.

Was he dead? Rufus worried, as he grabbed hold of Hack and shook him hard by the shoulders. But Hack remained inanimate. At that time, the Minié balls were whizzing everywhere, and the deafening explosions were close enough to easily feel their concussive blasts. *Is he alive? Move, Hack! Move!* But there was no movement or any other signs to indicate that his buddy was alive.

Come on, Hack! Move, damn you! Furiously, Rufus searched Hack's body for any vital signs to show he was not dead, but there were none. *He's dead for sure.*

Rufus sensed that he could not tarry there any longer, or he would surely get himself killed. But what should he do about Hack? He had to do something, but what? He could not very well abandon his best buddy, or could he? *Never! I've got to do something!*

As the dirt and dust and splinters showered down all around, Rufus reached under Hack and picked him up, threw him over his shoulder, and turned and ran as fast as he could go in the direction of the Confederate lines. He ran for his life, and he ran for Hack's life. He ran for Emma. He ran and ran as far as his strong legs could carry the two of them.

The menacing cannons continued to roar on both sides of the battle lines. Amongst the earsplitting explosions of artillery rounds and frantic cries and shouts of men fighting, the staccato clacking of rifle fire pierced the smoky air. Rufus looked anxiously over the battlefield to gain his bearings but saw only clouds of smoke and massed confusion. The retreating Confederate troops were barely staying ahead of the forest of waving Union banners, following close on their heels. Private Edmunston was disoriented and at a loss as to which direction to head. So he just lit out toward Petersburg with Hack draped across his shoulder. His only hope was to dodge bluecoats and find a safe haven somewhere behind the Confederate lines, if such a place existed after this fiasco.

Improbably, Rufus eluded the Union soldiers and just kept on making his way clear of the skirmishing and fighting until he broke into the clear near the outskirts of Petersburg. Pandemonium was running rampant in the city. Rebel soldiers fled through the streets, and civilians, realizing Lee's army had been routed, scampered in all directions trying to escape Grant's loosed cavalry. Seeing and sensing the mass confusion surrounding him and feeling extremely ill at ease with the deteriorating situation, Rufus did not linger for very long in Petersburg.

He found the railroad leading west, away from the city, and decided to follow it and take his chances. For more than an hour, he pursued the iron rails as far as his weary body could physically tote Hack. Finally, due to sheer exhaustion and dehydration, he trudged off the railway grade and collapsed heavily onto the ground, barely able to cushion Hack's fall.

At that point, Rufus knew his friend was alive. He had heard Hack's moans and felt his flinches as they had fled down the tracks. After catching his breath somewhat, he picked Hack up once again and moved him a safe distance away from the railroad, into a small thicket of pine trees. Stooping to his knees, he gingerly laid Hack down on the pine straw and then crumpled down beside him, grunting in relief and overcome with fatigue.

After taking several minutes to recover, Rufus scouted around and found some water in a nearby creek. Carrying the cool water in his cupped hands, he splashed it over Hack's soot-stained face and watched intently to see the reaction. At first, there was a slight twitch. Then, he watched as his buddy slowly blinked both eyes. Quickly, he flung more water on Hack's face. Directly, a low moaning sound could be heard accompanied with these faint uttered words, "What? What is this? Where—where am I?" Hack's eyes barely cracked open for an instant before shutting again.

Greatly relieved, Rufus moved to where his face was only a breath away from his buddy's and spoke. "You're with me, Hack. It's Rufus. It's me, Rufus." While waiting for a response, he scanned over Hack's body real good and could see no terrible shrapnel wounds or evidence of profuse bleeding.

"Rufe—Rufus—what—what happened?" Hack mumbled in a low raspy voice as his eyes opened slightly.

"You got yerself blown up, that's what you did! Where you hurting, Hack?"

"My head—the back of my head hurts somethin' terrible."

"Let's see now," replied Rufus as he gingerly helped Hack turn his head for an inspection. There were no holes or blood oozing out of it—that was always a good sign. Rufus detected what appeared to be an ugly abrasion behind Hack's ear. His first suspicion was that Hack might have suffered a hard knock to the head, as he tumbled to the ground in free fall following the explosion. He could have easily hit it against a rock or even a timber, but there was no sure way of telling. "Don't see nothin' that looks too bad, Hack."

"Well, it ought to look bad—bad as it feels. Can ye give me some more of that water, Rufe?" Hack whispered, as he strained to raise his head up off the ground.

Both Corporal Hartgrove and Private Edmunston drank their fill of cold creek water and rested in the shade of the pine trees. By nightfall, the corporal was able to get up on his feet and slowly amble around in the little woody copse. He was indeed fortunate not to have been hit by flying shell fragments. Actually, they were both extremely lucky in that regard. A bad headache was all the reward Hack picked up from the dangerous explosion, not counting the free lift on Rufus's wide shoulders out of harm's way. That night, while recounting the Confederate debacle and assessing the precarious predicament they found themselves in, the two Rebels made a thoroughly thought-out decision.

Believing the Army of Northern Virginia had been destroyed, they decided to head back to the Haywood mountains. It would have surprised them both to know General Lee had not lost his defeated army and would somehow manage to hold out for two more weeks before finally surrendering to Grant. But even if given that glimpse into the future, it would not have mattered to them. They had given their due—and more—to the Confederacy, and it had been to no avail. The two Highlanders were fed up with the damned war and wanted to go home and see their families. After that, they definitely planned to venture off and find their girls.

Chapter 26

In a Pig's Sty

Early spring had arrived, yet the wintry winds still blew up the East Fork River. Jesse was forced to pull a quilted blanket over his head to keep the cool air from freezing his ears off. The bed of straw he had piled and fluffed up was comfortable enough, but the crispy cold night breezes, whistling between the logs, were a little too chilly for comfort. It was such a crazy sentimental notion that drove him to sleep in the barn that evening. One of the Edmunston's work mules that Jesse had become attached to over the years was on its last legs. Actually, the animal was lying on its side, not very far away from Jesse, and its labored breathing was so pronounced and noisy that the young slave could not sleep atall. Lark had warned his son that ol' Jim probably would not make it through the night. So Jesse had decided to keep Jim company and, if need be, put the animal down if its suffering became intolerable.

Just as the sleepless African figured the time for merciful action might have arrived, he was startled by a strange commotion outside. Barking dogs and loud raucous noises shattered the usual nighttime tranquility. The distinctive sounds of horses on the move and men's raised, excited voices were unmistakable. This was a highly unusual occurrence, and Jesse was disturbed as to the meaning of the nocturnal disturbance. He jumped up from his straw bed and moved quickly to the barn wall. A gap between the logs was wide enough to peek through, and he strained to see out into the yard. What he saw was downright frightening.

Men—many men—on horseback carrying blazing torches were riding and surrounding the Den's main cabin and the slaves' shabbier quarters. However, the scariest part for Jesse was what he saw in the torchlight. The night riders' faces were hidden under black hoods, giving them the appearance of wicked ghouls. Right away, he ciphered the probable identity and purpose of this band of riders. He reckoned this was surely that outlaw Bugg gang. Bugg was an old nemesis of his—and Rufus's too—and he had heard tell that the mean old white-headed man had taken to marauding and thieving and killing. But he never dreamed Bugg would be so audacious as to attack the Den. Instinctively, he thought of Rufus and wished he were there, so they could both do something to stop Bugg.

It was an astute guess because, as it turned out, Jesse was correct. With the war waning drastically and the outcome all but assured, Amos Bugg had decided to make one more raiding swath through Haywood, before heading to the wilder west. There was too much uncertainty in the near future for the Southern states—freedom and welfare of the slaves, establishment of new local and state governments, financial retributions, a failing local economy, stepped-up law enforcement, and so forth. Bugg wanted no part of it. For certain, his chances of eluding the authorities and the hangman's noose would be much greater in the unsettled country west of the Mississippi.

Nevertheless, Bugg allowed that another month or so of plundering in the North Carolina mountains might suit his purposes well before moving on westward. He had waited a long time to get back at the Edmunstons, whose slights he had endured over the years. There was no way he could leave the Carolina highlands without paying back an old debt he owed—or rid himself of an annoying itch, so to speak. Tonight would be his last chance to do so.

Basil and Julia were sleeping soundly next to each other, when they both were awakened by the terrible crashing impact of the Den's door being busted down. Before either of them could make a move, they were staring at five hooded men and looking down the barrels of at least two revolvers. These men were awfully good at what they did!

"Outta bed—now!" came an order from one them. But the mean men did not wait for the couple to obey them. Two of the raiders rushed to the side of the bedstead and roughly jerked the startled couple to their feet. Hopping on one leg, Basil vehemently objected, "Stop! Leave her alone. We'll give you what you want. Give me my crutch over there!" he insisted, pointing to the wooden prop leaning against a wall. Basil always slept without his prosthetic leg attached.

About this time, another of the robbers was shooing Mary and Emily out of their lofty bed and down the steep stairs. A large hooded raider stepped closer to Basil and asserted his obvious leadership capacity. "Ye ain't going to tell us what to do, Edmunston! Now shut yer damn mouth and do what we tell ye! Ye hear me?"

Basil did not wince or express any form of emotion atall. He just stared directly at the cold shining eyes peering out from under the black hood. Obviously, not the response the man was anticipating, he reacted hotly. "Ye son of a bitch! Go ahead and set him down and tie him up in one of them chairs!" ordered the leader. "And take them three women out yender and lash them to that big oak."

At the same time the robbers were taking care of the white folk in the main house, there were about ten other riding and whooping outlaws rounding up the slaves at their quarters. The raiders searched diligently high and low for every last African and eventually were satisfied they had collected the entire lot. One man rode back to the Den to find the key for the smokehouse lock, while the others guarded the Negroes cowering under the light of their blazing torches. The thieving ravagers peppered the slaves with vulgar insults, while at the same time touching and feeling up the women. These unscrupulous men were the worst sort. But little did they realize, there was still one slave on the loose, watching them warily through a peephole in the barn. Jesse had concealed himself real good and was not about to be discovered, if he could help it.

As soon as Julia and the girls were taken outside and bound to the oak tree, Amos Bugg stripped off his black hood and sneered evilly at Basil. "'Member me, don't ye, Edmunston?"

Basil had known who this man was well before the unveiling. With his arms penned behind him and strapped to the chair, he glared back and responded, "I know who you are, Bugg. Appears to me you've come up in the world, haven't you? You've gone from being a land squatter to being a thieving murderer now. That about the size of things—is it, Bugg?"

Bugg did not immediately answer. The sneer disappeared from his face as he stepped toward Basil, rared his arm back, and punched the insolent captive hard in the face with his fisted hand. Then Bugg just backed away and watched as Basil shook off the blow and resumed an identical posture and expression as before.

"Ain't no need to hurt ye, I don't guess, 'fore I kill ye," and then Bugg was troubled by another thought, something he had almost forgotten. So he approached Basil again and hit him solidly in the face with another hard fist punch. This one was tougher to shake off, and Bugg just glared as Basil struggled to regain his senses. "That there is fer that damn son of yer'en. It's fer the beating he give me and Eli."

Bugg glanced around for Eli and quickly deduced that his son must be helping with the plundering work. Except for an accomplice who remained with Bugg to take good care of Basil, there was a guard with the women and one or two standing watch over the slaves, who had been locked up in the looted smokehouse. The rest of them were searching for plunder.

"Figured there weren't no need to keep my hood on, since it don't matter none if ye know who I am. Yes sir, we're going take good ker of ye. Ain't going be nothing ye kin do 'bout it, after we get through with ye, I don't reckon." Bugg had a big satisfied smile on his face as he teased Basil. "But don't ye worry yerself nary bit, Edmunston. We ain't going do no harm to them women folk of yer'en. It ain't my way."

Basil had no doubts his captor meant to kill him. Bugg was surely not bluffing. Evil ran deep within this man, who had killed Julia's mother and Burton's family. His hatred of Bugg was manifest, as he replied, "Mighty big of ye, Bugg, to look after the women. Can't figure out, though, why you didn't give the Deavers the same consideration. Maggie Deaver and her family—why did you kill them, for God's sake? She never wronged you."

"What—ye trying to judge me, Edmunston, or learn my thinking? Well—if ye have to know—reckon it don't matter none now, seeing how I'm going to kill ye. That ol' Deaver woman smart-mouthed me—she did. Weren't going to tolerate it—not nary bit. 'Sides that, she knowed who I was. And if that damned son-of-a-bitch Colonel hadn't got himself froze to death, I'd killed him instead, damn his hide!"

Two hooded men hurried through the door, one of whom urged Bugg on. "We're done, Amos. Ready?"

"No, we ain't ready! Ain't nary one of ye plundered this here cabin. Go ahead, ransack it and take what we need, ye hear? Go on!" Then the henchmen jumped to the work at once, pilfering and breaking and turning over everything that was not fixed down solid.

Basil tried to make their work easier. "You're not going to find any money or valuables here, Bugg. Got it locked up in the safe at the store."

Bugg just chuckled, "Makes no nevermind to me, Edmunston. Figured ye would do something tricky like that there. We're jest paying this here visit to take good ker of ye, is all." Then he turned to one of the men and queried, "Got them pigs all riled and meaned up fer Edmunston?"

"Got 'em ready, Amos. There's a bunch of 'em and some big ol' boars and sows. Eli's took a stick to 'em good and provoked 'em a sight."

That bit of news seemed to raise Amos's spirits. "Okay then, help ol' One Leg here out of his chair and give him a hand getting over to the sty. One of ye get this place ready fer the torch—and 'member, we don't set fire to it 'till we're on the horses heading fer the Shining Rock."

Julia, Mary, and Emily, who were lashed tight to the big tree in front of the Den, cried out hysterically as two hooded outlaws—one on each arm—dragged the one-legged Basil toward the barnyard. Illuminated by the torches, the whole horrific scene took on the air of a fantastic bad dream.

"Oh, Basil, where are they taking you?" Julia wailed.

Although Amos Bugg had re-donned his hood, he listened with peaked interest as one of the girls screamed, "Please, Mr. Bugg, don't hurt my father. Please don't hurt him. Please!"

So them girls think they know who I am, he thought. For a second or two, he entertained a notion of putting a bullet in all three of their pretty heads but then thought differently about it. Once word got out about this latest atrocity, the Haywood people and lawmen would recognize his work. So, it did not matter much what these womenfolk thought or knew. The heat would be on him again anyway. Besides that, he was about to kill the young girls' father and reckoned he felt a strange tinge of sympathy for them.

Over at the barnyard, where the murdering thieves had escorted Basil, they all gathered anxiously around the muddy pigsty. Inside the cramped pen were at least twelve hogs, snorting and moving about in ferment, excitedly waiting for something to eat. Eli and one or two of his buddies had been beating the pigs about the head with sticks to get them in a frenzied state of agitation. They also had fed a measly portion of shelled corn to the pigs to whet their voracious appetites and prepare them for the much larger meal to come. There were all sizes of porkers in that sty, with three or four sows weighing around five hundred pounds each, and a huge boar hog that was a good two hundred pounds heavier still. These ravenous beasts were excited, they were angry, and they were hungry. They were literally frothing-mad to be fed.

"Okay, men, bring the son-of-a-bitch over here and let's throw him in there," Bugg yelled out to Basil's handlers. "Wait! Hold up—hold him right there just a minute! Well, Edmunston, guess this is it fer ye. It's what ye deserve—or it's what ye're going to git, anyhows. The next time them girls up yender lay eyes on ye they'll be looking at a pile of pig shit. That's all that'll be left of ye—pig shit! Serves ye right, though—ye and yer kind." Bugg turned his head and hocked out a huge blob of spit. Then he scowled back at Basil and nodded his head. "Okay, boys, throw him in."

Basil was restrained so harshly that he could barely move, but he was able to shout back at Bugg, just as he was tossed over the split wood railing. "He'll get you, Bugg. My boy will get you! You'll pay for this, you son of a bitch!" And then Basil landed with a loud splat in the mud, as the pigs rushed toward the hapless victim. He tried to rise up out of the thick muck, but with just the one leg it was terribly difficult to get any traction or leverage—he could not even crawl! Basil was forced to cry out in pain and cover his head and eyes, as the larger hogs attacked and bit and chewed at his fleshy parts. Intuitively, he recognized that it would be only a matter of a few minutes before his entire body was consumed.

But even Bugg did not have the stomach to watch such a gruesome scene, and he did not wait around to see the grisly end. "All right, let's go!" he ordered and in just a few moments, the plundering Bugg gang was mounted and riding away.

Through the peephole in the barn wall, Jesse could see the Den ablaze in the distance. He had seen the whole thing—the entire tragic affair. But he had not shown himself or tried to help his Master, because he had not known what to do. In fact, there was nothing that he could have done to stop the Bugg gang. However, he now saw an opportunity to do something. It was as clear as day what he had to do. Like a bolt of lightning, he jumped across poor ol' Jim—still alive and suffering—and was through the barn door in a flash. In just mere seconds, he was climbing into the pig pen to help Master Basil.

Without any sign of fear or hesitation, Jesse leaped right into the middle of the feeding frenzy, kicking and trying to pull the pigs off of his Master. As he grabbed Basil by the arm to yank him out of the sticky sloppy mud, the ferocious hogs began biting into Jesse too. But at least he was able to partially tug his bloodied master from the quagmire into a sitting position. From there Basil took hold of the fence rails, and, using his arms and good leg, started pulling himself upright so that he could stand. In the meantime, however, Jesse had gone down.

The huge boar hog had butted him off his feet and was savagely tearing into his side and stomach. Basil on the other hand seemed to be out of trouble for the time being. There were severe gashes and bite wounds across his entire body, but, fortunately, he had been able to protect his face and eyes from the greedy animals. Frantically, he kicked and crawled and pushed with the one leg and, with his powerful arms, managed to hoist himself over the top rail and out of the sty to safety. But Jesse, poor Jesse, was in dire trouble.

As the giant boar ate away at Jesse's stout upper torso, the others fought over the bony feet and legs. He tried with all his might to get out from under the bulky animals, but even with his youthful stoutness, the slave could not beat them off. They were too heavy. They were too mad. And they were too hungry. He squirmed and flailed, and they fought him back, butting and stabbing into his body with their sharp protruding tusks. The filthy swine were not about to let this delicious prize get away. Under the porkers' enormous weight, Jesse began to sink lower and lower into the muck and shit, causing the pigs to grab hold of him with their teeth and ruthlessly jerk him back out of the mire. They began tearing and ripping his black carcass apart, piece by piece, as Basil attempted to right himself and find a weapon, or anything, to beat the attacking beasts off of poor Jesse.

He hopped over to the barn on one leg, where he finally was able to locate a heavy beating stick that might work. Using it as a crutch, he hobbled back over to the sty, as fast as he could hobble, with the intention of using the big club to knock the hogs off of Jesse. Alas, Basil was too late. By the time he got back to the sty, all that remained of Jesse was a bloody mangled torso with stubby pieces of legs and arms still attached. His head had been ripped away and the large organs and muscles were being devoured by more than one rabid porker. Upon witnessing this shocking sight, Basil collapsed onto the barnyard ground and began weeping in great distress.

It had all transpired so fast. Basil wished desperately that he had been the one eaten up and not poor Jesse. When he had barely been able to struggle out of the pen to safety, with Jesse's assistance, it had not crossed his mind that the strong boy would not be able to simply jump out of danger. If only he had known. If only he could go back and order Jesse to stay away.

Whimpering and babbling, Basil lamented his God's determination in this gruesome affair. "Oh God—why God have You taken Jesse and not me? Please! Please, God! Give him back and take me!"

There was plenty of sadness to go around at the Den in the immediate days following the Bugg gang's raid. In addition to Jesse's tragic demise, news was received at Deaver's Store that General Lee had surrendered his army on Palm Sunday, a little more than a week after the raid on the Den. For most, however, this was an expected development. It also meant that the war was as good as over, and at last things might soon return to normal. Their Rebel soldier boys—the few that were still left fighting—would surely be coming home now, just in time for planting. As for the Edmunstons, they could not wait to see the lanky tow-headed Rufus sauntering up the East Fork River path. His arrival would be just in time to help reconstruct their cabin and get the corn in the ground.

For the time being, the Edmunstons had temporarily displaced one of the slave families from a lice-infested cabin and were lodging in the filthy place. But not before the slaves had scrubbed down the walls and floor with boiling water and prepared new shuck-filled ticks for the new tenants. On one of these, Basil was stretched out so he could be attended to by Julia and the girls.

Immediately after the raid, Doctor Allen had come up and spent almost an entire day suturing and fixing the dozens of bites and gashes and other horrific wounds Basil had suffered in the pigsty. The Bee Woman was now paying daily visits to look in on the patient as well, and she routinely rubbed her magical honey-laced herbal pastes over Basil's traumatized body. Although it would be quite a while before the bedridden Basil could even think of taking up a crutch and moving about—his prosthetic leg had burned up with the cabin—the whole tragic mess could have been worse, much worse. Taking into consideration Jesse's ultimate fate, Julia and the girls were just grateful that Basil was still alive.

They and everyone else who heard the pigsty story counted Jesse as Basil's savior, and the slave's deed would be told and repeated and revered around Haywood for many years to come. Of course, Lark, Delia, and their ever-growing number of children were utterly devastated over the loss of Jesse. What few remains of his body could be recovered from the sty were boxed up and planted in a small burying ground overlooking the East Fork. Basil instructed the slaves to kill and butcher every hog that rooted in the pen that awful night and allowed the proceeds from the sale of the meat to be distributed equally among them.

Right soon after the young slave's burial, Basil and Julia tasked the grieving father with organizing the Africans into a work team to build a new cabin. The Master and Mistress of the East Fork meant to site the cabin on the same charred ground where the old Den had stood for so many years.

To be sure, there was plenty of grumbling and discontent among the Negroes, since some already considered themselves to be as good as emancipated. But Basil had Lark quickly squelch such nonsensical thinking. The South had not formally capitulated yet, and until that happened, every last one of the Africans was to consider himself or herself Edmunston property.

That was what Basil told Lark to tell them. And the ailing Master, also insisted on another thing. He directed that they get off to a good start on the construction work before Rufus returned home. So, only days after Bugg's ravages, the slaves were crawling over the mountainside hacking down huge poplar trees and hewing logs like a bunch of beavers in anticipation of the young Rebel's arrival. Surely, it could not be very long off.

Chapter 27

A Helluva Git

More than a week had passed since Private Edmunston and Corporal Hartgrove had decided to call it quits and head home from the war. During those last hectic days, the Virginia countryside they found themselves traveling through was far from lonely. Grant and Sherman's powerful armies of blue-coated Yankees relentlessly pursued the fleeing Rebel forces in southern Virginia and central North Carolina. Cavalry troops swarmed over the roads and through the rural farmlands and forests to bring the sesh to bay. Like two scraggly gray foxes before these relentless blue hounds, Rufus and Hack scatted along the railroad toward the hills.

The two Rebels on the run were indeed scraggly. Hack was fortunate enough to still be wearing the fine boots given to him by the benevolent, eggnog-bearing Yankee. Rufus, however, was completely barefooted and, like Hack, was hatless and his pants and shirt were tattered messes. They were so scruffy and ill-dressed that it tended to work in their favor in one respect. Sympathetic farmers along the way could not refuse to feed these two pathetic-looking soldiers and usually offered them encouragement and advice for the next leg of their long trek home. For this reason, nourishment had not been a huge worry thus far. It was a good thing, because dodging Yanks and bad men was plenty enough to occupy them.

Outside of Danville, Virginia, the two Highlanders stopped near the bank of the Dan River, after footing it for more than twenty miles that evening. They found a secluded hide overlooking the river where they could rest their weary feet and get some precious sleep. For the better part of the daylight hours they laid up, taking it easy and considering their options for crossing the wide stream. Just before dusk, however, gunfire in the distance aroused them from a light slumber. The shots could not have been very far away. At first, neither of them spoke and only cast curious glances toward one another.

Then Hack allowed, "What ye reckon all that there shooting was 'bout?"

"No idee. Appears it didn't take 'em long to settle the thing, though."

After waiting for another ten minutes or so without hearing any more shooting, Hack decided to go and investigate. "Rufe, ye stay here while I go take a look-see over there whur the shooting come from. I'm right curious 'bout it."

"Aww Hack, ain't no need to do that. 'Sides, gonna be dark 'fore long, and we need to get a move on." Rufus was obviously not keen on the idea of Hack sneaking around in the broad daylight with strangers about.

But Hack's mind was made, and as he got up and walked away, he offered, "Don't ye worry none 'bout me, Rufe. Jest keep resting them big feet of yer'en, and I'll be back 'fore ye know it."

"Now, don't you go getting yerself in trouble, Hat." Rufus was still in the habit of calling his friend Hat ever now and again, even though Hack's fancy colonel's hat was blown up and lost on Hare's Hill.

Not goin' to get into any trouble, Hack kept telling himself as he stole from tree to tree to see what he could learn about the little fight they had heard. Soon he came upon a gruesome sight by the side of a little-used trace. Peering out from behind a bare sycamore, Hack could see two lifeless Yankee bodies lying in gruesome postures near a dead horse. From his hidden vantage point, he perceived flies already swarming around the dead hosts, but nothing else was stirring. Determining that he must be alone and no dangers lurked in the vicinity, Hack stepped out from behind the tree and carefully approached the carnage.

The uniformed cavalrymen were dead all right, that was pretty easy to appreciate. But of more interest to Hack were the weapons that he immediately spotted. Holstered Colt revolvers were still belted to the bodies of the deceased soldiers. The first thing that came to mind was that he and

Rufus could definitely use these guns, since the most lethal implement in their possession was a pocketknife. As Hack stooped to begin stripping the pistols off the dead Yanks, he thought about how elated Rufus was going to be over this discovery. He totally lost himself in the looting work, rushing from body to body to horse's carcass, while rounding up the two handguns, a fine Spencer repeating rifle, and saddlebags full of ammunition. With his sense of wariness replaced by sudden elation over this good fortune, Hack understandably dropped his guard for a few minutes. But an instant was all that it took for him to be surprised by a single genuine Yankee swooping in on horseback!

"Surrender, damn you, Reb! I got you!" cried out a youngish-looking cavalryman holding a revolver in his hand, aimed directly at the stunned Corporal Hartgrove.

Absolutely shocked and at a loss as to his next move or what to say, Hack could only puff out his chest and bluster, "Yeah—yeah, ye've got me all right, Yank. And a helluva git ye got, too!"

Earlier, this same Yankee soldier had participated in the noisy mounted fight that the two Highlanders had listened to. He and a small band of Union cavalry had been chased off by Confederate horsemen. This cavalryman holding a gun on Hack had returned to the scene to learn what had become of his missing friends, and he was none too happy about finding Hack pilfering their belongings.

"You damn scavenger! Get away from those bodies—now!" ordered the Yankee horseman.

Hack slowly dropped his load of weapons and began moving in the direction the Yank was pointing to.

"I'm taking you prisoner back to—," and before the Yankee could finish the tirade about Hack's prisoner-of-war status, he was suddenly and unexpectedly whacked hard off his horse to the ground. The bluecoat had not seen it coming, and as he tried to scramble to his feet, Rufus dropped his heavy stick and pounced on top of the Yank like a big cat.

Hack reacted quickly too. As his partner delivered a series of hard punches, he picked up a loose revolver and held it on the horseman, yelling excitedly, "Okay, Rufe, let him be! I've got him covered!"

Heaving with giant breaths, Rufus got up off the young trooper and backed away a step or two. Looking over at Hack with a frown, he said breathlessly, "I knew you would get yerself into trouble, Hartgrove! Weren't any doubts 'bout it."

Hack just shook his head and then looked down at the Yank. "Ain't no need fer this. Been 'nuff killing and sech. The war's over, and we aim to go home. If we let ye go, Yank, will ye git and leave us be?"

Surprised at this offer of leniency, the Yankee hesitated for a few seconds before responding, "Yeah, I'll leave you alone. You're not going to shoot me then?"

Rufus jumped in. "Don't aim to, unless you can't leave us be. Sorry 'bout them punches, Yank. Got carried away, I reckon." The boy's face was bloodied a sight.

"Go on, git—git outta here 'fore we think twice 'bout it," Hack growled, as the Yank backed away from his two captors, slowly and carefully. The young man was filled with distrust for these sorry-looking Rebels, but he finally summoned the courage to turn around and run for it, and he never looked back.

There were no doubts that the Yank would return soon enough with reinforcements to retrieve their dead men. So Rufus and Hack immediately went into action and worked swiftly. First, they chased off the Yank's horse, because the last thing they needed was to be caught and hung as horse thieves. In a flurry, they each strapped on a newfound Colt pistol, and Hack threw the saddlebags full of ammunition over his shoulder. Rufus took proud possession of a pair of boots from one of the lifeless soldiers, and Hack grabbed the Spencer repeater. If need be, they could at least defend themselves now. Wasting very little time to admire the side arms or new footwear, the two Rebels strutted off with a spring in their steps in the direction of the Dan River. Darkness had already set in, and they planned to wade across the rocky shoals and penetrate into North Carolina that very night.

The pair of scraggly Rebels had other minor misadventures along the way home but managed to scrape through without killing or being killed.

Near Greensboro, North Carolina, they abandoned the gentle grades of the railroad and headed due west toward the mountains. Eight days after crossing the Dan River, the two Highlanders reached Caldwell County, where they stopped over to spend the night at the old Edmunston plantation—Fort Catawba. Rufus's grandmother, Louisa, was still alive and residing there in the large house, along with a few of her slaves that had not run off yet. Was Louisa Edmunston ever surprised to see them!

"Why, looky here who the cat's drug in. Hello, Rufus dear! It's so good to see you!" exclaimed Louisa after opening the door to see who had come visiting.

"Hello, Grandmother! We're heading home from the war," stated the grandson matter-of-factly, as he tried and failed to contain his emotions. They exchanged a long passionate hug, and Louisa showered her grandson with kisses all over his bearded face.

Then Rufus turned toward Hack and asked, "Grandmother, you 'member Hack Hartgrove, don't ye?"

"Of course, I do. Hello, Hack! Columbus was the best overseer we ever had out in Haywood—and one of Thomas's best friends, too," explained Louisa. "He came all the way over here with Colonel Deaver for the burying. It was so thoughtful of him. How's your father, Hack—and your family?"

Hack perked up and answered, "I'm not right sure, ma'am. It's been a coon's age since I heared from 'em. 'Spect they's doing all right though. Going to be seeing 'em right soon, I reckon—yes, ma'am, I reckon I am!"

"Of course, you are! Both of you are! You two fine-looking soldier boys are going to be back with your families before you know it." It was the polite thing for Louisa to say, but deep down in her bosom, she thought these two human specimens were downright pitiful sights. "Now come on in the house, won't you? We'll get you a bath and some proper clothes to wear, and then we can sit and visit a good spell. What do you say about that?"

They agreed with Louisa's notion and, once being reintroduced to soap again, were splashing around in the bathtub like two ducks, scrubbing off weeks of battlefield grime and road mire. Louisa found them some old clothes that fit tolerable well, and then she sat the two of them down to be fed. It was the best meal either had eaten in years, and they gorged themselves almost to the popping point. During bites and furious chewing bouts, the boys responded to Louisa's interrogation as best they could. And she was able to pass along some attention-grabbing news as well.

"Just heard from Julia about your father, Rufus. Says he's still laid up in bed—will be for a while," Louisa candidly stated, not even realizing that her grandson was unaware of the recent raid on the Den or his father's misfortune.

Rufus gulped down a huge bite, before looking toward his grandmother in astonishment and asking, "Sorry, Grandmother—what you mean laid up in bed? Has Father taken poorly?" He glanced at Hack and then returned his incredulous stare toward Louisa.

"Why no, he's—," and Louisa stopped in mid-sentence, as it suddenly dawned on her that Rufus was clueless about the latest tragedy to befall the Forks of Pigeon community. "Oh dear, you haven't heard, have you—about the Den burning down?"

The dumbfounded look growing over Rufus's face became even dumber-looking. "What? The Den burned down? No, I ain't heard nothing 'bout that! What happened?"

Louisa paused for a few seconds to formulate a truthful response that would be the least hurtful to her grandson. "There was another raid at the Forks, dear—it was at the Den—and a gang of hooded raiders burned down the cabin." Then with a painful sadness she added, "Oh, Rufus—Thomas and I built that log cabin sixty years ago, and now it's gone." Louisa daubed her watery eyes with a handkerchief, as she winced sadly toward her grandson.

Rufus and Hack both sat up on the edges of their chairs, listening intently to what the elderly matron was saying, but so far the details were sorely lacking. After considerately giving Louisa time to gather herself, Rufus probed for more information. "So what happened to Father? Did they catch the men who did it?" Nervously waiting for a response, he glanced at Hack, who was as disbelieving as he was, and then back to his grandmother.

"No, don't believe they've caught them yet. Your father says it was a man named Bugg who was the leader."

Bugg! That goddamned Amos Bugg, Rufus thought. *Well, it's all over for Bugg now. Just you wait and see.* He and Hack exchanged resolute looks, and then

Rufus repeated a question to his grandmother, "How 'bout Father, Grandmother? What happened to him?"

Louisa was mentally chastising herself for raising this sensitive and distressing subject. If she could have had her druthers, she would move on to talk about gayer topics—something less traumatic and nerve-racking. But in this instance, she could not have her druthers, so she proceeded to pass along to Rufus the horrible details he was so desperate to hear. "Those mean men threw him into a sty for the hogs to eat." Louisa stopped right there to let her words sink in. Then she continued, "One of the slaves—Jesse, I believe was his name—Lark and Delia's son—saved Basil's life. That's what Julia wrote. Too bad, though, he didn't make it—the poor thing."

Rufus then came alive more than ever. His patience had run its course, and he raised his voice, looking for answers, "What? Did you say that Jesse didn't make it? He was killed?"

"I'm sorry, Rufus, that's what Julia wrote. The pigs were so aggravated and aggressive they actually ate him." Louisa was terribly regretful for having to reveal this horrible news to her grandson.

Rufus buried his head in his hands and began to weep demonstrably. Hack's head just hung limp, with his chin resting on his chest. Then he too began to sob, as the harsh reality of his slave friend's death began to sink in.

The two ex-Haywood Highlanders got an early start for home the next morning, after bidding Grandmother Louisa Edmunston goodbye. An overwhelming sense of urgency to get back existed now, and for the final trek, they decided to travel in the light of day as well as the darkness of night. It was familiar country they would be passing through, and they would take the risk that Yankee cavalrymen riding and raiding out of east Tennessee could be avoided. The blue-coated troopers were reportedly swarming through the western mountains and willfully plundering, with the full sanctioning of their Union commanders.

Three days it took them to walk the final hundred and ten miles, and nary another Yankee did they see. The long hike from Petersburg had taken the whole of nineteen days to complete, putting them at Forks of Pigeon just six days after Lee's Palm Sunday capitulation to Grant. Inside Deaver's Store, Columbus Hartgrove heard—with his one good ear—loud shuffling and clomping noises of boots landing on the porch. It was nearly closing time, and he looked up in curiosity to see who in the world his late customers could be.

The heavy wooden door swung open and, of all things, in stepped Hack and Rufus with their Colt revolvers holstered at their sides. The two Rebel soldiers were sure enough worn out, but as they strode toward Columbus each sported a wide and ecstatic grin on their face. They had finally made it back from the war—alive and in one piece—and were mighty thankful for it. It was truly a sight to behold that Columbus Hartgrove's watery eyes took in. It was the boys. They had made it home, at last!

Chapter 28

Shining Rock

Well into the night, the Edmunston family celebrated Rufus's safe delivery from the horrible war. The crude little slave cabin overflowed with happiness, as they talked, giggled, hugged, and kissed. From his bed, Basil watched with pride and joy every move the boy made. It was almost impossible to comprehend—his son actually being in this room with them tonight. Mother, father, and sisters had been thinking and praying for this moment for two long years. Now, here was Rufus, safely immersed amongst them and a part of the family again. Only when sleepiness overwhelmed the tired young warrior and he was driven to a bed tick on the floor were the celebratory doings put on temporary hold.

"The Shining Rock, that's what Bugg said. They were heading for the Shining Rock to hole up—I'm sure of it, Rufus," explained Basil for the third time, while lying in bed with his head propped up on a pillow. The morning after the homecoming, Rufus had decided to get right into the story of the Bugg raid, and he sat in a chair at his father's bedside prying out the painful memories and details.

"I told the sheriff the same thing, and I expect he's already had a posse searching up the West Fork in that direction. Maybe you ought to check with him before you take off on your own, Rufus. Don't you think that would be the prudent thing to do?"

No, Rufus did not think it would be prudent. He thought it would be a gross waste of time. The sheriff had been trying to round up the Bugg gang for more than two years with very little success. Rufus was not about to lose a day riding over to Waynesville just to talk to the lawman, and then learn that Bugg had continued to escape all efforts to corral him. So Rufus replied to his father, "Yep, might be a right good idee, Father. We'll see 'bout it."

Time was of the essence, Rufus thought, and he needed to get after Bugg while the trail was still lukewarm. Over those last three days on the road, he and Hack had discussed at length what they should do about their old adversary. They had made a pact between themselves to hunt Bugg down—and his band of robbers, too—and bring them to justice. The brand of justice these ex-Rebels contemplated was akin to that dished out to the Yankees trapped in the Petersburg crater—no quarter would be given to the Buggs.

More than two weeks had gone by since Bugg burned down the Den and murdered Jesse. The man could be anywhere, and there was no way of even knowing if he was still in the area. The only thing Rufus had to go on was Bugg's careless mention of the Shining Rock destination, which his father had overheard. At the time, of course, Bugg had not counted on this key witness escaping his murderous designs. So Rufus was at least privy to Basil's helpful intelligence and had a reasonable idea where to commence the search for Bugg.

After a long discussion with his father garnering pertinent factual information about the raid, Rufus walked over to the cabin construction site, where he found the Africans hard at it. Lark was there directing the work of lifting and shoving huge sill beams in place. He allowed to Rufus that all the timber was cut and hewn, the oak shingles were split and ready, and, with the exception of the masonry work, he reckoned they should have the structure in the dry within a week's time. After a few short minutes of chatting about these business matters, Rufus got around to expressing his sincere sympathies for Jesse's death.

He allowed to Lark that Jesse had been his very best friend, besides Hack Hartgrove. "He sure meant a lot to me, Lark. I think you know that.

We was 'bout as tight as you can get—me, Jess, and Hack. I'm going to miss him terrible."

To which Lark replied, "Jesse thinks you's da biggest and shiniest star in da sky 'bove us, Massa Rufus. Why, we's believe—me and Delia—dat he thinks mo' 'bouts you's than do's 'bout us. When you's goes off to da war, he misses you's somethin' bad—real bad. He sure 'nuff do's! We misses Jesse real bad, too, Massa Rufus." Lark then took a moment to compose himself and wipe is eyes.

Rufus could hardly stand it. He was on the brink of losing control of his own emotions, and Lark's confessions and sentiments only made matters worse. So, he diverted the conversation and mentioned his plans to set out in the next day or two to catch the man responsible for Jesse's death. Lark was considered by many, including Rufus's father, to be the best woodsman in Haywood County. He had hunted wild beasts and chased stock all across the region's mountains, and no one knew the heavily forested ranges better than he did. Rufus wanted Lark to join his posse and help him find Amos Bugg, and he explained at great length what a valuable asset the slave would be to the effort.

"Think about it, Lark. You know them mountains above the West Fork better than the bears that roam 'em. Them trails to the Shining Rock, you can help us find 'em and watch 'em. Don't much believe we can catch up with Jesse's killers without yer help, and that's a true fact."

Lark was not only flattered, but he relished any opportunity to bring his son's killer to justice. "If you's wants me, Massa Rufus, den I wants to help you's find Jesse's killers. I wills find that mean ol' Bugg fo' you's. You's jest waits and see."

Rufus was elated to have Lark as a scout. "Good—good then. And, Lark, I ain't yer massa no more. You're as good as a free man now. Soon as we find Bugg and you and the boys get that cabin built, Father's goin' have to cut ye loose." Rufus paused for a moment to gauge Lark's reaction. The slave's eyes opened a little wider, and a puzzled grin grew over his face.

"We's wants to stay on here at da Den, if Massa Basil will has us, Massa Rufus."

"Don't 'spect there will be a problem there, Lark," replied Rufus. Emancipation of the slaves had not been discussed in the earlier meeting with his father, but Rufus figured a hard worker like Lark would definitely be welcome to stay on. "You ought to tell him yer druthers. He'll be right glad to hear that you want to stay on—I'm sure of it. Now, I 'spect these here other boys can keep the building work going while we go 'bout Bugg catching."

Two days later, Lark rode at the head of a small posse of five men ascending through the rugged wilderness toward the Shining Rock. Of course, Rufus and Hack were tagging along behind him, and so were two other former Rebels. Garland Henson and Francis Christopher had also fled back to Haywood upon the chaotic disintegration of the Confederate Army following the disaster at Hare's Hill. Pursuing an entirely different course to Haywood, they had actually beat Rufus and Hack home. However, their homecomings had been cut short by Rufus's coercing pleas to join him in the quest to apprehend Amos Bugg and his gang.

All of them were armed, including Lark. In addition to the Colt revolvers that Rufus and Hack wore on their sides, they each carried long single-shot hunting rifles, with the exception of the Spencer repeater Hack proudly toted. Lark had a deadeye when it came to hunting game, and the four former Rebels had plenty of deadly experience when it came to shooting down their fellow man. Facing down the murdering Bugg gang was nothing compared to what the four Highlanders had experienced during the war. Undaunted, they doggedly made their way along the high, precipitous trail Lark was blazing toward the Shining Rock.

Reflected sunlight glistening off a slick white quartzite outcropping on the bald summit had prompted the early pioneers to dub this mountain the 'Shining Rock.' Steep craggy slopes rising toward its peak were covered with dense growths of towering hardwood trees at the lesser elevations. As the altitude gained thousands upon thousands of feet, the deciduous woodlands gradually gave over to forests of evergreens, with thick blankets of scrubby undercover.

Spring in the highlands had gotten off to an unusually cold and slow start, so most of the thawing trees were still leafless, although the white blooms of the Mountain Dogwoods were beginning to fleck the lower stratums. Without the leafy canopies, visibility across the numerous high drainage valleys was bound to be excellent, so Lark endeavored to find a vantage point where he and his followers could observe the broad mountainside directly underneath the Shining Rock. If Amos Bugg and his gang were holed up somewhere around that high top and were moving about, then Lark figured they ought to be able to spot them.

A boulder-strewn stream brawled hundreds of feet below where Rufus and his band were camped. They were hiding out on top of a sheer rock ledge, watching and listening for some sign of Bugg or his henchmen. But the weather was not cooperating a bit. It had rained for two full days, and the misty clouds blocked their view of the rocky features of the Shining Rock, looming far away. In the meantime, the men had crouched and shivered under a damp rocky overhang, waiting impatiently for a break in the weather conditions. Refusing to light a fire for fear of giving away their position, measly portions of salted beef, bacon, and crusty cornbread were eaten cold. Even after bundling themselves under blankets at night, they still shivered to stay warm. These dreadful conditions were barely tolerable and were so remindful of the war just ended. As the friends sat hunched under their shelter, they talked and grumbled a good deal, just as they had every night for the last two years.

"Bit of bad luck this is, but it's bound to clear off soon—don't you reckon, boys?" offered Rufus as he vented and encouraged in the same breath.

The former sergeant, Garland Henson, responded first, "It sure better, Rufus. We need to get on with this Bugg-catching of yer'en. I've got me a Crabtree girl waiting fer me. Been thinking I might jest up and marry her right soon, if she'll have me."

"Don't ye feel none too privileged, Garland. I've me one waiting too," Hack added testily as he gave Rufus a glance. "Leastwise, I think I have.

She's a bit further away than Crabtree though. Soon as we get done catching Bugg, I'm heading up into Yankee land—to Massachusetts—to meet her."

Francis Christopher jumped in, "How do we even know Bugg is in these here parts anyway, Rufus? Why, he might have hightailed it out of this country by now. If I was one of them Buggs, I sure 'nuff would've."

All the talk about girls had gotten Rufus to thinking about them too. As always, sweet memories of the dead Tine were resurrected. But these were soon chased away by the pleasurable and sensual reflections of the angelic nurse, Emma. His unwavering love for her had not waned one bit over the long absence, though he could not fathom why she had not written to him. It had been ten months since he left her in Plymouth, the longest ten months of his life, for sure. Had they not confessed their love for one another and enjoyed an intimacy beyond human expression? *What in the world could have happened to her? Did she find someone else?* As he muddled over these confounding questions, his attention was aroused by one of his buddies.

"What ye say, Rufus? Captain said they were headed up here, that not right?" Hack asked, noticing his friend's distraction and trying to rouse him out of it.

Rufus snapped back to attention. "Yeah—yeah, that's right. He sure 'nuff heard Bugg say 'the Shining Rock.' So we know they were headed up here, but it ain't certain how long they planned to hide out. You're right 'bout one thing though, Francis. They may be long gone by now, but we don't know that fer a certainty. Don't rightly know what else to do. This is the only place we know where to look for 'em."

Lark was sitting off to the side staring into the mist as he listened to this banter. Then he turned to join in on the conversation. "Massa, I do's feels it in me's bones. Dis rain goin' be's gone from here by morning. I can feels it in me's bones."

The former Rebels looked from Lark to one another and nodded their heads, confident of the accuracy of the slave's prediction.

True to Lark's words, the following day broke clear and bright as the sun rose over the eastern mountains. The excited members of the posse stared intently across the gorge in front of them, and focused their gazes upward to the far-away rocky landscape under the Shining Rock. As the morning mist burned off, their careful inspections captured every feature of the mountain top that was gradually lit up by the rising sun. For hours on end, they watched and kept their eyes peeled for some anomaly or movement or maybe even a whisk of smoke. But as the sun slowly crested over their head and then continued on its descent, nothing suspicious or interesting was detected. One by one, the young soldiers became distracted and began fiddling about, until only Rufus and Lark were left peering out into the distance.

While holding his gaze outward, Lark commented, "If dey be's over dare, Massa Rufus, den we's goin' to sees something. I believes dey's holed up in a cave, but dey's not goin' stays dare forever."

Rufus was beginning to have some doubts. He was losing his patience too, and becoming more and more convinced that their vigil would lead to naught. "I don't know, Lark. I think we're too far away to spot Bugg. Maybe tomorrow we ought to climb down and hike over somers closer."

Lark did not reply, but just kept his searching eyes directed over at the Shining Rock. By late afternoon, Rufus had moved away to join in with the others, as they debated their next ploy and whether or not to build a fire for the night. But then, suddenly, just as the sun was about to duck below the mountains, the group was alerted by a sharp call from Lark.

"Come sees here, Massa," he cried out frantically to Rufus, while at the same time motioning toward the Shining Rock. As Rufus and the rest ran over and fell in beside Lark, he pointed for them to see something. "Dare! Sees! Sees dat!—Dare it bee's 'gin—sees!"

Rufus did see something, and so did the others. It was a series of glinting reflections coming from an area just below the top of the mountain. Although not definitive, it was a positive sign of human presence.

"Yeah, I see it, Lark. It's a reflection of sunlight fer sure," Rufus replied very deliberately, as he intently watched the glittering light.

Garland Henson added, "Probably off a piece of metal—a knife blade or ax head or maybe a gun—something like that."

"It's what we've been squatting up here in the rain and cold fer," a suddenly reinvigorated Hack Hartgrove added. "Damned if we didn't see something. Way to go, Lark. Let's go check it out!"

"Good job, Lark," Rufus said, as he patted him on the back. "Do ye think ye can get us up to that place yender?"

The whites of the former slave's wide-open eyes shone brighter than the Shining Rock itself. Staring big at Rufus with a smug look on his face, he replied, "I can, Massa Rufus. You's can be's sure I can!"

Chapter 29

Bugg Hunting

By the crack of dawn the next day, Rufus and his posse were already making their way toward the mysterious glimmering reflections Lark had spotted high up on the mountain. Although the drowsy black bears were just shaking off the effects of winter hibernation and there were deer and wolves and panthers and all sorts of other wild critters prowling about, the Bugg hunters were convinced that two-legged varmints were at the root of the phenomenon. Surely, it must be Amos Bugg and his gang hiding-out up in that rugged terrain, and Rufus and his party aimed to bag them. But the overwhelming problem of actually reaching the outlaws had to be surmounted. How in the name of hell had Bugg gotten up there in the first place? There had to be a trail of some sort, and it was left to Lark and his uncanny skills to discover it.

After a perilous crossing of a wild rocky drainage chasm and a mile-long climb through thickets of mountain laurel and rhododendron, the going got so steep and rough the horses had to be left behind. *It was no wonder the sheriff and his posses had failed to corner Bugg, Rufus thought. Those men would have had better sense than to break trails through wilderness such as this.*

While his thoughts were turned toward the sheriff, Rufus wondered whether the lawman would condone the sort of vigilante justice he had in mind for Bugg and his band of thugs. Against his father's and Columbus Hartgrove's advice, Rufus had not sought the sheriff's sanctioning for the manhunt. Time was wasting and there was Bugg killing to be done, he had rationalized. Besides, there was no need to get bogged down with a host of legal do's and don'ts. As far as Rufus was concerned, the murdering thief's fate had been predetermined, and all that remained to be done was to squash the damn Amos Bugg.

Higher up on the Shining Rock, just beneath its rocky summit, the occupants of a dark, deep grotto were beginning to stir. A narrow fissure about fifteen feet high pierced a lofty vein of granite and opened into an immense subterranean cavern where they had retreated. It was a hidden cave that over the past thousands of years had sheltered many an Indian and other wilder creatures. The current tenants had cruelly evicted the cave's previous inhabitants, shooting and killing a slumbering mother bear and her two cubs. But after being holed-up there for three weeks, these latest dwellers had become stir-crazy and restless. One of them, a hefty, grizzled man with a shock of hair the color of dirty snow, vented his frustration and impatience.

"Time to git up! Wake up, Eli! Git up, all of ye! It's another purty day breaking outside. We need to git off this goddamned mountain today. Come on! Let's git going!" Amos Bugg figured they had lain low plenty long enough, and the time had finally come to escape Haywood County. They had to get out while the getting was good, with their treasure trove of silver and gold species, bank notes, jewelry, and other stolen valuables accumulated and stashed away during the lucrative war years. The soldier boys would be coming back from the blasted war any day now, and there was no telling who all might come searching for him and his bunch. No doubt about it, the nervous Bugg reckoned. It was high time to skidaddle.

There were nine of them cooped up together in the cave—all that remained of the notorious thieving, murdering gang that had marauded and terrorized the western mountains during the latter half of the Civil War. After their final raid on the Edmunston's East Fork cabin, they had retreated to this lair to allow time for things to simmer down, before moving on to the lawless territories beyond the Mississippi River. Montana Territory is where Bugg aimed to go. He had heard there were mountains covered with gold just lying around for the taking, and a man could get rich—if the Indians failed to kill him first. But Bugg was not scared of the red-skinned savages one bit. He longed to test his meanness against Montana's wild natives, just as soon as he slipped out of these rugged Carolina highlands.

"We've starved long enough in this damned hole, and I've a terrible craving fer me some 'bacco. Plumb run out days ago. 'Sides that, them people's going to discover us sooner or later, so let's git a move on! Git yer things together, and let's go kitch what horses ain't been eat up by the damned wolves and paint'ers."

"They's still four of 'em down there, Amos. Least they wus yestidy, when I went to feed 'em," offered one of the outlaws, a particularly wretched low-life deserter from the Confederate Army.

Another of the army-dodgers chimed in, "Ain't no sane man goin' to come up here to get us, that's fer damn sure. But them snakes's goin' be crawling about right soon I 'spect. Don't ker a bit fer nary snake!"

Still another despicable man allowed, "I'm 'bout fed up to here with all this here male company. I want me a woman!" While pronouncing this sentiment, he puffed up straight and jerked his hand clear up to eye level to indicate his degree of aggravation and horniness.

After a few moments of general stirring and utterances of "Ye ain't the only one!" and "Me too," Eli Bugg asserted, "Ain't no'ens going find us up here, Pa. They ain't that crazy, don't ye reckon?"

"Can't say I'm a'feared of anyone going out of their way searching fer us— 'cept maybe that Edmunston boy we had the run-in with. He'll be coming home soon, if the Yanks ain't got him already. There ain't no telling what he'll do once he discovers we fed his old man to a bunch of hungry riled-up hogs. We got him back good, though, didn't we, Eli? Killing his father and grandmother ought to be payback enough fer the licking he give us! Yea, I reckon it should."

Rufus and the others were extremely hard pushed to keep up with Lark, who was scrambling way out ahead of them. He burst through the laurel hells and brush thickets, bounded over the smaller boulders, and scaled hand-over-hand up the larger ones. Seldom pausing for a breather to let the troops behind catch up, he just kept relentlessly plowing forward. Finally, after about three hours of excessive toil and exertion, the soon-to-be emancipated slave's excited voice could be heard ahead.

"Massa! Massa! Come looks! I finds da trail! I finds it!" The thrill in Lark's voice was evident to the four huffing Rebels, and they hustled up to see what he had discovered.

"Sees here!"

It was an obvious game trail that the slave eagerly pointed to. But there was no mistaking the evidence. They could easily see that men had recently trampled over this path. Distinct fresh boot impressions could be made out in the soggy bare earth. This was Bugg's trail—had to be. They were everyone sure of it, and their blood flow surged a good deal quicker as an intense survival instinct kicked in. Somewhere at the other end of this trail was a deadly foe—probably as deadly as the Yankees had proven to be—and the four war veterans began mentally preparing themselves for yet another fight. Lark was not exactly sure what he might be getting into, but he aimed to find the mean men responsible for his Jesse's demise.

As Rufus and his cohorts girded for battle and were about to continue their climb, Hack Hartgrove suddenly raised an arm and shushed everyone. "Shsshh—quiet! I heard something!" he said in an alert, hushed manner. For several seconds they all stood still and quite, listening acutely. And sure enough, faint far-off sounds were barely perceptible. It sounded like muffled voices and faint stomping noises, as if someone or something was moving through the forest. The racket seemed to be growing louder and getting closer, as if—as if that someone or something was descending the mountain along the trail toward them! Could it be Bugg?

Acting instinctively on the spur of the moment, an excited Rufus gathered the four others around him and hastily formulated a plan. "Move off this trail and find ye some cover," he directed coolly, keeping his voice low so that it didn't carry. "Let's hold our fire 'till we see 'em everyone. Don't fire unless they shoot first, hear?" he asked, looking around to make sure he was understood.

"Got ye, Private," answered Garland Henson. "Let's git." Then, they all scampered off the trail seeking safe refuge and concealment.

Several nervous minutes passed, as the distant tramping and voice levels gradually rose, until at last the first of the trekking bunch could be seen. One by one, the bearded, scruffy-looking characters came into sight, skidding and sliding down a steep incline. A half dozen or so slid to the bottom before Rufus spotted the familiar face of Eli Bugg come crashing down the slope. Then, right behind him and bringing up the rear was that evil-looking, white-maned father of his. Rufus knew he could not be mistaken. It was the same brutish man he had fought at the mill. He was sure of it. The very sight of the sinister creature stirred a deep emotional hatred within him that no other man, not even a Yankee, could provoke.

Amos Bugg stopped briefly to brush away the dirt and grime from his rear end, and then spouted out gruffly, "All right—keep it moving. Time's a-wasting. Them horses can't be too much further down."

Bugg and his men all carried weapons, but they were either stuck under their belts or strung across their shoulders. Intuiting that this must be the entire gang, Rufus decided to act while the unsuspecting outlaws were all bunched up. Without any second thoughts or hesitation, he sprang into action.

"Okay, you men—git yer hands up in the air! Git 'em up!" hollered out Rufus, as he jumped out from behind a large rock beside the trail and blocked the thieves' way. Before the nine startled thugs could think straight, they saw four more armed and fearsome-looking ambushers appear out of nowhere and rush in to surround them.

Rufus barked out again, pointing the revolver first toward one thief and then another, "I said, git 'em up! Git your hands up!" To accentuate his order, he casually moved closer to the younger Bugg and fired a deafening and unerring shot directly into the top of the vandal's foot.

Immediately, the eight others, including Amos Bugg, put up their hands, while the screaming Eli fell to the ground writhing in fury and pain. Then Rufus snapped an order, "Okay, Garland, take their guns and weapons. Keep those guns leveled at 'em, men," he continued, glancing down quickly at the wounded Eli while striding over closer to the father. Aiming the Colt revolver directly at Amos Bugg's head, Rufus stated matter-of-factly and assuredly, "If any of you makes a move, I'll gladly plant a bullet in this one's head."

Amos's glowering eyes revealed his contempt for this impertinent Edmunston, but there was no mistaking the threat. The war had meaned this boy up, and he meant business. The only move Bugg made was to instinctively jerk his arms a little higher in the air. And the same went for the other gang members, who were disarmed in short order. "Now then, Lark, why don't you bind and hobble them men, and then we can decide what ought to be done with 'em." Turning back to the elder Bugg, a sneering Rufus spoke in a most satisfied tone as he kept the revolver aimed at the murderer's head, "You're not as big as you think you are, you son of a bitch! You're a coward to fight the Yanks, and you're a coward to fight a fair fight." Pausing for a short moment, Rufus glanced around quickly at the others to see how the disarming and binding were going.

Then he turned his attention back to the wicked Bugg, "'Spect you don't know that my father is still alive, do you, Bugg? Them pigs didn't kill him like you planned, you good-fer-nuthin son of a bitch. Me and him's going to enjoy watching that son of yours swinging by the neck." Rufus stopped and stared at Bugg, watching the hatred inside the wicked man come to a boiling point, his face turning redder and starting to draw up and flinch. "But we've got something else planned fer you, Bugg—something real special," Rufus added. The satisfaction in his voice was manifest.

All went surprisingly well with the capture proceedings. In short order, Lark lashed the first seven captives' hands behind their backs and hobbled their legs. The incapacitated Eli persisted in crying to high heaven, and, for the time being, the slave skipped tying him up. Instead, he moved over to take care of the elder Bugg. Rufus could not believe how easily events were unfolding, and while pondering the good luck became distracted with Eli's loud ruckus. It was at the very moment when Amos Bugg was lowering his hands to be secured by Lark that things went dreadfully awry.

The vicious bandit realized that once the damn darkey bound his hands and feet, it was all over—the Edmunston boy would then have gotten the best of him. This notion did not sit well with Bugg atall, and he reacted in the only way he knew to get back at the uppity Edmunston. Violently breaking away from Lark's grasp, Bugg lunged head-on and straight into the distracted Rufus, bowling him heavily to the ground. Alas, Garland had not discovered a large hunting knife concealed inside Bugg's boot top and, in an instant, the thieving murderer was wielding the weapon and slashing out at Rufus. In one effective slicing motion, the knife severed his flesh and opened up a deep gash extending diagonally across his entire chest. It was a serious wound, directly over the heart, but Rufus did not fully appreciate the gravity of his injury. He was definitely in a bad way, yet focused on survival and fending off another violent knife assault.

Besides being seriously carved up, Rufus had lost the revolver, which had been jarred loose from his hand. So he was essentially weaponless and fought desperately to grab Bugg's stout arm—the one that was about to thrust the bloody knife blade deep into his body—one final time. The beastly Bugg maneuvered with lighting quickness to launch the mortal stabbing strike into his hated victim. He would show Edmunston what was what, who the better man was. But Amos was not quite quick enough. Just as the bandit's arm muscles hardened and quaked to initiate the knife's descending plunge home, the butt end of Francis Christopher's rifle stock crashed down hard against his head.

The leader of the thieving gang was instantly knocked senseless and collapsed lifelessly on top of Rufus. Immediately, Lark yanked Bugg's limp body away and fell upon his knees at his master's side, as did Hack. Looking on worriedly, they could see Rufus gasping for breath and wincing from great pain. They had good reason to worry. The grievous knife wound Rufus had suffered was plenty deep and bleeding profusely. But the former Rebel soldiers were undaunted. They had, of course, witnessed many such gruesome injuries on the battlefield—injuries much worse than this one. Immediately, they instituted diligent efforts to staunch the bleeding and provide aid and comfort to their buddy. Whether they could get Rufus off the mountain before he perished remained to be seen, however.

A half hour later and with the bleeding from Rufus's ghastly knife wound mostly stopped-up with linen scraps, Hack Hartgrove leaned over close to the patient and spoke lowly, "How ye feeling now, Rufe?"

Staring up at Hack with weak soulful eyes, Rufus responded wearily, "Hurting bad—how you think I feel, Hack?" Then Rufus gave his best effort to crack a smile.

"Yeah, 'spect ye're hurting right bad. It's a serious carving, Rufe. We've 'bout got the bleeding stopped, but ye've sure 'nuff lost buckets of blood. Rufe, we've got to get goin' and get ye off this here mountain and to a doctor. Built us a stretcher to tote ye on."

"Okay then, let's get going," Rufus replied. But then he thought of something and quickly asked about another most serious matter. "Got all them prisoners ready to go?"

"Reckon they're all ready. That youngest Bugg's foot is shot up right bad from the bullet you put through it." Then Hack added with undisguised sarcasm, "Too bad, don't ye think?"

Rufus was not very concerned about Eli's foot. He was sure the youngest Bugg could survive the difficult slog off Shining Rock Mountain and the much easier trip to Waynesville. And it was a gratifying feeling to know that the bushwhacking, murdering thief would soon gimp up the steps of the county gallows and swing from a hangman's rope. But Rufus was anxious about a much more delicate matter. "How 'bout Amos Bugg? Is he going to live long 'nuff fer our plan to work?"

"Yep, he's still alive and mean and ornery as ever. But I don't 'spect he'll survive this night," Hack answered, as he exchanged knowing looks with Rufus. "Me and Lark's done took care of the thing."

Chapter 30

WE WHO?

It was a tremendous undertaking to portage the wounded and suffering Rufus off Shining Rock Mountain. And not only that, the small posse had to marshal the Bugg gang down the precipitous wilderness slopes at the same time. Lark and the former Haywood Highlanders shared the burdens of this arduous ordeal and, more than once, had to stop and deal sternly with their captives' unruliness. However, by dusk, most of the horses had been rounded up, and the caravan had descended to an easier-sloping terrain.

That night around a large campfire, the Bugg hunters ate their first hot meal in days and were finally able to dry out their clothes and warm themselves. Dreadfully tired, they all turned in early as the fire's glowing embers died down—with the exception, of course, of a rotating guard to stand watch over the prisoners and mind Rufus. It was in the wee morning hours, a time of unusual profound quietness, when the most awful-sounding shrieks imaginable began to pierce the silent solitude of the heavily forested mountain. These strange howling cries, from somewhere high above them, were unlike those of any beastly critter Rufus and his buddies were accustomed to hearing in the wilds. Interestingly, the unearthly screams fell on some highly receptive and appreciative ears in the camp.

The wretched prisoners, understandably, were made uncomfortable by the horrible sounds and were filled with apprehensive forebodings. But the same could not be said for Rufus and his buddies. On the contrary, the eerie screams seemed to have a pacifying, or even satisfying, effect on the exhausted Bugg hunters—especially the much-suffering Rufus. They understood that these distant woeful cries, so wonderfully horrific and soulful, could mean only one thing. The business with Amos Bugg, which Hack and Lark had tended to, was playing out just as planned.

Turns out, the defiant evil Bugg had been strapped stark naked to a chestnut tree and abandoned in the rugged wilderness—but not before Hack and Lark had smeared bacon fat all over the murderer's body and tied generous bacon chunks around his neck, waist, genitals, and feet. The awful screaming sounds the Bugg hunters became so attuned to were actually those of Bugg himself, when the bears—or maybe a pack of wolves—discovered their midnight snack. Anyhow, before sunup, Amos Bugg's body had been reduced to a heap of slimy bones crawling with insects and bugs—real bugs! No trace of him was found, nor was he ever seen again, and Rufus and his accomplices would later swear to the inquisitive lawmen that, unfortunately, the thieving murderer had escaped them and fled into the wilderness somewhere.

That afternoon, when the first farm on the West Fork was reached, Rufus was gently laid on a bed in a tiny cabin. He was in an awfully poor way by this time, and Hack lit off like a bolt of lightning down the river to fetch the doctor. Several of the farmers living on the upper reaches of the West Fork were recruited to accompany Garland and Francis, as they escorted the notorious Bugg gang on over to Waynesville. Lark stayed at his Master's side. He knew Master Rufus was in dire trouble, and once Doc Allen arrived on the scene, this appraisal was confirmed.

The doctor adjudged Rufus's life was hanging by a poorly spun thread and immediately endeavored to mend him. For more than an hour, he stooped over the patient, doing everything within his capacity to save the young man. The doctor probed, felt, cleaned, and sutured the severe knife wound, while Rufus lapsed in and out of consciousness, shrieking in pain during his brief moments of awareness. When at last the doc was finished, he slowly stood up with a low grunt and stretched out real good. Then, he turned to address Hack and Lark. These two faithful friends had been ever watchful and attentive throughout the whole operation and were all ears as Doctor Allen began to describe Rufus's grim prospects.

"Done 'bout all I could for him, I'm afraid," he allowed, shaking his head slowly while looking down upon the patient, who had once again fallen into a state of slumbering shock. "He's lost a sight of blood, and I don't rightly know that his nasty wound can keep from getting infected bad. Matter of fact, it's done started festering."

Hack, who was terribly concerned, of course, did not reckon he knew too much about festering, so he got straight to the point and asked direct like, "What ye think, Doc? Reckon Rufe's going to make it? Ye stitched him up—closed that gash up right good, didn't ye?"

"Good as I could, Hack. But I can't do nothing atall about that festering. His wound has already got infected, appears to me. We'll jest have to wait and see how bad he'll get. Now, it's best we don't move him from here. I'll come up tomorrow to look in on him. You go on along and see about his folks. And please, if he gets any worse tonight, you or Lark come and fetch me."

For the next couple of weeks, the crude little West Fork cabin where Rufus was confined became his hospital, thanks to the accommodating folk who lived there and allowed it. When the farmer learned Rufus had been a Haywood Highlander and, besides that, was Captain Basil Edmunston's son—why, he and his entire family packed off for nearby relatives' houses. They meant to give the young Edmunston every opportunity to die in peace.

Soon as the Bee Woman learned of her nephew's plight, she rushed up the river to his bedside and began administering her special healing salves and potions. With Hack and Lark's assistance, Aunt Folsom attended to Rufus night and day, caring for him as he desperately fought off fever attacks and feebly clung to life. And they were not the only ones looking after Rufus.

A steady stream of concerned visitors rode up to offer their support, hopes, and prayers for survival. Julia, Mary, and Emily came up immediately and, with Lark's assistance, were even able to haul the still-tormented Basil in a wagon to visit at his son's bedside. Of course, Doctor Allen called on

Rufus, oft-times twice a day, and several Haywood Highlanders, Columbus Hartgrove, Horace Mann, and a few of the Edmunston's tenants, including the Andersons and Preacher Poston, made the trip. But no matter the good intentions of all these well-wishers, Rufus's condition failed to improve. On the contrary, he was getting worse, and Doctor Allen even suspected that pneumonia might be taking hold.

Well into the second week of confinement, the patient bravely hung on, while fighting infection-induced fevers and enduring ever-increasing coughing spells along with extreme breathing difficulties. But he stayed alive—just barely—and was somewhat aware of what was going on around him, as he was on this morning when Hack loudly entered the single-room cabin. Rufus was alert to his friend's familiar stomping steps in those fine Yankee boots of his and listened as Hack came closer and leaned over the bedstead. Then, he was able to make out his buddy's face and see the huge grin he was sporting.

Summoning up his reserves of energy, Rufus asked, "What's got into you, Hartgrove? You look like you jest received one of them love letters from yer Yank girlfriend." Almost out of breath, he wheezed and gulped in some air before finishing, "What's up?"

Hack could not shake the smile off his face as he kneeled down on his knees and rejoined, "Naahhh—it ain't that, Rufe—ain't that atall. But ye know how I've been waiting on ye to heal up real good, so's we can go up to Yankee land and meet Harriet—seeing how's we settled that Bugg business? Well, now I don't reckon ye're gonna want to go with me."

A puzzled look came over Rufus's tortured face. "What you mean? I'm still going with you to meet Harriet—," Rufus stopped to cough a few times and gasped audibly for air. *I must not have long*, he thought, yet he continued, "If I ever get up out of this here bed—I'm going to meet her, jest like we agreed we would go together. Soon's I'm able." Another bout of heavy congested coughing overcame him, as a hard awareness began to set in. It was all over. He felt certain he would never rise up out of the bed again—never leave it alive, that is.

Hack did not yet fully appreciate Rufus's dire situation, so with his expression sobering slightly, he blurted out excitedly, "No—no, ye're not,

Rufe! Ye ain't gonna want to go with me up yonder after ye see who's come here with me."

Rufus had no earthly idea what Hack was insinuating or what sort of joke was being hatched. "I don't much feel like being messed with, Hartgrove." Coughing and hacking, he went on, "Don't feel much like it atall." Pausing for several seconds to catch his breath, he finished his thought, "Who you hiding out there—that wants to see me? Who—who is it?"

"Okay, now close yer eyes, Rufe, and I'll go get 'em."

"Aww—quit your fooling around and—hurry up." Saying that, he turned his head to the side and rested it on a pillow, gasping to breathe.

"Hush up, and close 'em now—and keep 'em closed!"

Although he felt like a suffering fool—an exhausted dying one at that, Rufus obediently kept his eyes closed and listened to Hack quickly stomp over the puncheon floor and out the door. In a very short time, he could make out shuffling sounds in the outside yard. Soon, his ears tuned to low muffled voices and what seemed to him to be mysterious babbling sounds. Then, suddenly, there were more steps on the wooden floor again approaching his bed. *What in the world was that crazy Hartgrove up to*, he wondered, while gulping heavily for air.

"Okay—okay, now! Open them eyes, Rufe!"

Partially tilting his head on the supporting pillow, Rufus slowly opened them. And through his half-open weak eyes, he looked upon the most beautiful sight he could ever have imagined to see. Standing right there before him was Emma—tall, splendid, striking Emma! She looked more beautiful than ever—just as he remembered her—as she stood there at Hack's side. Suddenly, huge tears of joy welled-up and flooded down his cheeks. Never in his life—never—had he been so surprised or as happy as on this singular, momentous occasion. Curiously though, Emma and Hack held teeny babies in their arms.

"Emma! Emma! Is it really you?" a shocked, wheezing Rufus asked. It was really all he could utter out of his mouth, as he tried unsuccessfully to raise himself in the bed to get a better look.

Still holding the baby, Emma stepped over closer to Rufus. *Here he is at last*, she thought, *my young Rebel soldier who completely captured my heart and soul.* She leaned over his lanky frame and greeted the ailing young man she loved so dearly with a tender kiss to his forehead. "Oh, Rufus, we've missed you so." Tears were welling up in her eyes, too, and she wasted no effort to hold them back.

Rufus was absolutely stunned by the turn of events and tried frantically to formulate some sane notion of what was happening to him, as he smelled and felt Emma's presence. He was confused and could not get beyond wondering just what in the hell was going on. Then, he was overcome with another spell of hacking coughs, and he gulped frantically for air. Hartgrove reached down with his free hand to support the back of Rufus's head, in a mostly futile effort to provide some comfort. Finally, after regaining his breath, Rufus was able to mutter these intelligible words, "But Emma—you've come! It's you! You—," and then again Rufus had to stop for the coughing, which was getting worse. He could hardly breathe.

Doctor Allen had been right about the pneumonia. The debilitating knife wound that so severely cleaved Rufus's chest had opened his body for other infections to be introduced. Unfortunately, his natural defensive systems, weakened and vulnerable from the effects of the deep festering cut, had been unable to fight off a nasty pulmonary disease. His lungs were filling up with fluids, and he was literally on the verge of drowning.

When at last the coughing and sharp pains in his chest subsided sufficiently, Rufus gathered himself and continued again, "Ye look—so beautiful. But you said 'we'—did ye say 'we've missed you?' We who, Emma? What—what are these babies all 'bout?"

Again a prolonged bout of coughs stopped him. Emma just waited in confused shock, overcome with horror at the awful condition Rufus appeared to be in. Then having subdued the worst of the coughing, Rufus continued, "Whose babies—are they?" he asked while straining and looking first to Emma and then up to Hack in complete bafflement. Noticing that Hack's grin remained extended from ear to ear, he switched his gaze to stare at the tiny babes they were cradling ever so gingerly.

Then Rufus thought he heard these soft deliberate words emanate from Emma's pretty mouth. "They're ours, Rufus. These are our twin babies—a boy and a girl. I haven't given them names, yet, because I thought you would want to help me."

There was a pronounced silence as Rufus simultaneously grappled with this astounding message. He gasped hungrily for air and understanding. *Emma had said "They're ours." Did I hear her correctly? Does that mean I'm a father now? Well, it most certainly does, doesn't it?*

At once, he began mulling over the staggering implications. What a beautiful woman she was—Emma. She was exactly as he remembered her when they parted ways almost a year ago—an eternity it seemed like. Here she was again. She had come all this way to find him. She had not forsaken him as he had feared. During all those endless days and nights at Petersburg, with cannon and mortar fire exploding all around him, he had worried more whether Emma had forgotten him than he did about dying.

Thank God she has not forgotten me. Emma is here in Haywood—right now—with two babies. They're my babies—and hers. That's what she said. But—but it's too late. Emma's too late, he feared. *A life with her and those babes would be so wonderful. But it's not to be. Too late—*

Rufus could not breathe. He could not go on living like this. It was so terribly difficult to simply hold his head up, but he strained to do so. He had to. He had to gasp out one last thing—to Hack—one last thing.

"Hack," whispered Rufus desperately. "Hack," he wheezed and panted out again, while opening his eyes to make contact with his friend.

Hack heard him and in an instant his face was only inches away from Rufus's. "What is it, Rufe?"

"Take good—good care of 'em—fer me. Ye—hear?"

Hack had finally caught on that Rufus was in the throes of death and suddenly he became all emotional too. Tears flooded from his eyes down across his cheeks, as he replied to his best friend in the whole world, "Gotcha, Rufe. I will. I promise ye, I will."

"And—Hack—jest—one more thing."

"What is it, Rufe?" Hack replied, while bawling unashamedly.

And then Hack heard these faint, barely perceptible words slip out of his friend's mouth, "Goodbye—Hat."

Chapter 31

An Eloquent Proposal

Some would allow it was the Bee Woman's doings that had done it. Still others would swear it was Emma and the twins who had provided the necessary inspiration and will. Whatever the reason, no one denied that a glorious miracle had come to pass at the isolated West Fork settlement. It was said that Rufus Edmunston was the latest beneficiary of a glorious intervention. Undoubtedly, his God—not to be confused with the Holy Bible's all-powerful Christian protagonist or the various other gods worshipped by the religious faithful throughout the world—had looked favorably upon him this time. Who's to say why?

The gangly tow-headed Rebel had killed more than his share of Yankees in the recently ended war. There was no doubt about that. He had also killed Amos Bugg, putting an end to the evil man's reign of terror in Haywood County. Did Rufus's God reward killing? Probably not. Why, not even those religious zealots whose God they believed favored one side or the other in the late war dared to imagine their Almighty could condone the killing of fellow human beings. Rufus, in fact, did not believe his God or anybody else's God could be partial to killing. But his God had created him and put him on this earth for some reason—some good reason, probably—and, perhaps, His plans for Rufus were not yet realized.

Perhaps there was too much left undone that He wanted Rufus to finish—more good that He intended for the young man to dispense. Take that beautiful girl of his, Emma, and those two children of theirs. They certainly needed him in their lives right about now. Perhaps, Rufus's God meant for him to take care of them. That could be. Or there might be myriad other reasons. But inexplicably—miraculously—Rufus's life was spared, and he could thank his God for that blessing, along with a host of people in his life who loved him and would not allow him to die without a fight.

Upon hearing Rufus mumble that last sad "Goodbye," Hack screamed in alarm for someone to help. Immediately, Folsom was on the scene, working with a fury, applying her special healing powers to save her nephew. A new concoction of hers—a salve containing the blended powders of chinquapin nuts, peppers, and tobacco along with substantial doses of fish oil and honey—was applied as a plaster to his chest. The Bee Woman and Emma took turns rubbing the pasty mixture into his skin, applying a new layer every hour or so. Hack busied himself keeping a kettle of sassafras-and-honey tea boiling over the fire. Steaming cups of the brew were held close to Rufus's face, and the wafting vapors were fanned such that the patient inhaled them into his congested lungs. Doctor Allen, mystified that Rufus continued to cling to the very knife-edge of life, did what he could but mostly assisted the Bee Woman and others.

This care-giving team had no notions of Rufus's God or His plans for Rufus. These friends and other family members had only one thing in mind—they aimed to keep Rufus alive, one way or another, and that is exactly what they did.

On the verge of succumbing to the debilitating lung infection for nearly two days after Hack's urgent call to action, Rufus never gave up. He kept on breathing somehow, although with tremendous difficulty. Feeling the soothing hands of his dear Emma pressing against his chest and listening to her sweet encouraging words incented every breath he took. Gradually, little by little, he began to show signs of improving respiratory function. Inhaling the tangy tea fumes seemed to actually soothe his incessant coughing, making the simple act of breathing tolerable again. Moreover, the agonizing pain associated with the festering knife wound began to ease somewhat. All the signs were there. Rufus—who now had so much to live for and look forward to—appeared to be on the mend.

For another long week in the remote cabin, Emma stayed by her dear Rufus's side and helped nurse him back to good health. At least this time, he remembered who he was and knew how he felt about his beautiful nurse, and she knew where she stood with him. Eventually, Rufus was able to converse at length with Emma, with little consequence to his strengthening respiratory process. Whenever they had some precious alone time, they were able not only to enjoy intimate conversation but also to catch up on each other's lives. And the very first thing Rufus wanted to know was why in heaven's name she had not written to him.

During their long estrangement, Rufus had not heard a peep from Emma, just as she had received nary a letter from him. He had told Hack there would be a good reason for it—and sure enough there was.

Only a few days after Private Edmunston had rejoined the Confederate Army, Harmon Davenport had loaded Emma and the rest of the family aboard the *Hester* and set sail from Plymouth for the far-end of Albemarle Sound. At Elizabeth City, a river town still held by the Union, the Davenports settled in with some kinfolk. There Harmon and his two sons were able to escape the Confederate authorities and avoid certain conscription into the army. Straight away, the *Hester* was again plying the waters of the sound and hauling in bountiful catches of fish, to be sold to the local population and to the Union troops. And, needless to say, there was no mail service available from Elizabeth City to the areas of the country that fell under the auspices of the Confederacy, thus explaining the dearth of correspondence between Rufus and Emma.

At some point, just before Doctor Allen released the patient from his West Fork confinement, Rufus was compelled to pop the all-important question to Emma. It was the right thing to do—he was sure of it. They had even talked about it before their protracted estrangement, and she had given him reason to believe it was what she wanted. Certainly, it was what he wanted. So, during one of their long convalescent chats, Rufus came right out with it.

"Emma, you've put yourself to a passel of trouble to find me. And I feared all this time that you had given me up—but here you are—with them two babies of ours." Then, with a pensive hopeful look in his eyes, Rufus laid it on her, "You reckon we can get ourselves married off now?"

A marriage proposal expressed so eloquently, how could Emma ever refuse? Of course, she reckoned they could get married. Why else would she have packed those tiny babies across the entire breadth of North Carolina to the wild Haywood mountains? Those little ones needed their father to provide for them and protect them, and she desperately craved to rekindle her burning love affair with Rufus.

"Well, Reb, I do believe we can get ourselves married off. Can't think of anything better I would like to do right at this moment," replied an overwhelmed Emma with enormous satisfaction. The tear droplets were streaming over her cheeks, and her face glistened with sheer happiness.

Lark and Hack managed to load Rufus, Emma, and the twins into the back of the smelly old farm wagon and haul them to the East Fork quarters. Over the days and months to come, the goings-on and farming operations around the Den underwent a dramatic makeover as a result of the war and its aftermath. The Edmunstons' slaves were emancipated as soon as the last daubs of mud chinking were dried in the new log Den. Lark, however, elected to stay on with his former master, working for wages and his keep. The bond between himself and Basil was simply too strong for a war to break up. Besides that, Jesse's nearby grave needed regular tending, and Lark and Delia could never abandon that responsibility.

When at last Rufus and Basil recovered from their terrible injuries and were fit enough to travel, they made another long train trip to Wilmington where the prosthetic leg maker was promptly found and engaged. After being fitted with his new wooden limb, Basil was able to carry on with the domestic and farming responsibilities at the immense East Fork farm. But he could not possibly have done it, nor would he have tried, if not for the abiding love and assistance received from Julia and the girls. Of course, Rufus added his strong support when needed, but he was not usually within hollering range. For goodness sakes, the nineteen-year old prodigy now had his own quarters to worry about.

His eloquent marriage proposal having been accepted, Rufus got himself married off to Emma that summer. Immediately afterward, the couple moved into a spacious new cabin that Rufus, Lark, and Manson Anderson had fashioned on the Crab Orchard property. Driving this move to the Orchard was the fact that old Josiah Anderson, Rufus's grandfather and long-time tenant, was slowly dying. With his father's urging and backing, Rufus and Emma had decided to take on the farming duties at the Orchard and to employ Josiah's son, Manson, to help work the fields and look after the stock. Oddly enough, the site they chose for their log cabin was very close to the spot where poor sweet Tine had stepped into the rocky den of rattlesnakes. And it was not far atall from the Bee Woman's vacant shack.

Speaking of the Bee Woman, Folsom had finally consented to move to 'town' in order to set up housekeeping with Horace Mann at Forks of Pigeon. However, she did not forsake her healing work and continued to offer her unique and valuable services to an ever-expanding clientele base. She abandoned her bee gums altogether, leaving them for her nephew to fret over. Believe it or not, she was eventually able to teach Rufus how to properly rob the gums, so he could keep their crocks filled with golden gobs of delicious honey.

In the years to come, Rufus and Emma Edmunston raised their twin children, Nancy Louisa and Joseph Davenport, on their beautiful Crab Orchard farm and managed to procreate even more offspring. As their numbers grew, so did the bonds tighten that held them together. It would take a strong family such as theirs to face the hard times that befell Haywood County as a direct consequence of the failed rebellion.

For at least a decade following the cessation of hostilities, there was no end to the economic doldrums and other atrocities affected by an onslaught of Yankee carpetbaggers and the rule of military-backed governments. Worse still, racial hatreds stirred by emancipation spawned night-riding clans of terrorists, who extracted a hateful revenge on the newly freed Negroes. Of course, Rufus and Basil remained above such immoral, bigoted behavior. They and their families were bigger than that.

To bear up under the staggering difficulties of the South's reconstruction, the indomitable Edmunstons simply worked hard and always strived to interact amiably with tenants and neighbors alike. One might allow they persevered, and throughout this dark period and the years that followed, the East Fork Edmunstons remained a much-admired family in Haywood County.

The Rebel duo that gave the Yanks and the Buggs what-for also remained a powerful force of nature around Forks of Pigeon. Rufus's and Hack 'Hat' Hartgrove's tight friendship never slacked atall in the years ahead. Interestingly enough, Emma Edmunston grew mighty partial to the Hartgroves as well. She and Harriet, Beth, and the rest of the Hartgroves became the fastest of friends. That's right—Harriet and Beth. Turns out, Hat finally did go up North, and he found that Yankee correspondent he was so keen on. And danged if he didn't manage to win the girl's affection and convince her to take up with him—in the Haywood mountains, of all things.

The End

About the Author

Carroll C. Jones was born and raised in the mountains of Haywood County, North Carolina, in the small paper-mill town of Canton. He is a direct descendant of the Hartgrove, Cathey, Moore and Shook families who pioneered the Forks of Pigeon region of Haywood County (present-day Bethel, N.C.), the setting for *Rebel Rousers*. After attending the University of South Carolina in Columbia, where he played football for the USC Gamecocks and earned a degree in civil engineering, he began an extended career in the paper industry lasting more than three decades. Carroll's professional work led him out of the Carolina highlands to Brazil, South America and then back to the U.S. where he eventually settled down in Pensacola, Florida. Now retired and living in Morristown, Tennessee, he juggles weekend retreats to the North Carolina mountains and fly fishing with his love for writing. To his credit Carroll now has four award-winning books: *The 25th North Carolina Troops in the Civil War*, *Rooted Deep in the Pigeon Valley*, *Captain Lenoir's Diary*, and *Master of the East Fork*. You can find out more about Carroll and his books on his website at carrolljones.weebly.com.